I0641334

Daybreak at the Abyss

SENTINEL SERIES
BOOK TWO

RACHEL HAWK

Copyright © 2024 by Rachel Hawk

All rights reserved.

No part of this publication may be reproduced, distributed, or transmitted in any form or by any means, including photocopying, recording, or other electronic or mechanical methods, without the prior written permission of the publisher, except as permitted by U.S. copyright law. For permission requests, contact Rachel Hawk.

The story, all names, characters, and incidents portrayed in this production are fictitious. No identification with actual persons (living or deceased), places, building, and products is intended or should be inferred.

Book cover by James at Go On Write:

https://www.goonwrite.com

For my dear husband, who's constant support keeps me grounded enough I can let my imagination run wild. You have put up with my countless re-writes, my terrible puns and jokes, and my occasional need to randomly talk about folklore facts regarding trolls, goblins, and other creatures in the middle of dinner. Love you!

To my great friends and pseudo-beta readers Annie and Angie. Thanks for always being there to laugh with me (and occasionally at me). All your cheer and support keeps me sane - even when I was in the depths of writer's block.

And most of all, this book is for my boys, my two favorite troublemakers (my own little Menehune). Thanks for keeping me on my toes and providing endless inspiration (and silver hairs).

Lastly, in remembrance of our family's own little panther, Fergus. For a small cat you had a big personality. You will always be my magic cat.

Dream until your dreams come true!

Prologue

Family is not defined by blood; it's defined through love and commitment.

Arianna Greene stared at the rising horizon, the biting chill of the crisp briny sea air stung her cheeks, her golden hair whipping her face. A burnished mulberry pink sun peeked through the wispy grey clouds as the Ningen floated steadily in the crystalline ocean waters. Droplets like crystal prisms danced off the creature's bone white hide.

She took a fortifying breath. The large aquatic creature was off-putting when she first saw it. It was very massive, similar to a whale, but with spindly arms where fins should be. But, most of all, the Ningen had an eerily human face, a face that stayed a perpetually blank expression. It was eerie. She was uncomfortable at first, but after several days, she had gotten used to the quiet monster. It never spoke, never made a sound. It kept moving, taking Ari and Dain to wherever he requested. Oddly, she found solace in the silence, her mind fuzzy and hazy.

Until she decided to wake up.

Shivering, she hugged the cloak tighter to cut the biting wind. The soft, white fur tickled her chin. What animal it came from, she had no idea. She only knew it was the best fur because only the best was good enough for

Prince Dain. She rubbed her cheek against the cloak's velvety thickness, her sleepiness fading slowly. Questions began trickling in, one after the other, blending together. How far had they travelled? How much longer did they have to go? How many days had it been? What time was it at home?

Home.

Ari's breath caught in the salty air. Time flowed differently in the Veil, the world parallel from the human realm. For all she knew, she could have been gone for months. Pulling from her hazy brain and the misty sun, she gathered only a few days passed, but she could never be certain. She could never be sure of anything anymore.

Through the pounding noise in her waking mind, the Ningen remained silent. The only outward sound was the rushing of the waves and the trilling call of the sea birds flying overhead. Ari suspected they were heading south since the seas were turning a brilliant turquoise, the breeze warming. She sat down on the back of the Ningen and pulled a small notebook from the cloak's pocket along with a black crayon. Taking a deep breath of clear salty air, she began to write.

Dear Lily....

Chapter One

WHO ARE YOU?

Tinmiukpuk, the great Thunderbird, perched on a mountaintop, his prominent gaze resting on the rising sun. The soft beams rose higher, casting an effervescent glow over the emerald treetops. He spread his massive wings, shimmering golds and reds burning away the departing shadows. His eye drifted down, his fathomless ancient orbs ablaze. Consuming. A deep voice reverberated in the silence, even though the mighty Thunderbird's beak was closed, motionless.

Who do you wish to be Lily?

Thunder boomed in the distance. Dark clouds cloaked the light's rays, turning the world into shadow. The ancient's eyes sparked, lightning crackling from his wing tips. A screech pierced, accompanied by another thunderous boom.

The wind has changed directions. It is time! You must step onto the path young Sentinel.

BEEP...BEEP...BEEP

Lily groaned, burying her head beneath her pillow, the threads of her dream misting away. She threw her arm out to smack the blaring alarm clock into silence. Her inner voice whined.

Just five more minutes...

BEEP...BEEP...BEEP

"No..." she grumbled, her words muffled, but the incessant machine kept beeping away. Apparently, her termination efforts failed on the tiny, annoying device. She buried herself further, hoping it would go away.

This has to be the cockroach of electronics

Suddenly, the windowpanes fluttered, their clacking filling the room as the alarm cheerily beeped again. Lily stubbornly ignored it. Whether it was Brom, the house brownie, or the cottage she didn't know.

She scoffed. The cottage? Really? How silly was she to think houses were alive. If she were honest though, she didn't care who or what it was. She only wanted a few more moments of precious sleep.

"Good morning!" An automated voice calmly spoke through the small speaker. "The time is 5:15am on Friday, July 28. The temperature is a temperate 60 degrees Fahrenheit with a 5% chance of rain today. The humidity is set for-"

SMACK!

The offending object promptly stopped, Lily's second aim hitting true. She groaned again.

Okay...okay! I get it, I'm up!

She threw an arm over her eyes, that fleeting moment between dreams and waking holding her captive a few seconds more. For the last three nights the same dream plagued her mind. She dreamed the Thunderbird told her she needed to 'step onto the path', whatever that meant. She had no idea what to make of it. Tinmiukpuk, the real one, hadn't spoken to her since she came back from the Veil. One dream, she thought it was just that...a dream. Two days, coincidence. Three? At this point Lily wasn't in a position to dismiss it. Not after everything she'd been through this summer.

Let's get moving slowpoke!

Boy, her inner voice was becoming a real drill sergeant lately. With a determined kick, she knocked off the covers and quickly threw on her workout clothes. Within fifteen minutes, she was outside in the backyard. The dew dampened grass tickled her ankles as she started jogging. She never particularly liked running. Always preferred books and academia to quiet her mind. But recently, she found herself enjoying the

4

meditative, almost euphoric feeling of the physical exertion. She ran about a mile before ending up by the stream which separated the property from the immense forest beyond.

At first glance, one would think it was a normal woodland area. No one would suspect that stepping over the protective barrier of the boundary line would send you to the Veil, a place between worlds where creatures such as fae, dwarves, and monsters existed. The forest was deceptively beautiful, not revealing the monsters that dwelled under the sparkling surface. And it wasn't the first time Lily found herself staring across the water towards the emerald darkness, beckoning her.

That darkness that turned her entire life upside down.

THUNK!
An arrow whizzed through the air, embedding itself in the rough tree trunk. Lily pulled the bowstring taunt, the burn of her shoulder muscles familiar. She let out a soft puff, a whisper over the fletching, before letting another arrow fly. It hit, only inches away from the hand drawn red circle.

She panted, brushing her curls away from her sweaty forehead. At least she hit something today. Between Peri's intermittent lessons and taking a week of archery camp, she was slowly getting the hang of it. Notching another arrow, the grazing eyes of dawn began to light up the sky. She sighed, her mind recalling the events that led her to this point.

It was hard to believe that two months ago everything Lily knew was spun on its axis. Then spun again and flipped upside down. Her father, Dr. Tony Ambrosino, had gotten married to Tabitha Greene. Which was wonderful. she loved her new stepmother. The issue was when Tabby and her father went on their honeymoon.

Lily, left in charge, got into a momentous fight with her stepsister, Ari. After that, Ari ran away and got herself kidnapped. But was that the end of it? Oh no! Lily also found out faeries were real. And...her stepsister wasn't really kidnapped. She had gone willingly with a fae prince who planned to break the barrier between the worlds by unleashing an ancient monster. And by monster, meant an enormous horned snake that tried to devour both herself and Ari! Thankfully, with the help of her new friends and the Thunderbird, they were able to stop the plan from succeeding.

Unfortunately, to top off the cherry on this absolutely sticky sundae, instead of coming back with her, Ari decided to stay with that crazy prince. That same prince, by the way, who attempted to feed Ari to that snake monster! But hey, that's only a minor character flaw in the dating pool. No biggie. Lily mentally rolled her eyes, her arrow missing the tree as it wisped into the tall grass.

Focus Lil, she reprimanded herself, rolling her tense shoulders. But that didn't stop her overactive mind from wandering again.

So, she returned home, emptyhanded, with no stepsister. Since then, her mornings were spent stepping up her workout routine and practicing archery. Her stepbrother, Brandon, told her it seemed like she was obsessed. She denied it, but secretly she admitted she maybe was a tiny bit obsessed. But Lily was determined to protect her family. Did anyone know how terrifying it is to be the only one with no powers or abilities against a snake the size of a mountain? Her stepbrother certainly didn't.

Lily was reluctant to admit it, but everything did turn out reasonably well in the end, if you forgot the part of Ari not returning. She kicked a rock, her anger rising. Bringing Ari home was the whole reason she went into the Veil to begin with! And now her stepsister was still out there, somewhere in the Veil, with a crazy prince. And she wasn't exaggerating on the crazy. The guy tried to offer her as a main course, who was to say he wouldn't try something again. She gripped her bow. Maybe she wasn't prepared the last time, but that wouldn't happen again. She refused! And there would be a next time, Lily was sure of it.

This is temporary, she reminded herself, breathing out. *It's only temporary*. Ari just needed time. She would come home, Lily assured herself.

She hoped.

Panting, she wiped the sweat off her brow. The sun had finally risen over the trees, a sign that it was time to stop. She clutched at the antique pendant, the one that housed the Thunderbird, tightly in her hand. It warmed under her palm, a soothing balm to ease her brewing anxiety. She liked to think Tinmiukpuk was comforting her, in a small way.

Shouldering her bow, she took a deep, cleansing breath, then frowned. She leaned toward her shoulder and sniffed, her frown deepening.

Yeah girl, time to shower. You reek.

Chapter Two

"*FIORE*! LIL, IT'S TIME FOR BREAKFAST!"

Lily's father, Dr. Ambrosino, knocked on her door a few times.

"*Fiore? Sei qui?*"

Lily sat on her grandmother's dresser, rubbing a towel to dry her curls, her silver reflection staring back at her. She tossed the towel into the laundry basket.

"Be right down dad."

An enthusiastic squeak chirped behind her, accompanied by a furious rattling. She smiled warmly.

"I hear you Rox." She chuckled softly. "I'll get you something to eat too."

Her pet sugar glider Rox, jumped around his cage excitedly as Lily gathered some dried fruit. She giggled. While some things drastically changed in the last two months, there were things that remained reassuringly untouched. She reached in to give him some papaya pieces, smiling as he eagerly snatched up the tasty treat.

A cold hand tapped her shoulder, startling her. She yelped, pulling her hand back unexpectedly, scraping her fingers against the cage. Wincing, she cradling her scratched fingers. Rox squealed in fright and promptly ran to his hiding spot.

"Oopsiesss..." rasped a dry voice. "Sssorry..."

Holding her stinging hand, Lily turned around to find her stepsister's face staring back at her. Long strawberry blonde hair framed the big blue eyes of Arianna (Ari) Greene, who was munching noisily on a honeycomb, honey droplets falling onto the floor. Well...the person in front of her only looked like her stepsister. It was actually a doppelgänger. A scary changeling that was a carbon copy of Lily's stepsister.

Lily sighed, rubbing her temple. "Ang, what did we talk about with the sneaking?"

"Knock on door first. If no response, don't enter." Ang garbled through a mouthful of beeswax, honey dripping down her chin.

Lily tried desperately to school her expression while inside her stomach roiled. She must have failed as Ang raised an eyebrow. She bit her lip, immediately feeling bad.

"Sorry Ang, but please don't forget..."

Ang waved her hand, dismissing Lily's upcoming speech. "Yeah yeah. Keep clean. You humans are sooooo focused on being clean it's annoying," she grumbled, wiping her mouth with her sleeve. She perked up a little, giving Lily a sly wink. "But I think I'm doing a pretty darn good job sissy."

Lily nodded. "You know we appreciate it. It may seem weird, but if you're going to pretend to be human you need to adapt to how humans behave."

Ang rolled her eyes. "I get it, but you could be a teeny more grateful you know. This is a huge favor that his highness Prince Jacy asked of me. If Prince Dain learned I was helping you, I'd be in hot water."

Ang was right. She was doing them a favor, that is if you count being forced by the Forest Prince Jacy as a favor. By now, Lily knew 'favors' in the Veil weren't always what they seemed.

Ang was a changeling, a fae that impersonated a human. Her recent assignment was to pretend to be Ari until they found a way to bring Ari home. The last thing Lily needed was their parents finding out that Ari was missing. So, in reality, it was a huge favor. Major in fact. Lily didn't even want to entertain the idea if her stepmother got wind her daughter was not only gone, but off with a fae prince. She didn't know which was worse in her stepmom's mind: running away from home or running away with a guy. Lily certainly didn't want to find out.

She grimaced. It was hard to be completely grateful though. Maybe it was because of how they originally met Ang. In the beginning, she pretended to be Ari the day Ari was kidnapped so no one would know she was missing. To make matters worse, Ang was sent by Prince Dain to impersonate Ari, the same fae prince that started this entire mess. Lily didn't want to recall her first encounter with the changeling. Needless to say it didn't go that well, resulting in a bruised shoulder and a dented teapot. Lily rolled her shoulder, the memory unnaturally vivid.

She sighed inwardly. She really did have to work on not being so judgmental. She could tell Ang was putting a good faith effort. Even though the changeling still had a hard time grasping human manners, she was generally doing well. Sometimes too well, a twinge of caution snaking through Lily's brain.

She nodded her head, her shoulders slumping. "You're right Ang. I'm sorry."

Ang tsked, already dismissing her apology. "Eh forgiven. Now!" She clapped her hands excitedly. "Breakfast! Your dad made his delicious maritozzi! Get a move on sissy!" And with that, she ran out of Lily's room, slamming the door behind her.

Lily caught herself chuckling. Ang loved those sweet breads filled with whipped cream and drizzled with honey. The changeling adored her father's cooking. Or maybe she just loved sweets. Probably the sweets. Regardless, her father enjoyed making baked goods which quickly made him the changeling's favorite in the house. Her step-mother, Tabby, mistook Ang's appetite to Ari finally warming up to her dad. Unfortunately, it was only a fae with a notorious sweet tooth. Either way, seeing Tabby and her father smile so brightly when Ang happily ate whatever he cooked warmed Lily's heart.

She turned back to Rox's cage, throwing the remaining dried fruit in. "I'll be back Rox."

As she headed down the stairs to the kitchen, she pushed down the familiar sense of guilt of becoming more comfortable around Ang. It was conflicting. Maybe it was because Ang wasn't mean to her like Ari used to be. Sure, the changeling was grumpy and sarcastic. And blunt, definitely blunt. But she was never cruel or made fun of Lily. Rather, there was a mutual wariness of the other. But they were open about it, which was odd. The honesty of it all, to be honest, was refreshing.

But, it was still weird.

It was weird that she got along with someone who looked like her stepsister. She shook her head, rubbing her arms slightly. She made a point to call the changeling "Ang" because she needed to separate Ari from Ang. Even Brandon admitted he couldn't call her by his sister's name. So, they created a ridiculous excuse to their parents "Ang" was a nickname. Her stepmother, Tabby, assumed it was short for angel and thought it was sweet.

The siblings didn't correct her.

Lily rubbed her arms harder, an invisible chill glossing over her skin. If Tabby saw the real "Ang" she wouldn't think of an angel, but rather some demon right out of an H.P Lovecraft story. Claws, papery mangled skin, and empty eyes. Yup, Ang was definitely no angel. Thankfully, the changeling didn't mind the name. In fact, she actually seemed delighted, which suited the stepsiblings just fine.

A heady aroma of bacon and honey entered her nostrils as she walked into the chaos centered in Hemlock Cottage's little kitchen. Even though it was small, it certainly was abuzz with activity. Her dad was frantically setting up the table, his hands scrambling to hold various plates, cups, and silverware. Tabby was sizzling up bacon on the antique stove, even though the table already sported a huge pile of crispy meat drizzled with honey, a recent request from Ang. Fluffy biscuits with jams and butter were laid out along with fresh juice.

Lily sat down at her place and poured herself some of the citrus beverage, taking a tentative sip. The chaotic noise enveloped her, bright and cozy.

"Morning Lily!" Tabby called out over her shoulder cheerfully.

She smiled back. "Morning Tabby."

Her dad whipped around, finally noticing her. He scrambled to catch a dish that flew out of his hand, hunching over to protect the precious tableware.

"Hey *fiore*, any word from colleges yet?"

"Shush Tony," admonished Tabby. "The poor girl just woke up. Don't nag her first thing in the morning."

Her dad nervously fiddled with his glasses. "Oh...right."

In his distraction, he forgot his arms still held a few plates. The dishware slipped out of his hands, crashing onto the table. He yelped, scrambling to collect them. Thankfully, none were broken.

He cast a sheepish smile. "Sorry *fiore*, I'm excited for you."

"Really?" asked Tabby, raising her eyebrow knowingly, giving a teasing grin. "We didn't notice."

Tony Ambrosino flushed, pushing his glasses up. "Yes, it's just, I'm so proud of my little girl. I'm excited to see where she chooses to go."

Lily smiled softly. Her dad was a professor of archeology. Academia was his passion, his life. He loved to discover new things from the past. And until recently, for most of her life, that was what she had known and wanted for her own career.

"I know dad. I haven't heard yet, but it's only been a few weeks."

"*Sì!* Yes, of course! I won't ask again until you tell me." Tony grinned broadly, rearranging the napkins.

An excited voice whispered in Lily's ear. "Ten bucks says he'll ask you tomorrow."

She jumped, her heart skipping. A mop of shaggy blonde hair framing a pair of mischievous blue eyes twinkled at her. Her step-brother, Brandon, had silently snuck into the kitchen and sat down next to her. He was learning to be stealthier these days. Which only broadened his repertoire of usual pranks. She never thought she'd prefer the loud clomp of his shoes over silent heart attacks.

She put a hand to her chest, forcing her heart to slow down. You'd think she would get used to this by now, but obviously her racing heart failed her. She wheezed out, "Geez Brandon! Give me a little warning next time."

He shrugged in slight apology, unable to hide his grin. He whispered excitedly, "Ang says with more practice I'll be able to walk around the room and no one will know I'm there."

Lily groaned. "You gotta stop learning things from Ang."

"He's really good at sneaking," quipped Ang. She gave Brandon a somewhat proud look as she took a large bite of maritozzi, cream smearing across her cheek.

Lily palmed her face, already dreading how to explain table manners to the changeling...again. It took almost all her energy to wrangle Ang on a daily basis. Now to add Brandon to the mix? She inwardly sighed, her forehead moving closer to the table. She gave her cheeks a quick pinch. What else could she do? It wasn't like she could tell their parents.

For all public purposes, Ang was Ari. At least until Ari came to her senses and returned home.

She was still focused on her musings when a soft pull tugged her away.

Brandon shook her arm lightly, embarrassed. "Sorry Lil, I didn't mean scare you earlier. Ang says being stealthy is key in the Ve...umm, key in life."

They glanced around, making sure their parents weren't listening.

"Key for a human," interrupted Ang...loudly.

Lily gasped. "Ang," she hissed, glancing at her dad. Thankfully the adults were busy talking to themselves, away from the table.

The changeling shrugged, uncaring, and reached for another pastry.

"Yeah right," acknowledged Brandon. "I just need to level up a little more."

"This isn't a video game," said Lily firmly.

Brandon had always been a bit of a prankster, playing tricks on people, preferably teachers. Recently, he tried to take on more responsibility. Or more importantly, ever since Ari decided to stay in the Veil. He did not go into the Veil, but Brandon was determined to come next time. If there was a next time. She was already internally dreading whenever that day would come.

Brandon glanced over at their parents and leaned to whisper to Ang. "Ang, heard anything yet?"

The changeling shook her head. "Nothing."

Lily tried to squelch the familiar disappointment that came from hearing those words. Every day they asked the changeling, and every day it was the same answer. They heard not one word from Prince Jacy since Ang had come to live with them.

And what was worse yet. They hadn't heard a peep from their fae friends. Well...most of them anyway. She inwardly flinched, trying not to think too hard about Cabyll. She frowned. Where they still friends? He had not visited her once since she returned...or contacted her. Honestly, if it wasn't for Ang staring at them in the face, the stepsiblings could have easily thought what happened to them was a dream.

The changeling scratched her hair nervously, watching their dejected faces. "Look...I'm sure we'll hear something-"

BAM!

The front door to the cottage was thrown open with a loud bang. The entire family stood still and silent. A cheerfully forceful voice rang out.

"*Buon giornio*! Hello? Where is my *familia*?"

Loud footsteps echoed down the hallway as Lily caught a glimpse of a petite young woman effortlessly carrying a large backpack and an equally large suitcase. She was short, probably no taller than 5'3, and sported a thick, glossy mane of dark brown hair that curled down her back in waves. Deep brown eyes, almost black, crinkled with joy. Large lips sported a blindingly infectious grin. The woman dropped the suitcase to the ground with an audible thump. She put her small hands on her wide hips.

"Well? Cat got your tongue?"

The kitchen remained silent, everyone staring at the newcomer. Lily's father froze, his plate of bacon falling to the floor. Then, as if someone pushed the play button on a remote, a huge grin appeared on his face.

"Ravenna!"

He looked down with a yelp, realizing his bacon was on the floor.

The woman and the rest of the household laughed as Tony scrambled on the floor, frantically trying to clean up the mess.

Lily's Aunt Ravenna had come to visit.

And chaos resumed.

Hugs were exchanged, large boisterous hugs that made you feel your insides were being squeezed out. Words overlapped as everyone rushed to get out joyful greetings. Brandon almost fainted from Aunt Raven's python hug while she cried out joyfully.

"Aww! Brandon! Look how much you've grown! Tabby, you didn't tell me how tall he has gotten. He's already a little taller than me, but then again everyone is taller than me."

"Thanks..." Brandon wheezed out trying to get a breath in.

"Let me get you a plate Raven," said Tabby, walking back to the kitchen.

Raven shooed Lily's dad, raising her eyebrow. "You better help her *fratello.*"

Tony blinked, adjusting his skewed glasses. "Oh? Yes! Yes, I'll help!" He gave his sister a quick peck on the cheek before darting off.

Lily chuckled. Her aunt may be tiny, but she was tenacious. It came with the territory being a renowned deep-sea Biologist and Hydrologist. In a profession largely consisting of men, Raven never showed any signs of intimidation or hesitation. She was the first woman to free dive 168 meters in the Pacific. "Go big or stay home" was her motto. When Lily asked her aunt why she tried so hard, she was told it came from being so much younger than her dad and wanting to do everything Tony did. It was well known Ravenna Ambrosino was the "whoopsie" baby. Fifteen years younger than her father, her aunt wasn't even thirty, but determined to live her life to the fullest. Lily hoped to have a fraction of her aunt's confidence.

Raven released her constricting hug from Brandon, looking around. "And where is my *nipote*!?" Her eyes zeroed in on Lily warmly, sporting a wide grin.

Lily returned the smile. "Hi Zia Raven!"

She was instantly engulfed in a pair of soft, strong arms. A comforting blend of coconut and citrus surrounded her, her aunt's tight hug warming Lily's heart. Her aunt always smelled of warmth and sunshine.

Raven stepped back, still holding her shoulders. Giving them a slight squeeze, she peered into Lily's eyes, as if looking for something.

"Well would you look at that," she murmured. "Seems like something happened since I've been away."

Lily fidgeted under that intense gaze. She nervously tucked a strand of curly hair behind her ear. "Nothing happened."

"Oh really?" Her aunt's lip tilted upward. "You seem different sweetie."

Lily shook her head. "I'm still the same."

Raven raised her eyebrow. "I wasn't talking physically *nipote.*"

She patted Lily's heart. "I'm talking here." Then tapped her forehead. "And here. You do not have the eyes of a child anymore."

Brandon and Lily exchanged a quick glance, their eyes wide. Her aunt tended to say things that didn't quite make sense. They always dismissed it. But now? Now they didn't seem like ramblings anymore. Before Lily could say anything, Raven went over to Ang. Weirdly, she didn't hug Ang. She didn't smile either. Which was really odd as her aunt hugged everyone.

Raven crossed her arms, looking the changeling up and down. Her eyes narrowed, then hardened.

"Ari..." Raven drawled out in a surprisingly cool tone.

Ang gave an awkward smile, adding a small wave. "Uh...hi Aunt Raven."

Raven moved her head to the side slightly, her wavy hair falling down over her crossed arms. "You seem different too."

On the outside, Ang looked confident. She fluffed her hair, exactly as Ari would. She rolled her eyes with a scoff...same as Ari. But Lily noticed the changeling's slight shuffle of her feet.

Ang laughed, her voice musical. "Oh really? Maybe country life agrees with me. I just love it here." Her voice was syrupy sweet, like Ari when she wanted something. Honestly, Lily had a hard time seeing any difference between the changeling and her stepsister when the changeling was in performance mode. But, would it work on her aunt?

Raven stared long and hard, not saying a word. They narrowed further, almost into slits, darting around Ang and into the kitchen. The silence continued, awkward and tense. No one moved.

Ang looked warily back and forth, her eyes wide, silently calling out for help.

Lily jumped in next to her aunt, grabbing her arm lightly. She shuffled toward the stairs.

"Come on Zia Raven. Let's put your things away."

As luck would have it, her dad returned. His mouth was full of bacon, some pieces still in his hand. "Hey *sorella*! How long are you staying?"

Lily's nose wrinkled. Please don't let the bacon hit the floor. But if it did hit the floor...her dad wasn't known to waste food. She grimaced.

Don't think about it Lil...just don't.

In a flash, her aunt's calculating gaze disappeared. It was replaced by a beaming smile, full of warmth. Raven squeezed Lily's hand affectionately replying, "Only a few days roughly. I'm passing by before I fly over to Australia. The team is getting set up to research for oceanic sustainable solutions." She turned to Lily. "Have you heard about college yet sweetie?"

Lily sighed, dreading going through the explanation again. Everyone was focused on school. Two months ago, that's all she thought about too. It's funny how different things were now. Her mouth opened, ready to give the normal excuses again. She was cut off by another loud knock at the door.

"I'll get it!" Brandon zipped quickly to the door as the rest of the group moved to the kitchen.

Raven pursed her lips, taking it in the chaotic mess. "Seems like things have been really busy around here. How was the honeymoon?"

"It was wonderful!" gushed Tabby, handing Raven a plate and ushering her to sit down. "And you know the real blessing? Since the honeymoon the kids have been getting along so well. Ari has really bonded with Lily. She even has been helpful around the house."

Raven picked at the plate, her expression neutral. "That's wonderful news." That calculating, bland gaze landed on Ang. "Ari? Are you really feeling at home? Your mother mentioned you were having a hard time adjusting after the wedding."

Ang glanced quickly at Lily who gave her an imperceptible nod. It seemed like a logical question. But that didn't stop the goosebumps that prickled on Lily's arms.

Ang smiled, putting her arm around Lily's shoulders. "Yes, Lily is a great sister. Only took me some time to understand that."

Raven mused, taking a slow blink at the two stepsiblings. "Hmmm...sounds like Ari is a whole new person wouldn't you say Lily sweetie?"

Lily and Ang looked at one another before forcing a laugh.

"Of course not Zia Raven." She clenched her teeth, keeping her smile in place. Her inner voice yelled.

Darn it Zia Raven, please stop asking questions!

"Mail incoming!" Brandon raced back into the kitchen holding a stack of paper. He threw the letters down on the table, the various papers knocking over the juice pitcher, napkins spilling onto the floor.

"Brandon Greene!" admonished Tabby. "Pick these up! They're getting wet!" She hastily grabbed the envelopes, dabbing a few with a towel that soaked up spilled orange juice.

Lily let out a quiet breath in relief as the attention moved away from her and Ang. The adults raced to grab paper towels, napkins, anything for this emergency cleanup.

"Sorry Ma," Brandon apologized. "I was too excited."

Lily noticed his side wink. She mouthed a silent thank you. Now was the time to make a hasty retreat.

Ang and Brandon must have been thinking the same thing. They backed up quietly to head out the back door when they heard her dad call out excitedly.

"Lil? Lil!! Come here quick!"

Come on! What now?

Lily reluctantly turned around. Her father was holding up a grey envelope, his face beaming. Tony practically jumped up and down as he handed it to her.

"Maybe it's a college." His hands clapped excitedly. "Quick, open it up!"

Lily's eyebrows furrowed, confused. It didn't make sense a letter would come that quickly. She looked at the envelope. It was small and thin. It barely fit in the palm of her hand.

Oh...it's probably a reject, she thought glumly.

Upon closer inspection, it didn't seem like a normal letter. It was handwritten in silvery cursive script, with no return address. The back of the envelope was sealed in silver wax. The seal was a wolf's head howling upwards with a dragon flying above, wrapping in a circle that reminded Lily vaguely of a type of yin/yang combination. It was the strangest rejection letter she had ever seen.

"Come on dear, don't keep us in suspense," pressed Tabby.

Lily tore open the envelope, pulling out a thin sheet of parchment that crinkled around the edges. There in handwritten script:

Ms. Lily Ambrosino,

We would like to cordially invite you to visit Arachstone University.

Arachstone has a long history of cultivating the

brightest minds and honing impeccable leadership. We hope your visit will enlighten you on the various career possibilities Arachstone can provide. Our Sentinel program, in particular, is considered the elite of academia.

Please provide this letter upon your arrival.

Sincerely,
Headmaster Stoorworm

Her dad looked over her shoulder, clucking his tongue. "Arachstone University? Never heard you mention that school before."

Lily gulped. She quickly stuffed the letter back into the envelope, putting it in her back pocket before responding. "Yeah, guess it slipped my mind." She hadn't heard of the school either, but the word *sentinel* stirred her suspicions.

Suddenly, the lights flickered and winked out, leaving the kitchen with the morning sun trickling through the windows.

Tabby gave a little groan. "The power is out again. I thought you had this fixed Tony."

Her dad sprang into action, giving a salute. "Not to worry my dear. I'll get this fixed in no time." He threw her a thumbs up with a big confident grin, his shaggy hair falling around his eyes.

Tabby chuckled. "Okay you go fix it. Raven, let me show you to your room before I head out to work."

Raven smiled. "That would be great."

Brandon let out a choked breath as the adults disappeared from view. He shook his head, blinking. "Man! What just happened?"

"You mean the lights or the letter?" asked Lily.

Ang sniffed. "Isn't it obvious? Sissy here got a request to meet the Headmaster of the Sentinels."

Lily's brow furrowed. "Headmaster?"

A prim and proper voice called out. "Did you hear that? The headmaster himself?! Oh my! What an honor Miss Lily! An honor indeed!"

A small pop echoed in the kitchen as a small figure appeared on the counter. Standing a foot tall, the figure hurriedly smoothed down imaginary wrinkles from an already pristine white shirt and pressed brown overalls. His big black eyes blinked with excitement, the figure jumping from one foot to another.

Lily crossed her arms. "Brom, did you mess with the lights?"

Brom, the cottage's lead brownie, bit his lip. He took his weathered cap off his head as he tapped it softly, his eyes embarrassed. "Nothing truly dangerous Miss Lily, I can assure you. It was purely to distract your parents so I may speak with you."

She raised an eyebrow, then relaxed with a small smile. "Uh huh. So, what do you know about the headmaster?"

His large nose twitched as he wrung the cap in his hands nervously, silent. Very uncharacteristic of the usually talkative brownie. He had become extremely tightlipped after she mentioned being called a Sentinel by the Thunderbird. No matter how much she asked, questioned, demanded, Brom refused to give her so much as a hint. This was the most he spoke about it...ever.

If it was Parr, he'd tell me, Lily thought glumly.

Another brownie, Parr, had helped Lily when she traveled the dangerous forest to rescue Ari. He had become a dear friend. A dear friend who could never keep a secret to save his life. Unfortunately, Parr was away on a training retreat to finish his lessons in becoming a full-fledged brownie. Lily missed him terribly.

Brom shot her another guilty look, seeing her emotions play across her face. "Not too much Miss Lily." He raised his palms at her spearing glare. "Honest! I only know he's a very important individual. To have a personal invitation from him is seriously significant."

Lily rubbed her forehead, weariness creeping in. "I don't even know what I'm getting into. Maybe I shouldn't go." Experience, little as it was, taught her that dealing with the fae world wasn't always what it seemed.

Ang snorted, licking leftover honey from her hand. "That would be a mistake, Sissy."

Brom glared at the changeling, his big eyes following the slow drops of honey that stuck to the floor. "Must you be so crude?"

The changeling burped, wiping her chin.

He groaned, pulling his cap. "I *just* mopped those floors thank you very much. And, as you please, you have not an ounce of decorum about you and simply go and mess up my floors again!"

Ang merely looked at him, then slowly wiped her dirty hand on the wall.

Brom's eyes bulged. "Why you ignoramus-"

Lily closed her eyes, the pinpricks of a headache beginning. "Guys, enough...please."

By far the worst task she had lately was separating the brownie from the changeling. Brom believed Ang to be a heathen. Ang was simply messy. Really messy, but she never destroyed or broke anything. But, as Lily discovered, filthiness and messes were considered high crimes to brownies. She suspected Brom wouldn't bat an eye if Ang kicked a puppy, but heaven forbid if she dropped a fork and put it back with the utensils without cleaning it.

Brom gave a resigned sigh, pinching his nose. "As much as I hate to admit it Miss Lily, the neanderthal's previous statement is correct. This is a formal invitation by the Sentinel Headmaster himself. You must accept."

"What happens if she doesn't?" asked Brandon. "Does it mean she doesn't get accepted into the academy? Big deal."

"No...that's not what happens Master Brandon." Brom shook his head. He gazed imploringly at Lily. "Please trust me Miss Lily, you must meet with the Headmaster."

"And where is it?" asked Lily, exasperated. She looked at the letter again. Nope, not one reference where the academy was located.

Brom shuffled his feet, not meeting her gaze. "At the heart of the Veil."

She leaned forward, bending over the anxious brownie. "And that is...?"

He flushed, sputtering. "My apologies! I keep forgetting we have not reached the geography section in our lessons of fae history and culture. Which should probably have been first in our lessons. But then again, I was unable to accurately articulate the current events of your procurement of the Sentinel status. Oh my! I'll have to restructure the lesson plan at this rate..."

Lily took a quiet breath. "Brom..."

His eyes bugged out, contrite. "Oh, my goodness! How terribly rude of me because I know you dislike me mentioning how I cannot tell you things. Oh dear, oh dear..."

Lily lightly placed her fingers on his slight shoulders to stop the poor brownie from hyperventilating. "It's okay Brom. Let's start with the basics, okay?"

Brom's breathing started to slow down. He coughed for a moment to clear his throat. "Yes, you are correct. The thing to do first is the first thing." He took a deep breath, squinting his eyes shut. "The Sentinel Academy is in Iceland."

Brandon and Lily's eyes widened. Iceland? She wasn't expecting that.

She chewed her lip. "And how am I supposed to get there?"

Brandon jumped in. "A plane would be an obvious choice, right?"

She nodded. "True. But the problem is I don't have money for a ticket and our parents may get suspicious if I need to jet off to Iceland without them."

He frowned, realizing Lily's logic. The stepsiblings looked at each other, unsure how to move forward. Suddenly, things didn't seem so easy.

A vibrant, gruff burr called out. "Keep the heid! Stay calm everyone. Alasdair is here to help!"

Out popped a similar figure to Brom, but not nearly as tidy. Alasdair, the cottage's resident hob, raked his hands through his messy red hair before adjusting his wrinkled blue pants. He looked at them, giving a large grin as he rubbed his soot-covered hand over his stubbled chin.

Brom groaned loudly. "And what, pray tell, is your brilliant plan this time?"

Alasdair clapped his hands, giving a toothy grin. "Oye! Dinnae be such a blether Brommie. Did ye forget the lad and lass have their own transport right here?"

Brom blinked, then twitched. He reminded Lily of a little stuffed toy, his eyes pitch black with no pupils. "I'd rather forget, if that is what you are thinking. I must say Alasdair, that route is not necessarily the safest mode of transportation. It is quite unreliable and can be dangerous."

The hob shrugged. "Aye, but if ye have a better idea Brom I'd love to hear it. Especially since the auld folk are around. What's tae say what that auld skinny malinky longlegs would do."

Brandon frowned. "Longlegs?"

He jerked his thumb toward the basement. "Yer stepdad lad."

Brandon bit his lip trying to hold his laughter, but unable to stop a slight snort from escaping. Lily raised her eyebrows. He sheepishly looked away, ears red.

Brom stuck his nose up in the air, hands on his hips. "I am only imploring considerate caution. That way may be the most direct, but I want Miss Lily to be unequivocally informed."

"You two didn't mention what this option is," she pointed out.

"The mirror lass," Alasdair gestured upstairs.

"Oh..."

When she returned from the Veil, Brandon and the others told her the antique silver mirror in her room was actually a magical mirror that could help find people and send objects. But now it sounded like it could transport more than that.

Ang rolled her eyes, huffing loudly. "Yeah, yeah, fine. We get it guys. It's important for Lily to go asap and the best bet is the ambiguously dangerous mirror. Now that's enough of that. Can we move onto the most important thing we have to discuss? Like what is up with your aunt?"

Brandon scratched his head. "Probably jet lag."

Ang put her hands on her hips, frowning. "She seemed to hate me!"

Alasdair clucked his tongue as he quipped sarcastically. "Canny imagine why."

The changeling glared at the hob, giving a small hiss.

Lily put up her hands. "I'm sure Zia Raven was only being protective. She looks at me like a sister and knows how Ari treated me."

Ang shook her head, frowning. "It's more than that." She rubbed her arms up and down. "It was like she *saw* me."

Brom blinked. "To clarify completely. You mean you believe she saw your...raw I guess we should call it...appearance?"

"But that's ridiculous," protested Brandon. "No one spit on her right?"

Ang's brow furrowed. "Maybe I'm overreacting."

She sounded confident but the changeling rubbed her arms harder, the skin turning pink. Lily put her hand over Ang's, stopping the furious action. Her worried gaze met Lily's.

Lily tried to give a reassuring smile. "You did a great job. When you flipped your hair, even I forgot for a moment that you weren't Ari."

"Really?" She asked softly, her eyes uncertain.

"Really," Lily repeated firmly.

She puffed out her chest. If there was one thing the changeling loved more than honey and milk, it was compliments. "Well, yes...I am rather good, aren't I?"

Brandon gave a thumbs up and a toothy grin.

Brom and Alasdair rolled their eyes. Shaking his head, Alasdair rubbed his chin through his stubble. "While this banter is braw and all, 'tis time to get moving." He motioned to the invitation hiding in Lily's pocket.

Lily sighed. *Better early than never, I guess.*

Chapter Three

LILY ADJUSTED THE SMALL BACKPACK ON HER SHOULDERS, testing the weight to make sure it hung evenly. She glanced longingly at her bow in the corner, wishing she could take it with her. Brom assured her she would not need it for this visit.

She sighed, doubt rising. She really wanted to believe the brownie. Truly, she did. Unfortunately, the prickle of unease that trailed down her spine told her otherwise.

She squinted, the glaring sun peeking through the windowpane. It was fast approaching noon. Soon, the mirror would activate. Then, to Arachstone. She rubbed her hands nervously. Brom said the safest time was either the peak of day or the peak of night. Not that the mirror wouldn't work other times. But, according to both Alasdair and Brom, there were less 'accidents'. The brownie assured her this was the smoothest method and there was a high probability she would 'retain all her limbs'. Somehow, that reassurance didn't give Lily much comfort.

Tabby and Tony had left for work in a hurry a few hours earlier. They promised to be home by dinnertime; her father wanted to make carbonara. Would her dad come home early? The uncertainty of being caught certainly didn't help the already high level of anxiety she was experiencing at the thought of traveling by an unreliable magical object.

But if she was being honest, and she hated to admit it, this was their best opportunity to sneak there and back without being discovered.

There was only one outlier in this sensitive equation. Aunt Raven.

Brom had calmly reminded Lily, at least ten times, that Aunt Raven was sleeping. But was he really sure? Jet lag didn't always mean people slept for hours. She could only hope her aunt was in such a deep sleep that even a heavy metal concert couldn't wake her. Unfortunately, she couldn't recall if Aunt Raven was a light sleeper or not. She prayed she wasn't.

Brom clapped his hands together primly, gathering the group's attention. Brandon and Ang halted, still holding chairs they were moving out of the way to clear a space in front of the mirror. Brom clasped his hands behind his back, holding himself in a soldier posture. He clicked his heels together with a tight snap.

"Hurry up, hurry up everyone! The noon sun will not last forever." Brom glanced around the room, frowning as no one immediately sprang into action. He dramatically cleared his throat as he spoke louder. "Quickly!"

Soon the space was cleared of all furniture and debris. Lily bit her lip, shuffling from side to side.

Well...at least a chair won't hit me if something goes wrong.

Brom continued to bark out orders. "Please back up everyone. Back up! Give Miss Lily space within the circle and form yourselves behind myself and Alasdair." He glanced over at Lily. He must have seen her hesitation. His gaze softened, giving her a reassuring smile.

"It is time Miss Lily."

Lily worried her lip. "Is Barlow alright with this?" Barlow was the resident lob, ornery and blunt. He was very particular, especially about not damaging the cottage.

Brom pursed his lips, sucking in a breath. "Well...he's quite busy at the moment. Alasdair showed him some items that need fixing. He'll be preoccupied for a while." He gave a nervous, slightly forced, laugh. "You need not worry Miss Lily. Not to worry at all."

She raised her eyebrow. "He's going to lose it isn't he?"

Alasdair pipped up brightly. "Oh, aye lass. He's gonna be crabbit no doubt about it. But nothing for you to sweat over. That's our problem."

Brom reached out, gesturing her to stand next to him in front of the

26

mirror. Lily tugged her backpack straps lightly. The smooth silver surface stared back, her reflection unmoving. Brom remained at her side, patting her hand. He whispered, giving her a calming smile.

"Not to worry Miss Lily. You can handle this."

She gave a feeble nod. A weight caused her to look down, finding small blue stone nestled in her palm where Brom had patted her hand.

Brom gestured to the stone. "A tracking stone. When you need to return home, simply throw it on the ground at your feet." His tone suddenly serious. "That even means if you feel scared or are in danger. Do not hesitate. Do you understand?"

She clutched the stone before tucking it into her pocket. "I understand."

Alasdair scoffed. "Brommie, yer makin' it sound like she's going to war." He waved his hand dismissively. "You'll be fine lass. Find out what they want and come home."

"You got this Lil!" Brandon put up his thumbs, a big smile on his face.

She returned a wane smile, though it did little to settle her churning insides.

"Miss Lily, you need to focus." Brom tugged on her pants, forcing her to turn back to the mirror. When he was satisfied, he stepped back toward the sidelines. He pulled out a small, gold pocket watch. His eyes widened, pointing to the mirror urgently.

"Dear me, we're out of time. Okay Miss Lily, just like we discussed. Walk up to the mirror five paces, hold onto your pendant, and call out the destination."

The mirror started to ripple softly, then began to speed up, the silver surface rolling like waves. The air quickly picked up, Lily's curls bouncing and whipping around her face. Her neck warmed, the pendant glowing faintly as the heat spread through her palm. The ethereal, deep voice of Tinmiukpuk whispered in her mind.

Let us go young Sentinel. The first step is but the beginning.

Lily breathed deep. *Easy for you to say.*

She glanced over her shoulder. Brandon was still giving her a thumbs up with a reassuring smile. Ang nodded, her arms crossed lightly. Steeling herself, she took five tentative steps forward, the wind buffering against her pants as she called out.

"Arachstone!"

Her lungs squeezed tight for a moment, her entire body constricting way too tight. She forced herself to stay upright, the squeezing sensation growing. The room started to evaporate when she vaguely heard the slamming of a door. Straining, she thought she heard faint, muffled yelling.

"What is going on?!"

She frowned. Why was the voice muffled? Then, a small pop hit her body. Like a bubble burst in her ribs. And then, nothing but pitch darkness.

Chapter Four

LILY'S HEAD CHURNED AS HER HAIR SNAPPED AGAINST HER face. Her eyes clenched shut as biting wind stung her eyes. Only when her windswept hair settled over her eyes did she take a breath. Her curls were probably a fluffed-up mess, but she was afraid to remove her death grip from the pendant to check. She forced herself to take another shaky breath, but still kept her eyes closed. As if on cue, Tinmiukpuk's calm and resolute voice reverberated in her mind.

You can open your eyes young one. We are here.

Blue surrounded her when she cracked her eyes open. Nothing but a large, bright blue, cloudless sky. She bent over, clasping her stomach, as an uncontrollable wave of vertigo crashed over her. She stood on a natural rock ledge, black lava rock crunching under her sneakers. Pale, yellow tinged moss dotted across the rocks. The ledge dropped sharply behind her and as well as either side.

She gulped; it was at least a two-hundred-foot drop. In front stood a huge mountain covered in moss and more lava rock.

The mountain was massive, towering toward the sky. The thunderous roar of water engulfed her eardrums. She blinked, turning slowly in a circle, and looked outward. The mountain was in the center of several large waterfalls, gigantic waves cascading around her, disappearing into the mist below. Another wave of dizziness crashed over her.

29

Spots danced around her eyelids. If she didn't calm down, she would pass out.

Deep breaths Lil, take deep breaths.

"Easier said than done," she muttered to herself.

E-wee-ne-tu. Peace young Sentinel. Move forward, Tinmiukpuk commanded softly.

"Move forward to where exactly?" She whispered, exasperated.

"Hey there!" A voice called out, cutting through the haze. A real, honest to goodness voice that wasn't in her head.

Startled, she automatically turned back to the mountain, her balance teetering. The voice called out again.

"Wait, wait! Not so fast!"

Her heart thudded loudly in her ears. Pebbles from her sneakers fell down the cliff, the small echoes tinkling and disappearing into the waves. She gulped. That was definitely not a good sign.

The voice continued. "Alright! Now I want you to walk slowly. And I do mean slowly. Turn and walk towards my voice."

She turned around slowly, even so far as to lower herself to the ground and slowly stretched her arms out. Her pulse fluttered in her throat, making her want to curl up in a blanket and hide. She refused to look anywhere but at her hands, each one grasping and moving forward on the mossy rock, inch by inch. She never anticipated she was afraid of heights. But then again, she was never hundreds of feet in the air with only two feet separating her from a sheer drop. The voice kept talking to her.

"Oh, crawling? Okay I guess that works. Whatever floats your boat."

"Do I look like this 'floats my boat'?" she groused out.

"Hmmm. Actually, you look more like a worm," the voice replied matter of fact.

"You're being *super* helpful you know that!"

"Ooohhh. Someone woke up on the wrong side of the cliff this morning," tsked the voice. "Keep going, keep going. Almost there... Okay! Looks like you're far enough away. You can look up now."

Reluctantly, she lifted her head. Through the fine mist from the waterfall, she could make out a passageway carved and smoothed out from the jagged black lava rock, right in the face of the mountain.

Slowly, carefully, she raised herself up on shaking legs. As she finally made it to the entrance, she found the face to go with the voice.

He looked to be in his late twenties, maybe thirties, as there were some fine laugh lines dotting around his eyes indicating he smiled a lot. He was not too tall, but not short either, with short brown hair and brown eyes. He was of a thin build, but lean muscle defined his crossed arms. He was handsome, by normal, human standards. Maybe it was his eyes. Eyes that spoke of mirth and mischief. Sure enough, his eyes crinkled as he gave her a warm smile, showing a small dimple.

His voice was jolly with an accent she couldn't quite place. "Welcome, welcome! Lily Ambrosino, I presume?"

She stood still, awkwardly adjusting her backpack as she replied quietly.

"Yes, that's me."

She jumped as the man's hand darted out in front of her face, his fingers wagging. "Invitation?"

Silently, she pulled the invitation from her pocket, handing it over. The man shook the note a few times, his eyes narrowing as he squinted at the paper. After a beat he turned his gaze back to her with a smile.

"Yup, looks good."

The man, without sparing another glance, tossed the paper over his shoulder, right over the edge. He reached out to grab her hand, shaking it firmly. His smile grew wider as his handshake became more pronounced.

"My name is Dagur. Wow, I'm impressed you took the cliff route to get here."

"Cliff route?" she asked. Her arm began to hurt from it flapping up and down as she tried to disengage from Dagur's enthusiastic greeting. "There's another way to get here?"

His eyes widened as he dropped her arm with a flop. "Um...yeah. Most newbies take the other entrance. Folks who drop in from the cliff route either pass out or throw up. It's awesome you didn't do either."

Lily raised her eyebrow as she asked. "What other way can you get here?"

Dagur laughed. "Well flying, duh! Didn't your invitation tell you your flight date and time? We would have picked you up at Reykjavik."

Lily blinked. "No...I didn't see that." Not that she could have explained a last-minute flight to Iceland to her father.

"Well now you know, don't you?" Dagur laughed, clapping her on the back loudly. The air whooshed out her lungs, forcing a raspy cough. Lily began to rethink the 'not throwing up' part.

Dagur, completely oblivious to her plight, continued to usher her into the mountain passageway. "Alright come on. Let's get you to see the big guy!"

She followed him into the darkened passageway, rubbing her arms as the air turned slightly damp. Sconces dotted the black rock, their flickering fire lighting the way as they headed up the stone steps. After a few minutes of silence, save for the rushing noise from the waterfalls, she asked.

"When you said 'the big guy', did you mean Headmaster Stoorworm?"

Dagur shook his head, glancing at her over his shoulder. "Nope. I meant the big guy." He gestured up the stairs with his head.

She tried, and failed, to keep her mouth from gaping open. The dimly lit stairs curved in a circular pattern and continued up and up, ending on a platform that housed a giant door. The firelight illuminated the gigantic stone door, casting eerie shadows that danced and hid around the stone. It was etched with various depictions that were Nordic in design, swirls and runes that glowed in the dim light. The door was so massive, towering over Lily's frame, that a single human could not open it. But that wasn't the only sight that gained Lily's attention. It was *who* was guarding the door.

Dagur called cheerily. "Hey big guy. How's it going?"

Her gaze moved up...and up. A massive, shadowy figure loomed in front of the door. He, Lily assumed it was a male, was easily nine feet tall and almost as wide. He was clad in tattered brown clothes, reminding her of old sails from a shipwrecked vessel. He sported a large bulbous nose, small dark eyes, and large bat-like ears that held random tufts of black coarse hair. He carried an enormous stone club in his hairy hand that dragged on the floor while scratching his almost bald head.

The guard let out a long, drawn-out sigh, which sounded like the grinding of stone as opposed to puffing air.

Dagur chuckled. "Aww come on man don't be like that." He

32

elbowed Lily lightly in the ribs, making her jolt. "Jot here thinks I talk too much. But then again, trolls think anyone who talks more than a stone talk too much."

Troll? Lily forcibly took a gulp of damp air.

The massive guard, well troll, rolled his eyes accompanied by a rumbling vibration.

She blinked, shocked. A real-life troll. She was equal parts awed and terrified. Dagur must have seen her face as he called out.

"Hey Jot, mind telling the nice lady you're not gonna eat her." He covered his mouth and whispered to her...loudly. "He hasn't eaten a human in like five hundred years."

Jot snorted, his eyes narrowing.

Dagur put his hands up. "Sorry man! Just joking around. Trying to lighten the mood ya know?"

Jot, still glaring at Dagur, leaned toward them, his club rising slowly. The walls around them began to vibrate and rattle ominously.

Dagur, unbothered, rolled his eyes. He let out a large dramatic sigh. "Fiiiiiiine. I owe you a bucket of sheep's milk. We square?"

The troll straightened up, the vibrations settling. With a soft grunt, he crossed the club in front of him. When the last of the vibrations died down, Jot's stony gaze landed on Lily, unmoving.

Remembering her manners, she said softly.

"Hello Jot, my name is Lily."

Jot slowly tilted his head to the side, studying her a beat before finally nodding.

She held in her excitement. She was talking to a real, honest to goodness troll! Sadly, she couldn't fully process that feat when another solid clap hit her back, breaking her out of her musing.

Dagur smacked her back one more time as he exclaimed cheerily, "Well now that introductions are out of the way. Mind letting us in pal? Newbie's gotta see the headmaster."

Jot stepped to the side slowly, his feet making heavy thumps that shook the ground. Lily spread her arms to keep herself balanced, her legs shaking from the tremors. The troll really was massive. She kept a wary eye on the stone club as it grated against the floor mere inches from them. Dagur must have seen her staring at the club. He whispered into her ear in a reassuring tone.

"Not to worry. Even though Jot is one of the smaller day-trolls, he knows how big he is compared to us."

She looked over, shocked. This behemoth was one of the 'smaller' trolls?

Dagur's unphased tone continued. "Pull your jaw off the floor newbie. If you're gonna be shocked from a day-troll, just wait." He gave her a mischievous wink. "That's nothing compared to what you'll see when you pass through this door."

As the stone door opened with a groan, Lily saw what Dagur meant.

The door opened to a large cavern carved inside the mountain. Stone staircases spiraled upward and downward on either side of the walls. The black rock was illuminated with veins of variously colored rock; from gold, to silver, to blue, to green. The staircases rose so high it faded from eyesight. The floor opened up in a fairly large, circular hole in the center of the room with silver metal railings surrounding it. A beam of white light shone within the circle. It was strikingly beautiful.

But that wasn't all.

Trolls, humans, and a variety of other creatures that Lily couldn't identify were walking around, completely unperturbed and focused on whatever their agenda was for the day. No electricity could be found. Instead, fires were lit on tall sconces along with thousands of floating balls of light which danced in the air. They zipped from one side to the other, darting around the passersby.

"Will-o-wisps," he answered her unspoken question as he dodged a creature that looked like a cross between a fox and a cat. "Gosh darn it, watch where you're going dude! Skoffins am I right?" He chuckled at her as if he expected her to know what a Skoffin was. Lily warily backed up when the 'Skoffin' hissed at Dagur, long fangs bared. She frowned, noticing the creature had blindfold on.

Dagur wagged his finger. "Nu uh. Play nice. You're here on asylum remember?"

The Skoffin hissed again, his mangy red tail fluffed up, before darting up the steps. Dagur shrugged nonchalantly. "You'd think he'd show some appreciation for us taking him in, but noooo. He's still annoyed he has to wear the blindfold. We told him, no blindfold no asylum. For a smart guy, he knows his eyes could kill anyone. Maybe he got mange from his cat momma."

Lily blinked, her mouth gaped open.

Ignoring her, Dagur proceeded to walk toward a hallway that branched off the side. She scrambled to catch up to him, dodging creatures and humanlike individuals. Mumbling her apologies as she almost collided with a large humanoid male sporting bull horns but ended up smacking into another creature that looked eerily like a griffin.

Oh please, don't let me get eaten before I even get to the interview.

"Not much further," he called over his shoulder. They reached another set of doors, these were still tall and massive, but didn't look nearly as heavy. He pulled the door open, giving her a small, gentleman-like bow with a smile.

"Right this way."

Lily found herself in a large library, the largest she'd ever seen. The dim light cast a warm glow upon rows and rows of books that were stacked up tremendously high. In the center of the room, several tables made of stone and thick wood were strewn in front of an immense fireplace. The fire crackled and hissed, thawing the damp coldness seeping into her limbs. In a normal situation, she would bask in this discovery. She wanted to revel in the books and curl up by the fireplace with a cup of tea. But this wasn't a normal situation. Regrettably, she tore her gaze from the library's siren call and focused directly in front of her. There, in front of the fire, standing at one of the tables, was a group of people who looked to be in deep discussion.

There were four individuals; two men, a woman, and some creature that Lily couldn't identify. One of the men, she guessed a leader as his very presence dwarfed the others, caught her gaze briefly with piercing ice blue eyes. He appeared middle-aged; his cropped short blonde hair was peppered with silver. He was very tall, easily over six and half feet, as the other adults did not even reach his broad shoulders. He sported a well-tended beard.

As Dagur and Lily approached the group, the man said in a deep, cultured voice.

"As always, we appreciate the light elves continued support and alliance. Please tell your king I will be in touch with him soon." The tall man gestured toward the woman. "Chancellor Nightingale, please escort our esteemed friend to the gateway."

The woman, Chancellor Nightingale, stood up. Lily's eyes widened. She was almost six feet tall herself. The Chancellor sported dark silver hair that was tied up in a severe bun. Lily blinked. This woman was beautiful. Not your typical, fairytale princess beauty. But a striking, fierce beauty.

The Chancellor turned, the firelight reflecting her entire face. Lily did a double take. She wore a monocle over her left eye, which was milky white with no iris. Nightingale's right eye, a stormy grey, zeroed in on Lily. Lily's cheeks reddened, ashamed that she was caught staring at the Chancellor's blind eye so openly. If the Chancellor noticed, she did not comment. Instead, she calmly assessed both Lily and Dagur as they approached the table.

Dagur raised his hand in greeting. "Hey Night!"

Chancellor Nightingale ignored him, instead she mutely nodded over to the tall man. Silently, she inclined her head toward the creature to her left.

The creature was small, with a bald head and large eyes. It was pale, with a yellow glow gleaming from its skin. It stared at the Chancellor with its big eyes. Almost hypnotically, her monocle began to whirl. The monocle gave a few clicks, the glass becoming iridescent a moment before fading back to clear glass. Nightingale raised her gaze to the tall man and spoke in a calm, but very matter-of-fact tone.

"He expresses his appreciation at your sincere gesture. He will present this to the Elf King and will return with an answer."

The tall man gave a small bow towards the elf envoy. As Nightingale turned to escort the elf out, Dagur yelled after them.

"What? Not even a hi?"

Still ignoring him, she walked briskly out of the library, the small elf following behind her. The tall man turned back to a pile of paperwork on the desk, flitting through a few sheets.

"Wow..." Dagur whistled low. "That Valkyrie lance is shoved up nice and tight there isn't it."

No one answered him.

Dagur pouted. "Oh, come on! What did I say?"

The tall man, not looking up from his paperwork, interjected with a droll. "I believe Chancellor Nightingale is still displeased at your antics the other week."

Dagur plopped down onto the table with a thump. He put his feet up, crossing them, narrowly missing another stack of papers. The last remaining man squeaked in protest, quickly gathering them with a disgruntled huff.

Dagur, oblivious, gave the tall man a cluelessly thoughtful look.

"Really? Huh! Never thought she'd still be upset. It was a little joke. A little cayenne pepper in the morning tea stimulates blood circulation. It didn't hurt anyone."

Lily schooled her expression, mentally shaking her head. *All'oscuro...*

The other man holding the papers huffed again loudly, rolling his eyes. He was shorter than the rest with an average build. Thinning red hair graced the top of his head that matched a thick beard and mustache. "You are too childish Dagur. You're a professor for goodness sakes, act like one!"

Dagur tapped his foot in the air as he gave a wink. "Heya Dick, how's it hanging?"

The man's face flushed, dropping the papers all over the table. He gasped, grasping for the spilled paperwork, his lips peeling back with a snarl.

"See?! Childish! My *name* is Richard" He threw his nose up in the air. "Professor Richard Bonk."

"Don't get so testy Professor Dick," scoffed Dagur. "You're looking kinda swollen and red now. You may wanna calm down, it's not a good look."

Professor Bonk sputtered, his cheeks reddening further against his bright red beard. "You...you..."

The taller male gave a deep, long sigh. The type of sigh parents would give to unruly children. "That is quite enough Dagur."

"Sorry headmaster. I'll be good, scout's honor." He crossed his heart and mimed zipping his lip, eyes wide and innocent.

So, that's the headmaster.

"You were never a scout," mumbled Professor Bonk, his disgruntled frown hidden beneath his beard.

Ignoring them, the headmaster walked around the table, his hands clasped behind his back. As he approached, his electric blue eyes gaze caught hers. Lily fought not to squirm. It was hard though; his gaze was so intense it was palpable. It was like being assessed by a scientist observing a cell under a microscope. When he spoke, it was in a formal, but pleasant, tone.

"Welcome to Arachstone, Miss Lily Ambrosino. My name is Headmaster Stoorworm. Please forgive the spontaneous and," he glanced over at Dagur (who was giving Lily a thumbs up behind the headmaster's back), "rather eccentric greeting you have received thus far."

Embarrassed, Lily waved her hands in front of her. "Oh, it's alright."

The headmaster gave away no emotion as he continued. "I presume you have many questions."

She twisted her fingers, clasping them together nervously. "Ah...Yes, a few actually."

Headmaster Stoorworm nodded. He stretched his hand out, gesturing to the door. "Will you walk with me a moment?"

Taking her silence as agreement, he turned and strode out of the library. Lily pumped her legs to catch up with him, cursing her short limbs. She finally reached his side when they approached the main hallway. The bustling activity was still there. However, everyone gave them a wide birth. A very different experience from before.

She shook her head inwardly. *Hard to miss him, he's enormous.*

The headmaster spoke up with a very astute observation. "Miss Ambrosino. Your first question may be what this place is and who we are."

She blinked, surprised by how blunt he was. "Yes, I have been wondering what a Sentinel means."

Stoorworm nodded, his hands flexing slightly behind his back.

"Understandable, you are completely new to this old world. Simply put, Sentinels are guardians. Scholars, peacekeepers, defenders, and at times justice enforcers to the delicate balance between the human world and the Veil. We are comprised of both human and fae, bound by honor and oath as a neutral party to preserve that tenuous balance between the worlds."

She remained silent. *Okaaay...that's a lot to process.*

Rocking back and forth on her heels, she chewed her lip. "So, are you really an academy?"

"In a sense. We provide services to many Sentinels for their various needs. From defense training to lore history. Anything a Sentinel may need to preserve the balance and maintain the oath. But ultimately, we try to remain as autonomous as possible. Each Sentinel has their own path to preserve the balance. I prefer more...solitary pursuits."

"But you're the headmaster," she blurted out before she could stop herself. "Isn't there a hierarchy? Aren't there are rules that must be followed? You're the top official, right?"

Lily rubbed her arm as a gust of cold air washed over her.

Stoorworm quietly raised his eyebrow, not responding. After an uncomfortable beat, he slowly drawled out. "That may be. I may oversee the larger picture to preserve the balance and maintain the Sentinels as a whole, but that is all. I do not 'teach' as one would think. Nor do I give absolute directives. We are neither a school nor a court."

His tone was cold. Not unfriendly, but definitely not reassuring.

Lily had a strange feeling she was treading on thin ice. Her pendant warmed softly against her chest, thawing the chill. "Umm, sorry. I think I understand. This place is similar to Constantinople. A place of learning and guidance if necessary. But there's also a larger authority when your Sentinels need overall checks and balances." She paused, hesitant. "Am I right?"

The headmaster stared at her, then nodded, approving her answer. As his gaze lifted from hers, Lily took a breath when the cold wave disappeared.

Stoorworm resumed observing the area in front of them, the circle of light in particular. "Your second question I assume is why and how are you came to be a Sentinel."

Lily mutely nodded, figuring he was asking her a rhetorical question. But, honestly this was one of her biggest questions.

Stoorworm paused midstride. "Your home, Hemlock Cottage, was built on a ley line. One of those most powerful and oldest ones. The cottage, as well as the corresponding Veil doorway, has been a most powerful sanctuary for hundreds of years. It must be guarded. Which means, the cottage needs a protector." He leaned down, his large hand pointing at her. "To put it simply. The cottage chose *you* Miss Ambrosino to guard it."

Lily's eyes widened as she let out a protest. "Wait, wait, wait. What do you mean the cottage chose me? It's not alive, is it?"

The headmaster remained silent, seemingly unhurried to answer. He tilted his head, his gaze raised upwards toward the spiraling stairs. His chest rose and fell with a deep sigh.

"While I am still unsure as to why the cottage chose you, we must make do. You are not only a human, you are young. Young in both body and mind as to how this new world works. And that is precisely the reason I sent you the invitation." He resumed walking, Lily jumping to catch up. "You may learn from our educators on anything you require to protect and guard the ley line at your home. That will be your primary objective as a Sentinel. Though seeing you now, I must say I am impressed you have acquired such powerful help already." He gestured towards her pendant.

Frowning slightly, Lily grasped the pendant. How did he know about it?

Stoorworm put up a hand. "You can relax Miss Ambrosino. I'm simply speaking of an old friend. Or...do you not wish to say hello?"

Lily's pendant warmed, shaking slightly. In a burst of light, a tiny bird, no bigger than her palm, appeared above her head. It sported long feathers of shimmery red and gold. The bird landed on her shoulder, its talons giving her a comforting squeeze. Then it spoke in the Thunderbird's deep voice.

Stoorworm. It has been a while old friend.

The headmaster smiled formally, giving a slight nod to the ancient Thunderbird. "Indeed. I am most glad to see you Tinmiukpuk. May I confirm that Miss Ambrosino-"

The Thunderbird nodded. *Assisted me in defeating my ancient enemy...yes.*

"Intriguing," murmured Stoorworm.

Then the two became quiet, staring at one another, not blinking. Lily coughed, hoping to break the silence. Her eyes darted back and forth between them, but they remained still as statues.

Suddenly, as if a trance was broken, the headmaster's electric gaze rested on Lily once more.

"You may ask one more question Miss Ambrosino." He pulled out an old pocket watch from his cloak. "I am pressed for another engagement."

Another gentle squeeze from Tinmiukpuk's small talons on her shoulder gave her encouragement.

"How can I get my sister Ari back from the prince?"

"Prince Dain?" Stoorworm rested his fingers on his chin, rubbing his beard. "We do not interfere with the fae's court dynamics. I am afraid I cannot help you in that regard. However," he continued as Lily had slumped her shoulders, disappointed, "I did say Sentinels are autonomous. As long as the ley line remains safe and the barrier between worlds is intact, there is nothing stopping you from going on your own to look for your kin. Especially if there is a human remaining in the fae world through questionable means."

"But, you won't help me?" Her disappointed whisper seemed to shout into the open air.

Stoorworm's eyes softened slightly. "The Sentinel academy is a neutral party. We guide, protect, preserve, and maintain balance. But, you have everything at your disposal to learn, to grow, and train. You, especially, will need to train."

"Why?"

He nodded to the Thunderbird. "Ancients are rare. Rarer still are cases where ancients have made pacts to assist Sentinels to preserve the balance. For the wise Thunderbird to choose you Miss Ambrosino, that is a feat. But," he cautioned, "an ancient is a strain on the human body. You must train to help him as he helps you. As I see it now, you are not even close to being able to utilize the full potential of being a Sentinel. Let alone one that is bound with an ancient."

Be kind old friend, the Thunderbird interjected. *She is young. And she is my Sentinel. That means she has great potential. For our journey, we must take one step before the next. Eventually our destination will be reached.*

Stoorworm sighed. "You are correct old friend. My apologies." His gaze centered on Lily, his tone grave. "But until you learn what you need, I'm afraid even the mighty Thunderbird would have difficulty assisting you appropriately."

Lily's head bowed, her lips twisting in a grimace.

Stoorworm gave a small smile, almost in apology. "Do not fret. I also believe, from what my old friend has relayed, you have many allies to assist you. Oh...speaking of-"

A loud caw echoed from above. A large raven flew overhead, taking a steep dive straight for them. Stoorworm held out his arm as the large black bird perched effortlessly, its wings beating loudly.

A rare smile broke out from beneath his beard. "Huginn, what have you brought?"

Inside the raven's beak was a small bit of paper. The headmaster gently plucked the parchment, unfolding it with care. He blinked a few times, his eyes skimming over the message.

He handed the paper to her, his eyebrow raised. "I believe you are needed at home, Miss Ambrosino."

She took the paper, her heart thumping in her ribs as she read the short message.

> *Lily, I think I found your sister, coming to your house. -*
> *Cab*

Cab...

Lily shook herself, taking a deep breath. With trembling fingers, she tucked the note into her pocket. "You're right headmaster Stoorworm. I think I do need to get home."

Stoorworm nodded. "Take this, you may need it."

Reaching into his cloak again, he pulled out a rather weird object, placing it in her hand. Lily frowned. It was an old brass doorknob. It was round, with the beginnings of rust forming around the edges, which dulled the once brilliant, burnished copper. Confused, she stared at the random doorknob nestled in her palm.

"Place that in the cottage's attic door when you need to come to Arachstone. It shall open a corresponding door here on the general floor." His tone was matter of face, but a twinkle sparked in his icy eyes. "Let's not have you go through the cliff entrance again, shall we?"

Lily burst out a sigh of relief. "Thank you."

The headmaster bowed slightly. "You are welcome to return when your...activities are done. While we shall not force you, I am sure there is more we can assist you with this world. And, I must confess, I am quite curious about how these recent events will unfold. I would appreciate if you reported your findings to me." He checked his pocket watch again as the raven flew up into the mountain giving another resounding call. "My apologies, I must depart. Safe travels Miss Ambrosino. It was a pleasure meeting you and I wish you all luck and success as you learn to become a sentinel." He nodded to Tinmiukpuk. "Old friend."

Without another word, the headmaster walked up the stone steps. Lily waited until the headmaster disappeared from view before she circled around, holding the doorknob. Where was she supposed to go now? Tinmiukpuk clicked reassuringly before he disappeared back into her pendant with a small burst of light.

"I didn't know you could do that?" she whispered.

There was a short pause before the Thunderbird spoke in her mind.

It was unnecessary until now. It also takes quite a bit of energy. When you train, it will be easier for me to appear.

"Do what?" asked a voice behind her.

Lily yelped, jumping slightly.

Dagur's smiling face greeted her. He clapped, nodding in approval. "You got some good reflexes. That'll come in handy in defense training."

She looked at him skeptically. "Are you really a professor?"

Dagur put his hand over his heart. "Oh! You wound me with your doubts."

"What do you teach?"

Dagur smiled proudly. "I teach both defensive and offensive training. Plus, a bit of herbalism and basic medical." He must have seen her frown. "Just come to my early morning boot camp. I promise you I'll get you ready for whatever you'll come across."

Lily chuckled. "Maybe I'll take you up on that sometime. But I do need to get back in a hurry." She raised the doorknob. "Do you know where-"

"Oh yeah, no problem newbie. Follow me and we'll get you home lickity split."

Lily smiled, following the young professor. A fluttering hope expanded her chest. She had *finally* gotten some answers. She still had questions, but this was enough...for the moment. And Cab had information on Ari, which was a bonus.

Finally, Lily thought, *things are starting to become a bit easier.*

Chapter Five

"HOUSE AND HOME HAVE MERCY!"

Lily blinked, chaos descending as the familiar squeaky, cultured voice screamed.

"Begone foul beast!"

She took a deep breath. *Easier? Definitely not. What was I thinking?*

Dagur had escorted her to a room filled with various doors. He told her to pick any door and simply insert the doorknob. Skeptical, she did as she instructed and stepped through the door and ended up in her room. No fuss, no muss.

But instead of being greeted by her friends, as she expected, a blur of bodies flew past her crashing into a chair. Lily could only make out a tangle of limbs as more screams rang from all around. As her vision focused, it centered on the floor. There, grimacing and screaming, was Ang. Someone was on top of Ang, holding her down.

Lily's eyes widened.

It was Aunt Raven, her face eerily cold and fierce. Ang's legs kicked out underneath, trying to knock Raven off but to no avail.

Ang grunted. "Get off me you crazy woman!"

Her aunt growled back, cold and angry. "What did you do with my niece?"

Ang stopped struggling for a minute. "What?"

Raven bared her teeth, raising her arm, poised to strike. "Bring her back, or so help me you *donas de fuera*!"

Ang's face paled, her horrified gaze darting around. "I...I didn't do anything!"

Brandon ran to Aunt Raven's side. He pulled her arm desperately, but she wouldn't budge.

"Aunt Raven please," he pleaded. "Ang is innocent!"

Raven barked, gritting her teeth. "Step back Brandon! You don't know what she is."

Lily's mouth dropped. Her aunt really was going to pile drive Ang into the floor. Something tugged on her arm. Brom stared up, his face anxious.

The brownie was beside himself, wringing his hands as his words came in frantic gasps. "Miss Lily, thank the hearth you're here. You MUST do something about that wildcat of an aunt of yours before she banishes Ang."

Lily's eyebrow quirked up. "Banish?"

That's when she noticed the amulet dangling in Raven's grasp. It was oval with blue, white, and black swirled enamel resembling an eye. Lily remembered her aunt mentioning something called the *Evil Eye* a long time ago. But the superstition said it was for protection, not banishment.

She frowned. "Brom, that pendant doesn't actually work-"

Her words died down at Brom's terrified expression.

Ang grunted, struggling to keep the amulet away. The changeling's arms began to tremble as Raven's hand continued to press downward, the pendant coming closer. It wasn't that Lily believed the pendant could do anything, but it was the look of utter fear stamped on Ang's face which caused her to dash forward, throwing herself between them.

"Stop Aunt Raven."

For a minute, her aunt's crazed look pierced through her. Lily grabbed her aunt's shoulders and gave it a good shake.

"Zia Raven, look at me!"

Her aunt blinked once, then twice, before her eyes cleared. She frowned, shaking her head a moment before emitting a small smile of pained relief.

"Oh sweetheart! Is that you?"

45

She nodded, keeping her voice calm. "Yes, it's me."

Raven took a deep breath, checking over Lily, making sure she was alright. Suddenly, she wrapped her arms around Lily, squeezing her tight.

"I thought they had taken you away," she whispered unsteadily into Lily's neck.

"I'm fine." Lily patted her back reassuringly.

Someone cleared their throat, forcing Lily to disengage. Ang was still on the floor, her lips pulled up in a pained expression.

The changeling grunted. "Can you guys get off me please?"

Lily's eyes widened. *Oops.*

They were on top of Ang's legs, squashing the poor changeling's thin bones. Raven's arms tightened around her before lifting and twisting them away in some insane dance move, positioning Lily behind her aunt's small frame.

Ang began to get up on unsteady legs as Raven bit out coldly.

"Not so fast changeling..."

Ang rolled her eyes, grimacing. "As if I could. I'm hurting over here you know!"

Lily put her hand on Raven's shoulder, giving a comforting squeeze. "Zia Raven, Ang is a friend."

Raven tensed as she asked skeptically. "She's a friend?"

"Yes."

"Do you know she's not Ari?"

"Yes."

"And you know what she is?"

Lily paused before she answered. "Yes..."

"Yeah, we both do," Brandon piped up.

Lily found herself at the brunt of her aunt's angry gaze.

Oh geez Brandon...not helpful.

Raven crossed her arms over her chest, staring them down. "Okay kids, just so I understand. BOTH of you know *what* she is. AND you know she's posing as Ari. Which means Ari isn't here..."

Brom interjected. "If I may Miss Ambrosino. Your family, especially Miss Lily, has been ever so persistent in the finding-"

"And what is a BROWNIE doing allowing a changeling in his home?!"

46

Brom flushed, mumbling. "Well, circumstances required-"

Lily and Brandon gave a wordless glance, then started to back up to the door. Their aunt was a swirling storm that they did not want to be dragged in. Brandon's foot creaked on the floorboard and Raven whipped back to them, not missing a beat.

"Oh...no. I am not done with you two!" She motioned to Brom. "You – stay put." She pointed her finger at Ang. "Same goes for you!"

Her eyes narrowed, her sharp voice cutting through the air. "Sit down, both of you!"

Immediately Brandon jumped down to the floor. Lily stood, motionless.

Raven raised her eyebrow, her voice quieting in a singsong lilt. "Children...you both have some 'splaining to do."

Lily and Brandon sat on her bedroom floor, legs crossed. It reminded her of being scolded at grade school. They sat there, chastised, while they explained what had happened over the last few months. Her aunt remained silent save for one time when she motioned for Brom to get her some tea. By the time they were finished, Raven had drunk three cups, the last one spiked with something Lily couldn't identify.

"And that's what happened," she finished.

Her aunt stood there, quietly sipping the last remnants of tea, her expression neutral. Lily's anxiety grew as the silence continued. Everyone was staring at Raven, waiting to see a reaction. Any reaction. After a moment, her aunt took one last sip and handed the cup silently over to Brom, who hurriedly gathered it, blinking out of sight.

Lily groaned inwardly. There would be no help from the brownie on this one.

Coward!

Her aunt's face remained expressionless. "Well...that's quite a story."

No one responded. Lily and Brandon looked at each other, unsure how to answer. Brandon finally answered.

"It's not a story though. It really happened."

Raven raised her eyebrow, her voice sharpening. "So let me get this straight. You're saying that Ari went to the fae world, you traveled there, almost died, came back *without* Ari because she decided to stay with the fae guy that tried to sacrifice her. You are now considered a 'Sentinel' and just came through a portal from Iceland, AND that Ang here," she gestured her thumb over towards the changeling who flinched, "was sent here to pose as your sister until you got her back. Did I get the cliff notes version?"

"Well...yes. But we're not lying," Brandon said defensively.

Her aunt sighed, rubbing her temple. "I never said you were."

Brandon grumbled, "You don't seem convinced."

Raven looked at him patiently. "What I *said* was that you have quite a story. There's a difference between saying you're lying and processing what you told me." She thought a moment before she asked. "Your parents have no idea about any of this?"

Lily and Brandon looked at each other, then nodded.

Brandon spoke up. "But there's nothing to worry about. Ang is really good, Prince Jacy sent her himself."

Raven blinked. "Wait...Prince?"

Lily hesitated. "Yes...Prince Jacy sent Ang because he wanted to help since his brother took Ari."

Raven's eyes narrowed, accusing. "*Another* prince took your sister?"

Lily winced, realizing they failed to mention that little piece of info. Her aunt groaned, palming her face. Lily and Brandon kept silent, but she fully expected they would be grounded until the next year.

Raven grumbled a few more times to herself, raked her hands through her wild mane of hair, and closed her eyes. She took a deep breath before she finally addressed the group. "Alright then. What's the plan?"

Lily blinked, confused. "What?"

"The plan." Raven motioned with her hands. "To get Ari back. What's the plan?"

"So, you'll help us?" asked Brandon, eyes wide. "You believe us?"

Raven crossed her arms, a determined look on her face. "Of course, I do! Besides, Ari is family." She looked to Ang, who was keeping quiet the entire time. "No hard feelings?"

Ang scoffed, subconsciously rubbing her arms. "I'll think about it."

Lily's brow furrowed. Why was her aunt so calm about this?

48

When Lily first discovered Brom and Alasdair were real, she had a hard time adjusting. But her aunt not only took it in stride, she was also talking to Ang and the others as if she knew them for months. Come to think of it, her aunt knew what Ang was before anyone told her. How?

"Um, Aunt Raven? How do you know about the Veil?"

Raven stared hard for a beat. She opened her mouth but before she could speak, the familiar chime of the doorbell rang downstairs. She promptly jumped up, briskly walking out the room, her peppy tone returned. "Not the time sweetie! Not the time."

Lily scrambled to catch up as Raven descended the stairs.

"Wait! Aunt Raven-" she protested. She had too many questions. Why did her aunt have a pendant to banish fae? How did she know about brownies?

Raven got to the door, her hand pausing on the handle. She turned back with a reassuring smile, but her eyes were pleading. "I'll tell you when we have a moment."

"Promise?"

Raven nodded, turning the knob. "I promise."

Cabyll stood there, his tall, lean frame crowding the doorway. A slightly nervous smile graced his handsome face, making him appear shy and unassuming.

He was anything but.

Lily rolled her eyes, ignoring her slight catch of breath.

His tousled wavy black hair shined in the sun, the red tint gleaming. Maybe it was Lily's imagination, but his jeweled green eyes were even brighter as they anxiously passed through the sea of faces before landing on her. He held her gaze and took a calming breath as they both shared a smile. Lily never thought she'd be happy to see his rakish grin, but relief poured through her seeing him again.

Cabyll reluctantly removed his gaze from her, his attention quickly moving to Raven. A slight frown ghosted over his face before it smoothed over to reveal a charming grin.

"Hello, I'm Cab, Lily's friend from school. I wanted-"

Raven gave a deadpanned, "No-" before immediately slamming the door on his face.

Lily, wide-eyed, looked at her aunt who was wiping her hands together as if she threw out the trash. Raven turned, her expression fierce.

"A Cabyll?!"

Lily's cheeks heated. She didn't mention what type of fae Cabyll was, only referring to him by his nickname, Cab.

Oh man...

Another loud knock came from behind the door. His voice was muffled, but she could make out he was asking to open the door. Raven ignored it, still waiting for an explanation.

"Yes, but he's a friend. He helped me find Ari." Lily pleaded. "Please Aunt Raven, let him in."

Her aunt waited a moment, her eyes narrowed, before she sighed deeply. She palmed her face before turning back to the door.

Cab's eyes widened, his hand poised mid knock when the door opened again. He put his charming smile back on, ready with a suave remark, but Raven raised her hand interrupting him.

"Nope! Don't wanna hear it. Just come in and behave yourself."

He entered warily, keeping his distance. Lily came forward, giving him a brief hug. She pulled back but Cab's arms banded around her, tightening slightly. Before Lily could question it, he pulled away, but not before he leaned into whisper in her ear.

"That was quite the welcome. While it's good to see you, who's the hellcat?"

Lily hissed back quietly. "That's my aunt, be nice."

He straightened up quickly, his eyes wide. "Aunt?"

Her aunt gave a stiff nod, her eyebrow raised.

"Horse," she bit out.

He smiled back, his teeth blinding as he gave her a sly wink. "Only sometimes."

Raven, unimpressed, barked back. "Behave or I throw you out."

Cabyll kept his smile on, but the slight grinding of his teeth told otherwise. He gave a stiff bow, his jaw hard. "Yes ma'am."

This will be fun... Lily thought sarcastically. *Wonder how the suave flirt will get out of this.*

He turned back to her, his expression serious. "We need to talk about your...friend."

The air in the room grew heavy. The solemn weight pressed on Lily, her heart zipping up to her throat.

She swallowed, her mouth suddenly dry. "I got your note. Did you find her?"

"Is she okay?" interrupted Brandon, his eyes anxious but hopeful.

Cabyll put his palms up. "She's fine. At least, fine in a sense she's...well... she's around. An old business client of mine may be able to tell us more."

Lily frowned, her red flag meter blinking. "Business client?"

During the forest revel, she discovered Cabyll was a famous assassin. Famous meaning the number one assassin in the Veil apparently. It was still hard for her to believe, even if he was a great fighter. If he was talking about a client, that could only mean someone from his role as an assassin. Was it another assassin? Maybe some shady character that would double cross them?

Cabyll seemed to guess where her line of questioning was. He nodded, but his eyes turned frosty, his tone defensive. "Yes. Is there a problem little human?"

Lily bristled, ready to give him her two cents when Brandon jumped in.

"Nope man! No problem at all. So, where's this client dude?"

Cabyll shook his head. "He's not here. We must go to him."

Brandon clapped his hands. "Okay, so let's go. I want to see what that magic forest looks like."

"Ari isn't in the forest...eh em," Cabyll coughed, his eyes darting over to Raven. "What I mean is she's not there anymore." He ran his hand through his hair, mussing it up. His eyes peered through the tresses, finding Lily, an unasked question in his gaze.

Lily nodded, answering him. "She knows. You can tell us where Ari is."

He closed his eyes briefly before answering. "She's in the Pacific."

"The Pacific?!" Brom's outraged voice yelled from the kitchen, causing the group to flinch. "For a young, unchaperoned child to stray so far? That ghastly prince took her clear across the world!"

"Oh, the parenting brownie has returned," muttered Cabyll. He sidled over to Lily whispering. "So...your aunt knows, huh?"

She nodded, keeping quiet.

Alasdair's voice rang out from the kitchen too. "Oye Brommie! Let the kids talk without you mother henning everyone fer a second."

"Does she know about me," Cabyll's whisper tickled Lily's ear.

She elbowed him, hard.

"But the Pacific," protested Brom. A resounding metallic crash echoed with an accompanied "Oomph!"

The whispered grumblings from Alasdair and Brom continued. Pots and pans clattered and banged before Alasdair yelled out to the group. "Sorry to interrupt. We'll have lunch ready in five minutes. Lad, get on with it and finish up yer briefing."

Everyone's attention turned back to Cabyll, waiting for him to continue.

He crossed his arms. "My client said they would deliver the rest of the information about Ari, but he insisted to meet him. In person."

Aunt Raven who, up until this point was quiet, pushed herself from her leaned position against the doorframe. She kept her arms lightly folded as she approached Cabyll. She barely reached his shoulder, but that didn't matter as she stared him down. "Where in the Pacific?"

"Byron Bay," he replied.

Brandon gave an innocently puzzled look. "Where's that?"

"Australia," supplied Raven. Lily could swear her aunt's eye twitched.

During the entire exchange, Ang had been quiet. Quiet, but focused. Then she tensed, the hairs on her arms standing up noticeably.

Brandon frowned. "Hey Ang...you okay?"

Ang gave a blank stare before she cackled in a slightly manic tone. "How you humans manage to get into these situations astounds me. We're all gonna die at this rate."

Lily frowned. The changeling spoke in her typical snarky tone, but she couldn't hide the slight trembling in her hands. What was in Australia that would make the confident fae so nervous?

Cabyll continued, "We need to go. Today if possible."

"Should we use the mirror again?" She ignored how her stomach flipped thinking about it.

Brom's voice yelled out, a pan banging against the tile. "I forbid it Miss Lily! That was hard enough for you today. You need rest."

Raven's eyebrow raised before she muttered, "Nice to see at least the brownie is talking sense." She spoke louder. "He is right *nipote*. No more mirror trips for the moment."

Cabyll looked over to Lily, giving her a side wink. He raised his eyebrow, a smirk forming. "And you have a better idea?" His smirk immediately dissolved at Aunt Raven's icy stare.

"Would you care to repeat that?" asked Raven, her voice neutral.

They stared each other down before Cabyll's eyes fell to the floor as he mumbled, "Sorry ma'am."

Satisfied, Raven nodded. "In response to your rudely asked question. As a matter of fact, I do have an idea. We'll get there in no time."

"But Aunt Raven," Lily protested, "you're not coming, are you?"

Raven put her hands on her hips. "You bet your patootie I'm coming. This is about family. I'm here to support you, so I'm coming too."

She tapped her chin for a moment before her demeanor transformed back into her chipper, fast-talking self.

Raven raced to the kitchen, a spring in her step, as she yelled over her shoulder. "Get something to eat and pack a small overnight bag. There's a lot to do and little time to do it in. You have twenty minutes!"

Lily could only stare in wonder at her aunt's retreating back. Brandon and Ang quickly dashed to catch up with the petite drill sergeant, no doubt grabbing some food Brom prepared. Lily envied how her aunt took control so quickly and without hesitation. Could she become that confident someday? A nudge on her shoulder shook her from her musings.

"You're thinking too much again," Cabyll said gruffly.

"One of us has to," she quipped.

He gave a dark chuckle. "No need for that when I have my charm and wit." He winked at her, a lock of hair falling over his face.

She rolled her eyes, ignoring his antics. "Thanks for coming so quickly Cab."

His gaze darted away, shrugging nonchalantly, keeping his hands in his pants pockets. "Well...yeah. We're friends, right?" His eyes didn't meet hers, his ears slightly red.

She grinned, nudging him back. "Yeah."

From the kitchen, Raven barked a variety of commands to Brom and Alasdair, the brownie squealing indigently as the hob laughed. Even though her gaze was toward the kitchen, the warmth of their shoulders hovered next to each other.

Cabyll murmured into her ear, his breath tickling. "Your aunt seems crazy, no offense."

A resounding crash echoed in the kitchen followed by a string of Italian.

She sucked her breath through her teeth, then nodded. "You have noooo idea."

Chapter Six

HONK!

"Yo! I'm driving here! Learn to merge, you country bumpkin!"

Lily winced as their driver yelled again at a poor motorist who had cut off their cab from the exit to the Brooklyn Bridge. She wriggled her burning nose and rubbed her eyes. The stale cloud of cigarette smoke coming off the cab driver seemed to envelop the entire cab.

Tensely tucked between Cabyll and Brandon, she sat quietly, clutching her backpack and bow case on her lap. Her aunt and Ang sat opposite them, looking equally anxious. Maybe it was the road rage radiating from the driver. Maybe it was the anxiety of their trip. Regardless, the group sat awkwardly silent while the driver honked the horn another time for good measure, speeding quickly through the winding avenues towards the center of Brooklyn.

Hard to believe, but less than an hour ago Aunt Raven concocted a story to convince their parents to let them leave. She told them she wanted to take the children to the next diving site in Australia for the week. One last summer vacation for bonding time with the kids is what Raven told Lily's father. Lily was surprised her father and Tabby agreed so quickly. Her aunt explained their parents were hoping this trip would help Ari continue to emotionally grow.

Lily grimaced. If they only knew. So, with their parents' blessing

55

(and some dramatic sniffles from Brom), the group found themselves staring at a large grey weathered van. The scruffy looking driver grumbled as he threw their bags in the back with barely a glance where they landed. And with a hug and kiss goodbye, Lily's father hugging her again for the third time, the group left for the city.

Buildings flashed by, a whirlwind of brick and concrete. Finally, Lily broke the silence with a question that was bugging her since they got into the cab.

"Zia Raven," she began. "If we need to get to Australia, why are we going to Brooklyn?"

Her aunt waved her hand, a gleam in her eye. "Not to worry *nipote*. Sometimes a roundabout way is the straightest way. Besides, I figured these two," she gestured to Cabyll and Ang with her thumb, "may have had a hard time getting through an airport."

Lily glanced curiously at them. Cabyll looked at her, silently. Ang gave a huff before she reluctantly answered.

"Iron in those places. Not good."

Lily's eyes widened, remembering stories of iron being poisonous to fae. "Ah. That makes sense." Her gaze returned to the window, stone townhouses whizzing past her in a blur. Another question bubbled up.

"But, wouldn't dad and Tabby check if we got tickets?"

Her aunt chuckled, her tone flippant. "Not in a million years. Your father is so scatterbrained, he'll never check."

Cabyll gave a drawn-out sigh, crossing his arms, his hand brushing Lilys. "If we had listened to my idea, we would have been on our way by now."

"*Your* way involved mermaids," countered Lily, shaking her head.

"And?" he asked with glib innocence. "Marisha and Celeste owe me a favor. And they happen to love me." He flashed her a brilliant smile, his arms flexing slightly in front of his chest.

Lily rolled her eyes, refusing to look at him. *His ego is as large as ever.* She snorted, trying to put distance between them. "You think every woman loves you."

He gave a warm, deep chuckle as waved his hand dismissively. "I don't think. I *know* they do." He raised his hands in surrender as Lily glared at him. "My point is, they would have helped us." His eyes

56

lingered, traveling down Lily. "There are such beautiful things to see in the sea."

Raven snorted, her voice deadpan. "Yeah, help *you* maybe. For us their 'help' means to a one-way trip under the Hudson."

He scoffed. "You Ambrosino women are too skeptical and too serious." He turned to the window as Lily heard him mumble, "I wouldn't let that happen."

Her aunt ignored him. Instead, she reached out to the driver. Unfortunately, her arms were too short, so her fingers only grazed the plexi glass barrier wall between them as she shouted urgently.

"That's our stop."

"Sheesh lady, I hear ya! Hold your horses, I'm stopping." The driver growled as he made a sharp jerk to the wheel causing the car to skid into the side of the road.

Lily, unable to prepare for the sudden shift, slid over to the side of the car. Clenching her eyes shut, she braced to hit the metal door, but strong hands steadied her. She cracked them open to find Cabyll staring down, his arms carefully holding her shoulders.

"Thanks," she breathed out. She jerked back, holding her backpack in front of her, hoping her warmed cheeks weren't red.

He nodded, his gaze unreadable.

Horns honked as cars sped past them, people yelling out from their windows. The cab's four ways blinked annoyingly in tune with the corresponding honks. Not leaving the car, the driver reached out his hand, his sharp tone centered at Raven.

"Alright already, I stopped. Now pay me and get lost!" The cabbie muttered, not too softly, "Weirdos..."

Ignoring him, her aunt motioned for them to grab their bags. As they jumped out, Raven kept a bright smile plastered on her face while she addressed the surly man in an upbeat tone.

"Thank you so much for the drive." She handed a few bills over. The driver snatched them greedily with a grunt. Raven sweetly yelled out as the vehicle sped away, dust flying. "I hope you have a pleasant day."

Raven looked back at the group, a broad smile stuck on her face a minute before she exhaled, shaking herself. "Well...what an unpleasant man. Shall we?"

Brick and weathered stone buildings melding into one another. Graffiti mosaics were spray painted in a wash of bright colors, a stark contrast against the dull greys. Random shops littered down the street. As always, the loud bustling of the city rang a lively tune as people briskly walked past them, not paying any attention.

Brandon's eyes lit up. "Man, I missed this."

Lily tensed. Ari and Brandon loved the city, but she always felt suffocated by it. The noise was too loud, too overwhelming. What was her aunt thinking of taking them to this random place? Lily frowned, trying to keep focused. Speaking of, where was her aunt?

"Come on kids, this way."

Lily spun around in the direction of Raven's voice. Her aunt was already half a block away, waving her arms for them to follow. Quickly shouldering her backpack and bow, Lily ran forward into the labyrinth of the city. Her anxiety spiked as she weaved through the throngs of people, trying to keep pace with her aunt, not knowing where they were going.

It'll be okay. Zia Raven's smart, she reassured herself.

T*en minutes later...*
   She's outta her mind, she thought as she found herself in front of a broken-down store. She jumped, thinking she said her thoughts out loud, but it was only Ang.

"Wow, your aunt is out there. Think we gonna get robbed?" Ang twisted a finger in her ear to clean something out.

Brandon nudged Ang's side, shushing her. Cabyll stood next to Lily, his arms loosely crossed, his eyebrow raised in judgement.

"You humans sure are full of surprises," he said coolly.

Somehow, I don't think he means it as a compliment, Lily thought ruefully. But, she couldn't argue with him. She shook her head, debating whether her eyes were playing tricks on her.

The shop was old. Dusty-streaked windows painted teal, the paint fading and cracking in places. Discolored cement steps went downward towards a barred metal door. A large, faded overhang sign with the words, "**Anasi's Weave**", in bright gold paint gleamed in the sunlight.

Raven opened the door, the dinging of chimes echoing into the street.

"Come on kids, inside."

When Lily walked through the door, the warm, burning smell of cedar and cinnamon tickled her nose. Row and rows of aisles and shelves touched the ceiling and made the shop seem like a maze. Everything was adorned with bright cloths, beautiful beads, and various books. Several jars filled with crystals and other items littered about while bushels of dried herbs and spices hung from the ceiling. It was a treasure trove of the unknown. As Brandon gawked at a basket full of daggers, Lily noticed Ang and Cabyll were frozen in the front of the shop.

"Everything okay?" she asked.

Ang took an audible breath before she crossed the threshold. Her body jerked forward, her arms trembling. Lily gasped, reaching out to grab Ang's shoulder to steady her. Concerned, she glanced over at Cabyll.

"There's a magic barrier here," he explained neutrally before walking over the doorframe. Unlike Ang, he did not show any outward signs of discomfort, but his shoulders tensed. Her attention whipped back to Ang, who coughed.

"I'm fine," Ang panted slightly. "Just wasn't expecting it that strong."

A rolling voice spoke from the back of the store.

"Don't be frightened young ones. Simply making sure everyone here knows they gotta play nice."

Lily and Cabyll followed the voice to the back where a smiling elderly man stood behind an old wooden desk littered with candles and herbs. He looked perhaps in his sixties, weathered lines crinkling around his beaming face. His shining bald head was covered by a cream straw fedora that sported a deep purple band. The man rolled up his cotton, flowing sleeves as he rearranged some white and purple candles. He waved his hands over enthusiastically.

"Come come! Don't be hidin' back there. Let Papa Remy have a look at ya."

He beamed as the group approached, his full lips sporting bright teeth in a smile that was friendly and welcoming. He opened his arms

59

toward Raven yelling out, "Ah, Raven! *Itilite!* So delighted to see you. It's been too long."

Raven laughed, running up to give the old man a big hug. He pinched her cheeks in a fatherly gesture. His gaze drifted towards the others.

"And who might these little ones be?"

Raven grinned. "Papa Remy. This is my niece Lily and my nephew Brandon."

Lily waved shyly as Brandon let out a "Yo".

Her aunt continued. "The others are Cabyll and Ang. They are helping us with a problem."

"Problem you say? Hmm." Papa Remy raised his nonexistent eyebrow, his dark eyes too perceptive. "What problem do you have child that involves the fae and the otherworld?"

Lily tried to keep her expression neutral. Inside was a different story. *Does everyone and their mother know about the Veil?*

Raven fished a list from her pocket and handed it over to Brandon and Ang. "Can you two go and get me these herbs please." She waited until Brandon and Ang left before she gestured for Lily to come over.

"Our sister, Ari," Lily blurted out, her bubble of anxiety rising. "She's-"

"We need to get to Australia, Papa," her aunt interrupted. She gave Lily's arm a slight squeeze in warning. "My other niece needs us to help take care of a problem."

His twinkling eyes gleamed with interest, then softened. "I understand, *zwazo*. I won't press. I am neutral after all."

Cabyll glanced around the shop. "This is a sanctuary." It was a statement, not a question.

Papa Remy nodded, giving a slight bow. "*Wi*. I am but a humble priest. My duty is to make sure all those who mean no harm have a place to rest." He pursed his full lips, giving a low whistle. "You need a *Papòt* little Raven?"

Raven nodded. "Yes Papa. We need the doorway please."

Papa Remy hummed in thought, tapping his fingers on his temple. "Are you sure? As you know, *itilite,* nothing is free. What do you offer as tribute?"

Her aunt pulled a bottle of rum, a pack of cigars, and a bag of apple candy from her backpack. She set them down on the counter carefully.

Papa Remy's eyes widened with approval. "Baron Samedi and Anasi will be pleased. You are very considerate little Raven." He patted her hand affectionately.

He turned to the fae, his tone matter-of-fact. "And what do you both offer?"

Raven frowned. "I thought that would be for all of us."

He shook his head. "The Loa need something else from the fae folk. So-" his weathered finger tapped on the desk, "what do you offer?"

Silence spanned for a beat. Lily's heart thumped nervously as she flexed her empty fingers.

What is he looking for? A pound of flesh?

Cabyll and her shared an equally alarmed look.

What were they going to do when they had nothing?

Chapter Seven

"PAPA? I'M HERE!"

A bright voice cut in from the backroom behind the counter, slicing through the nervous silence.

The large, beaded curtain pulled back to reveal a very tall, beautiful figure. Clad in a tight, bright gold mermaid style gown, glittered with crystals from top to bottom, the figure sauntered toward the group. Their black, coiled hair was in an enormous bun on top of their head, sporting a golden sun headdress that branched out in what looked like a spiderweb throughout the rich black tresses. Heavy but artfully applied makeup adorned the person to sport large dramatic eyes and full, bright pink lips. Those lips peeled back with a blinding smile that, to Lily, looked awfully familiar.

The newcomer put an expertly manicured hand out to Papa Remy. A deep, rich voice rang out. "Papa, it's a pleasure darlin'."

Papa reached out to grasp the hand gently as he bent over. "Welcome as always *larenn*."

The newcomer looked up, finally noticing the group. Their bright eyes widened and, if possible, their blinding grin grew even wider.

"Hey y'all! What are you doin' here in this neck of the woods?"

No one spoke, unsure how to answer. The drag queen cocked their head to the side focusing on Lily. They placed their hands on their hips, their eyes kind.

"Lily sweetie, you're looking as confused as a goat on AstroTurf."

Lily blinked a moment, processing before she asked cautiously. "Randy?"

The drag queen burst with a whoop and clapped their hands together gleefully. "Oh darlin'! I knew you'd remember me. Just look at you! You're so sweet I could eat you up."

Before Lily could respond, she was enveloped in a large, perfumed hug. Strong arms banded around her, squeezing her tightly. Randy helped her a great deal when Ari was kidnapped by Dain. Lily loved the fae's enthusiasm and carefree nature, though not so much when she felt he was going to eat her the first time they met.

Poor choice of words. Bet he did it on purpose, she inwardly grumbled.

But that was all behind them. Toward the end of her time in the forest, Randy became a genuine friend. When they parted, he said he had several places to be but assured her he would be seeing her soon. If she was honest with herself, she actually missed the talkative fae. And, if she was really honest with herself, she was also a teeny bit envious how free-spirited he was. The fact Randy was here now, Lily could feel the stirrings of her anxiety melting away as his warm hug tightened around her. She smiled, holding unbidden tears, returning the hug with a heartfelt squeeze.

An exaggerated cough behind them dissolved the warm feeling as Lily found herself being pulled away until her back hit Cabyll's chest. He glared at Randy above her head, his arms banded around her shoulders. "That's enough spider."

Her heart thudded, her cheeks warming. She quickly ducked under Cab's arms to move quietly to the side. He stared at his empty hands for a moment before placing them on his hips, his lips downturned.

Randy blinked innocently, a guileless smile in place while smoothing out the black wig and adjusting the headdress. "It's so nice to see you too Cab. Do you want to hug me too? I have plenty to go around handsome."

Cabyll rolled his eyes, ignoring the jibe. "Spider...what are you doing here?"

Randy pouted and tapped a perfect pink nail on Cabyll's nose.

Randy dodged when Cabyll tried to swat the nail away. "Doing here? How rude! I believe I asked you first, but since I'm the wonderful individual I am, I'll answer you. Why Cab, my man, this is New York City!! Need I say anything else?" Twirling in a flourish, Randy's skirts billowed around in a delightful dance.

Randy sighed dramatically at Cabyll's deadpan stare. "If you must know, Mr. Grump, there are events going on in Hell's Kitchen I *need* to attend to. I mean my adoring public just *can't* live without me."

Cabyll palmed his face with a sigh. "Randy..." he groaned.

"That's Randee Candee to you darlin'. With two 'e's' if you please. And don't forget I'm a queen at this moment so treat and call me as such."

Randy, or Randee now, blew a kiss at Cabyll, giving a sly wink.

Cabyll shook his head, but he couldn't stop a small smile forming before he hid it behind another frown.

Papa Remy nodded. "So, they are your friends...Randee is it?" He raised his eyebrow with a knowing grin.

Randee blushed, fixing her wig. "Yes Remy, they're my friends." She coughed slightly, smoothing her dress. "Now what y'all doing here?"

"They want to use the doorway. But they," Papa Remy gestured towards Cabyll and Ang, "do not have the sufficient offering."

Randee placed her hand on Papa Remy's shoulder, looking at the offerings. She picked up a piece of apple candy, taking a bite while she said softly.

"They're friends Papa. No need for that."

Papa Remy paused. "You know you'll have to talk to the Baron."

Randee scoffed, flipping her dark wig behind her with a flourish. "That'll be easy as pie. The Baron may be a few pickles short of a barrel, but he loves me. No one will bother my Lily girl, Cab, or their friends."

Papa Remy chuckled before turning towards Raven. "It seems your niece has very good friends in high places. Your offerings will suffice."

Randee blinked, eyeing Raven, finally noticing her for the first time. "Wait! Niece?" Her gaze darted between Lily and Raven. "Wait one collar pickin' minute here. You Lily's aunt?!"

Raven smiled kindly, putting out her hand. "Ravenna Ambrosino, wonderful to meet you, Randee."

Randee clasped her hand warmly. "Oh my! Aren't you sweeter than stolen honey darlin'." She glanced over at Cabyll. "All these Ambrosino women are so polite! And," she turned back to Raven, her eyes burning, "gorgeous! Girl you are just glowing. What do you use?"

Raven laughed. "When we have time, I'm more than happy to have drinks and chat. I'd love an apple martini."

Papa Remy laughed as Randee blinked in surprise, a slight blush staining the drag queen's cheeks.

Cabyll grumbled loudly, interrupting them. "Can we get a move on here? Need I remind everyone we have a time crunch."

Randee smirked, giving a side wink at Lily. "I have nothing but *time* darlin'."

Cabyll scoffed, rolling his eyes.

Lily swallowed, glancing nervously at her aunt. She left out a few things about Randee when she gave her aunt the backstory. If Raven found out Randee played a game where the result may have ended up with Lily as dinner, her aunt would blow up. Scratch that. Her aunt probably would throw Randee in the Hudson with cement shoes.

She glanced over at Cabyll, wordlessly spearing him a look, hoping he'd understand.

A slight smirk quirked his lip. His shrewd eyes took in her aunt and Randee, contemplating.

Please let it go. Let it go!

She stomped her foot, her glare palpable.

He groaned, rolling his eyes. "Look, we have places to be and this human," he gestured his thumb towards Raven, "has already wasted time with useless pleasantries. We're wasting time."

Lily's eyes widened. *Idiota.*

She tried to get his attention before it was too late, but the warm air suddenly cooled about ten degrees.

She gulped. Too late.

Raven whipped her head, her smile turning down into a sharp frown. She shot him a piercing look that contradicted the false sweetness in her tone. "If you're so impatient, why don't you go tidy something up around here. Put those so-called muscles to use. I'm sure Papa needs some boxes moved or something."

Dismissing him, she turned back to Randee and Papa Remy, apologetic. "My apologies. Looks don't always equal brains I'm afraid."

Randee's eyes widened before laughing loudly. "Oh, you're a delight! Don't apologize darlin', this fella and I have a long history. Would take more than his handsome gruffness to fluff me. Cab, you're so lucky meeting these ladies."

"Yeah yeah, lucky," he muttered, crossing his arms.

Papa Remy chuckled softly, turning toward Raven. "*Curieux.* Your party is very intriguing *zwazo.* While I wish you would stay longer, I do sense the underling urgency."

Then, he suddenly stopped talking. His eyes became glassy, unfocused.

Lily frowned. What he okay? Suddenly, he took both her and her aunt's hands in his wiry fingers and squeezed them tight. The scent of warm tobacco and bright citrus tickled her nose.

Papa Remy spoke low and direct. "The Loa tell me it's imperative you make this journey. You will face hard choices, but keep faith in the heart-thread that binds you together."

Raven hesitated before she gently patted Papa Remy's weathered hands. "We will remember Papa."

Lily could only nod, too emotional to speak. The air was heavy and thick. Could the priest see the future?

She jumped, a loud thump landing beside her. Brandon and Ang had returned with a pile of herbs, throwing them on the counter.

"This all you need Aunt Raven?" asked Brandon.

Raven glanced over the bundle. "How much Papa?"

He waved his hand, his eyes returning to normal. "No *zwazo.* No need for payment for this."

"But Papa-" she protested.

"Consider it a gift from me to help you on your journey. Oh, I almost forgot. Excuse me children, this old brain isn't what it used to be."

He reached into his pocket and pulled out a few candy wrappings. He handed the tiny treasures to Lily, Brandon, and Ang. "Here little ones. These are sour tangerine drops." He gave a conspiratorial loud whisper with a quick wink. "I find having a little something sweet and sour helps in these in-between moments."

Ang frowned. "Got any honey flavored?"

Lily held the brightly colored wrapper before putting it in her pocket. She nodded her thanks even though she had no idea how candy was going to help. But, better to be polite.

Ang raised her eyebrow, squinting at the candy before putting the entire contents, wrapper and all, in her mouth with a crinkly crunch. Brandon laughed, quickly unwrapping his own candy and popping it in his mouth with a toothy grin.

Lily shook her head. *So much for no candy from strangers.*

Papa Remy got up slowly, grabbing his cane. He gestured toward Randee with a kind smile. "*Larenn*, these old bones of mine may take a moment. Can you please escort them to the doorway? I'll be with you in a minute, children."

Randee blew a kiss with a wink. "On it, Papa. Come on y'all!" She pulled back the curtain, beckoning them behind the counter to go into the back of the store.

🌀

Lily stepped through the beaded entrance and came into soft darkness. Wispy smoke floated around her head smelling faintly of earthy myrrh and patchouli. Peering into the grey darkness, she could make out the faint outline of larger shadows. It was chilly, but not from the temperature. The room itself seeped her inner fire, leaching it from her core. Almost as if the dead itself was sucking her life. She jerked, her heart speeding up. Warm fingers wrapped around her shoulder. Raven squeezed in reassurance.

Randee's voice pierced the darkness, but Lily couldn't see her. "Time for a little light."

A soft snap of fingers followed by a burst of candlelight illuminated the eerie gloom. In front of them was a large door. A huge, wooden and stone gateway sported a semi arch which was surrounded by obsidian stone pillars. Various filigree adornments dressed the face of the door. Lily squinted harder in the dim candlelight before her eyes widened in concern. Skulls. Hundreds of skulls seamlessly wove themselves in the filigree throughout the entire door. She gulped, her inner chill burning brighter.

This is not a door. This is a tomb.

Brandon whistled softly, pulling her from her thoughts. "Cool man!

67

This looks like something outta a video game. Ouch!" He rubbed his head where Ang smacked him.

The changeling hissed.

"Be respectful kid. There's power here." Ang clamped her lips shut, eyeing the doorway warily, rubbing her arms.

Cabyll nodded in agreement. He glanced over at Randee, motioning to the door. "You trust this?"

Randee stood silent a moment, unable to look away from the doorway. "Don't worry Cab," she cleared her throat. "I got your backs."

Lily whispered to her aunt, her nerves rising. "Have you traveled through this before?"

Raven shook her head, biting her lip. "I haven't. Papa told me about it, but it's only for emergencies. I think this counts, right?"

"It certainly does little *zwazo*."

Papa Remy shuffled forward, the sharp click of his cane echoing against the walls. His other hand carried a bundle of small parcels. He stopped next to Lily and Raven, smiling gently as he carefully handed over the packages.

"I added a few things to your supplies. I hope you don't mind."

Raven gave a grateful smile. "Never Papa."

Lily fumbled with the packages, her cold hands shaking. "Thank you!"

Papa Remy nodded, his eyes grave. "I hope you won't need it, but I want to make sure you're prepared. The other side is not safe and must be treated with both respect and caution." He motioned to the door. "Same with using tools such as this."

He shuffled toward an alter that Lily failed to notice earlier. Half burned candles graced the table, the wax melted into various places. Papa Remy laid out the gifts carefully.

He breathed deep, his tone serious. "We need to ask the Baron to open the doorway. Once that happens, you need to hold each other's hands. Think of a chain. Do, not, let, go. No matter what. The spirit doorway is known to be unpredictable."

"Spirit?" asked Brandon. "I thought this was like a transport door."

Papa Remy's lip quirked slightly. "It is...but it is for the dead *pitit*,"

"Wait! The dead?!" exclaimed Lily, mouth dropping. This was not a great idea. Maybe they should use the mirror again. She'd take the risk.

Or maybe they could swim to Australia. Swimming with great whites seemed safer than traveling through a doorway meant for the dead.

Papa Remy put his hand out, his calm tone soothing. "The spirit doorway may be a doorway to the Underworld, but it can be repurposed to send you to the Veil. Not always, but it can be done. Accompanied by your fae companions should not make it too difficult, but the human soul is tricky. Remember...do not let go or you could be lost in limbo. You may also feel slightly nauseous when appearing on the other side. Eat your candies right before you enter." He gave an apologetic smile. "It'll help the nausea."

Brandon jumped up and down, his excitement making Lily more nauseous. "Cool. Wait, I ate my candy. Can I have another?"

Papa Remy chuckled, handing him a few more to which Brandon popped them immediately into his mouth. Lily shook her head. She opened her mouth to protest when her aunt cut her off.

"This is the fastest way to get there, sweetie," she gently reminded.

Cabyll rubbed the back of his neck. "As much as I hate to agree, she's right." His eyes bore into Lilys. "We need to travel far and fast if you want to find her."

Lily took a deep breath, resigning herself. She grabbed her candy and with shaking fingers, she unwrapped the orange treat and promptly put it in her mouth. A burst of sweet tart citrus exploded on her tongue, but it did little to ease the sour pit in her stomach.

Papa Remy nodded, satisfied. He motioned the group to hold hands. He directed his next question to Cabyll, who was at the front.

"Where are you going?"

"The Nalu Realm." Cabyll grabbed Lily's hand, holding it firm. Maybe it was her imagination, but it seemed like he was holding a little tighter than necessary. As if he didn't want to let go.

She shook her head. *Don't overthink it. It's just Cab.*

Papa Remy gestured toward Randee. "When I open the doorway, it's probably best you sweet talk the Baron, *bon*?"

Randee laughed. "Oh, I got him Papa. You don't worry your handsome little head."

"Aren't you coming with us?" asked Lily.

Randee shook her head, apologetic. "Not at the moment darlin'." She gave her a slight nudge when Lily's shoulder's slumped. "But no need to fuss on account of me. I'll meet up with you when I can, come hell or high water." She winked, her golden eyeshadow sparkling in the dark. Her eyes began to glow with an eerie light. "I have a feelin' this new chapter of your story is gonna be a doozy."

Lily, while disappointed, couldn't help the smile that pulled the corner of her lip.

Cabyll tugged her hand, pulling her a little closer.

His brows slashed down, his tone impatient. "Anytime now Spider."

Randee rolled her eyes, giving a little chuckle. She clasped her hands together giving a low whistle while nodding to Papa Remy.

Without another word, the old man closed his eyes. He began mumbling softly in a language Lily couldn't recognize. His eyes became vacant and opaque, his mumblings growing in volume. The massive doors began to slowly open with an ominous creak. More wispy smoke emanated from the crack, the inside pitch darkness. Soon, the dark began twisting and swirling until it resembled a pit of rippling ink. A deep, smokey voice echoed.

"*Kikyes ki rele'm*? Who calls me?"

Randee whistled sweetly. "Howdy Baron sweetie pie! It's little ole me."

"*Arenyen*? Is that you?" asked Baron, the voice sounding slightly confused.

"Yes, it's me you handsome devil." Randee flipped her hand through her wig, giving a little twirl, her dress catching the dim light.

There was a short pause, a slight breath sighing in the dark. "You're sporting a new look. I like it *cheri*, it suits you being gilded in gold."

Randee laughed, waving her hand up and down. "Aw, you sweet talker. How's the fam?"

The voice chuckled, and Lily could smell hints of cigar notes of earth and cloves.

"You know the Gede. Dancing and drinking *cheri*. I'm actually missing some sweet banda and a jug of my favorite rum for this summons."

"And how's the lovely Maman Brigitte?"

The Baron drawled out dryly. "You know that old maid. Probably drinking like a fish. I wouldn't be surprised if she's tripping over herself while dancing the banda."

Randee tsked, wagging her nail. "Be nice! That's your wife after all."

The Baron groaned, and Lily could practically hear the massive eye rolling.

Randee continued. "Baron sweetie, we called you here cause we need to travel the doorway."

"I see your companions *cheri*, and they do not seem dead to me." A long, drawn-out breath accompanied by a trail of smoke billowed out, covering the group. "Not even close to dead, *ki jan malere*. Very unfortunate indeed. Do they need a hand? Mine is firm and warm."

"No, no, Baron!" Randee held up her hands, chuckling awkwardly. "They only need the doorway to travel to the Veil. The Nalu Realm in particular."

She glanced at Cabyll, eyes questioning.

"The opening near Byron Bay," he supplied.

The voice exhaled loudly, more smoke filling the room. Lily coughed, tugging her hand unconsciously. Cabyll squeezed tighter, refusing to let go.

"Ah...*mwen konprann*. I also notice not all your companions are entirely human. This makes sense. But you know *Arenyen,* this is not normally done."

Randee twirled again, her dress billowing, flashing a bright smile. "Aw, since when were you ever a stickler for rules?" She gave a conspiratorial wink. "I guarantee this group is not boring, entertainment in spades with these folks."

The Baron chuckled again, a smooth velvet rumbling that raised the hairs on Lily's arms. "Sounds intriguing, and you know I cannot refuse you little one. Okay, I will let them pass." There was a pause, then the Baron continued, his voice sweetening. "I also see there's other pretty *fanm* with you. And I simply cannot refuse pretty women in need."

The doors burst open. The black inky swirls lightened until a grey-white cloud illuminated the entrance. Hidden behind the clouds was an outline of a very tall, slender man with a tall top hat. Lily squinted. She couldn't make him out, save for a shadow of a wide eerie grin as the man tipped his hat. The dark voice rang out in a seductive lilt.

"Go with my blessings *timoun yo, Arenyen*. I will see you at the crossroads."

The figure's eerie smile disappeared, along with the shadow.

Lily swallowed, trying to hold down the nagging fear that bubbled up her throat.

Randee turned to them, nodding her head toward the door. "Time to leave folks. Keep a tight hold onto your hands and I'll see y'all later."

Lily, distracted, bit her tongue. She grimaced; the pain combined with the tart tangerine spearing through her throat.

Cabyll tugged her forward, but she held back. Maybe this wasn't such a good idea. There were so many red flags they could cheer on a sports team.

Cabyll gave her hand a reassuring squeeze, his gaze focused on the doorway. "It'll be alright Lily. I won't let you go," he promised softly.

She closed her eyes, her shoulders shaking. Without realizing it, her head leaned down to rest on his back. He tensed, his muscles taunt against her forehead. Dimly she knew she should pull back and apologize, but her fear overshadowed it. Her inner voice did not get the memo. It yelled at her the second her head moved.

Get a grip girl. Breathe and pull yourself together!

Sucking in a mouthful of air, she lifted her head. Her cheeks warmed, but thankfully Cabyll's back still greeted her, so her embarrassment was short-lived.

Move it or lose it!

Ugh, her inner voice really was a drill sergeant. She gripped his hand tightly and walked into the mist.

Chapter Eight

GRITTY SAND SMACKED HER FACE.

Hard.

The air whooshed out of her lungs, her head spinning. Through the vertigo, she dug her hands in the sand, her subconscious knowing she was sprawled on the ground. Her muscles quivered, the coldness of the gate permeating through her bones, even though the hot sun beat down on her back.

Then came the nausea.

Bile rose in her throat, her mouth filling with salt. She heaved, acid burning her chest. Her arms trembled while she slowly tried to pick herself up, but failed. Her shaky limbs crumbled as she fell back onto the hard sand. Her eyes pricked with tears. Through the watery haze, a hand appeared in front of her, opening to reveal another tangerine candy. A worried voice spoke above her.

"Eat this Lil."

Blindly she grabbed the candy. Almost immediately, the nausea dissipated and her freezing limbs slowly began to warm. Carefully, she turned onto her back, her chest heaving. The low piercing calls of seagulls and lapping waves soothed her. The same voice asked her.

"Can you get up?"

She grimaced. *I don't want to. Don't make me.*

But she did anyway. With steady, deliberate movements she sat up. Breathing in fresh ocean air, she cracked her dusty eyes open. She held in her gasp, only because she was aware of the coarse sand kernels stuck to her lip.

Crashing turquoise waves frothed in a lively dance, twirling around a snow-white shore. Her peripheral vision beheld bright aqua fronds of towering palms dotting the tropical landscape. Vivid orange, red, and purple flowers dotted the blue-green jungle backdrop. The cream, white sand tickled her hands, sticking to her cheek. She squinted. The sun was bright, annoyingly so. The brilliant ocean sky welcomed her, almost too blue to be real.

"Wow," she whispered.

It was paradise.

A strong hand wrapped around her, picking her up. Startled, her eyes met Cabyll, who held her arms securely. He opened his mouth but jerked back as Brandon stepped between them, pushing him out of the way.

Brandon ignored Cabyll's glower. Instead, her stepbrother grabbed her hands, spinning towards the shoreline.

"Lil! This is so rad!" His eyes were bright, excited.

"Ah...I'm here too," Cabyll remarked dryly.

Brandon kept ignoring him. "Wasn't that trip a trip? It was something out of an excellent adventure right?!"

Lily cleared her dry throat, wincing. *Nope, it was nothing like that. Not at all.*

Brandon continued, oblivious. He pointed to the shoreline. "And do you see those waves? That is some awesome surfing. Well, if I knew how to surf. Think we can try before we go?"

She couldn't help smiling. "I don't know. Maybe?"

Cabyll huffed, his frown deepening. "I'm going to scout the area. One of us needs to remember why we're here." With a roll of his eyes, he turned and moved inland, keeping his back to them.

She flinched, ashamed. He was right. This wasn't the time for sightseeing. Her voice morphed into teacher mode. "Remember what we came here for."

Brandon waved his hand dismissively. "Yeah, yeah Lil I get it." He tugged her arm, trying to pull her to the crystalline waves. "But, some-times we have to take the moments while we have them. And swimming won't take too long. I mean it's such a waste to let this go to waste. Ya know?"

She blinked, wondering if she heard right. Brandon sounded way too mature at times.

"So he says before he gets eaten by a Yara-ma-yha-who," groused Ang, appearing over a small dune. She grimaced, shaking her hair as flakes of snow-white sand billowed around them.

Brandon called over his shoulder. "Aw! Don't be such a debby downer Ang. You gotta admit, this place is pretty awesome."

Ang's eye twitched as she slapped her shoulders, sand bouncing off. She gave a resigned sigh as a reluctant grin ghosted her face. "Yes, it is pretty." Her eyes hardened. "But remember, just because it's pretty doesn't mean it's not dangerous."

A lesson Lily knew all too well. Unfortunately, it didn't seem to resonate with Brandon.

He motioned to the waves. "You wanna at least get your feet wet Lil?"

She shook her head, the rolling waves triggering her stomach to do flips and flops. Maybe she needed another candy. "I...I think I need a minute for my stomach to settle."

His eyes widened, finally noticing her pale complexion. "Oh...yeah? You feeling okay? Did the trip make you sick? Funny I don't feel sick."

Ang, deadpan, replied, "That's probably because you have a cast iron stomach."

Brandon pursed his lips, paused, then nodded. "Yeah, probably." He dropped Lily's hands, kicking off his shoes. "Why don't you rest a minute while I go test it out." He ran to the waves, giving a little excited jump.

Ang yelled, exasperated. "You know there are things in these oceans that like to eat human toes!"

He shrugged off Ang's warning with a jubilant wave as he reached the water. He grabbed some smoothed pebbles and began to skip across the frothy surface. Ang and Lily shared a glance before Ang groaned, taking off after him.

Lily frowned. Someone was missing. "Zia Raven?"

A voice groaned from another sand dune. "*Ahia!* Ouch! I'm over here."

Raven emerged, stumbling forward. Her lips were pinched in pain as she approached, rolling her shoulders in a slow stretch.

Lily raced over, worried. "Are you okay?"

Her aunt smiled, waving her off. "Bah! I'm fine. Just a little bruise nothing more." She looked up to the sky and waved her fist in the air. "Don't think I didn't get the joke! Seriously," she mumbled, "landing on a natural seawall with barnacles is not a fun way to drop in."

Lily opened her mouth when Cabyll appeared at her shoulder, his heat startling against her back. She jumped, giving a small squeak. He was way too silent for her liking.

Is that on the checklist for best fae assassin, she wondered wryly.

He crossed his arms over his chest, giving a small, snarky smirk. "Maybe you should stay here then if you're hurt." He looked his nose down at Raven. "No need for you to slow us down."

"Cab," Lily admonished.

He turned his head sheepishly, shrugging his shoulders. "What did I say?"

Raven rolled her eyes. "What a charmer you are. This little bump isn't gonna stop me."

Lily's attention drifted. The scenery was beautiful, gorgeous, other-worldly. Similar and yet different from her time in the forest. Any other time she would have loved to swim, but if the Veil had taught her anything was that looks could be deceiving.

Ang and Brandon were playing by the crystalline waves, Brandon's loud laughter harmonizing with the crashing tide. Holding her smile, Lily scanned further. Then she frowned, her concern growing. There was nothing. Nothing but stretches of sand, trees, and sea for miles.

"Cabyll?" she asked warily. "Where is this person we're supposed to meet?"

His gaze narrowed down the sand strip. A hard glint sparked, making his eyes seem like emerald chips. He shook his head, his frustration evident.

"He should be here. This is the spot he said to meet."

"Where is the nearest place with people?" asked Raven.

"There isn't." He frowned. "He picked this place specifically because of its isolation for security reasons."

Lily tried to keep her heartbeat calm, but it thumped hard against her chest. "Cab, if he's not here..."

He refused to look at her, his shoulders tensed.

Raven lightly touched Lily's arm, steering her towards the shoreline to grab the others. "Let's not waste time then. We need to move before-"

A rustling shook the brushes behind them. Facing the thick fronds, Lily peered into the massive jungle. They stood still as Brandon's whooping laugh faded in the background. Lily glanced over to Ang.

The changeling had stopped as well, sniffing the air. Ang went very still, throwing her arm out in a jerky motion to quiet Brandon. Raven gripped Lily's arm, squeezing a little tighter as a shadow jumped down from the tall branches. It scurried and darted so fast Lily's eyes strained trying to keep up. She scanned frantically, her eyes watering from the strain, but it disappeared.

Lily whispered, not moving. "Cab? Did you see that?"

He nodded, his calm gaze focused.

A voice rang out. "Hey dude!"

Lily jumped, turning to find a smiling Brandon talking to an unknown figure.

The figure was tiny, almost childlike, but wrinkly like an old man. Bright red skin stood out in the blinding sun, a burnished crimson against the azure sea. It sported a huge head, bald and shiny, with white paint dotting its forehead. It had no nose, but slitted nostrils above a perceptively wide mouth. Long lanky limbs with equally long fingers looked disconcerting against its enormous belly. It was drastically disproportionate and, Lily grimaced, disturbing.

Brandon, oblivious, walked up to the little creature. "Hey man...or creature dude...think you could help us? We seem a little lost."

Lily tried to call out a warning, but the words stuck in her throat. "Uh, Brandon..."

Not hearing her, Brandon kept moving until he was within arms-length. The creature stayed still, simply watching with beady eyes.

Brandon frowned, scratching his temple. "Sorry dude, do you not understand me?"

Ang yelled out. "Brandon, get back!"

She jerked him backward the same moment the creature struck out with its long fingers.

Lily gulped. The fingers sported suction cups, like an octopus.

Yuck! I'm not going to look at calamari the same again.

Ang, still holding the collar of Brandon's shirt, glared at the creature, and hissed. The creature's eyes narrowed shrewdly before opening its mouth.

Lily's eyes widened.

The creature had no teeth! And by no teeth that meant nothing but ugly yellowed red gums. The creature's lips parted, emitting an eerie howl that echoed over the waves, toward the jungle.

Brandon, eyes wide, stammered out. "Ah...Ang? What's going on?"

Ang shook him by the collar, hard, as she gritted out. "You wanted to know what a Yara-ma-yha-who is? Well congratulations, you got to meet one." She gave another warning growl at the creature.

"And what does this Yara-ma-yha-who do?" asked Lily. It whipped its head to stare at her, its lips splitting into a creepy grin.

Cabyll grimaced, his lip curled in disgust. "Another name for them is the Outback Vampire."

She blinked. "Vampire?"

Well lucky ducky us. I don't like reading about vampires let alone meeting one.

Raven tilted her head. "It doesn't seem too dangerous."

Lily nodded automatically. What her aunt said made sense, logically. The little vampire didn't look like it was strong or particularly agile as it patted its bulging gut.

"That's if there's only one," remarked Ang. "But let's hope there's-"

A rustling intensified behind Lily. Well, shucks, she forgot to keep an eye on the jungle. Slowly, she turned.

Her blood hardened, her feet frozen in place. At least a dozen of little vampires appeared, surrounding them.

"Not more of them..." Ang trailed off, groaning.

Cabyll slowly unsheathed the scimitars from his back. Blue lights sparked in his eyes as he called out. "Everyone, listen up. Their mouths can swallow you whole, so don't get too close. And whatever you do, do NOT get touched by their fingers."

"Let me guess, the 'vampire' part is they suck your blood from those suckers," answered Raven dryly.

"Not too dumb for a human," snarked Cabyll.

"Cab! Not the time." Lily groused as she pulled her bow from its case, slinging it onto her back.

"Little human, I've got nothing but time for you." He winked.

She scowled. "Will you quit with the flirting or so help me I'll shove this bow-"

He smirked, his eyes leisurely moving up and down her frame. "So *bul gat-eun*. Save the fire for the vampires Lily. Though I'd be impressed if you managed to land an arrow in the sand."

His eyes sparked bewitchingly at her.

"Will you focus?!" She bit out, ignoring the slight flip to her stomach.

"Oh, I am *very* focused. Are you? Your attention seems to be more on me." He gave another flirty wink. "I am quite distracting."

Lily groaned, rolling her eyes. *Incorrigible, flirty, self-absorbed...*

She nocked her arrow, keeping her gaze on the Yara-ma-yha-who in the front, its eyes locked on hers. She took a breath, her thoughts racing. Did these vampires attack the person they were supposed to meet? Was that person...

Hold that thought girl. Dozens of red vampire leeches monkey thingies are in front of you. Deal with the other problems later, she admonished herself.

"Focus human," chided Cabyll, tearing her from her paralyzing thoughts.

Her eye twitched. "You focus!"

Ang growled, interrupting them, her fingers lengthening into sharp claws. "Will you *both* focus!" She threw Brandon behind her as two more Yara-ma-yha-who joined the original, advancing toward them.

Raven pulled out from her pocket a pair of fingerless fighting gloves, quickly slipping them on. She cracked her neck to the side, bouncing on the balls of her feet.

"Alright then," she turned to Lily, a bright smile gracing her face. "Ready *nipotina*?"

Lily wordlessly nodded as she pulled the string taunt, eyes narrowed.

She steadied her breathing, though her heart thumped loudly in her ears. Her inner voice yelled.

No! Not ready!

She took a deep breath, letting out the air slowly, tickling against the fletching of the arrow. She steeled herself as the first vampire jumped.

But, here we go.

Chapter Nine

UGH...HERE WE GO.

A voice echoed out, scratchy and whispery. "Miss Ari? Miss Ari? Where are you?"

Ari ignored the voice, as she had done often the past few days. Was it days? Weeks? She couldn't recall time anymore, and frankly, she was too tired to care. Her eyes took in her boring surroundings for, what felt like, the billionth time. There were no adornments, nothing but a threadbare bed and a washing room. However, the room itself could be considered a piece of art.

Brilliant shades of red, yellow, orange, brown, pink, and pure white sandstone streaked the walls and ceilings in a kaleidoscope of colors. Frankly, it hurt her eyes. She rubbed her temples to erase the impending headache she knew would come from staring at the busy pattern.

Listlessly, her gaze rested outside her window, if you could call it that. It was a stone opening, where below a winding sage blue river greeted her calmly. No balcony or safety barriers. It would be so easy to fall out into the river.

She leaned forward for a closer look.

A large shadow drifted under the bright surface, right under her gaze. It was the fifth time she saw the shadow, which meant something was circling her window.

She slowly leaned back, hugging herself.

Yeah, no thank you.

"Miss Ari? There you are."

She heaved a sigh, pulling her shoulders back to face the voice.

"Aput. I know what you're going to ask, and the answer is no, I'm not going."

Aput crossed their arms, bending their head down. Their antlers brushed the ceiling as they entered the room. Furry nostrils blew out the sandy air, dust scattering in the wind.

When Ari first met Aput, she had cringed in horror. Aput was an Ijiraq, a monster from the furthest northern region of Dain's territory. Somewhat humanoid, Aput stood on two legs, covered in brownish black fur. Black warrior robes wrapped around their torso and covered their entire body. Long red-brown braids framed a pronounced face ending with a snout and striking grey eyes on either side rather than in front, similar to a reindeer.

Standing at least seven feet tall, even taller with the caribou antlers sporting their head, the Ijiraq towered over Ari. They were a fae of nightmares. But, ironically, she found herself getting used to the fearsome fae with the quiet, whispery voice.

Aput sighed, the deep sound rustling against the sandstone. "Miss Ari. You really need to go outside and get some fresh air."

"Is Dain back yet?"

Aput closed their eyes, shaking their head.

She turned away, her hair swinging against her shoulders. "Then I don't want to go anywhere," she pouted. "I want to see Dain."

Aput took a deep, patient breath. "You do not need Prince Dain to explore. To live."

She crossed her arms, slinking back. "I do not want to go Aput. I don't want to be around...those...things."

She shuddered. Last time she went 'out' with Aput, the creatures she saw scared her. Even now, the thought of seeing them again made her squirm and shiver.

"You shouldn't judge the fae by appearances Miss Ari," admonished Aput. Their antlers shook in emphasis, steam coming out of their nostrils.

82

Ari blushed, shamed. "Sorry Aput. I know you're not bad. But the others..."

Aput's shoulders dropped as they stepped toward her, their eyes intense. "Your term 'bad' is relative. We just...are. You're not in your world anymore Miss Ari. You must remember that."

She merely nodded. It was hard to forget she was no longer in New Jersey. Images of her mom and Brandon pierced a corner of her heart quietly. She rubbed her chest absently. Did her mom know she was gone? Was she upset? How did Lily explain her disappearance? Ari could recall vividly the day when Lily came to 'rescue' her. She had never seen her stepsister so worried. For her. Lily even almost died trying to save her from the horned serpent.

Ari rubbed her chest again.

"Miss Ari? Are you in pain?"

Ari's brow furrowed. She knew she made the right choice. Dain cared about her. She forgave him for the horned serpent incident after he explained everything. At first, she was a means to an end. But she was important to him, she was special. She clenched her hands, her finger-nails biting into her palms. She *was* special, she knew it.

"Miss Ari?"

She shook her head, clearing her thoughts. Wiping away her family from her forethoughts, even if it was temporary, she smiled faintly.

"I'm fine Aput."

Aput tilted their head to the side, their antlers dangling down, the braids underneath like red ivy trailed down the downy fur. They contemplated Ari's sad gaze a moment before straightening up, covering their mouth to emit an exaggerated cough.

"Miss Ari, I forgot some important news."

Ari's bright blue eyes zeroed on the Ijiraq.

They continued. "Prince Dain *should* be returning tonight."

Her eyes lit up, her lips splitting into a beautiful smile. "Oh! Aput why didn't you start with that sooner. Can I have dinner with him? Please?"

"I'll see what we can arrange."

She clapped her hands, twirling merrily, her happiness rising. Her mouth hurt she was smiling so wide. Just the thought of seeing Dain made bubbles dance in her stomach.

Aput soundlessly drifted to the exit, ready to leave. They bowed slightly, careful with their antlers. "How about I send up some tea and treats while you wait."

"Oh, sure, that would be wonderful. Oh, Aput?" She called out before Aput disappeared. The Ijiraq, being a creature of shadows and mist, could dissipate soundlessly. Mist had already engulfed Aput, but they stopped, turning back. She blinked, a hopeful smile on her face. "Can I make some strawberry sugar cookies for Dain? He seemed to like them last time."

"You wish to bake?"

Ari nodded, clasping her hands eagerly.

"We do not have strawberries here I'm afraid," they responded reluctantly.

Ari's face fell.

"But-" Aput continued, their deep gravelly voice vibrating the room. "We do have lemon aspen. Perhaps you know recipes to utilize that fruit?"

She bit her thumbnail, thinking hard. Her eyes widened. "I know a lemon pound cake cookie recipe. My dad loved eating those in the summer."

Aput whispered. "I shall let the cook know to prepare the ingredients."

She beamed. "Thank you, thank you Aput." She turned around, quickly heading toward the washroom. "I need to get ready for Dain."

Aput vanished, quietly, into the shadows.

Torches emitted a firefly glow in the spaciously open dining area. Carved within the gorge, the sandstone glowed in the dim light.

A large stone table spanned the middle of the room, unique flowers etched and painted in various colors on the surface. Ari sat at one end, staring up into the open night sky. Thousands of stars flamed blindingly in the blue darkness. Maybe it was her imagination, but the stars seemed brighter, more colorful.

She smoothed her dress down, keeping her nervous hands busy. She wore a beautifully spun pastel blue gown that accentuated her bright eyes. She had curled her hair in golden ringlets down her back. Overall, she knew she looked good. Not just good. She looked fabulous.

She frowned slightly. Too bad she was the only one who seemed to notice.

Dain sat on the other side of the table, deep in thought. His long, elegant fingers swirled his glass absently. His burnished rose-gold hair shined in the dim light, giving an ethereal halo.

She blinked, tearing her gaze away. Sometimes she had to stop herself from staring. Dain was so handsome he took her breath away. Problem was, he hadn't looked at her once since she sat down. Instead, his mind seemed elsewhere.

She set her utensils down, the metal clang of the silver ringing in the silence.

"Dain?"

Silence.

"Dain?!"

His head jerked up. His normally arresting, red-gold eyes were cloudy, as if a fog passed through his pupils.

Ari blinked, pausing mid-sentence noticing the familiar signs. Dain was not called the Prince of Prophecy simply for a fancy title. He received prophecies, predictions, and forewarnings of future events. And his prophetic episodes were occurring more frequently after his failure to release Uktena, the Horned Serpent.

She got up, rushing over. Usually, he was fine after a vision, but there were rare occasions there was a physical side effect. She would never forget the first time she witnessed his seizures. After that, she refused to take any chances.

She motioned to Aput, who nodded before disappearing. Almost immediately they reappeared, a pitcher of liquid in hand.

Dain neither moved when she reached him nor responded when she tentatively placed her hand on his arm.

She took a breath and waited, knowing not to force him out of the vision. Sure enough, it didn't last long as Dain blinked, the fog clearing to reveal his blinding molten eyes. He blinked again, shaking his head slightly.

"Ari?" he asked softly, confused.

"I'm here Dain." She motioned Aput for the pitcher of fresh raspberry infused water. Aput bowed, pouring some into Dain's glass. Ari noticed the bright red berries helped stabilize him after an episode.

Gently she placed the cup in Dain's hand, wrapping his cold fingers around the stem.

She waited as Dain quietly sipped, before she finally asked, "What did you see?"

He paused, taking another slow sip, before putting the glass down. He waved his hand dismissively. "Nothing to concern yourself with."

"But Dain, I want to help," she protested, wincing at her pleading tone.

His eyes narrowed, biting. "And how can a human help me? You were supposed to help with Uktena, but we failed to release him."

She reared back at his harsh words, pushing down the hurt. He was always cranky and irrational after a vision. He didn't truly mean it.

She worried her lip. "We talked about this. I thought I was going to be eaten."

He sighed, exasperated, rubbing the bridge of his nose. "Your step-sister would have saved you. Do you really think I would have let you be eaten when there was another human there who could suffice?"

Ari bit her lip harder, tasting blood. As much as she wanted to, no needed to, believe him, it still didn't settle right. Especially with his nonchalance of Lily being sacrificed. Yes, Lily was a nuisance, but she didn't want her to die. Her vision went blurry as tears started to well up.

Dain quickly got up and put his arms around her shaking shoulders, his biting tone softening. "There, there. Do not worry. The visions are more intense than normal. I do not wish for you to cry."

She rubbed her eyes, her voice wobbly. "I know. You have...a lot of pressure."

He rubbed his temples, his eyes tired. "Immense pressure. There is still much to be done for the next event. We have no time to delay."

Her eyes widened. "Is it time? Can I go out with you? Finally?!"

Dain gave a small smile. "Yes, you still are an integral part of this *petit oiseau*. We must make the preparations."

He gestured to Aput, who nodded and disappeared into the shadows. Dain rose, taking Ari's hand and bowing over it in a courtly manner. "I shall take my leave, please get some rest."

He turned around and walked briskly away into the night air.

She sighed, rubbing her arms. The chill of the night air was empty and lonely. The stars blinked again. Here she was.

Alone. Again.

She already missed the soothing coolness of Dain's touch.

"Miss Ari? Shall I escort you back?"

Aput's whispering voice echoed in the night air. Even though they weren't physically with her, the Ijiraq seemed to possess an ability to be in multiple places at once.

She reluctantly smiled. Maybe she wasn't truly alone. She took a last glance at the brilliant night sky and back down to the table, her lemon cookies untouched.

"Yes, let's go Aput."

Chapter Ten

LILY VOWED SHE WOULD NEVER EAT OCTOPUS AGAIN.

Or, anything with suction cups that remotely resembled the clingy Yara-ma-yha-who that stuck to her leg. She kicked it soundly, her foot sinking into its soft protruding belly. She frowned. No matter how much she hit them, they were never hurt. It was as if they were boneless. Nothing phased them, their squishy bellies and heads absorbed any impact.

In front, Raven kept back several of the outback vampires with a flurry of kicks and punches. Her aunt was amazing. But again, the monsters did not seem to tire.

Beads of sweat dripped down Lily's forehead; she hastily wiped her eyes, closing them for a split second. A blur of red streaked past her, ending in a resounding thunk.

"Will you pay attention!" Cabyll growled.

Blinking, Lily dimly registered one vampire had sneaked up behind her. Before it could stick itself against her back, it was pinned against a tree by several knives, squirming.

Cabyll's eyes sparked, his arm outstretched. The rational part of her brain vaguely wondered how that many knives could fly that fast.

Oh yeah...that's right. Assassin. Forgot that little fact for a moment.

"Thanks," she panted.

Get it together girl.

He grunted, grappling another vampire and throwing it into the brushes. "Stop thanking and start helping."

Her eyes narrowed. *I'm gonna ignore that...*

"They're not stopping," she replied instead.

His eyes narrowed, twirling his scimitar slowly. "I noticed."

Lily glanced at the group. Her aunt was breathing heavy. Ang's chest was heaving, her hair sticking to her face. Brandon shoulders slumped, his throwing slowing. Not to mention Lily's arms began to tremble from launching arrow after arrow.

She bit her lip, hating to admit it. "We are slowing down Cab."

"I noticed that too," he said flatly. He spun, his scimitar taking out another vampire.

"Any thoughts?"

"Blow them up?" he answered dryly as he nonchalantly wiped something black from his cheek.

Lily tried not to gag.

"I'm up for that!" Brandon yelled behind Ang, who was struggling with five of the little leeches. He stomped on one that tried to sneak past, the vampire hissing angrily before jumping back.

Lily groused out. "Can we *not* resort to something that could potentially take us out too?"

Raven spun around, effectively kicking a Yara-ma-yha-who into the jungle. She rolled her shoulders before calling out. "I agree with Lily. Let's not resort to def con tactics."

"Then what, pray tell, do you suggest?" Cabyll snapped as he threw a few vampires off his shoulders.

Raven raised her eyebrow. "Fight or flight correct?"

His lip curled, insulted. "I do not fly."

"Yeah, you swim or gallop or something right?" Brandon quipped. "Aren't you a water horse?"

Cabyll growled, his eyes glowing. He spun around, ready to yell, then stopped as an arrow whizzed past his face to land on the foot of a Yara-ma-yha-who who was about to pounce from his blind spot.

Startled, his eyes widened, landing on Lily.

Lily put her bow down, her eyes stern though her arms were jelly. "Giving up a fight doesn't mean giving up. We need to move. We're pinched in and you know it."

For a moment, she may have glimpsed a proud smirk on his lips. But it must have been a trick of the light. His nose quivered before he growled out. "Fiiiiine. But let it be known it is because of you humans requested it. Not me!"

She began to roll her eyes but stopped as they widened, alarmed. She wasn't lying when she said the Yara-ma-yha-who were pinching them in. What she didn't realize was now they were effectively caged, the ocean at their back. They had nowhere to go. Dozens of little red vampires formed a half circle, cutting them off from the rest of the beach and the jungle.

"Ah...Cab..." This wasn't good. Definitely not good.

He turned around, grimacing as he came to the same realization. "*Jangnanhae*?!"

She backed up closer to him. "Uh...Maybe you should blow them up."

Desperate times called for desperate measures, right?

He shook his head. "They're too close now and we're next to the water. Unless you're fine with your brother being zapped." He pursed his lips, "I could..."

Brandon shook his head, yelling. "No! Not fine over here! Not fine with that plan!"

"Too bad," muttered Cabyll.

Her chest warmed as a deep voice echoed in Lily's mind.

Perhaps I can assist young Sentinel.

Lily held her breath. *Tim?*

I cannot do much, the Thunderbird replied, *but let me assist in this small way.*

She jumped when her arrowhead suddenly crackled, encased in a blazing blue fire.

She took a deep breath; it was her last arrow. *That'll help Tim, thank you.*

Keep calm little one. Breathe, and let the arrow fly.

Before she could think, one vampire jumped forward, and Lily released the arrow. It fell in front of the Yara-ma-yha-who, right into the sand. The fire caught quickly, spreading fast and far to create a temporary barrier separating them.

The group huddled together, back-to-back. The Yara-ma-yha-who giggled, their rasping hissing voices slithered across Lily's skin.

They climbed on top of each other. Her eyes widened when she realized they were going to jump over the flames. Goosebumps prickled her arms as she clasped her bow in front of her like a shield.

Her aunt kept her hands up, fighting position at the ready.

Raven yelled, "Well?! Come on you little slugs!"

An eerie silence fell over the group. Lily stumbled, a forceful pull at her back, her feet sinking. What was going on?

She gulped.

The tide.

It was the tide pulling her backwards. But it was too strong. The group dug their feet into the sand while the Yara-ma-yha-who stumbled forward, grasping for purchase.

Their eyes widened, their gaping mouths falling open in surprise. Some began to shake, a few fell backward scrambling. A tap on Lily's shoulder pulled her attention away from the present horror.

"Ah...Lil?" Brandon's quivering voice put her on high alert.

Slowly she turned.

The ocean waves parted, leaving a stretch of the seabed visible, as if someone carved out a chunk of the ocean. Shells and coral lay bare, open to the air. But that wasn't what pulled Lily's gaze upward. The missing strip of ocean water had risen, high above their heads. It twisted and turned, like a whip.

Lily whispered, fear lacing every word. "Cabyll. We're not dealing with another Iya, are we?"

She still had nightmares of the disease water demon they encountered in the forest. Sometimes she woke up in the middle of the night in a cold sweat, swearing sulfur and burning leaves lingering in the air.

Before she could ask again, Cabyll pushed her head down yelling out.

"Down...everyone!"

The ocean struck violently, like a cobra. Salty droplets danced on

Lily's arms as the wave raced over their heads. Clutching her eyes shut, the howling screams of the Yara-ma-yha-who faded within the increased roar of the ocean's torrent. Finally, the surging sounds dwindled, the calm rushing of gentle waves remaining.

Lily peeked through a burning salty haze, meeting Cabyll's glowing green irises.

He gently tucked a strand of curly hair over her ear. "You okay?"

Lily nodded, his other hand still resting on top of her head. She tried to get up, but the combo of his hand plus her shaky legs resulted in an inevitable flopping onto the soft sand like a beached fish.

Cabyll pulled his hand back quickly, averting her gaze as he ran his fingers in his hair, messing up his shaggy mane.

Lily wanted to bury her face in the sand, wishing she could hide.

Raven stood up, dusting granules and a strip of seaweed off her shoulder. "Looks like the little vampires are gone."

Indeed, they were, the wave having swept them away. Whether into the ocean or into the jungle, Lily couldn't tell. But she was sure they wouldn't be coming back anytime soon.

Or so she hoped.

"Dude. That...was...awesome!" Brandon jumped, his eyes bright.

"Ouch!" He rubbed his head where Ang smacked him.

Ang frowned, looking around, still wary. "Keep alert. Something caused the waves to do that. Something powerful."

As if the ocean heard her, the waves began to swell again. Lily braced herself.

Oh geez, what now?

She was pulled from her anxious thoughts as Cabyll chuckled softly. He pointed on the rising wave, this one so high it was a surfer's dream.

His bright eyes cut into hers, that familiar arrogant smirk and twinkle returned. "Took him long enough."

A figure emerged from the surf. Riding the swirling foam, a man surfed back and forth effortlessly. The wave crested above them, causing Lily to cover her head anticipating the crash. Then, with a soft dip, the wave descended in front of them, landing the figure firmly on the shore, the waters dispersing around his feet.

"Woah..." Brandon exclaimed, awed.

Lily silently agreed. The figure in front of them was imposing.

Almost seven feet tall, the young man towered over the group. She guessed he was maybe in his thirties. But, if she learned anything, looks were deceiving in the Veil.

Flowing shorts covered by a black lavalava wrapped around the man's immensely muscular frame. He was shirtless, his sun kissed skin covered head to toe with tattoos. Various tribal markings swirled around his body, too many Lily couldn't identify. All she could see clearly were turtles, ocean waves, arrows, and suns. His long, dark red hair gleamed a ruby crimson against the sapphire backdrop. He had it tied in a topknot, strands falling down over a chiseled jaw. Brilliant violet eyes shown through a half face tattoo displaying arrows and spearheads that trailed from his left eye, curling up around his head down his neck.

"You're late," Cabyll quipped, running his hand through his hair dusting off water droplets.

The man merely raised one eyebrow, crossing his arms over his massive chest, his muscles stretching.

Cabyll rolled his eyes. "Still as talkative as ever I see."

The man spoke, his deep voice rumbling like a wave. "Only when necessary." He reached out a massive hand. "Good tidings Cabyll."

Sheathing his scimitars, Cabyll grasped the man's forearm in a firm handshake. "Good to see you as well."

The man's gaze grazed over the group in a tactical fashion. Lily squirmed; the disinterested assessment palpable.

The man continued, "So *this* is the group you said could help me?" He raised his chin up, crossing his arms. "I am having doubts Cabyll."

"Kye, I know they don't look like much." He put his arms out in a placating gesture while Lily glared. "But you do need them."

"Doubtful," Kye scoffed.

Raven snorted, coming forward. "Well, lookie here. If it isn't Mr. Tall, Handsome, jacked up more than a Mac Truck."

Kye frowned, confused. "Mac Truck?"

Raven waved her hand dismissively. "Not the point Muscles. Point is, I think we started off on the wrong foot."

She looked down at his large, bare feet. "Yes, wrong foot. Sheesh you have big feet."

Kye frowned. "How does one have wrong feet?"

Raven laughed. "Oh *tesoro*, you're a hoot. First let me thank you for helping out with those vampire calamari things."

Lily giggled softly. The man, Kye, had appeared so cold initially. But now, he seemed utterly bewildered by her aunt's ramblings.

He shook his head. "Yara-ma-yha-who are quite harmless in small numbers. They usually keep to themselves. It is disturbing to find a large clan in this area."

"Well, be that as it may. Thanks a bunch, Muscles." Raven's chirpy smile was met with a frown.

"My name is Kye. Prince Kye. Address me properly." Again, he put his chin up in the air, intimidation radiating off of him.

Oh... Lily inwardly groaned. *Another prince. Gosh dang it.*

Raven shrugged. "Kye, Muscles, tomato/tomato."

He glared at her, his violet eyes burning.

Her aunt rolled her eyes, unperturbed. "But if you *insist* your majesty, fine."

Everyone in the group, even the prince, gawked. Lily put her hand over her mouth, hiding her laugh. She remembered the first time she met one of the Veil's princes. She had been terrified. They were beautiful yes, but dangerous. This prince practically screamed dangerous with a side of fatal death. And here, her aunt just plowed through the prince's warning like she was handling a toddler's tantrum.

Her aunt really was fearless.

Raven caught Lily staring. She smiled warmly, then jumped to concern. "Oh gosh sweetie! Are you alright?" She reached out, patting Lily's shoulders looking her over. "They didn't hurt you did they?"

Lily laughed. "Yes *zia* I'm fine."

Raven sighed in relief before turning to Brandon. "You okay sweetheart?"

Brandon gave a thumbs up. "A-okay."

"I'm fine too thanks for asking," drawled Cabyll.

"You should be. If you're not then what good are you," Raven snarked.

Kye's voice boomed. "I *am* still here you know."

Raven called over her shoulder. "*My* family. Which means more important, got it your Majesty Muscles? I'll get to you in a minute."

Kye's shoulders tensed. "It is your highness, not muscles."

Her aunt snorted, whispering to Lily. "Such babies the fae are."

Lily covered her mouth to hold another giggle.

Kye gritted his teeth, his question directed at Cabyll. "Is this human woman always this aggravating?"

Cabyll groaned. "You have no idea."

Raven straightened, placing her hands on her hips. "This *human woman* has a name Muscles. My friends call me Raven but you can call me Ravenna."

"You are frustrating...*woman*." Kye ground out.

"I'm awesome and fantastic thank-you-very-much." She flipped her hair back, mirroring the prince's arm cross.

Lily knew her aunt and the prince would probably go toe-to-toe in a fist match if no one stepped in. Honestly, she wasn't sure who'd win, but she didn't want to find out.

She quickly interjected. "Are you who we were supposed to meet?"

Kye's eyes narrowed, still focused on Raven, his irritation evident.

"...your highness," Lily finished with a neutral smile.

He reluctantly tore his gaze from Raven's unblinking stare. "Yes, unfortunately I was delayed."

Cabyll raised his eyebrow. "I'm assuming it wasn't a normal delay?"

He nodded. "You are correct. I suspect my delay is tied to your unfortunate encounter with the Yara-ma-yah-who. We must speak before-"

A large rustling within the jungle tore the group's attention. Everyone tensed. Was it more vampires? The fronds parted to reveal another Yara-ma-yah-who scrambling forward.

Since she was out of arrows, Lily raised her bow like a club, ready to hit it. However, the little vampire was lifted off the ground, it's legs flailing, by a massive hand.

A huge fae, larger than Kye, appeared. Similarly dressed to the prince, the man sported a kilt made of grasses and flax. He was also covered in tattoos. One that stood out was a large Tiki emblazoned on his chest. The sides of his head were closely shaved, the rest of his midnight black hair draped down his back with the top being tied tightly on his head. Swirls covered his entire face. He was imposing, a warrior built in every way. He carried a club in one hand, pale white with a tinge of yellow.

Looking closer, Lily shuddered.

It was bone. The smooth white bone club rounded out to a tip that could also be used as a blade. The fae silently held the squirming vampire in his meaty hand as his gaze rested on the prince, waiting.

"Any others?" asked Kye.

The fae shook his head, his dark rumbling voice replied. "Cowards."

"*Maika'i loa*. That's good." Kye spoke over his shoulder, answering the unspoken question. "He killed them all."

Lily's mind skipped. *Wait...they're all dead? And that's good? Seriously!?* Granted she didn't want to run into those creepy vampires again but wasn't that a little extreme.

Kye continued, almost in disappointment. "Waru, why did you leave this one alive?"

The massive warrior shrugged. "To question him. I figured you wanted answers. We didn't need all of them to answer our questions."

"True. Did you question him already?"

Waru nodded. "I have the information we need. I believe we need to relay this in private don't you, your highness?"

"Yes," Kye replied. "Let us move. But first, let's take care of the trash."

Waru bowed respectfully. He threw the Yara-ma-yha-who at the feet of the prince. The outback vampire shook violently, covering its face and bowing.

Kye stood still, his aura growing, his eyes glowing indigo.

His voice boomed, like a crashing wave against the rocks.

"Do you know what you have done traitor?"

The vampire skittered, speaking in various chirps and howls. Lily didn't know what it was saying, but she knew from the look in its beady eyes it was scared.

Very scared.

Kye's lip curled up in disgust. "It does not matter. There is no redemption save for your life to return to the Void. Your soul is not worthy, but I hope you find redemption in your next spirit life."

The little vampire bowed, resigned, tears springing from its eyes.

Lily's heart pulled seeing the creature so dejected. She bit her lip, warring on what to do. Finally, her eyes grew determined.

This isn't right.

She stepped forward.

"Wai-"

A hand clamped over her mouth. Cabyll was behind her, his warm hand holding her firmly in place. She pulled, trying to break free, but he held tight. Glaring, she grabbed his fingers, giving them a good pinch.

Should I bite him? Seriously, I think I'm going to bite him.

Her heart stopped when his gaze grabbed hers. They bore into her, dead serious, before he slowly shook his head. He bent down, his hair tickling her forehead while his voice whispered in her ear.

"This is not the time *Nari*. Prince Kye is not someone you want to get on his bad side. This is their way. You need to adapt."

She struggled before finally sighing, the air trapped by Cabyll's hand. Her shoulders slumped, frustrated tears welling up.

He cursed silently, his thumb rubbing softly against her cheek, wiping away a stray tear.

"*Budeuleoun ma-eum...*"

Lily stood quietly, not fighting anymore. That didn't stop the weight in her heart from pulling at her chest. He removed his hand slowly, moving to her side.

The air charged, the salty breeze swirling. Towering over the vampire, Kye raised his hand. In tandem, the waves seemed to become alive. A water plume rose, mirroring his hand movements.

The Yara-ma-yha-who began babbling, shaking uncontrollably.

Kye, with no emotion whatsoever, flicked his wrist forward. Like a snake, the water plume shot out, wrapping around the vampire's throat. The creature struggled, but it was no use. With another flick of his wrist, the water plume threw the creature over the group's heads, straight into the ocean with a faint splash.

Lily blinked, stunned.

The Yara-ma-yha-who flailed, yipping desperately. She bit her lip, a glimmer of hope peaking in her chest. Maybe the creature could swim. If he swam fast enough, he could make it back to shore. But no sooner than the hope appeared, large bubbles began to froth and foam around the little vampire. The water darkened as a large shape emerged from the depths. Then something, Lily didn't know what, sucked the wailing Yara-ma-yha-who down into the deep.

In a flash, the little creature was gone.

She clutched her arms, goosebumps peppering her skin. How the fae could be so cruel was beyond her. Staring at the stone-cold Kye, Lily realized Cabyll was right. This prince was not someone to cross. She didn't even know where to begin about Ari. What do you say after that?

Thankfully, she didn't have to as Brandon blurted out.

"Dude...you have like water-powers. That's so awesome!"

Lily swallowed, her throat dry. Did he not just see what happened?

Ang groaned. "Brandon, not the time."

"But...but he's like a muscle-bound superhero with water-powers! Come on Ang, you can't tell me that's not cool."

She palmed her face.

Waru tilted his head to the side, as if finally realizing the group's presence. "Is this the group *tou nui*?"

Kye's eyes reached the heavens as he reluctantly answered. "Yes, they are the humans that will assist us."

Waru shook his head. "Weak..."

Brandon frowned. "Hey dude, just cause we're human doesn't mean that we're weak. Have you ever heard of hero stories where like humans overcome all obstacles and stuff like that?"

Waru raised his eyebrows. "I never said you were weak because you were human. You are weak because you could not defeat the Yara-ma-yha-who."

Brandon opened his mouth. "Oh...fair point..."

Waru rubbed his chin, tilting his head. "But you are also very small."

"I had a growth spurt."

"Still small."

Brandon frowned. "I'll get another growth spurt."

The warrior pinched his fingers together. "Your arms are quite little."

"I'm lean!"

"Like a wet noodle, flimsy..."

"Okay I get it Maui wannabe," grumbled Brandon, his cheeks flushed.

Waru pursed his lips, confused. "My name is Waru, not Maui."

Ang chuckled, elbowing Brandon in the gut, his cheeks flaming. "I think I'm going to like these guys."

Kye clapped his hands. Immediately, Waru quieted, bowing his head.

"That's enough Waru," the prince snapped. "We have much to discuss, and no time to speak." His striking gaze scanned the area. "This was supposed to be a safe haven, but since the Yara-ma-yha-who are here tells me one thing."

Cabyll nodded. "I get what you're going to say Kye."

Lily looked at him, confused. "What is going on?"

He sighed. "It means things just got harder."

"But," protested Lily, "we came to find Ari."

Kye's cold tone could freeze the sea. "Understand this human. You help me and I will assist you with finding your sister." His dismissive assessment rose Lily's hackles. She tried to ignore it, but it was proving difficult. "My brother told me of your bravery, but I will be honest...I have my doubts."

Raven glared. "For us, it's family first Muscl- I mean, your highness."

Kye gritted his teeth as he ground out, his fist smacking his chest. "Can you understand, you frustrating woman! My *territory* is at stake. We are talking one person versus millions. Remember well that what happens in my territory inevitably will affect your world."

A breeze tore through the group, ruffling hairs. Kye's gaze steered to the jungle. "We must move. The jungle now has the ears of my enemies. Let us go, now!"

Kye raised his arm again, his violet eyes blazing. The ocean parted, opening a tunneled path into the seabed. The seawall on either side towered over Lily by several feet, connecting above in a watery arch. Various colored fish, manta rays, and sea turtles swam the edges, staring at them curiously. A school of blue grouper even jumped from one side to the other, like a fish rainbow.

Lily gaped at the sea tunnel. Did he really think they would simply walk into the ocean?

Kye stepped forward, his head grazing the watery ceiling. He commanded over his shoulder, never breaking stride, "Let's go."

The group cautiously walked into the ocean. Brandon jumped with excitement, as he noticed a massive black manta swimming above him. Raven moved forward calmly, her eyes doubting. But by the time she was fully in the tunnel, Raven was running her hands on the water wall, a fascinated twinkle in her brown eyes.

Lily hesitated, images of drowning racing her mind. Was this safe? Probably not.

Cabyll remained by her side, whistling softly. It didn't fail to escape her attention that his gaze centered on her aunt, his eyes warring in indecision.

Lily lips pinched as her senses tingled. "Cab?"

He turned, his startled eyes meeting hers briefly before a crafty arrogant smirk emerged. "Oh, did you want me to hold your hand?"

She shook her head. "Don't."

He blinked innocently. "Don't what?"

Her eye twitched. *Oh, acting all innocent now you two-faced flirt.*

She put up her finger, wagging it back and forth. "No drowning, you promised."

He ran his hand through his hair, covering his face briefly. He chuckled, warm and low. "Oh? Of course. I promised, didn't I? I would never drown *you*." He winked, his lips pulling back in a devastating grin.

She frowned. *This sly horse.*

"Not me!" she barked. "My aunt."

His eyes widened, surprised. He scratched the back of his head, refusing to look at her. "Um...well..."

"No."

"A splash?" He pinched his fingers together. "Just a little?"

"Don't even think about it!"

"Fine, fine." He put his hands up in surrender. "I wasn't going to drown her."

He flinched when Lily glared harder. "Just a little dunk, that's all," he muttered, disappointed.

She poked his chest. "None of it, Cab. I mean it."

He sighed dramatically. "Fiiine. You're so serious."

"You must hurry."

Waru's deep voice called from behind, startling her. For a guy so big, he was awfully quiet. The large fae leaned forward, his eyes intense. "Prince Kye is closing the tunnel behind us to prevent unwanted guests."

Cabyll reached out. "Let's go Lily, you get to hold my hand after all."

She speared him a side glare. Ignoring his outstretched hand, she lifted her head and stomped into the tunnel.

Waru barked a choked laugh.

Cabyll jogged beside her, giving a wink. "You'll forgive me, I'm too handsome to be angry at."

She closed her eyes and counted to ten. *Save me from the whims of crazy fae.*

Chapter Eleven

ARI CLASPED HER SHAKING HANDS AROUND THE LEATHER straps, desperately trying to hide her nervousness. She squeaked, her equilibrium teetering where she almost tumbled off her ride.

Her very much living, breathing, ride.

"Miss Ari, you must hold tight to your mount," chided Aput, their voice muffled by a large cloak covering their face from the blaring sun.

She grimaced, straightening the reigns of her mount. 'Mount' was a loose term. She shuddered as the warm scales under the reigns grazed her fingertips.

Dain sighed a long, drawn-out breath. "The burrunjor will not do anything unless I say so."

In emphasis he patted the side of his massive mount, the burrunjor snorting in response.

Ari shook her head, biting her tongue. *Yeah sure...he doesn't know these things are supposed to be extinct.*

Earlier, she was excited. She was finally helping Dain. That excitement quickly ebbed when she realized she would have to ride an animal.

She didn't like animals. They were smelly, dirty, and never seemed to like her. But she'd try, for Dain. Then she saw the creature she was riding. Was it a horse? Nope. She even would have preferred a donkey. Instead, slitted yellow eyes narrowed at her, accompanied by razor sharp teeth on a huge upright scaly body. She thought she was being subtle, but then Aput had begged her to stop screaming.

Thinking back Ari's cheeks flushed, and it wasn't from the hot sun.

How did he expect me to react? He thought I'd be fine riding a T-rex?

But, she didn't want Dain to be upset with her. Biting the inside of her cheek she held on firmly to her burrunjor. She was going to prove she was the leading lady. A smooth scale grazed her ankle.

She flinched.

But why did it have to be a reptile? Ew ew ew!!

Dain raised his eyebrow, irritation evident. "Do we have a problem Ari? We cannot delay, time is imperative."

The words stuck in her throat, choking her. He was mad at her again. Why? She was trying so hard. Her gaze lowered, her mind spinning.

"Your highness," interjected Aput, moving their mount between them. "Please remember Miss Ari has not encountered a burrunjor before. I would say she has shown remarkable adaptable behavior for the task at hand. Remember Sylias?"

Dain smirked, irritation melting away as a soft chuckle escaped him. "Yes, that fool just walked up to his burrunjor and got his arm bitten off. He screamed quite loud."

He moved his mount faster, a gleam in his eye, the last few minutes forgotten. "We're almost there."

Ari let out a breath, giving Aput a grateful smile.

"Thank you," she whispered.

The Ijiraq shook their head, antlers rustling. "Do not thank me. His highness is like the snow. Beautiful but becomes cold quickly. You must learn to adapt faster."

They clicked their feet against the mount, urging the burrunjor to pick up the pace.

She nodded and followed. She whispered to her mount, "Don't you dare knock me off." An answering angry snort had her quake slightly before adding. "Please?"

With a jerky nod, the burrunjor took off.

A ri's breath came in gasps as the sticky heat became suffocating. The burrunjor had taken them far away from the gorge, through arid open land, past a brilliant beautiful coastal lagoon to finally rest at an adjacent freshwater lake.

The lake was enormous, surrounded by low brushes with arid landscapes. The water was a brilliant deep blue save for parts covered with a thick film of green algae.

The burrunjor arrived at the far edge. High rock spikes dotted the rocky shore where the algae lay heavy and thick. The mounts reared back, roaring in unison. She tugged, but her mount refused to go further.

Dain's eyes took an excited gleam, the red-gold irises burning bright. His lips split in a blinding smile.

"We're here."

He jumped off his mount, patting its hind. The nonverbal cue signaled the burrunjor as it hastily ran away.

Ari scrambled to get off her escaping burrunjor, her legs flailing. She finally disengaged, hopping on one foot, as her mount disappeared into the jungle.

Dain's warm laugh curled around her, tugging her heart. His cold hand wrapped around her waist, keeping her steady. She sighed in relief as his magic cooled her burning skin which had taken a beating from the relentless sun.

"You can be so clumsy little one," he murmured. His smile was still in place, his eyes a warm gold that melted her fears.

She returned his smile. This was the Dain she knew. Sweet and warm who made sure she was okay. He was having a bad slump from his visions, she reasoned. But as quickly as he steadied her, he removed his hands, leaving her back in the suffocating heat.

He turned around, clapping his hands in anticipation. "Now!" His eyes began to glow softly. "Let's get started."

She looked around, finding nothing. "What do we do?"

He rubbed his chin, muttering. "We need to get his attention."

Aput shook their head. "Then we must wait your highness. The Muldjewangk is nocturnal. He does not normally wake until night approaches. My estimates indicate we have a few hours."

Dain's face was unreadable before his eyes briefly flashed white. He blinked, shaking his head. "We cannot wait."

His shoulders tensed before he asked over his shoulder.

"My dear?" His question directed at Ari. "Do you have any thoughts?"

She blinked, stunned. He was asking for her opinion. Quickly, she blurted the first thing that came to her. "Maybe trick it? Let it think it's night?"

He hummed, pondering. "And how do you purpose I do that? My powers may be strong, but they aren't limitless."

She blushed, embarrassed. Of course he was right. There was no way to do that. She chewed her lip, her mind blanking.

Dain's eyes softened, a small smile emerging. "Do not worry my dear. Why don't you take a quick walk on the bank, clear your mind."

Aput opened their mouth, but Dain interrupted. "Aput, I need to speak to you in private. Come!"

Ari eyed the water warily. "But isn't there something in the water?"

Dain waved his hand. "Not to worry. As Aput said, the Muldjew-angk is nocturnal. Go take a quick walk. The lake air will help clear your head from the long journey. We'll be right back, I promise."

She soon found herself alone by the lakeshore, staring out into the wide, murky water. Here she was, alone again. She scrubbed her foot against the grainy shore, berating herself. Trick it to thinking it was night? Gosh...how stupid.

She sighed, her breath coming out in a choked gasp.

Lily wouldn't think it was a dumb idea.

She shook her head. No, she did not need to think about Lily right now. Or anyone in her family. Here she was, in a beautiful, magical place and she was going to change the world with a love story just like in the novels she read. Dain was gruff, but he was secretly sweet. She had to keep showing him she was on his side, that she cared.

She clenched her hands, nodding to herself. She could do this. She was Arianna Greene for goodness sakes! She didn't need her family. Not her silly little brother who still thought fart noises were funny. Not her stepsister who would rather investigate dead languages. No thank you, she didn't need any of that weirdness. Dain and this magical world were worthy of her. She deserved this.

But...try as she might to hide it, a tiny corner in her heart ached.

Ari, still caught up with her thoughts, failed to notice the slight rippling of the water. Her toe kicked a few stones into the lake, little circles plopping, breaking up the algae. She sighed, turning back inland, wishing Dain and Aput would return soon.

That was when she noticed the silence.

An eerie silence. The type where the birds, the animals, all the white noise, disappeared.

Goosebumps rose on the backs of her arms. A strange presence loomed over her. Little droplets hitting her hair and shoulders, like a whisper of a kiss. She blinked, the water stinging her eyes, then frowned. It couldn't be raining, the sun was shining.

Ari tensed, her heart thudding in her chest heavily, her shoulders beginning to shake. She tried to be still, praying that whatever was behind her couldn't see as long as she stayed utterly still.

You're thinking about dinosaurs again, she admonished herself.

That's when a large tree limb moved in the corner of her vision. Her lip began to quiver. Why did the tree limb have green markings on it? Did someone paint it? As the tree got closer, her heart stilled. It wasn't a tree limb, but an arm! A massively long, lithe arm that sported long black claws. Those sharp claws slowly tipped over a palm tree that was larger than Ari's entire body.

Her entire body quaked, her lower lip trembling.

Oh my god! Oh my god! What is that?!

But as much as she wanted to know what was attached to that massive arm, she was too frightened to move. A deep, dark, raspy voice echoed behind her.

"Well...Hello little quokka..."

Ari clenched her eyes shut. *Nope, nope! Not listening.*

A devilish chuckle shook the ground under her feet. "How adorable. I do so love when my food shakes so much. Makes them more tender. But...I would like to see your eyes sweet quokka. It is only polite."

She refused to move.

"Now!"

The booming command made her yelp, jumping around. She paled, her jaw dropping.

106

The deep voice chuckled darkly.

"Oh, you are so delightful little quokka."

Ari's heart began skipping, jackrabbiting inside her chest. Her body shook so much she fell down, the sharp rocks biting into her legs and palms.

The creature - the Muldjewangk - the fast-fading rational portion of her brain realized, stared at her. Its slitted, teal eyes narrowed dangerously.

It must have been as long as four school buses and Ari couldn't even fathom how tall it was as it blocked out the sun. Strong, long limbs covered with teal markings were stark against grey-brown skin. The skin seemed leathery, similar to a marine mammal. While the Muldjewangk had arms, it had no legs. Instead, it sported a massive whale-like tail.

It flapped lazily in the lake, tearing up the algae. And if that wasn't terrifying enough, his face was truly the most horrific. A prominent forehead, almost reminding Ari of a squid, sported similar teal markings. Jutting brow bones covered slitted eyes to end with a massive mouth that held thick, long fangs. That fanged mouth curled into a devilish smile.

"Oh? What's this? A human child I see. It has been ages since I had a human. I believe since right before the Sentinels banished me back into the Veil."

His slithery smile melted into a hissing frown.

She scrambled backward, her palms stinging. Her mouth opened and closed like a fish, but no sound emerged. Her back hit something, hard, stopping her in her tracks. Her eyes widened. She had thrown herself right in its claws. And those long claws curled around her, clutching her tightly.

Ari's stomach dropped as weightlessness took over, her feet dangling in the air, while being pulled high toward the awaiting Muldjewangk. He chuckled darkly while Ari shook, from either the hand or her fear she wasn't sure which.

"You poor, little human," he tsked. "So adorable yet so fragile. I promise I will make this as painless as possible." His mouth opened, a massively long tongue snaking out to lick her face.

Tears poured down her cheeks. She grunted, struggling in his grasp. Desperate to get free.

No...no, no, no! Dain where are you?!

Maybe she said the last part out loud, she couldn't recall, but a crack split the air. The temperature instantly became colder. A cold, lazy voice drawled out behind her.

"Hello Yarramundi."

The Muldjewangk, or Yarramundi, paused. His tongue slithered back into his mouth, his head tilting slightly. His eyes widened in recognition.

"Prince Dain? What brings you to this territory?"

"I came to see you of course." Dain's gaze grazed Ari, turning back to Yarramundi with a dismissive wave. "This is such a distraction. Could you please put the human down so we may speak?"

Yarramundi lowered his massive head until he was eye-level with Dain, his eyebrow bone raised. "My apologies prince, but I am hungry."

Dain shrugged. "Why didn't you say so?" With a snap of his fingers, the bushes parted, revealing two large figures.

Ari peered over her shoulder. The figures were taller than an average man. They walked upright on two legs, however that was where their similarities ended. Covered in white and grey fur, they walked on paws instead of feet. Long snouts sporting sharp, glistening fangs shone in the bright sun. They were humanoid werewolves, covered in leathers.

Her puzzled gaze warred with a shuddering unease. Her mind whirled, trying to place them. When they gave a nod of deference to Dain, it clicked. They must be the Adlet. Dain told her they were his personal guards. His elite force, next to Aput.

She frowned. But what were the Adlet doing here? They were supposed to be guarding Dain's territory. A prickling uneasiness grew, droplets of doubt growing. Dain was not surprised to see them. The question was, why didn't he tell her?

Ignoring Ari, who was still clutched in Yarramundi's grasp, the two Adlets carried armfuls of raw meat in their large, claw tipped hands.

Yarramundi stared, unblinking, as they carefully placed the meat in front of him. Back and forth they came, more bundles of raw meat piled on top of each other.

Ari grimaced. If she wasn't vegan before, she would be now.

When the Adlet finished their task, they put a clawed hand on their chest, looking at Dain. The prince nodded, the unspoken command evident. They bowed, then disappeared into the bushes.

Dain gestured to the pile. "I heard you have a fondness for lamb, am I correct?"

Yarramundi blinked, his slitted eyes expanding, surprised. "Lamb?"

The Muldjewangk hesitantly sniffed the pile, his tongue snaking out to grab a piece. His eyes closed in bliss, a humming sound rumbling the water's surface. A breath or two later, one eye peeked open. "I have not had lamb in hundreds of years. It is still as good as my memory serves." His gaze snaked toward Ari. "Not as good as human, but still a delicacy I have long missed."

Dain crossed his arms lazily. "By all means, please eat your fill. Then we can discuss business."

Yarramundi shook Ari, giving her a sly grin.

"Next time little quokka."

With a flourish, he uncurled his claws. With a yelp, Ari's stomach went up to her throat as gravity took over. Clenching her eyes, she braced for the hard impact. Her breath flew as she landed on something hard but giving.

A whispering rasp coughed underneath her. "Miss Ari, are you alright?"

She found herself on top of Aput, their body cushioning her fall. She scrambled up, reaching out to the help the Ijiraq. Aput hesitantly grasped her hand, standing upright. They both glanced at Dain and Yarramundi.

The Muldjewangk was tearing into the pile of meat ravenously. His long tongue wrapped around large chunks, swallowing them whole.

Ari's shoulders shook, shock kicking in. She trembled, frozen as piles of meat disappeared in the monster's cavernous maw.

That could have been me.

Aput put their hands on Ari's shoulders, pulling her backward. Slowly. "Let us move back here Miss Ari. At a safe distance."

She nodded mutely, too stunned to protest.

Dain continued, not looking back at them. "I have heard you acquired some valuable knowledge. Knowledge that I need."

Yarramundi's tongue reached out to wipe his cheek. He chuckled darkly. "I am too old to play word games, young prince. I know what you seek."

Dain's eyebrow raised. "Oh? Do you?"

Yarramundi's shoulders shook as his rumbling chuckle echoed in the lake. "There have been whispers across the territories that you tried to awaken Uktena. When you are as old as me, it wasn't hard to figure out what you want."

Dain pursed his lips, blinking innocently, before he drawled out. "Well then, if you know what I seek, will you assist me?"

"What do you offer me?"

Dain gave a half smirk. "What if I said freedom?"

"Do not mock me," he growled, his fangs gleaming. "My freedom was taken from me, by those blasted Sentinels."

"But what if I could offer it back? Back to the human world?"

Yarramundi scoffed. "Is that what you told Uktena? That went well young prince."

Dain tsked, examining his nails. "While that plan did not go exactly as anticipated, your banishment is not the same as Uktena. Yours is simply isolation in this lake, unable to move to a ley line to return to the human realm. I need only move you."

"If it was that easy, I would have done it long ago."

The Muldjewangk's tail splashed up and down steadily in agitation, belying the calm tone of his words.

Dain continued to examine his nails, unconcerned. "What if I said I have a portal stone?"

The tail stopped abruptly, Yarramundi slowly asked. "You have a portal stone?"

Dain yawned. "The same portal stone that can create a fissure in the Veil, allowing you to pass into the human world." His eyes took a calculating glint. "Do you not miss it?"

Yarramundi hummed. "I do miss eating humans at night. I miss my old lake."

"Plus, you could take revenge on the Sentinels."

The Muldjewangk's eyes took an eager gleam. "What a mind you have young prince. I admit I do like that suggestion. If you have a portal stone and put me back in my old lake, I will give you what you seek."

Dain smiled, pulling out a smooth pebble from his pocket. It

110

gleamed like an opal, its iridescent sheen sparkled. Yarramundi's eyes grew wide as his clawed hands flexed, holding back from reaching out and snatching it.

Dain held out the pebble, just out of reach. "Give me what I seek first."

Yarramundi nodded. He turned, passing his clawed hand over the lake. The lake hissed and bubbled until a column rose above the surface. A small obsidian box lay on top.

Yarramundi, with two claws, carefully plucked the box and placed it in Dain's hand the exact same moment the prince passed the pebble.

His tail flapped excitedly, his gleaming eyes fixated on the stone. He shook his large head, focusing back on Dain.

"You know it is worthless without the fire."

Dain shrugged, unperturbed. "That will not be a problem. I appreciate your assistance."

Yarramundi's slitted eyes narrowed. "Young prince, is there anything else you want? This stone is worth far more than what is in that box as you may never get the fire."

Dain chuckled, holding the box tight. "That is where you're wrong old one. I will succeed, the visions have told me so. But to your question of what else I can ask of you." His eyes took a cold, calculating gleam. "Just do what you do best when you return to the human world. I hope you feast to your heart's content."

Yarramundi waited a minute, his body tense. He opened his mouth, fangs extended...and laughed. A deep, thunderous laugh echoed around them, shaking both the Muldjewangk's body and the lake in loud waves.

Ari shuddered. It was an evil, maniacal laugh that made her blood ice over.

"Oh, young prince," A long claw wiped a lone tear. "I see I made a good decision to hand that over to you. I will keep that promise."

His dark eyes zeroed back to Ari, who still huddled behind Aput. He gave her a sinister wink. "I have missed quokkas."

With a flash, the Muldjewangk sank back into the lake, the waters rippling. After a moment, the water glowed, a bright shining white. The water swirled and bubbled. Then, after a few minutes, it grew still, the light dimming. The algae slowly came back to cover the surface once again.

"What happened?" Ari bit her lip at the few lingering ripples disturbing the water.

Aput shook their head. "Yarramundi returned to the human world. He used the portal stone."

She frowned. "But...Aput. Didn't they say he was going to eat humans?"

Dain sauntered up, flipping the box up and down lazily. "Of course, that's what he does. We need as many of our allies on the other side as we can."

She opened her mouth to protest but he interrupted. "You know what must be done for this new world, *right* my dear?"

Ari held her breath, ashamed. She knew sacrifices needed to be made, but...

"It's just...he tried to eat me."

Dain clucked in sympathy. "You must have been frightened."

She pouted, clenching her fists. "Where were you Dain? You said you would be back."

"And I did come back, in time of course. I figured your sweet smell would lure out Yarramundi."

Ari paused, shocked. "Wait...you left me to lure him out?"

Aput ducked their head, confirming her suspicion. Her voice pitched higher. "You KNEW he would try to eat me?!"

Dain waved his hand. "We were watching. There was nothing to worry about."

"But why didn't you tell me?"

He shrugged his shoulders, unperturbed. "Your reaction needed to be convincing, or else he would have known something. I only had one shot to convince that sly slug." He held the box, his eyes molten. "And we succeeded! All thanks to you."

She drank in the praise, her anger dimming. If it wasn't for *her* they never would have lured out Yarramundi. With big doe eyes, she pleaded. "You won't do that again though, right Dain?"

"I won't let you be eaten by a Muldjewangk."

She sighed, relieved, before running to his side, hugging him. She relished his cold arms holding her tight.

Aput coughed lightly. "Is it truly the vessel?"

Dain slowly opened the obsidian box. There, nestled in the stone was a small jar. It was made of a brilliant, blood red jasper with a quartz stopper set with a rope inlaid with buttery yellow sulfur crystals.

"Hello beautiful," he whispered.

Ari stared, a warm pull from her belly tugged softly. It was beautiful. She had never seen anything like it. Intricate spirals were carved into the jasper, soft and ethereal.

She found herself reaching out, hoping to touch the spirals to see if it was truly as smooth and soft as she knew it had to be. Her fingertips grazed the smooth surface. It felt surprisingly warm. A slight shock hit her fingertip, like an electric charge, and zipped up her arm.

Aput interjected. "It does look to be the vessel your highness."

She blinked, the warm pull disappearing slowly. She lowered her hand awkwardly, thankful Aput and Dain didn't seem to notice. She absently rubbed her hand, still feeling the slight tug, her gaze remaining on the jar.

Dain carefully lifted the vessel and placed it around his neck, tucking it underneath his shirt. He turned back to the group, his eyes bright, his smile dangerously wide.

"Let us go get some fire Aput."

Chapter Twelve

"THINK THIS GUY'S GOT A FIRE OR SOMETHING WARM AT THE end of this thing? Cause I'm freezing!"

Brandon rubbed his arms, puffing out air in small wisps.

Lily shivered, agreeing. They had been walking for what seemed like hours in the magical water tunnel. It was amazing at first. Out of this world really. Schools of beautiful fish and glowing creatures swam around them. But after looking at it for an hour, and a sneaking shark that seemed to follow them for a good while, Lily was ready to get out.

Her aunt had stopped several times to ask various questions about the unique creatures. It got so bad that Kye, grumbling and growling, stomped over when Aunt Raven, who wasn't paying attention, was asking Waru about a monstrously large dome shaped turtle that sported a long neck with a twelve-foot-long fish tail. Without a word, he plucked her up by the waist, ignoring Raven's protests and kicks to his stomach, and proceeded to carry her for several miles. They bickered and growled at each other for a long time. Ang and Brandon snickered when Raven got a good shot to Kye's kidney. Waru even burst out laughing when Raven called the prince a '*biscotto figlio di una scimmia*' (after Lily quietly translated it for him).

Finally, Raven relented, slumping over the prince's shoulder with a pout. When he noticed her protests stopped, he gave a reluctant sigh and put her down. Both of them refused to look at each other.

The hike continued in silence.

Lily had to hand it to her aunt. She was definitely not intimidated or impressed by the prince. Even after how ruthless he was with the outback vampire, her aunt did not treat him any different from anyone else. Likewise, the prince seemed unsure how to handle her aunt. Lily couldn't blame him. No one knew how to handle Ravenna Ambrosino.

"Did no one hear me? I'm cold guys," complained Brandon, bringing her back to the present. A puppy dog pout began to form on his boyish face.

Raven dug in her pack, looking through the supplies. She handed Brandon an herb that looked somewhat like jerky.

"Start chewing that sweetie. That'll help for the time being."

Brandon frowned, eyeing the herb with distrust. Finally, he shrugged, shoving it in his mouth. His eyes widened.

"Oh wow. I'm feeling like I took a warm bath. This is great Aunt Raven." He noisily chewed the herb, marching ahead with renewed energy.

"Are you okay *nipote*?" Raven's concerned brown eyes bore into hers, gesturing to the herb. "Do you need some too?"

"I'm okay Zia Raven." She put her hands up at her aunt's narrowed gaze. "I promise. It's not too far until we're there, I'm assuming."

"I would think so..." Her aunt tossed over her shoulder with a syrupy sweet tone. "We do not have much further to go do we Mus... oops...I mean your 'highness of everything surrounding us as far as the eye can see which is as big as his ego'?"

Kye cracked his neck, his nostrils twitching.

Waru coughed into his hand behind them, his shoulders shaking slightly.

The prince took a calming breath before stopping in front of a wall of water. He looked up, his gaze scanning the depths in front of him. "It is just beyond here. I need to open a door. Waru?"

The unspoken question hung in the salty air.

Waru nodded. "Humans, stay next to me." He gestured to Cabyll and Ang. "If you are strong enough, you'll be fine."

Lily frowned. That didn't sound promising. "And if they're not?"

Waru shrugged. "They're not worthy."

Ang rolled her eyes. "Enough with the macho stuff. Let's get this over with."

She took a large breath, holding it.

Lily blinked. *Wait...no. Why are we holding breaths?*

Cabyll smirked, cracking his knuckles. "This will be fun. Have at it Kye!"

Before Lily could ask what was going on, the prince raised his arms and the tunnel collapsed.

Her eyes widened as the torrent rushed over her. *Oh crap...*

"Remind me...'cough'...the next time we...'cough'...go into a magically created water tunnel...'cough'...to not go!"

Lily's chest burned as sea water poured out of her lungs, making her speech difficult.

As she tried to catch her breath, her mind replayed the last few minutes. She vaguely remembered Kye raising his hands, pushing water forward to open a door. However, that meant the entire tunnel disappeared, torrents of water pouring over them.

Waru clapped his hands together, making tiny bubbles. The bubbles encased the human's faces, essentially creating an air pocket helmet for them to breathe.

Cabyll had changed into his horse form, swimming effortlessly in the sea, doing flips and dives in the current as the rest of them struggled to move.

She clenched her teeth. *What an arrogant, self-centered, showboat.*

Ang held her breath, zipping through the water, heading towards the newly formed, glistening door up ahead. Waru grabbed the humans one by one, swimming each one toward the door.

He reached for Raven first, but she shook her head, pointing to Brandon and Lily. Waru nodded, grabbing Brandon and safely delivered him through. Raven and Lily waited, patiently, pushing through the water.

Unfortunately, the current proved to be too strong for Lily, as it carried her away. She kicked hard, but to no avail. Panic settled in.

Raven pushed forward, reaching out to grab her, their fingers brushed before an undertow grabbed Lily. Raven tried to reach again, her eyes fearful as Lily was carried further and further into open sea.

To make matters worse, her air bubble helmet began shaking, gradually pressing inward. The logical part of her brain deduced there was a time limit on how much air was left. Maybe she could get to the surface. She looked up but couldn't see anything in the dark water. Even if she swam as fast as possible, she wouldn't make it. Not to mention she wasn't sure how heavy the water pressure was. She grimaced, not wanting to think of what would happen if the helmet would pop.

The current continued to carry her, bubbles blocking her sight as the dark blue depths crept in. The helmet shrunk further, almost touching her nose. Lily realized she only had seconds before it would pop.

Desperate, she inhaled loudly, taking in as much air as she could. The bubble burst, water rushing into her eyes. She squinted, saltwater stinging as she tried to keep her eyes open. A shadowy figure emerged from the dark, racing toward her.

Please don't let it be a sea monster.

As her eyes closed involuntarily, her lungs burning for air, she could make out a familiar mane of black and red tinged hair.

Which brought her to the present with her current state coughing up at least a liter of sea water. She tried to speak again, but the fiery pricks in her lungs stabbed her ribs.

Shaking hands grabbed her shoulders.

"*Nipote*? Are you okay, dear?"

Warmth embraced Lily as Raven held her tight. "I thought I had lost you! *Mio dio!* I tried so hard to get you. If Waru hadn't grabbed me...I swear I'm going to break that prince's squarely defined jaw."

Lily coughed, an involuntary laugh breaking out. Wincing she held her side as clean air jabbed into her lungs.

Cabyll's chastising voice came from above.

"You should give her some space."

Raven glared, not letting Lily go. "I'm only allowing your rudeness because you saved my niece's life. No illness or injury stops an Italian's hug, *fata!*"

Lily tried not to laugh, the stabbing in her ribs not relenting. She clutched her chest, her hand hitting her pendant. Her very cold pendant. Her lungs seized. Why wasn't the pendant warm? Shouldn't the Thunderbird have helped her. Did something happen to him?

Tim? You okay?

His deep voice echoed, a little faint.

I'm here little Sentinel.

Why were you quiet?

I'm sorry young one. Per an oath I took, I can only intervene in human affairs when my kind is a threat to them.

So...that means... Lily bit the inside of her cheek, trying not to breathe too fast.

His remorseful tone answered her unspoken question.

It means the current was natural, not magical. And the water was not caused by a magical entity. I was unable to do anything.

Her shoulders sagged as Stoorworm's warning came back. She did have a lot to learn. Guess that meant she was on her own when it came to any natural disasters. Though she couldn't help but grumble to herself.

So, I have this ancient super-powered immortal that can only work in specific situations. Lucky ducky me.

The Thunderbird chuckled deeply. *There is the humor young one. Now, I believe there are others who are concerned about you.*

She breathed in a lungful of fiery air before looking up.

Cabyll wasn't being snarky or arrogant for once. His eyes, concerned, trailed over her.

She put a trembling hand on her aunt's arm, keeping eye contact with Cabyll.

"I'm okay Zia Raven. But can we agree to never do that again."

Raven nodded, laughing shakily.

Cabyll reached down, offering his hand.

Grateful, she reached out. She teetered on unsteady legs, but he didn't let go. "Thanks for saving me. Again."

He huffed, pulling back to ruffle his hair. "I promised I wouldn't drown you." He muttered under his breath. "That includes you drowning in general."

She raised her eyebrow.

Cabyll, flustered, blurted out. "You owe me so much you know that!"

She nodded, hiding her grin. "Just put it on my tab."

Her gaze strayed over their heads, her mouth widening. "Woah..."

They were in a dome. A huge underwater dome. It reminded Lily of being in a snow globe, only with the water on the outside. In the center was a structure surrounded by coral and mother-of-pearl. Large coral pillars stood on the perimeter of the area, sporting large tear drop larimar crystals. The larimar glowed, a soft rippling blue that pulsed faintly.

"Where are we?" she asked.

"No idea. Wherever *Prince* Kye wanted to go," Raven replied drily.

"Everyone else is inside. Let's go." Cabyll let go of Lily's arm as he moved toward the structure.

Lily and Raven stayed back. Lily pursed her lips. "Think this is safe?"

Her aunt sighed. "Remember what Papa Remy said *nipote*. Nothing here is safe. But what choice do we have sweetie?" Her gaze grazed over the dome, a smile peeking through. "This is pretty amazing though. We should take in the good moments while we can *va bene?*

Lily nodded, taking in the wonderous view of a pod of dolphins playing from above. "*Va bene*. Let's go and get Ari."

Raven smiled, patting her shoulder affectionately. "That's my strong niece."

Lily entered the structure, not sure what she'd find. Large crabs? Octopus? Small bright sea slugs and snails crawled on the damp seabed. Her foot squished on the wet sand. This whole place was probably underwater just recently, so where were the things that considered this place home?

Well, this is unexpected.

The circular structure was large, but very open. The interior was completely open and spacious as well with coral and barnacles naturally embedded the walls. But...it was surprisingly plain. Functional, but plain.

When they entered the center, intricately woven beds of seaweed were wrapped around the floor. It took Lily a moment to realize they were thick enough to sit on.

Kye was sitting toward the center of the structure, casually sipping something from a clay cup. He inclined his head to Lily and the others.

"You have found the other human."

Cabyll nodded. "Yes."

"She is unharmed?"

Lily's eye twitched. *He knows I'm right here.*

She replied instead, "I'm fine your highness."

Kye merely raised his eyebrow, motioning with his arm to the group. "Have a seat."

Lily bent forward to sit down, before a distant growling reverberated around the space, freezing her in place.

The deep, animalistic growl grew louder, until two emerald eyes glimmered in the darkness behind Kye. The large shadow passed over the prince who, unconcerned, proceeded to take another leisurely sip from his cup.

Lily's eyes widened when the figure appeared in the dim, oceanic light.

Dios mio!

It was a panther.

Well, not a normal panther. It was big, extremely big. Black midnight fur shone against large glowing green eyes. It was by far the largest cat Lily had ever seen. Even from far away, Lily surmised the panther's head was larger than her shoulders. It easily must have weighed over eight hundred pounds. It was beautiful.

Beautifully dangerous.

Kye must have seen their stares. He tilted his head toward the large cat.

"This is Aka. Keep your distance, if you'd like to keep your limbs."

Lily breathed out the breath she was holding, keeping an eye on the massive paws...and claws.

Not a problem from this end.

Unfortunately, her aunt didn't seem to get the memo. Raven stepped forward, a beautiful smile blossoming.

"Oh, *che bello*! Hello Aka, you handsome kitty!"

She put forth her hand, palm down.

Kye frowned. "That is not a-"

Aka's ears flattened, dropping his head down slightly. His gaze narrowed on Raven, his body tensing.

Lily's blood froze. She anxiously looked at her aunt, who still was wearing a warm smile at the man-eating cat. She opened her mouth to yell when the panther pounced.

Kye jumped up, alarmed, but he wasn't quick enough. The panther covered Raven until there was nothing but black fur.

Lily's heart stopped.

Then she heard something.

Laughter.

Her aunt's laughter tinkled, muffled under the large cat.

"*Basta basta*! You're tickling me."

Her aunt's head peaked around the massive head. Aka was licking her shoulder, butting his head against her hair, messing it up into a wavy mop. Her aunt laughed, halfheartedly pushing the panther back, but Aka was not having it.

Kye's mouth opened in shock. He quickly smoothed his face, taking on a familiar frown as his eyes narrowed into slits.

"Aka! *Alu ese*."

The panther snorted softly, reluctantly retreating from Raven as she stood up, dusting off her clothes.

Kye growled at her. "Foolish human! What did you do?"

Raven tilted her head, innocent. "What do you mean?"

Kye stabbed his finger toward Aka, accusing. "What did you do to Aka? Are you a witch?"

She scoffed. "I did nothing. He's a cute kitty."

His eyes widened, shocked. "Kitty?"

Waru snorted, his shoulders shaking. He wiped a tear from his eye. "Miss Raven. That 'cute kitty' is one of the most dangerous creatures in our territory."

Raven pondered that for a moment, then shrugged. "Still cute."

Brandon stood in awe before whispering. "Aunt Raven, you're awesome."

Lily held in her chuckle, agreeing silently.

Raven beamed, giving a delightful wink.

The prince palmed his face, growling. The air grew damp and wet as his eyes sparked. He directed his next question to Cabyll who, like the rest of the group, stood watching the exchange in shocked silence. "Are humans always this difficult?"

Cabyll whistled low. "Well..."

He stopped with a grunt, bent over, holding his chest where Lily elbowed him in the ribs, hard.

"I'll let you be the judge," he wheezed out.

Waru cleared his throat. "Perhaps we should focus on why we're here *tou nui*."

Kye nodded wordlessly, rubbing his temples.

"Yes, you're right Waru. Please sit everyone, there is much to discuss."

Ang grumbled, rubbing her arms. "No offense your highness, but we're kinda cold. Especially the humans."

She gestured to Brandon, who was shaking, his lips beginning to turn blue.

"See?" She shook her head. "They won't be able to speak. Their teeth will be chattering instead."

The prince, unperturbed, tapped on a seaweed basket next to him. "Sit near the baskets, you'll warm up soon enough."

The group sat down hesitantly. Aka had left Kye's side to sit next to Raven, a deep purring echoing around them. Kye glared, but Raven paid him no mind, scratching the large panther's ears to Aka's delight.

Lily looked at the seaweed basket near her. It was filled with golden amber. She picked one up, shocked. It was warm and, to her surprise, gave a small pulse of heat. It was a dry warmth that soothed the chill in her bones. It was pleasant.

Ang hummed in approval, checking on Brandon whose lips were regaining their normal color.

Waru chuckled. "Very frail skin these humans are. Like infants."

Kye shook his head at the group, disapproval evident. "Frailer than infants Waru. They cannot even withstand the basic elements. This does not bode well."

Raven snorted delicately. "Not frail. Humans biologically are not predisposed to deep oceanic water. I mean we don't even have fur." She took Aka's large furry face in her heads making kissy noises. "Not like your soft beautiful fur you kitty witty sweetie."

Aka purred, his tail thumping in happiness.

Kye's lip curled in disgust. "I will find out what tricks you did to my beast. Mark my words human."

Raven ignored the prince to rub her nose against the large man-eating cat. She continued speaking to Waru. "Our skin is not thick or have layers of insulation." Her eyes widened. "Wait, does that mean you have evolved with those characteristics?"

Waru tilted his head. "What do you speak of?"

She scooted forward toward the large warrior and poked his bicep.

Waru's eyes widened, shocked. Cabyll palmed his face. Ang merely raised her eyebrow. Lily choked on a laugh when she noticed Prince Kye's mouth gaped open.

Raven, oblivious, continued to press Waru's bicep, her eyes taking on a clinical glint. "Is the muscle similar to whales? Maybe not fat per se but perhaps-"

Lily hissed a warning, seeing the increasing anger rising from the prince. The prince had jumped up and began stomping toward Raven. Actually, Lily gulped, more like stalked. "Zia Raven..." she warned.

Her aunt ignored her, which didn't surprise Lily in the least.

"What are you doing woman?" Kye thundered, snatching her hand away from Waru.

Raven rolled her eyes, giving a huff. The prince stared at her, shocked. Even when meeting his furious gaze, she merely huffed at him. Lily gaped. Her aunt really was either oblivious or fantastic. She was leaning toward the latter.

Raven wagged her free finger. "We went over this. Not 'woman', it's Ravenna. There is absolutely no need to be rude. You may be handsome but that doesn't trump over rudeness. Oh, my!"

Her gaze went back to Waru, her arm still dangling in the prince's hand. "I'm sorry Waru that was rude, wasn't it?"

Waru started to laugh but choked as the prince's angry gaze zeroed on him.

Ang shook her head, mumbling. "You think?"

Raven continued, contrite. "I'm sorry, it's a flaw of mine. When I get on a scientific hypothesis, I'm like a dog with a bone."

Waru smiled large. "No need to be sorry Miss Raven," he gave a jolly wink. "I'll show you my arms any time."

The group groaned in unison.

"Waru!" barked Kye.

The warrior's eyes downcast, his smile fading.

The prince's glare returned to Raven. Still squeezing her hand firmly, he gave it a small shake. "You are infuriating! First my beast and now this. Do you not have any regard to the seriousness of this situation?"

Raven's eyes narrowed, her voice taking on a dangerous edge. "Oh, I'm aware all right. I'm distracting myself to calm down, but I still have half a mind to tear into you about that stunt you pulled back at the tunnel. You almost killed my niece and nephew...and you didn't tell us your plan before you did it!"

She continued, her voice becoming steel. "You may be used to everyone listening to you, no questions asked, but it is obvious you have never met an Italian woman. I may be half your size, but you put my family in harm's way like that again I'll cut you off at the knees you *idiota*!"

Lily put a hand on her aunt's opposite arm, trying to calm her. It wasn't that she was afraid of the prince's reaction. Rather, Lily was worried her aunt would make good on her promise.

Kye shook his head, unable to keep up with the conversation, his grip loosening. "Sorry?"

Raven suddenly smiled, pulling her hand away. "Apology accepted."

He frowned. "I didn't -"

Raven clapped her hands, dismissing him. "Now, let's sit down and get all nice and dry, shall we?"

Lily shook her head, almost pitying the confused prince. Her father knew better than to go toe-to-toe with her aunt. He always told Lily fighting with Ravenna was like fighting with the tide, there was no way to go against it. One minute she was calm, the next she was a storm.

And Prince Kye was certainly getting a taste of the storm that was Ravenna Ambrosino.

Waru's laugh cut through the tension, a deep booming laugh that filled the space.

Kye grumbled, rubbing his temples again before sitting back down.

"I...apologize for the unconventional entrance." He gave a pointed look at Raven, who resumed petting Aka. "This place isn't meant for others save for Aka and me, let alone for humans. But this was the only safe location for us to speak freely."

Cabyll raised an eyebrow. "Care to share Kye? Not that I'm not used to you being tight lipped, but this is a lot even for you."

Kye sighed. "You're right. Do you remember the last time we walked together?"

Cabyll concurred. "Yes. It was when you decided to go on a walkabout."

"And?" the prince prompted.

He tapped his chin. "Hmm...You established the Council."

Kye nodded, his fingers steepled to his lips. "I have been keeping an eye on the Council over the last few centuries. I have kept my interference to a minimum, as promised. I wanted them to find their way just as I have continually strived for."

Cabyll flicked a barnacle off his shoulder. "And I've told you all the walking in the world won't bring enlightenment save for a sore foot."

Lily tried to keep her expression neutral. *Centuries?!* Just how old was he?

Kye continued. "But, it has come to my attention there is turmoil in my territory."

Waru stepped in. "There has been talk about returning to the human side of the Veil."

Cabyll frowned, crossing his arms. "There are fae that go back and forth from the Veil all the time. That's not new."

Waru crossed his arms. "That may be true. But there are those that do not want to live, but to conquer the human realm."

Kye's eyes were intense. "If you remember, there was a faction within my territory that lived for the thrill of creating fear and nightmares amongst humankind in the past."

Cabyll scratched his head. "But you created the Council to provide order. Laws. This is the very scenario the Council would handle. Am I right?"

"You're correct." Kye paused, raising his eyebrow. "However, what if I told you the Council was compromised?"

Brandon jumped in, eyes wide, whispering excitedly. "Like a spy? Like in those action movies?"

No one responded.

Lily coughed, bringing the attention on her. "Your territory would dissolve into chaos, wouldn't it?" The prince didn't answer, so she kept going. "If your people cannot trust their governing body, then who can they trust."

He remained silent, weighing her words.

Waru answered, his tone serious and gravely. "Not only that, but the accords would be broken."

Ang cursed under her breath.

"What accords?" asked Brandon, confused.

"Between the Veil and the peacekeepers of your world, the Sentinels," Waru replied as if they should have known.

Lily gulped, clutching her pendant. What were the accords? Silently she put that on her checklist of things she needed to learn at Arachstone.

Kye's violet eyes glowed a brilliant purple, centering on her. "I need a Sentinel to stop the accords from being broken, without directly interfering with the Council. As you can tell, this is a delicate situation and I cannot create panic among my people."

He glared at the group. "I will be honest, I have my doubts. You are not warriors. You have no experience, no combat skills. You are lacking in every way."

"Tell us how you really feel," Brandon mumbled. Ang shushed him.

"But," interjected Raven, "based on your story, the faction happened long ago. Wouldn't they have given up after centuries? Had time to reflect?"

Kye's hands gripped his seat, muscle cords tight. "Those beings are not human. Fae do not simply 'reflect'. We're neither good nor bad. We are instinct and nature." His eyes narrowed on Aka, before holding hers. "Remember this, we are simply animals. Deadly ones."

Brandon began juggling the amber stones. "Then why us? Why Lil?"

Kye continued, reluctant. "Jacy vouched for you. He would never give his word lightly. You greatly assisted his people." His glare returned as he gritted out. "That is the ONLY reason I am still entertaining this preposterous idea."

Cabyll rubbed his chin. "So *that's* why you agreed to help find Lily's sister. I will admit I was surprised you were willing to offer help to a human."

Kye shrugged. "She is a Sentinel," as if that answered everything. "Albeit a young one. As much as I hate to admit it, it may work in our favor. If I approached the elder Sentinels, it could cause a diplomatic incident."

His gaze locked onto Lily's. "I will assist you to find your family, and in turn, you help me save mine."

Lily tensed, unsure. Her pendant warmed, Tim's voice wrapping around her.

It is fine little Sentinel. Let us help the young prince. He may be gruff, but his heart is noble.

She squared her shoulders. "What do we need to do?"

Kye's own shoulders relaxed. He turned to Waru. "They can be trusted now Waru. Speak on what you have found out."

Waru struck his right fist against his chest, nodding. "The vampire was very talkative. The rebel faction has gathered in number from whoever is backing them from the Council. Prince Dain is on the move and gathering the pieces."

Kye's eyes narrowed. "What has he gotten so far?"

"The vessel," Waru replied.

The prince cursed, slamming his cup down. "How?!"

Waru crossed his arms, disdain dripping. "Yarramundi."

Aka growled low, his fur fluffing in parallel to Kye, whose form grew slightly in the dreamy oceanic light. The prince snarled low, his voice deepening like a wave.

"And where is Yarramundi?"

Waru gave a sigh. "He was freed and returned to the human world."

Kyle's voice suddenly became eerily quiet.

"What?"

"Your brother apparently was able to do it *tou nui*. Yarramundi gave him the vessel as payment."

Kye bared fanged teeth as Aka gave an answering growl. "I should have killed that slug when I had the chance."

Waru shook his head. "Mercy is not weakness your highness."

Lily tried not to stare at the vampiric fangs but couldn't repress a shudder as Kye barked.

"Send your best to hunt for Yarramundi before the human population, or the Sentinels, find out."

Raven whispered over to Waru. "How would they find out?"

"When Yarramundi starts eating the locals," he spoke out of the side of his mouth.

Louder Waru responded, "I will send word as soon as we reach the surface."

Brandon raised his hand. "Um, excuse me? Can we back up a minute? What vessel are you guys talking about?"

"A vessel that holds something so powerful even the ancients are too scared to speak of it," Waru answered gravely.

"Well...that's dramatic," quipped Brandon.

Kye gritted his teeth, his growl louder. "He only needs the fire."

"Fire for what?" asked Lily.

Waru's solemn look gave her goosebumps. "The fire to resurrect a god."

Kye stood up fast, knocking his chair over. "There is no time. We must get to the Council."

"And do what?" asked Cabyll, rolling his eyes. "You said it yourself you don't know if you can trust them. You want this to be delicate right? You can't go in fighting on this one Kye."

Kye gritted his teeth, remaining silent.

Raven sighed loudly, tapping her cheek. "Here's the problem with being the strong silent type." She pointed her finger at Kye. "*You* need help, but you keep your cards to the vest. So, I can only assume from your faces that this 'god' of yours has been dead-"

"Slumbering," interrupted Waru.

Raven rolled her eyes. "Slumbering, whatever. My point is, you need to tell us everything so we can help you as best we can. My niece needs all the information to make the best decisions. This isn't all about you, Muscles."

Kye's jaw ticked. "You already know my brother Dain tried to awaken the ancient serpent within Jacy's territory. What you do not know is my territory houses creatures far more dangerous than the ancients. It holds powerful beings that were once called gods by humans. These fae were creation makers in our world. The one my brother wants to resurrect...if that god sides with him...the Veil and your world would burn."

He rubbed the back of his neck, giving it an audible crack. "The Council and myself are the only ones who know the information how to resurrect that god. A god of cataclysmic damage, mind you." He sneered at Raven. "Is that enough information?"

Raven got up, giving Aka a pat on the head. With measured steps, she approached the prince. He towered over her, her head not even reaching his shoulders. She slowly reached out, careful as if handling a wild animal, and gently patted his hand.

"That's a start," she said softly.

Ignoring his shocked expression, Raven turned back to Lily. She gave a calm, reassuring smile.

"Sweetie? What do you wanna do?"

Lily fidgeted, aware of all the eyes on her. This suddenly was much bigger than simply finding Ari. That seemed small in comparison to 'cataclysmic damage'. But, more importantly, could she do this? She was only human. And without any training, which was made abundantly clear during the last fight. What could she do against a god?

Tim's deep voice whispered in her mind.

Do what you do best. Follow your heart young Sentinel. I am here with you.

She closed her eyes, his support fueling her. Looking up, her determined gaze rested on her aunt and Kye. "Like I said before, what do we need to do?"

Raven beamed, winking at her.

Kye nodded, satisfied. "You do have heart little one. Let's hope it remains steadfast. Since my brother found the vessel, we must change course. We need to find the fire before he does."

Cabyll mused. "So, now we have three missions."

Brandon scratched his head. "Three?"

Cabyll uncrossed his arms, checking off his fingers. "We need to find the traitor on the Council, locate the fire before Prince Dain, and find Ari."

Brandon looked down, counting his own fingers, mumbling. "Oh... three. Gotcha."

Ang groaned. "What is with you guys? Why can't we have something easy?"

"But how do we find this fire?" Lily pondered.

"When I created the Council, I gave each member a piece to finding its location. So only by a vote in dire situations would they reveal their piece. No one member can locate the fire alone," Kye explained.

Lily brows furrowed. "So that means you know the location?"

Kye shook his head solemnly. "No. After I spoke to each of the Council members and obtained their oath, I had my memories erased."

"Well, that's super helpful dude," Brandon said sarcastically.

Kye shot him a glare, which prompted Brandon to quickly stare at the floor.

His frosty tone was fierce. "I did that for the safety of all."

Raven merely raised her eyebrow. "Why?"

"My purposes are my own," he grunted, keeping them at a stalemate.

Raven's singsong lilt did not hide her sarcasm. "Keeping cards to the vest..."

"Infuriating woman," he muttered.

Cabyll sighed, raking his hand through his hair. "So, how do we convince the Council to give us the location?"

"No," Kye rejected firmly. "We cannot risk them revealing what they know to the traitor. I created a failsafe in case the Council was compromised."

His voice drifted off as he stared into the distance.

"And that is?" prompted Ang.

Waru looked warily at Kye, who had remained silent, unfocused. "Something far more dangerous than simply asking them."

Finally, Kye sighed deeply. "We need to petition the one who took my memories."

Lily didn't know what creature was strong enough to erase a fae prince's memories, but she wasn't sure she wanted to find out. The mention of the mysterious creature seemed to make even the warrior prince uneasy.

She closed her eyes, overcome with fatigue. *Nothing is ever simple in this place, is it?*

Cabyll jerked her out of her musings. "Kye, we can't do all that."

"You're correct," the prince reluctantly agreed. "We need to split our forces. As much as I hate dividing us, it must be done."

Ang took a big swig of her cup, wiping her chin. "Well, let's get this show on the road. Who is going where your highness?"

The prince paused, his brow furrowed before focusing on Lily.

"As a Sentinel, you must be the one to retrieve my memories."

Lily pointed to herself, confused. "Why me?"

Waru answered. "You can act where we cannot. A Sentinel carries weight in our territory. We all," he paused, "well...most of us, put the accords on our highest level of promises."

She bit her lip, a sour pit forming. *There they go with the accords again.*

Cabyll stood by her shoulder. "I should go with her."

Kye shook his head. "I need you with me to engage the Council."

Cabyll rolled his eyes. "You don't need me there."

"Yes," the prince insisted. "I do."

"And for what purpose?"

Kye stared at him, hard. "To do what you do best...subterfuge. I need you to be charismatic to the members, especially the ladies." He rubbed his chin. "Maybe if that human sister is there you could persuade her to revealing my brother's plans."

Lily's heart slowed, a pit of unease growing in her stomach. So, he would have to flirt with Ari? She knew she shouldn't be surprised, but she couldn't understand the stone in her stomach at the thought of him acting that way with Ari.

Cabyll stiffened next to her, refusing to look her way. "Seriously?"

"This is important Cabyll," reminded Kye.

He gave a resigned sigh, pinching his nose. "And why would you go to the Council? Shouldn't you be the one to retrieve your memories?"

Lily tried not to jerk at the obvious change of subject.

"I swore I would never return to retrieve my memories. That was the only detail I was allowed to retain. I gave my vow," the prince said firmly.

"But you also gave your word you would not interfere with the Council," Waru calmly reminded.

Kye groaned. "You're right. I did, but I did not swear an oath. I will not interfere as promised, but I must go regardless."

"They will be suspicious," warned Waru.

"I will disguise myself, they will never know." Kye pulled out a ring. It was a simple thin gold band, completely innocuous. "This will help disguise Aka and myself."

"Forgive me your highness, but what can a ring do?" Ang asked skeptically.

The prince lifted it high. It twinkled in the light, revealing etchings inside the band.

"A powerful spell was placed on it. This will hide not only my appearance, but my aura as well." He turned to Cabyll. "Which is why I need you. I must remain hidden, but your presence will keep them on edge. That is what we need for the traitors to mess up and reveal themselves."

Cabyll tensed, ready to protest again.

Lily stepped in. "It's okay," she breathed deep, "I can do this."

"Alone?" he quipped, unconvinced.

She held in the urge to kick him in the shins.

Waru shook his head. "She will not be alone." He smacked his fist over his chest. "I will be her shield."

Lily blinked. *That is kinda extreme...*

Brandon jumped up. "I'm going too!"

Cabyll pointed his finger at Brandon. "Sit."

Raven piped up, "Oh no you don't mister."

"That," Kye interrupted them, "is an excellent idea."

Raven yelled, "Excuse me?! He's a *bambino*."

Kye's loud voice boomed. "Enough!"

He continued when it went silent. "He may be young, but warriors already fought battles at his age."

"When was that? With the dinosaurs..." Raven mumbled.

Kye cut her a hard look before motioning to Brandon. "He should go with the Sentinel. Waru will accompany him along with one of our allies who will join us tomorrow."

A voice cut in. "Not without me."

Ang took another swig, a loud burp resounding. Lily grimaced as wet tracks trailed down Ang's chin.

Ugh, I told her to watch her manners.

Ang wiped her chin with her sleeve. "I'll go with the kids." Her pointed stare drilled into Waru, who returned hers with a smile.

Raven raised her eyebrow. "And me?"

Kye sighed, clearly resigned. "I guess it can't be helped. You will join me on the journey to the Council along with Cabyll and our remaining ally."

"Ohhhhh no..." she barked, startling Aka who scrambled away from her with a dejected whimper. "You will NOT separate me from the family do you understand? I'm responsible for these kids."

"Zia Raven..." Lily interjected.

She continued, not listening. "What if they get hurt, or fall down a cliff, or drown, or this thing that took your memories tries to slice a limb..."

"*ZIA!*" Lily yelled.

She turned, her startled eyes catching Lily.

Lily took her aunt's shaky hands, leading her away from the group. She whispered, "Zia Raven, I need to go."

Raven shook her head. "But sweetheart, what if-"

"I *know*," She paused, hoping her breath wasn't trembling. "But we need to find Ari. And if she's with Dain, that means she may be with the Council. One of us needs to be there. Besides," she said ruefully, "she may react better to you than me."

Her heart dropped a little. It wasn't an easy thing to say, but it was true. She took another shaky breath, whispering. "Honestly, you should be retrieving his memories instead of me. You're brave."

Raven frowned, "Oh Lily, that's not-"

She closed her eyes. "If I wasn't a Sentinel...I wouldn't be going. I'm not special. Not like you Aunt Raven. I hope...I...I just don't want to mess this up."

She jerked as her aunt's arms enveloped her, squeezing her tight. Lily trembled, breathing in Raven's warm, comforting scent. Too soon those arms pulled back and shook her shoulders lightly, her aunt's expression beautifully fierce.

"Don't you EVER say that about yourself sweetheart. You are so special. If anyone can do this, it's you. Never compare yourself to anyone, you hear me?"

Lily could only nod as Raven wiped a small tear from her eye before straightening up.

Clearing her throat, Raven's voice rose for the others to hear. "If that's where you need me *nipote*, then I'll go. But-"

She turned to Kye, her eyes narrowing. "If ONE hair of my niece or nephew's head is out of place when I see them again, I will tear your perfect hair from your scalp. *Capisce*?!"

Waru nudged Brandon, speaking softly. "Your aunt would make a formidable warrior."

Brandon smirked. "Dude...you have no idea how right you are."

Cabyll groaned. "And how will we explain her?" He jerked his head at Raven scowling. "Don't you think it'll look suspicious bringing Lily's aunt, especially if her sister is there?"

Lily chewed the inside of her cheek. He did make a good point. How could they make a probable story?

Raven waved her hand dismissively. "Don't worry your little head. I'll figure something out."

"That is not comforting," Cabyll griped.

Ang impatiently slashed her hand down. "Figure it out later! So, what do we do now?"

Kye stared off into the ocean, his gaze distracted. "As much as I hate to wait, we must rest tonight. Let the humans gather themselves. Tomorrow the remaining members of our company will arrive. Until then, we prepare."

"Prepare for what?" asked Brandon.

"Strategic warfare young human," Waru cracked his knuckles, an anticipatory gleam in his eyes.

Kye raised his glass. "So marks our bargain. Rest well humans! We rise tomorrow."

Aka roared in agreement.

Chapter Thirteen

CLINK!

Lily grimaced; her arrow glanced off the barnacle covered driftwood that was her makeshift target. Her arms ached, remembering how much effort it took to drag the driftwood into place. She rolled her shoulders, loosening the pain in her neck. Taking a deep breath, she settled her mind and drew again.

The morning sunlight danced above her, the bright rays piercing through the watery tides that drifted around the magical bubble surrounding Kye's sanctuary. A bale of sea turtles swam overhead, followed by a playful sea lion family. The smallest pup in particular hovered around Lily since her early morning run, which proved difficult amongst the coral and debris. She finally gave up after almost twisting her ankle for the third time and focused on her shooting. After the last fight, she was more determined than ever to get better.

Waru was kind enough to give her more arrows since she lost them in the last fight. She ignored how the arrow shafts were made of an eerily similar bone white material as his club. She twirled the arrowhead, watching the way it caught the light and sighed. All night she tried to calm her mind, but the memories of yesterday were on constant replay. Her inner voice kept telling her the things she could have, should have done. Just thinking about it rose her anxiety, a familiar ache settling deep in her chest as the weighted cloak of responsibility blanketed her.

Forcing herself to take another calming breath, she closed her eyes and counted to ten. Notching the arrow, her gaze centered on the driftwood. She blew out slowly, about to let it fly, when a familiar voice called out.

"Keep focused human."

She jolted, the arrow flying astray. Frowning, she could only watch as it disappeared into the distance. She turned, glaring as Cabyll slow clapped, a familiar smirk gracing his handsome face.

"Wow," he scoffed lightly. "You haven't improved much."

She glared, already on the defensive. "I managed to hit a few of those red vampires. I think I'm doing pretty decent, thank-you-very-much."

He raised an eyebrow. "Decent? Decent gets you killed in this world."

His amused smirk disappeared as his gaze narrowed, motioning toward the target. "You need to be better. A lot better. You can't let distractions rattle you."

"What do you think I'm doing right now? I've been practicing all morning." She crossed her arms, the bow awkwardly hanging from her shoulder before falling into the sand with a thud. Her cheeks warmed.

Real smooth Lily.

Cabyll merely eyed her up and down before sneering. "One morning practice and suddenly you think you'll master it. Doesn't happen...especially for a human."

She rocked back on her heels, muttering. "Never claimed I'd be a master." She looked up, fire fueling her. "But forgive me Mr. Perfect, I bet you weren't so great when you started."

His arrogant tone bristled. "Of course I was. A prodigy actually. Though, I do understand it takes a long time of practice and dedication for others to be a fraction as good as me."

Lily closed her eyes, holding her sigh. *Why am I not surprised?*

She pinched the bridge of her nose, searching for patience. "Let me guess, it takes years?"

A roguish grin graced his face, his dimple winking. "Years? Try a few centuries."

Oh...must be nice to live for hundreds of years to get good at something...

He continued, waving his hand flippantly. "Don't worry, you'll never be as good as me so do not set yourself up for disappointment. Humans have such short lives, it is really quite sad."

A tick pulsed above her eye. "That is only your opinion."

"What? You don't agree?" His eyes twinkled with glee at her rising anger.

"Of course not!" She clenched her fists, her nose scrunching up. "I don't believe the value of someone's life is based on how long they live. It's what they do in the time they have that counts."

He snorted before mumbling. "*Gamsangjeon-in.*"

Lily bit her lip. She hated when she couldn't understand him, but from the cynical tone, he was mocking her. Shouldering her bow, she notched another arrow.

"Look, if you're not going to help or have anything nice to say you can leave," she snapped. "I need to practice so I don't get skewered by whatever I'm going to be facing."

Silence stretched for a beat, the soft rushing of waves rolling above them. She refused to look behind her, trying to focus on the target. But it was hard. His gaze was palpable.

He mumbled something under his breath, too soft for her to catch.

She called over her shoulder, biting. "What? I didn't hear you?"

He snarled softly. "Ugh...fine, I'll help you."

"I didn't ask for your help."

He huffed. "Well, you're getting it anyway. First, you need to bring up your elbow slightly. You won't shoot straight with that posture."

She changed her stance, pulling her arm higher. "Like this?"

"No," he replied curtly.

She tried again. "This way?"

With an exasperated grunt, he circled behind her. Lily tensed as his fingers brushed lightly against her arms. Gently, he moved her elbow, positioning her limbs like a marionette. His chest pressed against her shoulders.

She stayed silent, holding her breath, but his crisp scent of salt and rain did little to cool her warming cheeks. He was too close...way too close. Should she kick him? Maybe she should.

"Like this," he said softly, his breath tickling her ear.

Slowly, he let go of her arms, but his heat remained at her back. "Try again. Focus."

Easy for you to say. She clenched her eyes. *Get a grip Lil, he's a flirt to everyone. This means nothing to him. Ugh, why doesn't he back up a few feet?!*

She let out her breath slowly, focusing on the target, and released the arrow.

It went flying and hit the mark dead center, the arrowhead embedded in the wood.

She hit it! She really hit it. Smiling, she turned.

Cabyll had his arms crossed, backing away a little. His face was flushed, his hair all disheveled as he ran his hand through it.

He groused out. "There, now remember that and maybe you won't shoot your foot."

She rolled her eyes. "Why are you so grouchy?"

He refused to look at her, his hand tearing through his hair again. "I'm not."

She placed her hands on her hips. "Look, just because I'm human doesn't mean I can't handle this. I'm going to do my best and Waru will be there and-"

"But I won't be!" He yelled out, startling her, his voice echoing around them.

She tilted her head, confused. "What?"

Cabyll's cheeks pinked, his gaze at his feet as his voice quieted. "I won't be there to help you. What if something happens and you need my help. You always get into trouble."

Her shoulders relaxed, her gaze softening. *Oh, is he worried?*

She put the bow down, putting a hand on his shoulder. His gaze jumped up to hers, startled.

She spoke quietly. "I get it. I'm nervous too. I wonder all the time if I'm good enough to do this. Believe me, I'm the first to doubt myself."

He frowned, "That's not what I-"

She continued, interrupting him. "But Kye is right. I have a role to play and so do you." She paused, looking into his intense eyes. "Tell me this Cab, do you trust Kye?"

He held her gaze. She could see his mind working on how to respond. Wordlessly he nodded, his expression grave and solemn.

Her lips quirked up slightly. "Then the best place for you to be is helping Kye and my aunt. Find Ari. Keep my family safe. Please Cab? As my friend?"

His shoulder's slumped, exhaling. "You really are one of my only friends...you know that right?"

She snorted a laugh. "That's cause you have such an award winning personality."

His lip tilted upward. "Of course I do." He gave her a devilish wink. "You are lucky to be my friend, human."

She shook her head. *Arrogant fae...*

"You didn't answer me, Cab."

He sighed dramatically, the tension evaporating. "Fiiiine. I will do as you request. Though I do not know if the others in this party will be sufficient in helping you."

"I was going to ask if you knew who is coming."

He crossed his arms. "All I know is they should not be incompetent fools. Kye knows better than to associate with less than superior warriors. But if they are not good enough, I will speak with him and-"

THWAK!

Another arrow whizzed between Lily and Cabyll, slicing into her arrow, breaking it in half. Lily blinked, unable to register what just happened. Cabyll growled, sparks flying from his fingertips.

Suddenly, a solid form flew into Lily, knocking her over. Thin, strong arms squeezed her as a high, tinkling voice squealed in her ear.

"My goodness!! There you are Lily pie!"

Lily blinked. A haze of silver hair obscured her vision as the scent of peppermint and sugared berries tickled her nose. Violet eyes hovered above hers, twinkling with mirth.

"Peri?" asked Lily, her foggy brain slow to register.

She gasped as Peri's arms banded tighter.

The little fairy squealed in glee, snuggling into her neck. "Lily sweetie I missed you sooooo much! And look at you! Practicing like I taught you. I'm so proud of my little sweet innocent Lily, I could just squeeze the dickens outta you!"

Lily gulped, taking in little tufts of air. Her friend, as little as she seemed, was a lot stronger than she looked. Lily knew if she wasn't careful, Peri could actually squeeze her so tight a few bones would break. Purely by accident of course. Peri was just a bit insane, but in a sweet crazy way.

A deep, rolling voice interjected.

"That's enough Per. You're gonna suffocate her." A huge hand deftly plucked Peri off.

Peri pouted, kicking out, her legs flailing as the large hand held the little fairy by the nape of her gossamer shirt. "Spykie poo! Let me down! I missed Lily and I need to fill up my hug quota!"

The large fae laughed, the deep vibrations echoing into the waves. Lily eyes twinkled, grinning from ear to ear. Spyke was just as she remembered. The eight-foot-tall warrior tossed his tawny red hair to the side. His eyes crinkled in warmth, the long scar down his left eye stretching.

"It is good to see you Lily," he said affectionately.

She laughed, getting up slowly. "I'm glad to see you too Spyke."

A firm hand grasped her arm, helping her regain her balance.

Cabyll kept hold of her, glaring at the two fae. "I'm still here," he retorted snidely.

Spyke nodded. "Of course. Prince Kye informed us you'd be on this mission as well Assassin Cabyll."

Cabyll raised his eyebrow, ignoring the title. "You know why you're here then?"

"His highness disclosed the nature of the missions, yes. The fire must be found and protected," replied Spyke. "We are all needed on this quest."

Peri stuck her tongue out. "Yeah, yeah. I guess that includes even stupid Cabyll who makes my sweet Lily's life so complicated."

Her disgusted gaze raked him up and down. "I can't believe you're still hanging around her. Lily," she blinked innocently, "you're too sweet for your own good you know that?'

Cabyll's eye twitched. "And I can't believe Kye let a peri fairy into his sanctuary."

Peri shot her nose up in the air. "He does when we are official emissaries of Prince Jacy." She took her hand and pulled her eyelid down, sticking out her tongue. "So, nah nah!"

Spyke sighed, giving her a small shake. "Per, we talked about how to speak as official representatives of his highness."

Peri rolled her eyes, jumping out of his hold. She landed gracefully, going up to Lily to hug her arm.

"But it's only Lily and stupid Cabyll." She put her hand over her heart, big eyes widening innocently. "I promise to behave at the Council. Scouts honor."

Spyke shook his head. "You were never a scout Per."

She tilted her head. "But I did take out many scouts." She started counting on her fingers, getting up to nine. She held them up. "That counts right? Remember the most recent time? Back when we were in Crete-"

"Not the time Per," he interrupted.

Peri pouted. "Spoilsport." She turned her gaze to Lily's, her pretty pout pleading. "Lily pie you haven't said a word to *me* yet. Didn't you miss me too?"

Lily shook her head, smiling. She patted Peri's arm that was linked with hers.

"I missed you too Peri. I'm happy you're here."

Peri smiled, satisfied. She laid her head on Lily's shoulder. "Of course you are!"

Spyke sighed, palming his face.

Lily grinned. She wasn't lying when she said she missed Peri. Even though the anxiety pressed down on her chest, the weight of the mission stealing her breath, the genuine warmth of her friend's hug lessened the burden. She took one more cleansing deep breath, her frantic heart calming.

Peri spoke nonchalantly, but knowing eyes focused on her. "You calm now Lily pie?"

Cabyll mocked, sarcastic. "Of course she is. She's a human going off on a dangerous quest, she's practically skipping with glee."

Spyke came forward. "You will not be alone. I heard Waru is accompanying you, he is an honorable warrior."

Lily nodded. "Brandon is going too."

Cabyll muttered, "Yeah one warrior and a child..."

Spyke shook his head. "Not just one warrior. I will go as well."

Cabyll and Lily spoke in unison. "You?!"

141

The large fae nodded, his gaze on Lily. "Yes, I will assist Waru in protecting you and your brother."

Lily blinked. "So...does that mean Peri is going to the Council?" Her gaze, as well as Spyke and Cabyll's, warily rested on the peri fairy clutching her shoulder. A pregnant pause filled the air. She bit her lip. "Alone?"

Cabyll smirked. "Then that settles it. I guess I'll have to go with Lily so *you*," his pointed gaze rested on Spyke, "can babysit the ticking time bomb."

Peri snorted. "I'm older than you Cabyll. I'm not a baby."

In a very unPeri-like fashion, her tone grew serious. "Spyke, you need to protect Lily while I'm at the Council."

"And what are you going to do to contribute to the Council?" scoffed Cabyll.

"Save your butts when things go belly up." Peri gave an air kiss to Lily. "Don't think I don't wanna be with you Lily pie, but Spyke will keep you safe. And I'll make sure the rest of your family is too."

A deep voice cut through. "Are we all ready?"

Prince Kye appeared, Aka beside him. Everyone else was following behind.

The prince's gaze landed on Peri and Spyke. "Jacy's emissaries, you have the sending stones?"

Spyke raised his palm, a smooth stone nestled within.

Kye gave an approving nod. His booming voice rang out.

"Everyone! Gather with either the peri fairy or the Thunderboy so we can be sent to our destinations." He continued, his tone firm. "Remember, once we leave this place, nowhere is safe...and no one can be trusted. Only trust those who you see in this space. We need to root out the traitor and retrieve my memories so we can obtain the fire before my little brother. Time is of the essence. Waru, remember to return to the Council within three days."

"Why three days?" asked Brandon.

"Because my brother needs a fire festival for his ritual to work and the next one is in three days. After that he would have to wait until Beltane which is many months from now." Kye's lip curled. "And I know my brother, he will not wish to wait."

"Isn't Beltane in May?" asked Raven.

"You are in the south Miss Raven," explained Waru. "Technically it is winter here."

"Winter in August? Awesome!" Brandon's grin split.

Ang elbowed him.

Kye's voice boomed, startling them all. "Time is critical. We must go now." His gaze finally landed on Lily, a frown gracing his full lips. "Sentinel, are you sure you are ready for this?"

Cabyll frowned, opening his mouth to speak but Kye cut him off.

"Let her speak Cabyll."

Cabyll crossed his arms, his long fingers tapping on his forearm. He looked at Lily in silent question, his eyes warming.

Without a word, Lily went to the makeshift target and tugged out her arrows. Tucking them away, she focused on her aunt, Brandon, and Ang. They all looked at her in equal parts concern and encouragement.

Tim's comforting voice cut through her thoughts.

Time to set off young Sentinel.

Lily chewed the inside of her cheek silently. *You have my back?*

A soothing chuckle tickled her head. *Always. As you have mine.*

With renewed determination, she replied. "I doubt I'll ever be ready. But, let's do this."

Kye raised his eyebrow, surprised. "Very humbling."

Apparently satisfied, the prince nodded and took his position. Aka's rumbling snort filled the space as the large cat moved beside the prince, creating an intimidating pose.

Raven enveloped the kids in a huge hug as she whispered in their ears.

"I love you both. Remember. Trust each other. Take care of one another. Family is all we have right now."

Brandon and Lily returned her hug. As Raven stepped back, she gave the changeling a pointed look, fingering her evil eye.

"Watch out for my family, got it?"

Ang rolled her eyes. "I get it, put that away will you? Sheesh." She nudged Lily's shoulder, a half smirk gracing the changeling's face. "We won't get killed right sissy?"

Lily chuckled. "I'll do my best."

Ang nodded, going to Brandon, wagging her finger. "And you! Don't do anything stupid."

143

Brandon put his hands behind his head. "Come on when have I ever-"

"Don't even finish that sentence," she interrupted, then frowned. "Look, I'm only one changeling. I don't know Waru, but Spyke isn't so bad. He's as good a fae as you can get...and we're not that great."

"Aw Ang, I think you're pretty great," Brandon winked.

Ang covered her red face. "Go on, you crazy kid. Knowing you, you'll annoy the enemies to death."

He smiled, giving a mock salute while Ang groaned. "I'll try!"

His face smoothed, his eyes unexpectedly serious as he patted Ang's arm. "Hey...Don't worry Ang, we got this."

She squeezed his hand back in silent agreement, still refusing to look at him.

Kye interrupted the mood as he clapped his hands, impatient. "Alright everyone! Are we ready?"

Raven fired back. "Just one collar picking minute impatient pants. So help me if you interrupt an Italian family's goodbye, you'll regret you took me with you."

"I may regret it already," he muttered.

Peri's bright eyes took in the exchange. She whispered loudly, "O... M...G! Who is this beautiful fiery woman?"

Lily smiled. "Peri, meet my Aunt Raven."

"Your aunt?!" Peri's eyes lit up. "Oh, I love her already! We're gonna be second best friends cause you're my favorite Lily. Wait! No, third sorry cause I can't forget Spykie poo."

As Peri kept talking, everyone took their positions. Lily moved forward, but a hand grabbed her wrist, jerking her back slightly.

Cabyll's held her gaze, his expression fierce.

"Keep safe, will you?"

Lily blinked, unable to respond before Cabyll continued, his voice picking up, becoming harsh.

"I mean you're so clumsy and small. You can't help but get into a life-or-death situations every five minutes."

Anger began to prickle in Lily's veins. *Really? He can't say one nice thing, can he*

"It's not five minutes," she grumbled.

144

He muttered softly, his frustration evident. "Look, I'm saying. Well...just...I just want you safe, alright?"

The hand that grasped hers trembled, belying his harsh tone.

Lily's anger melted. She covered his fingers, giving a reassuring squeeze. "I'll be fine. I'll see you in three days, okay? I bet when I see you, I'll even be able to hit a bullseye."

He raised his eyebrow, a sly smile slowly gracing his lips. "A bet you say?"

Her eyes widened. *Well fudge...*

"I...I didn't mean it!"

"Too late, you made the bet." His green eyes gleamed. "What do you bet?"

She sighed, clearly losing this battle. "If I win, then you be nice to my aunt."

He rolled his eyes, groaning. "So boring. Why can't you think of something more exciting?" His hand pressed slightly on her wrist, his warm fingers wrapping firmly around her pulse point. "Fine, but when I win..."

"*If* you win."

His lip curled, dimple on display. "Then I get that scarf you have in your backpack."

She frowned. "How did you...? You mean the one I made?"

"Yes, I want that one."

"Why?"

Lily didn't know what to pack before they left, so she packed a little of everything just in case. When she came back from the Veil, she needed to keep busy and her mind calm. One attempt was learning how to crochet, but she realized early she was terrible at it.

The scarf was an absolute mess. The green, blue, and purple threads were mashed together, some of the threads escaping. She only packed it because she wasn't sure if she needed something warm and it was the first thing she found. Why would he want that ratty scarf?

Cabyll nodded firmly, not deterred. "I want it."

Raven's voice called out. "Come on you two!"

Lily's cheeks flushed. "Fine," she bit out, tugging her arm.

Cabyll rolled his eyes but reluctantly let go. Right before they parted to their groups, he whispered against her ear.

"Be safe Lily. Remember…three days."

As if I could forget, she groused inside, rubbing her wrist absently.

The groups looked at each other solemnly as Peri and Spyke stood in front, holding stones that were clasped around their necks.

"Alright everyone. Hang on tight." Spyke called out.

Peri blew a kiss. "Good luck sweeties. See you soon!"

Bright light engulfed them, Lily squinting as it burned her eyes. Peri's tinkling voice called out as they faded out.

"Oh! And don't forget to kick some butts out there. Spykie poo make sure Lily pie is safe or I'll never speak to you ever again."

The last thing anyone heard before they vanished from the sanctuary was Spyke groaning.

Dear Lily,

I know this probably won't reach you, but I couldn't think of who else to write. Brandon wouldn't take me seriously enough. Mom would be crying too much. Is mom doing okay by the way? I wonder how she is from time to time, if she's thinking of me too. Or if she's upset…

Oh!

Lily did you know the sun shines even brighter on the ocean? I thought the sun was bright in the sky, but I was wrong. The reflection, it's magical. Isn't that funny I said magical? After everything that's happened. Something so ordinary I took for granted, the sun and water seem more radiant than I ever saw before. Think it's because it's in the Veil?

Chapter Fourteen

SMACK

"Ouch! You'd think in a magical place they'd have some magical bug repellant," groused Brandon. He rubbed his arm where another mosquito bit him.

Ang sighed. "It's just a little bite. This is nothing."

"Nothing? I'm getting eaten alive dude!"

SMACK!

Brandon smacked another offending bug from his calf, a few red welts already dotting along his skin.

Lily couldn't help but silently agree, batting at a bug. After separating from Cabyll and the rest of the group, she found herself transported from the underwater sanctuary to the middle of a dense rainforest.

Heavy, green fronds covered tall canopy trees that blanketed most of the sun. Streams of hazy afternoon light kissed portions of the ground at her feet. Her nose tickled with the scents of hibiscus and jasmine lingering in the thick, humid air. Bright red and orange flowers dotted the emerald landscape, but she couldn't admire it. Her focus was on the sticky sheen of sweat that clung to her, the faint whispers of itchiness settling in. Instead of hearing the tinkling of the bird songs echoing in the trees, she only could focus on the stinging high-pitched buzzing of insect wings grazing her eardrums.

SMACK!

She grimaced as the trickling of wet goo from the squashed insect dripped down her arm.

"Stop being so dramatic," Ang scoffed, before mumbling. "You'd know if you were being eaten alive..."

Lily gave a side-glance. *Yeah, not comforting Ang. Definitely not comforting.*

She rummaged through her pack, looking at the various supplies her aunt threw in before they split up. Her hand hit upon a small bottle with a balm-like substance. She handed it to Brandon.

"Here, try this."

Grateful, Brandon began to spread the balm over the raised red bumps that dotted along his legs and arms. He sighed, his relief evident.

Waru's deep voice jostled the peace.

"Are humans always this fragile?" He shook his head, a smirk splitting his face. "Fear of little bugs, how cute."

"Our skin is thinner than yours, I suspect." Lily replied. She really was beginning to hate the constant barrage of being told humans were weak or frail.

He shrugged. "Thin...weak...sounds the same to me."

"I just have amazing blood, like totally the best man. It's just golden," boasted Brandon, his pep back now that he wasn't constantly scratching.

Ang groaned. "Do you even know what you're saying?"

Spyke interrupted, his voice broking no argument. "We need to keep moving."

Waru lazily swung his club in a slow circle. "Agreed. I'll take the lead. Spyke, take the rear. Humans, keep in the middle."

Ang raised her eyebrow, giving a humpf.

Waru bent his head slightly. "Apologies, changeling. Since you look like a human for the moment, I forgot. Keep in the middle to guard the humans."

Now," His kind face morphed into a serious expression. "The creatures here are dangerous. More dangerous than you've ever dealt with. Do not trust what you see and alert me or Spyke to anything unusual.

And keep to the path. This is the most important. Do *not* stray from the path."

Brandon saluted. "Or we get lost, right?"

Waru deadpanned. "Or you get eaten alive or killed by the elements, your choice."

Brandon blinked, putting his arm slowly down. "Dude, buzzkill much."

Ang smacked the back of his head, hard.

Waru started heading down a worn dirt path, motioning them to follow. "Let's go. Three days are not much time."

Brandon and Ang followed, their feet stomping down the trail. Lily hesitated. She knew she needed to move, but her body refused to budge.

A strong hand gently rested on her shoulder. Spyke's kind eyes peered down.

"It's okay Lily." He nodded over to Waru. "Warriors tend to be blunt. No time for fancy words during battle. Eloquence means death. But, if it helps, you can do this." He smiled encouragingly. "I'll be by your side. Be vigilant and acknowledge that fear, only then can you overcome it."

She nodded, forcing her feet to head forward into the jungle.

A few hours passed. The thick, humid heat misted through the dancing beams of light. Lily wiped her forehead for probably the billionth time, the salty sweat stinging her eyes.

Stopping briefly, her hands rested on her sweat coated thighs. She grimaced, hating the gross feeling of another layer of dried, salty sweat caking her skin. Her chest heaved, taking in sticky air, when something pushed her shoulder.

Spyke nudged her forward, his kind gaze sympathetic. She nodded, grateful for the push. Occasionally during the trek, Spyke's large hand fell on her back to hold her upright before she stumbled. But again, no one spoke.

She frowned, oddly bothered by the quiet. Usually by now Cabyll would be teasing her for how slow she was walking. She shook her head. Why was she thinking about that? She must be getting lightheaded.

Water. Yes, she needed something to drink. She reached into her pack, but before she could pull her thermos out, Waru held up his hand, forcing the group to stop.

His voice smacked Lily's eardrums, probably because of how long they walked in silence to the jungle's beat.

"Grab some water quickly."

He pointed downward, the pathway opening slightly from the dense fronds. "We need to get through this area before we can rest for the night."

Brandon plopped down on the dirt with a thud. Ang handed him a flask. After a few sips he poured some in his hands and splashed his face. "Dude, how far do we need to go?"

Waru chugged a mouthful of water. "As far as we can get boy."

Brandon panted, taking another swig. "Can we chill for a few minutes? We must have gone far since we haven't stopped yet."

Waru shook his head. "Maybe for a human. I've been taking it easy so you can keep up."

Brandon choked, spitting out water. "Easy?!"

Ang smacked his back, Brandon's cough echoed in the trees.

Spyke crouched down, filling up the flask. "We could go much faster if it was just us." His sidelong glance bore into Waru. "But we have been going at a decent pace."

Waru conceded with a slow nod.

Lily bit her lip, the water suddenly tasted bitter at the thought they were falling behind.

Spyke continued, his gaze resting on Lily as if reading her thoughts. "Don't be discouraged. We can afford a few minutes rest." He looked back up to Waru, his eyebrow raised. "Right?"

Waru sighed dramatically. "Fine. It's like watching over babes."

Ang rolled her eyes. "If they were babies, they would listen."

Brandon, still coughing, protested. "Aw, come on Ang! If I listened, it wouldn't be so fun – OUCH!" He rubbed his shoulder where Ang smacked him again.

Waru rested his club on his shoulder. "Rest humans. I'll scout ahead. When I return, we move."

And with that he went into the jungle.

Spyke's deep sigh rumbled. "I might as well check behind us to make sure we are not being followed." He tilted his head, his gaze questioning. "Are you okay that I leave Lily?"

"We'll be fine." She smiled, shouldering her bow for emphasis.

He chuckled, ruffling her hair affectionately. "Forgive me, I'm used to reigning in Peri. I don't mean to be overprotective. I should remind myself that while humans are physically weaker, it does not mean you're weak."

"Thanks for that." She made a shooing motion. "You better get going. I have a feeling Waru will be back before we know it."

His warm chuckle faded as he disappeared silently into the jungle.

Lily shook her head. For big guys they were pretty quiet. It was undeniably creepy.

Brandon must have read her mind as he echoed. "Man, they're like ninjas."

Ang sighed. "You are fascinated by the strangest things."

Lily's concerned gaze rested on the changeling, who was rubbing her temples, looking pale. "Are you okay?"

Ang waved off her concern. "It's just the heat. I'm not made for this type of weather, but I'll be fine."

SMACK!

A wet thud hit Ang square in her face. She spit angrily, clutching the offending object. "What is this?"

Lily wiped her wet hands on her thighs, tucking her flask back in her pack. She gestured to the underbrush. "Lay down. Put that washcloth over your forehead. Hopefully that'll help."

Ang grumbled, a slight reddening dotting her cheeks. Whether it was from the heat, Lily wasn't sure. She did manage to hear the changeling mumble something under her breath like, "too caring", but she wasn't sure.

"Come on Ang," she insisted. "We'll be here, don't worry."

Reluctantly, Ang laid down, placing the washcloth on her face. "Don't do anything stupid okay?"

Soon, soft snores drifted into the breeze.

Lily breathed in the humid air, leaning back against a tree. She grimaced, wiping the sweaty curls stuck to her neck. She peeked over at Brandon, and he was staring back.

She gave him a half smile. "We haven't had a minute to talk, have we?"

He stood up, twisting his fingers nervously. "Well...yeah. But it's been kinda crazy ya know?"

He took his flask and drank again greedily before coming over. He leaned against the tree, standing next to her in silence.

She peeked out of the corner of her eye. His blonde hair stuck to his forehead, his cheeks flushed. When did he get so tall? He was already at her eye level, which was slightly disconcerting.

"Yeah," she finally conceded. She leaned her head back, staring up at the canopy. "It has been a little crazy. This hasn't been exactly a normal summer."

His bright blue eyes twinkled. "But it's been super cool!" His cheeks flushed as he tousled his hair, embarrassment evident. "Though I don't mean Ari getting kidnapped of course."

"Of course," she agreed, hiding her smile.

He continued, his pace increasing. "But you know, weird thing is I've been really happy. Getting to know Ang, Brom, Barlow, and Alasdair. Also, spending time with you. I'm really glad we can spend some time together." He cautiously peeked over through his blonde strands.

She chuckled, reaching over to pat his shoulder lightly. "Same here. I'm glad we're getting to know each other. I've always wanted a brother."

He blinked, his smile dimming. "Brother?"

"Yeah. I've been alone for a long time. It's nice having siblings."

He kicked a stone, mumbling to himself. "Sibling..." His voice got louder. "Uh, yeah...definitely Lil." He grinned as he dramatically pointed to himself with his thumb. "You know you can count on me!"

She laughed. The anxiety of Ari's situation sat in the back of her chest, but she was grateful for the bubbles that rose up with the laughter. She could always count on Brandon to lighten the mood.

Suddenly, Brandon froze.

He leaned in, whispering.

"Did you hear that?"

She squinted, straining to hear through the bird songs. Faintly, the rolling sound of rushing water overrode the ambient noise. Her gaze lifted to meet Brandon's excited grin. He dangled his now empty flask in her face, shaking it.

"Let's go fill up."

She hesitated, sparing a quick glance at Ang who, thankfully, was still sleeping. "Waru and Spyke told us to wait and not stray from the path."

He scoffed, pointing. "It's not far. See?"

She followed his finger and, indeed, she could catch within eyesight the reflecting sunlight from water. She bit her lip. Her own flask was almost empty, and the heat was getting worse.

Brandon nudged her with his shoulder. "Ang will be okay. She needs water too. And there's two of us." He held out his palm. "Five minutes tops."

She raised her eyebrow, skeptical. "Five minutes?"

He put his hand over his heart. "Cross my heart. Promise!"

In the end, it was the bitter salty taste of sweat that dripped off her nose that convinced her. She laid down her pack, keeping her bow on her back, and grabbed her flask.

Brandon grinned brightly. "Let's go!"

With no hesitation he jumped off the path into the jungle.

At first, Lily thought something would grab them immediately when they stepped off. Waru didn't stop reminding them the dangers, but when her foot crunched onto the fallen limbs...nothing happened. Some nervous energy remained, but she breathed deeper as she continued to follow Brandon. Maybe this would be quick and painless.

Please, please let it be nothing...

Brandon called out ahead. "Wow...Lil hurry up! You gotta see this."

The blinding sun burned her eyes as the jungle opened up. Her mouth dropped. It was a lagoon, tucked between the jungle and the ocean. But that wasn't what had her gaping. The water was pink...bright pink. White froth surrounded rose-colored tourmaline and purple shades that starkly contrasted the bright blue sky.

"This is beautiful," she whispered, still hiding within the edges of the jungle.

"I know right! This is so cool. Pink water!" He went to the edge and scooped up a bit, the water trailing down his fingertips.

She held out her hand, cautioning. "Wait Brandon we don't know-"

He took a gulp, grimaced, and promptly spit it out.

"If the water is good," she finished lamely.

He stuck out his tongue, gagging. "Yuck! It's salty."

She rocked back on her heels, letting out a long breath. She sucked in her teeth, hoping she was sounding sincere. "Oops, that's inconvenient. Well...I guess we should go now."

While she did love the view, she was eager to get back. The lagoon was too still, too quiet. She rubbed her arms absently, wishing Brandon would get the hint.

"Yeah, sure..." He frowned, his disappointment palpable. "I only wanted to be useful."

"You didn't know. And you did find a cool spot," she said brightly, wanting to cheer him up.

She turned back, motioning him to follow. "We'll just ask Spyke..."

A faint sound broke through the stillness. She stopped, whipping her head toward the far side of the lagoon.

Voices.

Someone was approaching from the water. Eyes wide, she waved to Brandon, hoping he'd get the hint. He shook his head, clearly not understanding.

Lily pumped her arms up and down frantically. She didn't want to yell, but she was ready to. Finally, after a few more awkward charade moves, Brandon's eyes widened before he nodded. When he got to her, she reached out, jerking him behind a large tree when the voices got closer.

He leaned over. "What is-mumpf!"

She clamped her hand over his mouth, shushing him to keep him still.

A little green boat, made of banana leaves, drifted into view. On the boat, there were two small figures, humanoid in nature. They seemed to be about two feet tall. Lily's eyes narrowed. They reminded her of the brownies back at home, but different.

These fae had larger ears, sporting a short bulbous nose. Their dark, sun-kissed skin matched their long dark hair which hung down under faded, red caps. They were barefoot, wearing cream, canvas shorts. They were also shirtless, their bodies strong and muscular for their small frames. Large brown eyes were filled with mirth and mischief visible even from Lily's hiding place.

One of the figures called out, their voice excited and loud.

"Look Pika! This is the perfect spot to catch some shrimp."

The other, Pika, jumped up, rocking the boat. Completely unperturbed, he peered into the pink water until his nose almost touched the surface. "You're right Peni. There's a whole mess of them under us!"

Peni slapped his hands together. "It's gonna be a feast tonight."

Pika bent down, getting nose level with the water. "I'll grab the first one."

Peni protested, slapping his hands on the side of the boat. "No! I will!"

"No, me!"

"Arm wrestle for it?"

Pika rolled his shoulders, flexing his bicep. "Let's go."

Suddenly the two started to arm wrestle, the little boat jostling. Lily wouldn't be surprised if they scared all the shrimp away with how loud they were. Brandon scooted closer to get a better look.

"Are they brownies?" he whispered.

She shook her head. "I don't think so. Could you imagine Brom shirtless?"

Brandon snorted into his hand, holding his laugh. "That's true. So, what do you think they are?"

"No idea." Honestly, she hadn't the faintest clue. There were some similarities, but tons of differences. She found herself wishing she read more books. Why didn't she think about that before?

Brandon shrugged, unconcerned. "Maybe they know where to get some water. Should we ask them?"

She backed up slowly, pulling further back into the fronds. "No, I think we should get back as quietly as we can. Stay out of their way."

She turned around to go up the hill, keeping her steps quiet. Her unease grew as the time ticked on with them not on the path.

Brandon pouted. "Fine...I guess so."

Disappointed, he turned to follow when a frightened squeal cut through the jungle.

Lily closed her eyes, shaking her head silently. *Nope, nope! Keep moving forward girl. Pretend you didn't hear it.*

Another louder, more frightened squeal pealed the air.

"Ah...Lily?" Brandon tapped her shoulder.

Just ignore it Lil, just ignore it.

But she turned back anyways.

The two fae, Pika and Peni, had stopped wrestling. They stood in the middle of the boat, hugging each other frantically, their eyes wide. Their faces squished together as they spoke out of the side of their mouths.

"Peni, grab the oar and hit it."

"No, you do it!"

Ripples circled around the boat, small bubbles trailing in the pink waters. The two fae clutched each other tighter, shaking. The ripples grew faster, the bubbles bigger, until something broke the surface.

It looked like a cross between a seal and a dog. A shaggy black coat draped over wet sealskin. It had a rounded head, like a dog, with large ears and whiskers. It lifted its head, and its neck went up.

And up, and up.

Lily blinked. The creature's neck was long, making the four-foot animal more like six foot in length. That neck turned almost in a circle before resting in front of the two little fae in the boat. Yellow slitted eyes narrowed at them. Its mouth opened to reveal small tusks and rows of sharp teeth.

She gulped. *Well...merda...*

The little fae shivered, calling out.

"We're gonna die!"

"Someone help! Help!!"

The creature hissed in dark delight. It reared its long neck back, like a snake ready to strike, when a rock flew out of nowhere and struck it on the head. The creature reared back, shaking itself. Its neck lashed back and forth, trying to find the source.

Lily turned, finding Brandon on the bank holding another rock, his eyes hard.

She hissed, "Brandon, get back here."

He shook his head. "Can't let those little guys get hurt, Lil. You know that."

She warred between hitting him and dragging him back by the scruff of his neck. Yes, she knew that was the morally right thing to do. But

156

what she didn't want was Brandon stepping right in the middle of this dangerous mess. Before she could respond, the creature zeroed in on Brandon, its eyes widening.

Che cavolo!

With a flourish, the creature dove back under the water, the ripples heading straight for Brandon.

The little fae yelled over. "Watch out kid!"

The other pumped his fist. "Hit it good."

The water rose up as the creature lunged out from the surface, aiming for Brandon. He gritted his teeth, ready to throw another stone when the creature yelped and fell backward into the lagoon, an arrow protruding from its shoulder.

Lily notched another arrow, breathing deeply. She yelled, jerking her head in the direction behind her. "Come on everyone. Move!"

The little fae didn't need to be told twice. They paddled like crazy, their muscular arms pushing them to shore before she could finish her sentence.

Brandon shuffled them along into the jungle. "Come on little guys, let's get you outta here."

"Little?!" yelled one. "Kid, we're older than you!"

The other scolded the first. "Pika! Focus!"

A loud roar rose from the water, the creature regained its footing back and launched itself onto the white shore.

Lily grimaced. It was even more ugly than she thought. Spindly limbs sporting webbed paws dug into the sand. Frothy bile dripped down its jaws. Its angry eyes centered on her, particularly at her bow.

Pika gulped loudly. "Yup...you're right Peni. No time to worry about. Let's run kids!"

And run they did.

But they didn't get far.

Brandon panted, leading the charge uphill. Breathless, he wheezed out. "Lil...the path!"

Another growl rumbled through the trees.

Her heart skittered. Biting her lip, she whirled around, lifting her bow, hoping to buy them some time.

Brandon yelled out, skidding to a stop. The little fae bumped into his legs with a grunt, falling backward.

In front, appearing from the fronds, was another of the creatures. Frothing lips peeled back, its growl growing.

"There's *more* of them?!" shouted Brandon.

The fae clutched to each of his calves, shaking. One replied. "Um... oh yes! Bunyip usually are in pairs, or a pack. Let's hope it's a pair."

"A pack?!" Brandon's eyes bugged.

The bunyip in front rumbled, slowly advancing forward.

"Stop scaring the kid Pika. If we die, let him have a little hope," admonished Peni.

"I didn't tell him about them ripping us apart with their tusks, did I?" protested Pika. He pulled Brandon's leg backward, avoiding a nip as the bunyip took a quick jump, then retreated.

A pack? Seriously?! Lily mind swirled, but she kept her eyes focused on the one behind them. They were pinched in, the bunyip slowly advancing, giving a weird huff that sounded oddly like laughter.

Her eyes narrowed, anger building.

They're toying with us.

"Will you both stop it?" Brandon yelled at the little fae, trying to keep his balance. He grabbed another rock. "Lil? You ready?"

She notched her arrow, her eyes laser focused on the larger bunyip. "I am." She didn't know if they'd make it, but she'd be sure they would regret it.

The bunyips growled low to each other, communicating something.

Probably trying to figure out the best way to eat us, she groused to herself.

Brandon threw his rock, hitting the one in the face. It shook its head, blinking, its paw lifting to rub its eye. "Well...that was cooler the first time," he said, backing up slowly, his back touching Lily's.

The bunyip snarled again before they pounced simultaneously. Lily fired, her arrow hitting her bunyip right in the leg. But she didn't stop the creature's momentum. It was flying straight toward her.

She flinched, bracing herself, when a deafening roar rang out. Before it hit her, the bunyip whimpered as it was knocked sideways, rolling down the jungle incline. A familiar, large back covered her vision.

"Sorry I'm late." Spyke glanced over his shoulder, his club raised. "Are you okay?"

"Yup, just peachy." Lily notched another arrow. She called over her shoulder. "Brandon, you good?"

"Fine and dandy! Waru just lopped off this one's head. Kinda messy, but cool."

She groaned, not wanting to see behind her...at all. More rustling in the jungle greeted her, growing louder.

"Um...Spyke?" Her eyes scanned around the area warily. "We were just told these things are bunyip."

Spyke nodded wordlessly, his eyes darting.

She continued, "And we were told they sometimes are in a pack..."

Her sentence drifted off as more growls grew closer.

"Well...there is my answer," she groaned, fear turning her blood sluggish.

Spyke called out. "Waru?"

"I'm here."

She jumped, startled, as Waru's large presence appeared behind her. These guys really were too silent for her liking.

"I'm clocking about four over here," said Spyke.

"Five to our right," Waru's deep voice replied, excited. "This will be a fine fight!"

Brandon picked up another stone. "Ah...hey? Waru? Not to be a buzzkill or anything, but can we get back on the path before any epic fight scenes?"

Waru cracked his neck, stretching his shoulders. "What is this buzz you refer to have killed? I have never heard of a Buzz, but you should be proud of your title."

The snarling reached a fever pitch, drowning out Brandon's moan. One bunyip leapt to attack Spyke, only to meet another massive thud from his club, sailing far behind them with a pained yip. Another tried to spring from a tree, which Waru caught by the throat. It howled painfully before the warrior threw it down the hill.

Lily angled her bow, tracking another as it stalked Spyke who was already engaged with one. The arrow flew true and hit the bunyip's foot mid jump. However, it did not stop. Fear took hold of her as the wounded bunyip's mouth opened wide, ready to clamp onto Spyke.

Lily blinked as a rush of air hit her from above, messing up her curls. "AH!!"

Ang screamed loudly, launching herself on the bunyip that landed on Spyke's back. She hissed, claws out, slashing the monster over and over.

The bunyip howled, dropping from Spyke. Ang rolled gracefully into a crouch, her arms with claws spread out. She hissed again, her fangs gleaming, at the remaining bunyips that remained around the perimeter.

The two little fae hiding between Brandon and Lily squealed. Lily blinked, forgetting they were there.

"Oh my Pika, is that a changeling?!" exclaimed Peni.

"Yes Peni. Let's hope it doesn't want to eat us! Uh, hello? Do you want a shrimp?" They shrank back as Ang's feral gaze latched onto them.

Brandon nervously glanced at Ang. "Um...hey Ang. Sleep good?"

Ang growled, her nose twitching. "Don't Brandon. Just...don't."

"Mmkay...got it!" Brandon mimed zipping his lips shut, before throwing another rock.

"Um, guys?" Lily notched her bow again. "Maybe Brandon has a point about the path."

"Oh, you mean the path you were *supposed* to stay on," Ang groused sarcastically.

Brandon sucked in through his teeth. "Well...about that..."

Ang hissed louder, taking a swipe. She pointedly ignored him to bark out, "Waru! Can you stop messing around and take care of this!"

Waru let out a warrior whoop, smacking his chest. With a burst of speed, he raced around the group, taking the hook of his club and scooping up the remaining bunyip in one large haul.

With a flourish, he spun around several times, the bunyip whining pathetically as the sheer force kept them stuck on the hook. Then, Waru planted his feet before flinging them high over the group's head. Their plaintive howls echoed faintly in the distance, before hearing a soft splash.

Waru cracked his neck again, his smile wide. "Well, that was a good warm up."

Lily's mouth opened slightly, still unsure what she just witnessed.

Ang scoffed, her pointed stare burning into Lily and Brandon. "I take one nap. ONE! And this happens!"

Brandon held up his hands. "Yeah, I know we said we'd stay, but...here's the thing. We wanted to get you some water. It's really hot, are you guys really hot?" He tugged on his collar, giving a pained grin. "It's suddenly getting warmer isn't it..."

"Brandon..." Ang growled in warning.

He continued rambling, "And when we went to get water, we found this really cool lagoon. It's totally awesome. Did you know it's pink? You should check it out. Oh, probably not if those monsters are back there. Oh, by the way, did you know the water was salty? And...well..." He motioned to the two little fae at his feet. "And we saved these guys!"

"Hello..." The two waved awkwardly.

Waru knelt down, tilting his head. "Looks like you rescued some Menehune."

Brandon scratched his head, confused. "Mene-what now?"

Spyke interrupted, leaning on the butt of his club. "The Menehune. Similar to brownies in this territory. They're not affiliated with a home. They live outdoors and like to create mischief."

One pointed to himself, asking innocently. "Who us?"

The other scoffed, blinking rapidly. "We would never..."

Spyke crossed his arms, raising his eyebrow. "You have no idea why a bunyip pack was after you?"

The Menehune gulped audibly. The one, Pika, raised his hand hesitantly. "Maybe because we pranked them the other day."

Peni's eyes widened. "Oh, I thought that one was familiar!"

"That's right Peni! We were racing sleds down the mountain and-"

Peni continued, "We blew the big horn to sound like a Yowie."

"Bunyip sure do hate those things."

"And then when he heard us-"

Pika spread his arms like he was flying. "That bunyip jumped off the cliff into the reeds, howling he was so scared!"

The Menehune doubled over in laughter. They clutched their bellies, falling onto their backs as their legs kicked out, arms flailing with mirth.

Waru chuckled. "Typical Menehune."

Lily slowly closed her gaping mouth. Seriously? She caught Brandon looking at the duo in amazement. She squeezed her eyes shut, willing her thoughts to reach Brandon. *Please don't ask them how they did it.*

Waru wiped his hands and dusted his knees off. "Well then, no harm done." He placed his hands on his hips, addressing the humans. "Let's not do that again shall we?"

Brandon and Lily both nodded. It was achingly familiar of when her father chastised her.

Waru turned around, wagging his finger at the two newcomers. "And you two...stay out of trouble for at least an hour."

The duo nodded vigorously.

Ang frowned. "No harm, huh? What would have happened if we were late?"

Waru shrugged lazily. "A Sentinel should be able to handle a bunyip."

Lily flinched, her stomach knotting up. Was a bunyip that weak that it should be simple for her? She clenched her hands, fighting to keep her face neutral. That wasn't simple, not one bit. And to make matters worse, she hadn't heard one word from Tim. How was she even supposed to fight efficiently when she didn't even know how to utilize the tools she had? Her face flushed as she twisted her fingers. A massive hand covered hers, dispersing the negative thoughts.

Spyke gave a reassuring smile, giving her hand a comforting squeeze. She took a deep breath, calming herself. When she relaxed, he pulled back, his kind expression melting away to a professional tone as he addressed Waru.

"Remember Waru, we are protecting nonwarriors. While Lily is a Sentinel, she is still learning about our world. Have a care."

Waru scratched his head with a small grimace. "*Pouri*. Apologies, I keep forgetting. It has been a while since I had to protect someone so small."

Brandon mumbled, crossing his arms. "I'm not that small. I grew 5 inches this summer."

Spyke interrupted, his gaze tracking the sun. "Let us keep moving. We have lost enough time as it is."

Peni and Pika piped up. "We can help!"

Peni coughed dramatically, clearing his throat. He puffed his chest, taking on a dramatically formal tone. "Since you saved us, you can stay at our village for the night. It's only a short distance."

Pika giggled, giving a stage clap of approval as Peni blushed.

Waru bowed, the air growing serious. "We would be honored to accept the Menehune's invitation."

Lily whispered to Spyke, confused. "This is a big deal, isn't it?"

He nodded. "Their village is cloaked with magic blessed by the water goddess. No outsider may enter save his highness or those the Menehune invite."

"So, a big deal then," she reaffirmed.

"Will there be food there?" Brandon oblivious, patted his stomach. "After that fight I could go for something to eat. I'm starving."

Pika's eyes gleamed. "Lots! Oodles and oodles of food!"

Brandon winked. "You had me at the first 'oodles'."

Ang groaned.

Lily shook her head, hiding the unwanted smile that was forming. She shouldn't be laughing about mini-Brandon replicas, but she couldn't help it.

"Let us go," interrupted Spyke, ushering them up the hill toward the path. His own answering smile coated his tone. "I'm hungry as well."

"Get the shrimp!" cried the Menehune.

Chapter Fifteen

"MISS ARI, YOU MUST MAKE HASTE, OR YOU WILL BE LATE for the welcoming Feast of Lights."

Aput's feathery whisper snaked into her ear. She smoothed her dress again, a nervous habit she could not shake. Dain said this was very important, pressing that she needed to be on her best behavior. She chewed her fingernail absently.

They were meeting the Council tonight.

They were visiting under the guise of trading agreements for goods only found in Dain's remote territory. The real reason was Dain needed to consult with his ally to find the fire. What this 'fire' was, Ari did not know. All she was told was to charm, behave, and follow his lead. She was to play the role of the token human the Prince of Prophecy took a fancy to.

She smiled, pushing away self-doubts. *I can do this.*

But, that imposing feeling when they arrived at the Council's Convocation reared again. She gulped, remembering that day.

When departing the lake, they rode up through the jungle past sand dunes and arid planes. There, seemingly in the middle of nowhere, rose a gigantic monolith of red and purple sandstone. Dain stood in front of the rock-face and, with a wave of his hand, the wall melted away to reveal a carved doorway, allowing them entry.

The inside was a smoothed honeycomb; a kaleidoscope of oranges, reds, purples, and yellows streaked the walls that were decorated with clinging jasmine and plumeria vines. Torches lit their path as they moved further into the monolith, every so often small openings appeared allowing Ari to see outside. She noticed they were getting higher and higher. Finally, when she became thoroughly lost, a small humanoid lizard appeared, waving them wordlessly to their rooms.

❀

Fast forward to now and here she was, getting ready for dinner to meet the Council.

She bit her lip, her stomach flipping as panic rose. *I can't do this!*

"Miss Ari?"

Shaken, she looked up.

Aput materialized in front of the door, still hidden in the shadows. While she couldn't make out their expression in the dim light, their tone dripped with concern. She took a breath and held it, trying to calm her nerves.

"Sorry Aput." Her shoulders slumped before admitting in a reluctant whisper. "I'm just really nervous."

The Ijiraq tilted their antlers to the side. "Why would you be nervous?"

She shuffled her feet, twisting her hands. "What if I mess up. These are important people."

"Not people. Fae, monsters, demigods perhaps, but not people."

Demigods? She shook her had. "Well...regardless. Dain said they're important, right?"

Aput nodded. "His highness does require assistance to secure the fire."

Again, what was this fire? She bit back her pout. No one told her anything. She was supposed to stand and looked pretty. She could do that with her eyes closed. Even now she knew she was beautiful in her soft, flowery pink ensemble, her hair decorated with ribbons and flowers. But, what she wanted was to be included, to be trusted.

She chewed her fingernail, pushing aside the tiny pricks of anger that flickered inside. "That means everything must go perfectly."

Aput let out a long breath. "To acquire the Council's approval, impeccability is a necessity."

"That means I have to be perfect."

"Miss Ari…"

She hugged herself. "You can't lie Aput."

Aput sighed deeply, their breathy voice barely a whisper. The answering silence confirmed her suspicions.

Her breathing grew shallow, her shaking hands twisted her hair. "I…I need to check my hair again."

"Your hair is fine Miss Ari."

She snapped over her shoulder. "Then my makeup!"

"Nothing is out of place," Aput insisted. "You are visually stunning Miss Ari. We must leave-"

"I need another minute!!" She smashed her hands down on the dresser, knocking over her toiletries.

Silence.

She slowly turned. Would Aput be angry? Maybe she should apologize. After all, Aput was only trying to help. She looked up to an unblinking stare, the Ijiraq stood unmoving and unphased.

Nothing bothers that Ijiraq does it? Her bitter thoughts ripped into her head.

Aput drifted into the room until they were about an inch away, making no move to touch her. They bent down, their antlers dangling above her.

"Do not do this to yourself."

She frowned, her eyes narrowing. "Do what?"

Unperturbed, Aput continued in a calm tone. "Make yourself less. Do not underestimate yourself."

Her rising anger popped like a deflated balloon. She closed her eyes, ashamed. "But what if I mess up?"

"Then we take it as it comes. His highness always has a contingency plan."

Awkwardly Aput's clawed hand patted her shoulder, clearly uncomfortable. "Do not fret."

Ironically, that did seem to help. Her hands shook less, her breathing evening out. Aput was right. She had nothing to worry about, Dain always had a plan. Everything would be fine. Yes, everything would turn out exactly how he wanted.

"Thanks Aput."

They jerked back, retreating to the shadows by the door. Aput cleared their throat, but it came out more like a rusty growl. "Good. We're late. Let us be off, shall we? The Mo'o always prepare a spectacular feast."

Ari was having serious doubts on the Ijiraq's taste in food. She eyed her plate suspiciously, poking her fork subtly at the unknown food gracing her plate. More small lizard servants, the Mo'o, came out with trays of various food, placing them on a long banquet table.

Aput was right to say the Mo'o created a huge, spectacular feast. However, a lot of food seemed to not want to stay on the table as Ari speared a writhing tentacle before it rolled off her plate. Aput had prepared her food, telling her they would only provide the rarest delicacies. The tentacle fell off with a soft thud.

Rarest? Ari gagged. *This goes beyond rare. It's just eww!*

A Mo'o servant startled her, appearing noiselessly. "May I get you something else my lady?"

She eyed her plate again, trying to hide her disgust. "Some fruit please?"

The servant nodded, disappearing.

Leaving her alone.

She was informed Dain and the Council were still in a meeting and would be a few minutes late. She breathed another cleansing breath, especially after that disgusting food. Having an extra minute to 'digest' the situation, she was certain she could remain calm and collected when the Council arrived.

Like Lily.

The thought surfaced, unbidden. Her eyes narrowed, batting the unwelcome thought away. Why was she thinking about Lily? Well... maybe because Lily always had her act together. It was one of the things about her that annoyed Ari. How could Lily act like everything was fine when it wasn't? It made no sense. Pretending things were okay was not okay.

Murmured voices approached the dining hall. The servants scuttled around, quickly pouring empty cups with fresh drink and making last minute touch ups.

She gulped, her palms beginning to sweat.

The Council had arrived.

Dain, along with five figures, walked in. Dain brought up the rear, still speaking with the last member. Ari took a moment to observe them while they gathered around to enjoy the feast. She tried to recall the names Aput told her, attempting to put a face to the fae that were powerful enough to oversee a territory.

"Oh, look at this. The Mo'o never disappoint. What lovely dishes they prepared for us in such a beautiful display."

The soft, lilting voice belonged to a stunningly beautiful woman. Ari suspected she was Hi'aka, who humans considered the goddess of hula.

She was short, much shorter than Ari, sporting a slim figure with prominent curves. She wore a green grass dress that was decorated with red hibiscus flowers and bright bird of paradise that accentuated her glowing caramel skin. Her long, dark hair fell down her back in soft ringlets that was graced with a beautiful flower crown of yellow and pink sweet scented plumeria dotted with purple hibiscus.

Ari was getting used to how stunning the fae were, but she was intimidated by this woman's sheer beauty. Hi'aka dripped femininity in every way that any other woman would be shown lacking.

Ari pushed her plate to the side, suddenly having no appetite.

A tall figure across from her let out a droned sigh, the sound reminiscent of the rustling trees. Actually, Ari thought the figure was a tree at first. Standing around seven feet tall, his brown skin was rough-hewn with a bark-like quality. Green, vine-like braids fell down his shoulders covering green tattoos resembling ivy and leaves. This must be Tane, who humans regarded the God of the Forest.

His black, depthless eyes – excluding small yellow pupils - closed reluctantly. He sighed again. "I do hope they provided more vegetable or insect dishes this year. Last year poor Ruru did not have much to eat. Isn't that right Ruru?"

"*Quork-Quork*!" A hoot chirped kindly. A little brown speckled owl, no bigger than Ari's palm, peaked through Tane's green braids. It tilted its head to the side, its yellow and orange eyes wide.

Hi'aka giggled. "Don't worry little Ruru. We'll make sure there's something for you."

Tane remained silent, his hand absently reaching up to brush under the owl's chin.

A loud voice boomed. "*Talofa*! Hey! What does a gal have to do to get some drinks around here?"

Tane's expressionless eyes narrowed. "Must you be so loud Nafanua? The Mo'o can hear you just fine at an appropriate level."

A woman came up, clapping Tane on the back...hard. He wheezed loudly, his owl flapping its wings excitedly before settling down. The woman laughed deeply before sitting next to him.

"Tane, it's a feast! Unclench your tree bark for a minute."

Tane, panting softly, straightened himself up stoically. "You are such a heathen sometimes."

"Love ya too *uo*." A servant handed a big tankard to Nafanua who happily tilted her head back, gulping down the contents noisily.

Tane gave a slight, pretentious grimace.

Ari stared in awe. Aput told her Nafanua was a human chief turned fae, one of the only ones known in history. She was by far one of her people's best warriors, with her reward being granted immortality to live in the Veil.

Nafanua had a large, muscularly built body topped with a head of thick, messy brown hair held up by a headband that framed large, crinkled brown eyes. She was tall, not much smaller than Tane, wearing a simple leather tunic and pants. Dangling at both her side and her back were two weapons: a wide hook that had four pointed sharp teeth facing sideways and a war club shaped like a spear with jagged looking edges on both sides. Ari chewed the inside of her cheek, holding in her excitement. This woman was the one she wanted to meet.

Nafanua's dark eyes gleamed merrily, yelling behind her, a loud burp resounding. "Kamohoali'l! Come join us! Don't sit there and talk business anymore with his highness."

Behind her, the figure speaking quietly with Dain stopped. He towered over Dain, easily reaching over eight feet tall. Ari couldn't say he was stunningly beautiful like Hi'aka, but he sported a wild, raw beauty. He was striking, his black eyes zeroed on the group.

Nafanua, unperturbed, waved him over. For a large fae, he moved quite stealthily. This must have been the Council member Dain wanted to speak with. Kamohoali'l, the infamous Shark God. He sat down, the table shaking a brief moment as his large frame settled.

He motioned to the nearest Mo'o servant.

"A large plate of *uala* and *wana* please," his deep voice boomed. The tiny lizard shook slightly, quickly filling a plate of sweet potatoes and sea urchins, laying it in front of the large fae. With the neutral look the Shark God sported, this had to be his normal voice. Ari didn't want to know how loud his voice got when he was angry.

He really was impressive, and not just the muscles on top of muscles. Long midnight black hair hung down straight over his shoulders. Grayish blue skin was dotted with white raised tattoos that Ari speculated were carved, not inked. His large hands tapered off into claws which dug into the sea urchins, tearing off the outside with little effort. Soon another plate came to follow the first as the Shark God devoured the food with gusto.

Dain proceeded to sit next to her, not saying a word.

Nafanua raised her tankard again, her eyes glittering. That must have been a signal everyone was waiting for. Soon the rest of the group began eating with a flourish.

She slammed her tankard down, yelling over her shoulder.

"Kamehameha, I know you don't eat, but you don't have to sit in the shadows hovering. We have guests so please sit down with the rest of us."

"You're implying just because we have guests he can sit?" Tane scoffed, his condescending tone evident.

Nafanua glared. "You always take things so literal, Tane. Kamehameha is part of the Council and is always welcome at the table. I gave up trying to force him a while ago."

"Was it the time you tried to drag him to dinner, and it ended with you both battling it out?" Hi'aka asked flippantly, fixing a flower in her hair.

Kamohoali'l snorted, hiding a chuckle. He slurped down another sea urchin. "You mean when she almost beat to death a leader of the dead?"

Tane rolled his eyes. "Must you be so crude."

A growly dark voice interrupted. "Need I remind you that I am, indeed, here?"

The last member had Ari gulping, cold shivers racing down her arms. Out of the shadows came a tall, lithe figure. Deep skin, so rich it was almost a black hue, could be seen in the shadowy mist which cloaked him. He was tall, not as tall at the Shark god or Tane, but certainly taller than the average human. He was shirtless, his muscles defined under a tattered gray shoulder cape that draped over his neck, held together with a coconut shell necklace.

Ari could not make out his face as it was covered by a helmet. But, she shuddered, it wasn't normal. The helmet was bone white, shaped like a skull, the edges tinged yellow and red that covered the fae's entire face save for half his mouth. On his back he sported a deadly large scythe shaped like a fishhook.

Ari rubbed her arms, hoping to get rid of the sudden chill. This was Kamehameha, the leader of the Nightmarchers.

The leader of the ghostly dead.

Kamehameha crossed his arms, barely moving an inch toward the table.

Nafanua rolled her eyes. "Come on sour puss. How about we arm wrestle?" She paused, showing her bicep with a grin. "I promise I'll go easy."

"Then the honor of winning has no meaning if you do not try," quipped Kamehameha dryly.

Nafanua slammed her fist down, cracking her knuckles. "Do I need to drag you?"

Tane shook his head. "You know how this feral child is. Don't rile her up Kamehameha."

Kamohoali'l gestured for another plate, three empty ones piled up. "Last time she was this riled up she broke the table." He gave the Nightmarcher a side look. "It's the Festival of Lights, *hoaloha.*"

An audible sigh rose before Kamehameha drifted over to the end of the table, the empty plate untouched. "You know I do not do well..." he glanced over to Dain and Ari, "with the living."

Ari flushed, glancing downward. She clenched her hands under the table, her heart beating fast.

Dain, not looking at her, reached over and grabbed her fingers. His calm and haughty demeanor evident.

"I understand Kamehameha. The living can be quite noisy and pointless." He dramatically looked over to her, a smile gracing his handsome face. "But I can assure you, our company is anything but. Maybe some merriment and amusement perhaps, but our presence is not pointless."

His gaze rested on Ari and her flushed cheeks. "This living creature is special in ways we have yet to know." He ended with a soft kiss on her knuckles, his golden red eyes aglow.

The intense stare of the Nightmarcher leader pierced into her, taking in the exchange silently. She tried not to visibly shake, the physical pressure of his gaze pressed down on her. Her lungs constricted; everything was so tight.

Suddenly, she breathed out, the pressure lifting as Kamehameha's gaze moved to address Dain. "The living are not pointless your highness. What will be will be. The cycle is inevitable."

There was a deep pause. Kamehameha continued. "I must admit you bringing a human into the Veil is rather, unexpected."

His gaze turned back to Ari, the pressure returning. He tilted his head, taking in her shaking limbs. "I do apologize, my presence is rather much for the living. I should take my leave."

Nafanua waved him off, dismissive. "Stop your whining. You're fine. Just sit." She raised her tankard again. "More drinks please!!"

Dain's finger swirled the top of his wine glass absently. "Yes, another drink is very appreciated."

Time passed as the drinks flowed as along with the conversation. After a time, Dain paused in his conversation with Tane. He took a leisurely sip of wine, his eyebrow twitching, a clear sign the wheels turned within his mind. His voice rose to catch the table's attention.

"This Festival of Lights has been most impressive. Truly we appreciate such gracious company tonight. Though I must ask," he paused, motioning toward three empty place settings near Nafanua, "are we expecting more company?"

Hi'aka daintily popped a sugared lychee in her mouth. "There should be some delegates from Prince Jacy's territory arriving correct Kamohoali'l?"

"Yes, they should be arriving shortly," he replied, not looking up from his urchins.

Dain tapped his finger absently on the table, slowly. "Oh really? May I ask why?"

Tane held up some seed for Ruru. "We have an agreement your highness. We keep your confidence regarding trade agreements. We do that for others as well. Remember, we keep our contracts seriously and with confidentiality."

Dain held up his hands. "Of course, of course. Though, you could see why I would ask of my brother's people being here. Especially due to recent...misunderstandings."

"There is nothing for you to worry about your highness. This is a neutral, sacred space," said Kamohoali'l firmly.

Dain put his hand over his chest, a handsome smirk in place. "I am not worried, for I know the power of the Council is indeed great."

A small Mo'o servant scuttled out from the entrance. She coughed discreetly, garnering attention to primly pipe out. "Dear esteemed council members, the emissaries from Prince Jacy have arrived."

The servant bent down with a short bow, her arm out as the Forest Prince's party walked into the dining hall.

Ari twisted her head, peering over her shoulder. She held in her breath, hoping these fae were not from the fight they had with Dain's brother. First stepped in a handsome fae with dark hair and green eyes.

She frowned. *Wait...* It was the fae that was with Lily. He was almost as handsome as Dain, she reluctantly admitted to herself. Cabyll was his name, right? According to Dain, he was one of the best assassins in the Veil. Was he here with Lily? She straightened, lifting her head...but no sign of Lily.

Another large, muscled male Ari did not recognize walked in, accompanied by a huge black dire wolf. Tall, with long green hair and lightly browned skin, he was handsome, but nothing really stood out. Except he had a quiet, deadly aura that made goosebumps pepper across her skin.

Another fae walked in behind him. This one Ari did recognize. It was the little, winged fairy that clung to Lily at the revel. What was her name? Per? Peri? Yes, Peri! She bit her lip. That fae didn't seem to hate her when they last met, but she wasn't sure. Finally, the last figure came walking in, looking her dead in her eyes. Ari's jaw dropped.

"Well sh-"

"Language sweetie! I know I surprised you, but here I am." Aunt Raven's quirky grin speared her across the table. To everyone it looked like a kind smile, but the slight twitch in Raven's eye spoke otherwise. Ari gulped. She was in trouble.

Big trouble.

Raven gestured to the empty space across from Ari. "May I sit here?"

"Of course. Please, let's get them some drinks!" Nafanua's boisterous tone and smile welcomed the group.

"A drink sounds amazing!" Raven plopped down, letting out a relieved sigh.

The tall, green-haired fae sat next to her, his eyes piercing at Raven. She ignored him completely, stretching her legs and arms with a groan.

The little fairy sat next to Ari, a sugary sweet smell wrapping around her. Ari cleared her throat, the words sticking in her windpipe.

Peri winked, her large lips quirking upward.

Dain's keen gaze landed on Cabyll first, narrowing. "Fancy seeing you here Cabyll."

Cabyll smirked, putting his hands behind his head lazily. "Same to you Dain."

"Prince Dain," he corrected.

Cabyll shrugged. "Suit yourself."

Dain raised his eyebrow. "Are you here on your human's business?"

Ari held her breath. Was Lily here?

Unblinking, he merely replied, "She is not my human."

Dain's tone took on a dangerous edge. "Then are you here for *my* human?"

Cabyll chuckled, his eyes resting on Dain and Ari. "I'm here on the other prince's orders. Though your human is as lovely looking as she was back at the revel."

His eyes held Ari's before giving her a small wink. She blushed, warmth burning her cheeks.

Dain smirked, appearing carefree. However, he squeezed Ari's fingers a little too hard. She held her wince as he said tightly. "Of course she is. She is beautiful for a human."

Cabyll's lip quirked. "I see." He lifted his hands with a shrug. "To your other question. As you know, *Prince* Dain, I go where the money is."

Hearing that, Dain relaxed, his grip lessening. "Fair enough Cabyll, fair enough." His gaze turned to Raven. "And you? You seem to know my *petite oiseau* am I correct, human?"

Raven's eyebrow raised. "Human? My name is Ravenna Ambrosino. My friends call me Raven. And you must be Dain correct?"

"Prince Dain," he corrected again, his teeth gritting slightly.

Raven stared, unblinking. "Okay, Dain."

"Ambrosino?" he murmured to himself. "You are related to my human?"

Raven opened her mouth then immediately shut it with a grunt. After giving a side eye to the male fae next to her, she nodded. "I am her aunt."

Her big brown eyes turned to Ari, questioning. "You doing okay sweetie?"

Ari merely nodded, the words stuck in her throat. Whether it was because she was happy to see a friendly face or terrified of her aunt's possible wrath, she didn't know.

"Family?!" Nafanua's eyes lit up excitedly. "Did you know your aunt was coming?"

Dain replied for her. "No, I'm afraid we didn't." A chiseled smile plastered on his face, which belied the tightening of his hand over the wine stem. "But I can imagine it is a joy for my special human to see her family. Though this is quite...abnormal. Tell me, Aunt Raven-"

"Ravenna," interrupted Raven smoothly. "But you can call me Ms. Ambrosino."

Ari bit her lip, almost choking on her drink. In the short time she knew her aunt, she never had people address her formally.

Well...this isn't going well.

"I must admit, I am curious as well. What brings you here Ms. Ambrosino," said Hi'aka, her slender hands resting under her chin.

Raven's brilliant smile rested on the council members. "You can call me Raven. I must say those flowers are simply beautiful. That color combination is fabulous!"

Hi'aka preened, fluffing her hair at the obvious praise.

"She came with us because she's special." Peri jumped up, grabbing a cup and drinking the contents down in one gulp.

Tane's disinterested tone pierced the folly. "I think the question is, what made this human special. We were told the reason for his highness's human, but," his suspicious stare landed on Raven, "you have not given us a logical explanation as to you being in the Veil."

The large green haired fae cleared his throat, his wolf growling softly. He looked at Raven, unsure, before speaking up. His deep voice was hesitant. "The reason is that-"

Raven grabbed the large fae's muscular arm, her hand unable to wrap around his bicep. Her grip must have been hard because the male grunted, stopping mid-sentence. She motioned for him to take a drink. As he reluctantly began to sip, her gracious smile beamed at Tane.

"The reason is that we fell in love."

The man coughed, spitting out the contents. A Mo'o quickly cleaned the mess, disappearing into the shadows.

Ari's eyes widened. Aunt Raven? In love?

Oh, my goodness! You've got to be kidding me.

Peri giggled merrily. "This is amazing. Give me another drink!"

"Same here!" concurred Nafanua. "I do love a good love story, and Prince Dain has been quite tight-lipped about his romance."

Dain slowly sipped his wine, his eyes narrowing on Raven's hand on the male's arm. "I prefer not to kiss and tell. But I must say, this *is* interesting." He tapped his chin lazily. "You say for love? I am intrigued. If you're my human's aunt and your name is Ambrosino, you must be related to the sister, correct?"

"Correct," said Raven cautiously.

Dain smirked. "So, you are here on your other niece's orders, correct?"

"I'm here for myself Mr. Confident," replied Raven. "No one orders me around."

"Your highness," corrected Dain, a dangerous edge creeping into his tone.

Cabyll speared Raven a look when she began to roll her eyes.

Inside, Ari stomach clenched, the fruit tasting sour. Why was Aunt Raven here anyways? Was it really for love? Or was it for her? She stamped down the bubble of happiness thinking if it was the latter.

She's not your aunt, remember that Ari.

Dain clapped his hands, laughing. He turned toward the male. "Then I guess it must be true. I have noticed this human line is quite formidable."

The green haired male mumbled, "You have no idea."

"May I have your name?" Dain asked.

The large male stared back, unshaken. "You may call me Okena."

Dain twirled his glass. "And what are you doing here Okena?"

"When his highness, Prince Jacy, sent his envoy, he included Thunderboy representation," replied Okena.

"A Thunderboy? I've always wanted to meet one of you." Nafanua smirked. "You are true warriors the legend tells."

"Okena is an awesome Thunderboy, aren't you handsome?" Raven's cute tone went up a notch. Okena seemed to tense up while Peri giggled.

Raven patted his arm, addressing everyone. "Forgive him, he's a little straightlaced. That's why we fit so well. Opposite attract you know."

Her big eyes rested on Nafanua before catching Hi'aka. "Back to your question about us. I am an explorer. I happened to be exploring the forests, delving into the lakes, when suddenly I came upon a circle of trees. I didn't realize I had walked into the Veil. After walking, lost, I ended up at a beautiful lake with fireflies dancing around. That is where I met Okena."

She turned to the large fae, his eyes getting wider in surprise. She smiled brilliantly, her eyes sparkling. "He was so kind to me, so considerate. He offered to help me find my way home." She paused, her eyes catching Okena's shocked ones as she gave him a lovey dovey smile, cupping his chin. "It was when he saved me from a pit of poisonous snakes that I knew I was in love. Prince Jacy was so generous and said I could follow Okena on his latest mission before we would return to my home."

Nafanua sat transfixed, her cup frozen at her mouth. She slammed it down, the drink sloshing onto the table. "What a story."

"Yeah, quite the story," mumbled Okena, his gaze never leaving Raven.

Peri clanked her glass against Nafanua's excitedly. "This is soooo awesome! It's like dinner theatre." She addressed a small Mo'o servant with an excited whisper. "Think you guys have popcorn here or something? This is too good."

"Peri," warned Okena.

Raven patted his tense arm lightly. "Oh, don't mind Peri sweetie. She loves hearing this story."

Cabyll groaned. "Don't give that natural disaster anything that will dull her little senses."

Peri pouted, her hands landing on her hips. "Spoilsport!"

Nafanua chuckled, "Don't listen to them little peri fairy." She started to pour from her own cup into Peri's empty one. "Have some of mine. It's stronger than this other watered-down stuff."

Tane grumbled, palming his face. "Your stuff could peel bark off a tree."

"You'd know," quipped Nafanua.

Hi'aka smiled dreamily. "That is so romantic. I always do like the rare dalliances with the human world."

Tane scoffed. "Won't last too long."

Kamehameha nodded. "Human lives are indeed short." His intense gaze filled the room. "Treasure every moment."

Raven blinked, taking in the Nightmarcher leader. Without hesitation, which surprised Ari, her aunt's unwavering gaze met the formidable Nightmarcher.

Raven smiled. "You are a sweetheart, aren't you?"

Silence.

Loud laughter rang out as the Nightmarcher turned away, shoulders hunched.

Kamohoali'l's deep chuckle rang. "I never thought I'd see this old man get unnerved."

"Hush Kamohoali'l," rasped Kamehameha, refusing to look at them.

"Raven is definitely not your ordinary human," replied Okena, his unreadable gaze resting on her.

Kamohoali'l' smiled, clapping his meaty hands. "Alright everyone. At this successful Festival of Lights, let us eat, drink, and enjoy the merging of company. For tonight, it is about creating bridges and pathways toward a better life for our territories."

The guests raised their glasses high.

"CHEERS!"

Ari quietly sipped her drink, reeling. Within minutes her aunt effortlessly charmed the entire Council. She chewed her lip. That was *her* job, and here she was failing miserably while her aunt swept them off their feet.

She glanced over at Dain. He wasn't happy. Yes, he was smiling and laughing at Tane. But it was the slight squeeze of his glass and the flash of a twitch on his bottom lip that told a different story.

He gave her a side-glance, his eyes narrowed slightly. She flushed, ducking her head down. It was only when Dain laughed again that she dared to peek up. Raven's concerned eyes caught hers. She raised her glass to Ari, mouthing the words, *We need to talk young lady.*

She gulped, her throat burning. *Well crud...*

Chapter Sixteen

SUGAR DUCKS...

Lily took another sip of banana milk, yelping to regain balance as a group of Menehune children zipped past her. She wobbled, her unsteady feet trying to remain planted on the ground. She closed her eyes, which proved to be a mistake. Her head swam, forcing her to open them, focusing on the scenery before her.

The Menehune village bustled with infectious energy. The village chief, who happened to be Peni and Pika's grandfather, was overjoyed to hear how they saved his family. The village welcomed them with open arms, inviting them to enjoy the Festival of Lights.

Lively music and animated voices drifted through the jungle trees into a beautiful bower that sported little banana huts that were strewn about. On the far side of the village, beyond a border of brushes and brambles, ocean waves lapped against the shore. And in the center of the village, a substantial lagoon glistened in the moonlight. Bright blue bioluminescence glowed on the lagoon's surface, creating a spectacular display of lights. Fireflies and moonlight illuminated the village from above in a cool, ethereal glow.

She was told the Menehune never handled fire. Their Festival of Lights was celebrated with the stars, the moon, and the creatures that lit the night. Lily's gaze rested on the little Menehune children surrounded by fireflies. They giggled, their cherubic faces alight with excitement as they played a game Lily couldn't identify. Their laughter rang out, innocent and happy.

She smiled before the familiar pit of guilt settled.

I wonder if Ari is having fun right now. Did Zia Raven find her?

She shook her head, clearing her thoughts. She stared at her glass of banana milk. How many did she have? Was this her second glass? Third? When Peni and Pika handed her the first glass, she thought nothing of it. They giggled, saying all her worries would melt away. She laughed at the time, but then the fizzing feeling began to bubble in her chest and tickled inside her head. She vaguely realized they must have infused the milk with magic. Nevertheless, she took another sip, the sugary sweetness melting on her tongue.

She smacked her lips, her thoughts fuzzing as she chuckled. *We're in the Veil. Of course the milk isn't normal.*

A hand appeared in front of her, *or was it two?* and swiftly grabbed the cup before it hit her lips. She sputtered, protesting.

"Be careful with this." Spyke sat down next to her. He wagged the cup in front of his nose, briefly sniffing. "It's spiked with something."

"Says Spyke," she giggled, enjoying her little pun.

He shook his head, smiling softly. "How much have you had for you to make such jokes?" He chuckled, his gaze trailing over her face. "But it is good to see you smile." He turned away from her mumbling, "It's very pretty."

Lily's nose crinkled, a small hiccup escaping. "It does feel nice to laugh. And not have anything try to kill us for two seconds. Or is it four? I never know."

She pursed her lips, mimicking a frown and ended up giggling again. Spyke followed suit with a deep chuckle.

"Hey guys." Brandon called out, sitting down next to Lily with a thump. He eyed the drink in Spyke's hand. "Is that the banana milk? No one will give it to me. Can I have some?"

"NO!" Lily and Spyke yelled in unison.

Brandon held up his hands. "Geez fine. Ang said I couldn't have it and I thought she was just being Ang." He put his finger on his chin. "Although maybe that's why she's passed out."

Lily's eyes bugged. "She what?!"

Ignoring her, he continued. "Guess I'll stick to the watermelon juice." He pouted. "Though it's not as fun."

A lively drumbeat filled the air. The Menehune jumped up, moving toward a large, open space where banana trees swayed, and the fireflies buzzed overhead. The energetic dance began, the locals chanting and clapping with the beat.

Brandon's eyes widened, turning to Lily. "Hey Lil, let's dance!"

Maybe it was the music. Maybe it was the banana milk. Or maybe a combination of both, she didn't know. Regardless, bubbles rose up in her chest, her mouth widening with an anticipated grin. Her smile grew as she jumped up, grabbing Brandon's hand. She failed to notice the stunned look on Spyke's face.

She tugged Brandon's hand. "Let's go." Turning back, she waved her hand. "Come on Spyke, let's dance."

He gave an embarrassed smile, shrugging his shoulders. "That's alright. I don't really dance."

She ran over and grabbed his hand. She gave it a small tug, but he refused to budge. She tried again, encouraging. "Don't worry, just follow the rhythm. You can't mess it up."

Face flushed he pulled away, tugging his hair nervously. "Last time I danced, I knocked over a few tables. I'm good where I am. But you two go and have fun."

Brandon clasped her hand. "Come on Lil."

Lily gave him one last look. "You sure?"

Spyke nodded, waving them off.

With a little hesitation, she let Brandon pull her toward the dancing Menehune, laughter trailing behind her. She tentatively moved her hips to mimic the young female Menehune who patiently showed her the complicated dance steps. She got the hang of it quickly.

Soon, both Lily's legs and face hurt from having so much fun. The drumbeat thumped in her chest as she weaved with the other dancers. Every so often, she would look over at Spyke to make sure he was okay. Sure enough, the large warrior sat there, her cup in his hand. He looked menacing, a statue unmoving. Save for his eyes. His eyes were merry watching them.

I wonder if Cabyll can dance?

The thought crept up, unbidden, her dance faltering a beat. Being a good dancer would make women practically fall at a man's feet. Of course he knew how to dance. If he was here, she bet he would tease her to make her fumble. Then, he would catch her and twirl her around masterfully. She found herself chuckling, imagining it.

Maybe he's dancing with Ari or someone else right now...

Frowning, she shook her head. *What am I thinking? Get it together Lily!*

The lively music took away those worries, her mind on the present. She kept dancing, moving her hands in an intricate pattern and swaying her hips so fast she lost her breath.

Finally, when the song ended, Brandon and Lily were both gasping, sporting huge smiles. Another fast beat immediately picked up and they had to plead with the dancers for a break. Laughing, they returned to Spyke.

"I didn't know you could dance like that Lily," he said gruffly.

She beamed. "Of course I can, I'm Italian."

She laughed at his blank stare, clearing not understanding. Brandon laughed as well, and soon Spyke chuckled too.

A voice broke the pealing levity.

"Are you enjoying the feast?"

The question came from the wizened old voice of the village chief, Luano. He sported a white beard underneath a headdress of brightly hued flowers and feathers. He held a staff made of coconut wood etched with beautiful designs, his kind eyes sparkled merrily.

Spyke bent his head down in respect. "Indeed, Chief Luano. Your hospitality is beyond generous."

Luano waved his staff dismissively. "Oh hush! You saved my grandsons. It is the least I could do." His keen eyes winked at Lily. "Besides, the great Namaka spoke of your arrival."

"Who's Namaka?" asked Lily.

The chief gestured toward the lagoon, which sparkled and danced under the moonlight. "She is there." He pointed above. "She is here. Around us, surrounding us. Always eternal, even when we are gone."

Brandon tilted his head, confused. "But aren't the fae immortal?"

The chief shook his head, smiling kindly. "Nothing lasts forever young child. Even the fae. But the great elementals, such as the sea, came in the beginning. And they will be there until the final ending. Even after time has washed us Menehune away."

"Is this Namaka a great elemental?" asked Lily.

Luano put his finger to his nose, his eyes merry. Lily's gaze returned to the lagoon. It pulled and pushed against the moonlight, dancing in a beautiful rhythm she couldn't identify. Was it Namaka? Or was it just her imagination? She scoffed. At this rate it could be the banana milk. But one thing was for certain, the pull to go to the water was undeniable. To see down into its depths.

A loud, boisterous crash resounded, interrupting the solemn moment. Peni and Pika fell in front of them, a bunch of shrimps falling at their feet.

The chief sighed. "Boys, what did I tell you? Make multiple trips to get more shrimp. Don't try to gather everything at once."

"But *Kupunakane*...Grandfather, we were hungry," protested Peni.

"Don't worry Pops, it's still good!" Pika smiled, taking a fallen shrimp and popping it in his mouth.

Lily shook her head, covering her smile behind her hand. *These two are seriously Brandon 2.0.*

The chief must have noticed, he wagged his finger at her. "Don't encourage them young Sentinel." He took his staff, bonking the boys lightly on their heads. "Get up! Show some respect to our guests. What would your great grandfather Ola say hmmm?"

"Ouch!" they both yelped, clasping their heads.

"Fiiiiine," grumbled Pika, rubbing his forehead.

"You win *Kupunakane*, we'll behave," conceded Peni.

Lily snorted, coughing into her hand. She didn't have the heart to mention they were crossing their fingers behind their backs. With the look the chief was giving them, he probably already knew.

"Away with you. Go!" He turned back to the group, a warm chuckle shaking his shoulders. "Children."

The chief looked back briefly, his grandsons running ahead. He sighed, appearing older. "You just want to protect them. It comes across harsh sometimes, but just as I teach them, I learn from them as well."

Lily blinked, confused. *Did he mean...?*

"Yes Sentinel," replied Luano sagely. "I know why you are here."

Spyke leaned closer to Lily, slightly putting himself between her and the chief.

Luano smiled, holding up his hand. "*Maluhia* warrior. Peace. I am only speaking truth. Not to intimidate, but to inform."

Brandon's eyes grew wide. "Woah! Are you like a mind reader or something?"

"Youth," Luano chuckled. "Such an imagination. No young human. I was informed by the *'uhane.*" Brandon gave him a blank look. He twirled his staff in the air, indicating the dancing lights. "The spirits."

"Oh..." Brandon exclaimed, "You mean like ghosts?"

Luano coughed, hiding his laughter. "Something like that."

"More like the sacred beings of their ancestors that assist the living," mumbled Spyke.

Lily nudged him. "Hush."

Her movement was a calculated mistake. The fizzy bubbles from the banana milk rose up again, tickling her throat. She covered her mouth, a giggle escaping. Her body tilted sideways, her arms outstretched to find balance.

Warm arms steadied her, keeping her from falling. Shocked, she remained still as Spyke held her effortlessly against him. Slowly he removed his arms, tucking her against his side.

"Here, use me as a wall until you get your balance back." He clasped his hands together in front of him, his voice gruff.

She smiled, leaning her head against his arm to stop the swirling that rammed into her brain. Spyke was always so kind and considerate. "Thanks, right now everything is whirling and swirling like a soft serve ice cream."

"What's ice cream?" asked Spyke.

Brandon jumped up. "Only the best thing ever! Uh...Hey Lil, you sure you're okay. You can lean on me too ya know." He gave Spyke a side eye.

"The days of youth," muttered Luano. "Sweet and fleeting like a spring morning."

Spyke coughed loudly. "And what did the spirits tell you Chief?"

Luano's tone grew somber. "They told me where you are going and what you seek. And more importantly, *why* you are seeking Prince Kye's memories."

His wizened eyes bore into Lily. Suddenly her whizzing head cleared, the bubbles dissipated as if they popped simultaneously.

"It is imperative that you succeed," he continued. "Which is why from the great advice of the 'uhane and the great Namaka, I gift you with this on your journey."

He fished a small bracelet out from the pocket of his robe. Inlaid with light green serpentine stones held a beautiful pearlescent seashell. Etched on the shell was a beautiful black coral design that was embedded within the ridges.

The chief saw her staring. "It is black coral that resides deep within the heart of the ocean. The coral is sacred to us as it is one of the creations closest to Namaka."

The chief gently wrapped the bracelet around Lily's wrist, securing it tightly.

At that point words faded from Lily's ears. The chief's lips were moving, but she couldn't hear anything...except waves. The ocean crashed and roared in her eardrums, drowning out all other noise. It was as if a seashell was propped against her ears, leaving everything muffled and dissonant.

She frowned, smacking her eardrum. Her chest heaved as a rushing cold saturated her body. A pull tugged her belly, pushing her forward. Her legs moved on their own, brushing past Spyke and the startled chief, bringing her briskly to the lagoon.

The water lapped softly against the shore, a contrast to the crashing waves that roared in her ears. She tried to yell for help, but her lips wouldn't move. She had no control over her body. Startled, she found herself stepping into the cold water, shoes and all.

A small flicker of panic rose up as she moved forward, inching deeper into the lagoon. Her eyes widened, she couldn't pull back. Water lapped at her hips, the blue glowing bioluminescence swirling around her. Her chilled heart thumped madly. At the rate she was going the water would be over her head in five more steps.

One step. Her mind yelled out.

Cosa nel mondo?!

Two steps.

Water splashed at her shoulders. Hands tried to grab her to no avail. From the corner of her eye some unknown force pushed Spyke and

Waru away. They both fell backwards onto the grass, their concerned faces stabbing her. Her heart fell down to her stomach, the coldness seeping further into her bones.

Think Lily, think! You're smart. You can figure out how to stop an unknown, probably a spell, thingy. Right? Just figure out how to disrupt the blockers that are freezing your limbs.

Three steps.

Okay forget it, let's go with plan B.

Her mind cried out.

Tinmiukpuk? A little help?

Four steps. The cold water splashed against her lips, her pendant cool.

TIM!

Fifth step.

The water raced over her head, cresting above her eyes. The roar of the waves quieted as she sunk beneath the water, the stillness blanketing her. The swirling outline of the moon flickered above the rippling surface. The blue glow of the bioluminescence danced in patterns around her.

She blinked, the water surprisingly clear. There was another soft glow, a greenish white, that pulsed by her side. *What is that?*

Her body was now frozen in place as the water held her, the surrounding glow accompanied by the dancing moonlight. It was, ironically, peaceful. Her mind yelled at her.

Peaceful? Am I nuts? I'm drowning here!

She held her breath, bubbles escaping her lips as the faint burn for oxygen rose. How much longer could she hold it? Just when she was ready to release her breath, a warmth rushed through her veins, dispelling the unnatural coldness.

Hold on young Sentinel!

As if a cord was cut, her locked limbs suddenly relaxed. Then panic roared to the surface as Tinmiukpuk cried out.

Now Sentinel, to the land. Hurry!

She kicked hard, pushing herself backward as she raced upward. Her heart constricted painfully.

Almost...there...

Bright, crisp air hit her lungs. She coughed, gathering as much oxygen as she could. Grass met her eyes, water falling into her lashes. Tim manifested next to her in his small bird form. He nudged her head comfortingly as she expelled more water, her limbs shaking.

Large hands picked her up, warmth surrounding her. Spyke held her gently, one hand rubbing her back, not saying a word.

"Lil! Are you okay?" Brandon's worried gaze caught hers.

Waru crossed his arms, concerned. "That was unexpected. You could have died little human." Spyke's arms tightened around her, but Waru continued, "Were you bewitched perhaps?" The warrior's keen eyes scanned over the area before narrowing down at Lily. More importantly, at her arm.

She alternated between coughing and gasping for air. Looking at her side, the bracelet from the chief shimmered the same greenish white light that had pulsed around her in the lagoon. She shivered, and she wasn't sure it was from the water. If she had enough strength, she would have ripped the thing off, but she didn't have enough energy to lift her hand yet.

Chief Luano, panting, raced up to them. Peni and Pika were in tow behind him, their eyes concerned. The chief held his knees, taking a deep breath. "I...can...explain."

"Please do Chief," Spyke's calm tone belied his hard eyes and clenched jaw.

Luano's eyes widened at the glowing bracelet. His mouth opened slightly before he shook his head. "Never in my life have I seen this."

"What is this Chief?" asked Waru.

"The bracelet is from Namaka. It has been passed down through generations of chiefs." He frowned, concern evident. "This bracelet is meant for protection."

Brandon glared. "Protection by drowning? Dude that's messed up."

"Drowning isn't protection," scoffed Pika. "You're a few coconuts short of a tree aren't ya human?"

Peni nudged Pika, whispering loudly. "That is not what he meant Pika."

Pika thought a moment, confused. "Then why did he say it?"

"This has never happened before," interrupted Luano, shaking his head emphatically.

His gaze landed on Tinmiukpuk. He blinked, stunned, before

hastily bowing. He glanced over at his grandsons, who stood still as stone. He smacked them on their calves with his staff. They yelped, immediately falling down into a clumsy bow.

Luano spoke calmly. "Forgive us wise ancient."

Tinmiukpuk screeched low. *My Sentinel was in danger. How do you explain this?*

The chief kept his head bowed. "We do not know the reasoning for this."

The Thunderbird stared at them in silence. The hibiscus perfumed air was stifling as the seconds ticked by slowly. Finally, he blinked, breaking the atmosphere before nodding at the Menehune.

The chief sighed in relief, leaning against his staff.

"Does anyone have a theory?" asked Lily, her voice raspy. Spyke patted her back lightly, more water coming out from her lungs with a cough.

Tim's deep voice echoed in the glen, although his small bird form did not move a beak.

I believe this is the work of Namaka.

"The goddess of the seas?" Waru frowned slightly, rubbing his chin. "But she disappeared centuries ago. No one has seen or heard from her."

Tim flapped his wings, landing on Lily's shoulder lightly, pushing warmth into her. She closed her eyes, burrowing further in Spyke's arms. The combined warmth thawed her chilled body

Just as I sealed myself away, Namaka could have done something similar.

Tim's gaze landed on the bracelet, which was still softly glowing. *Even if it was a small piece of herself, it would be enough.*

"But why now?" asked Brandon.

Everyone focused on Lily. She swallowed, wincing as her throat burned. "Don't look at me guys." She shook her head. "I don't have any special powers you know that."

Luano pondered a moment before raising his staff. "Namaka only knows."

"Cop out," whispered Brandon.

Lily narrowed her eyes at him. *Not that I don't agree, but you don't say it, Brandon.*

Brandon flushed, turning away as he whistled loudly.

Tim nuzzled against her, his voice entering her mind for just the two of them.

You may not have powers little Sentinel, but your soul is strong. We will find Namaka's purpose in due time.

Lily pursed her lips. *Not soon enough for me.*

Tim butted her head. *We will figure this out together.*

She took a deep breath, comforted by that simple sentence. "I do not like drowning, thank-you-very-much, and I've had two...count them TWO times this has happened. So," she raised the bracelet with a small jiggle. "I'll just take this off and keep it safe in case we need it sound good?"

She tugged.

It would not come off.

She pulled harder, panic rising. No matter how hard she tried she couldn't take it off. She cursed slightly under her breath. "Why...won't...you...come...off?!"

Luano gently laid his hand over her wrist. His kind eyes grounded her. "Namaka has a purpose. What that is I do not know, but it looks like you are part of that young human."

She drew a shaky breath, her eyes pleading. "Does that mean I could drown again?"

He patted her hand in a fatherly gesture. "All I know is, until her purpose is fulfilled, the bracelet will remain on."

Tinmiukpuk's loud screech had everyone freeze as his voice boomed. *I will not let the sea goddess hurt my Sentinel.*

Luano and the other Menehune bowed low.

Her shoulders slumped, a headache forming. "Great, another puzzle to solve to add to the list."

"No need to be so down little human," said Waru. "We shall tackle this the same way as any other challenge."

"Please don't tell me it's books." Brandon's lip curled up in disgust.

"With our fists!" The warrior punched the air with a whoop. "We shall defeat anything that comes in our way."

Brandon's eyes lit up, raising his fist too. "Now that's what I'm talking about!"

Lily whispered to Spyke. "He's a hit first, talk later kinda guy, isn't he?"

His chuckle rumbled against her back. "Most of us warriors are."

"But you're not," she protested.

He looked down at her, their eyes meeting a moment. He cleared his throat, pulling away to stand. He held out his hand, helping her up but refused to meet her eyes.

"I used to be," he quietly admitted. "I've had years of regret to change my view."

She chewed the inside of her cheek. She was insanely curious, but it wasn't her place to ask.

Spyke patted her head, an unbidden smile quirking up. "Don't frown. Waru is a skilled warrior. He knows not all issues are resolved with his fists."

He gestured toward Waru who was showing Brandon some punches. Soon the group was stamping their feet and yelling loudly, the previous tension dissolved.

The light bulb clicked. "Oh, he did it to calm everyone."

Spyke nodded. "In a sense. But," he interrupted, his large hand lightly resting on her shoulder. "Remember. We are fae warriors. We will do *anything* for our mission. And our mission is to protect you and obtain Prince Kye's memories. Do not forget that, Lily. Our compass is not the same as yours."

She smiled, patting his hand lightly. "I guess it's a good thing I'm here to remind you then."

He chuckled. "Yes, indeed it is."

As the dancing resumed, Lily stared down at the bracelet. Of course, there was another puzzle to solve. Why was nothing ever easy in this place? The bracelet had dimmed, looking completely normal now.

She sighed. *One thing at a time girl. Take it piece by piece.*

They only had two more days. Her thoughts drifted again, settling on Cabyll and her aunt. Did they find Ari? How were they handling the Council. Or, more importantly, how was the Council handling Peri?

She held in a giggle thinking what Peri was doing at that moment. But then, another nagging thought emerged. How was Ari? Was it everything she wanted?

Maybe she is happy with Dain...

"I think I'm going to get some rest," she said, her chest tight.

She was a few feet away before she tripped over something. Something large.

"Lily? You okay?"

Spyke ran over, deftly plucking her up in his arms. He set her down on her feet carefully. She rubbed her knees, trying to dispel the ache and her embarrassment. How many times would Spyke be helping her on her feet tonight? She made a resolution right there to never touch banana milk again.

A groan rose from the ground. There, lying in a puddle of banana milk and honey, was Ang.

Lily grimaced, still rubbing her knee. *Oh geez, she looks terrible.* Guess that meant she was not going to bed anytime soon.

Ang smacked her lips, taking a dirty sleeve to lazily wipe her face. Her bleary eyes cracked open, trying but failing, to focus on Lily and Spyke.

"So...." her wobbly voice ended in a hiccup. "What'd I miss?"

Spyke palmed his face.

Chapter Seventeen

"MISS ARI, IT IS TIME TO WAKE UP."

Ari rubbed her face, grimacing. Her other hand was tangled in her hair as she tried to scrub off the gritty remnants of the previous night. Her mind was fuzzy, the cobwebs slowly untangling. Maybe she had too much of that sparkling drink. Maybe it was the dancing. She wasn't sure which, but whatever happened, she did not care for the massive headache she had. She squinted, barely making out the shape of Aput standing over her bed.

"Shall I get you a tonic for your head?" Aput's antlers titled to the side, questioning.

She moaned, her mouth too dry to answer.

Immediately, as if by magic (and it probably was), a small cup appeared in her hands. She held it up, twisting the glass as the emerald tonic sparkled in the morning light. It was beautiful.

She put it to her lips, but quickly pulled away, her nose wrinkling. It smelled awful! How could something so pretty be so disgusting? That didn't seem right.

"It may not taste good," Aput acknowledged, "but it will help."

Resigned, she pinched her nose. *Here goes nothing.* She grimaced as she took a dreadful gulp. Soon her head cleared, the pressure lifting almost immediately. She sighed in relief, her body relaxing.

Aput didn't wait long. They made a delicate cough, which for a terrifying fae such as them, making such a dainty nose was almost as startling. "Miss Ari. It is time."

She frowned, rubbing her temple. "What do you mean?"

Aput breathed out, speaking slowly but patiently. "Do you remember what you promised his highness last night?"

She blinked, thinking back...

The first thing she remembered was the lights.

The firelight twinkled high above her head, the candles floating. Music was drifting through the main hall, a large expansive structure of sandstone gleaming in the twilight. After dinner, the Council decided that light revelry was needed. Well, to be fair, it was Hi'iaka, Nafanua, and Peri who insisted.

Tane grumbled as Hi'iaka pulled him onto the floor. His reluctance melted away as the tall forest fae began to twist and sway. Kamehameha flat out refused, Kamohoali'I slapping him on the back with a deep laugh. Soon, many fae were out on the floor, swaying to the tinkling strings of music plucking over the air.

Ari smiled. She loved dancing. Apart from the disastrous ending of the last one, she loved the revels. Eager, she turned to Dain, hoping to get him to dance.

He grasped her arm lightly, his gaze hard to read.

"Would you like to dance petit oiseau?"

Without waiting, Dain swung her around to the vibrant beat. Her heart lifted. How she missed this. Just him and her. The string notes swirled, his hand warm against her back. Her head grew fuzzy, the lights blurring.

"Poor little Ari," he whispered. "I believe the drink has muddled your senses."

She could have sworn he looked concerned. She blinked, but his eyes were unreadable. It had to be her imagination.

"Things are a little fuzzy," she admitted. She clutched his arms tighter, trying to keep her balance.

He merely raised his eyebrow. "I'm sure it was a surprise to see your aunt."

She could only nod. She didn't want to talk about that now.

His eyes, half-lidded, continued in a quiet voice. *"Do you really believe she is here because she fell in love?"*

She shook her head. *"Aunt Raven can be emotional. She could fall in love fast, but I don't think she would leave her family."* Unlike her, but she refused to think about that.

Dain twirled her around. *"I agree,"* his tone laconic, already tired of the conversation. *"She must be here to check on you, which means your sister may not be far away."*

She ignored the twinge in her heart when he mentioned Lily. Her gaze remained downcast.

He continued, *"What I'm concerned about is Cabyll. If he is still in league your sister, this could spell trouble for us."*

She looked up, centering on the famous Assassin of the Veil. He stood on the sidelines, his arms casually folded, taking in everything...and everyone. When his bright green gaze caught hers, she glanced away, her face heating.

Dain's eyes followed hers, narrowing on Cabyll. His hand gripped hers a little tighter, his brows slashing down. *"He cannot interfere."*

His lips pursed a moment, giving off a small hum. Then, his eyes took a cunning gleam.

He pulled her closer, whispering in deep purr. *"Did you not notice he is looking at you?"*

She blushed, shaking her head.

Dain chuckled. *"So adorable. And how could he not?"* His fingers came up to tap her cheek. *"You are beautiful my little human. But,"* his eyes sharpened, *"he should watch his eyes."*

Her breath caught, barely able to contain her happiness. Of course she was pretty and guys took notice. They did all the time. But to hear the jealous tone in his voice, she was weirdly flattered.

He bent down, his crimson eyes level with hers. *"I need your help, petit oiseau."*

Her head snapped up. She was not expecting that. He needed her help? Yes! She must have spoken out loud because he laughed.

He wiped his eye, still chuckling. *"You know I must get more of the Council on my side. In order to do that, Cabyll must not interfere."* He smiled, his lips curving upward like a crescent blade. His purr trailed down her spine. *"Will you distract him for me?"*

195

She opened her mouth, ready to agree, but stopped. He wanted her to flirt with Cabyll? Why? She was with Dain, wouldn't that be betraying him?

"But," she protested.

"You only need to keep his attention," he interrupted smoothly. "You are so delightful I'm sure he will not stay away from you." He paused, lifting his hand, caressing her cheek. "You can do this for me right?"

"Um, yes. I can do it." She bit her lip, forcing herself to smile. "I promise I'll do a good job Dain."

"That is my good girl. Now," He twirled her, then abruptly stopped, letting go of her hand. "I'm off for business." He winked, gesturing with a small nod over to Cabyll. "Why don't you get started as well."

He blew her a kiss before heading toward Kamehameha at the edge of the floor, talking quietly with the other Council members. He did not turn around, leaving her in the middle of the floor.

Alone.

Ari stood there, awkwardly. What should she do? Nafanua had pulled Raven away from an intense dance with Okena, the Thunderboy's eyes following Raven's every move. The two women jumped around, laughing cheerfully. Tane had removed himself from the dancefloor, his little owl flapping merrily. Hi'iaka was dancing with another unknown male fae. Peri danced by herself, perfectly chaotically content.

A flush crept up Ari's throat, embarrassment soaring. She didn't want to see her aunt, but she may not have a choice. Before she could decide where to go, a hand tapped her shoulder. Cabyll's handsome smirk filled her vision. Ari tilted her head up, surprised how much taller he was than Dain.

His deep voice rolled over the music. "It's a shame a lady such as yourself was left alone." He gave her a playful wink. "Mind if I have this dance?"

Her gaze strayed back to Dain, who was talking to Kamohoali'l. She took a breath, mentally slapping herself. Remember, she reminded herself, flirt with him. She turned back with a sunny smile, flipping her hair behind her.

"Of course!"

As they danced, the tempo picked up. Drums began to beat lightly, an

196

earthy beat pumping steadily. She marveled how well he could dance. For a formidable killer, the man commanded the dance floor well.

He gave her a roguish grin. "You seem to be settling down in the Veil quite nicely Ari."

"I absolutely love it here," she gushed. "Everyone has been so welcoming. It's just perfect."

"Perfect hmm? That is an interesting choice of words." He tilted his head. "Do you miss your family at all?"

She scoffed, her lower lip pushed out. "I'm sure they're just fine without me. Besides, Lily can be real salty you know."

His brows furrowed, a stray hair falling over his eye. "Salty? Do humans taste like salt?"

"Oh! Sorry, that's just a phrase. She's bitter, mean, and all around just not cool."

"Hmm," He pursed his lips. "I do admit, she is sometimes too serious for her own good."

Her eyes lit up. "Yes, that's right." She looked at him through her lashes, pouting dramatically. "It must have been really hard to put up with her for as long as you did."

Cabyll's eyes were unreadable. "She is definitely not a typical human. I have never met a woman like her."

"So...did she come with you?"

"No, she did not come with me. I left her behind."

His gaze strayed to Okena. "I was sent by his highness to assist with the talks. Like I told Dain, I go where I'm paid."

So, he wasn't with Lily? He really did leave her behind! But he looked happy with her the last time she saw them together. Was she wrong?

Her fingers tightened around his arm.

"Do you know where she is?"

He shrugged, nonchalant. "I do not know where she is. Not my business."

Ari bit her lip. Was she okay? Was she in the Veil? She mentally smacked herself. There is no point thinking about Lily. Why did she even imagine Cabyll and Lily were together. Obviously not. It was clearly just business. But why couldn't she help the slight pinch of shame crawling up her throat?

She cleared her throat, shaking her hair to the side. "Well, better she's gone. She'd drag this entire party down with her sullen attitude. No one wants her anyways. Her sour face would scare everyone."

His hands tightened on her waist...painfully.

She flinched, surprised. "Ow!"

Cabyll loosened his grip, his eyes blank. His lip turned upward in a small smirk, almost cruel. "Forgive me. I sometimes forget how frail humans are. You are like a snowflake."

He leaned down, the song ending, and pulled her hand out to give an air kiss. Ari almost sighed, the move right out of a novel.

She blushed. "It's okay. Honestly, it barely hurt."

He stared at her a moment, his eyes mesmerizing, before he extended his arm, escorting her off the dance floor.

Ari's gaze strayed to find Raven and Okena. The huge warrior's face was beet red. She couldn't make out what they were saying, but he didn't seem pleased. Turning around, Raven walked away, heading toward Kamehameha. The Nightmarcher leader appeared surprised, staring down at Raven who had her hand on her hip, her other pointing at him. Kamohoali'I laughed, deep and loud, slapping Kamehameha on the back, pushing the Nightmarcher forward. Kamehameha awkwardly took Raven's outstretched hand onto the dance floor.

She frowned. "What is Aunt Raven doing?"

Sure enough, Raven was smiling, encouraging the Nightmarcher to dance. The intimidating fae was awkward, his limbs stiff as he tried to mimic Raven's moves. Nevertheless, she smiled brightly, clapping her hands to cheer him on.

Cabyll shrugged. "I do not understand your aunt's actions. But she is a force that is for sure." He winked at her. "I hope you're ready whenever she talks to you."

Her lips curled. "Not really." She batted her eyes upward, trying to seem cool. "But...I hope we get to talk more."

He raised his eyebrow slightly before a roguish smile slowly appeared. "Of course, perhaps tomorrow by the training courtyard."

With a parting wink and a bow, he left, calling over his shoulder. "Have a good night."

. . .

198

Ari rubbed her forehead, the memories flooding in. Aput still stood in front of her, unmoving. "Oh yeah...that's what I promised."

Aput sighed. "Did you agree a place to meet?"

"The training courtyard."

Aput looked outside. "Then you must hurry."

She flopped back down, trying to put the covers back over her head. "Ugh! Why?!"

"Because the training yard becomes hot at noontime."

"So?"

"Do you understand what I mean by hot?"

She rolled her eyes. "I'm not dumb Aput. We're near the desert. It'll be warm."

They shook their head. "The training yard is for the most skilled warriors in this territory. The nearby volcano heats up the training yard for maximum endurance. It is almost as hot as magma when noontide rises."

Aput's eyes bore into hers, somewhat amused. "If you think you can tolerate the heat of the volcano, then be my guest, Miss Ari."

Her eyes widened. "Oh...uh...yeah that sounds hot."

Aput nodded. "Very hot."

She chewed her lip, tugging her hair around her finger. "So, I guess I should go huh?"

"Very wise Miss Ari."

Reluctantly, she threw the covers off, jumping toward the closet, her nerves tight.

Time to look pretty.

Ari smoothed her flowing dress for the twentieth time as she quickly headed toward the training courtyard. Thankfully she wasn't too late; a helpful Mo'o servant had found her and offered to escort her. The honeycomb maze was so complex she had gotten lost multiple times.

She grumbled to herself. Why didn't they give out maps?

She hid her disappointment that she hadn't seen Dain yet. When her memories cleared, she remembered Aput had taken her back to her room, mentioning Dain was working hard to increase support. He never even said goodnight to her after the festival.

Her hands clenched the silky fabric tightly. *He is just busy. He has an important mission and I have to help him. When I see him, he'll see how well I've done. He'll be so proud of me.*

She was still lost in her thoughts when she realized the servant had stopped, staring at her expectantly. Gesturing in front, the servant bowed and disappeared.

Ari, hesitant, peeked out of the enclave. Her breath caught. The training ground was open to the elements, the large, blinding sun shining down. A blue sky was shockingly bright, with not one cloud dotting the perfect canvas. Vibrant yellow and red sand swirled in intricate patterns on the coarse, sandstone floor.

Wisps of steam rose from the red stone, glistening against the beams of light. A large mountain rose in the distance, the plush jungle in-between. Rushing water trickled in the background, but she couldn't find the source. And there, in the middle of training field, was Cabyll.

He didn't notice her. He stood in the center, his bare feet outside the red swirls. He was shirtless, holding two scimitars in front. His eyes were closed, his breath even. Then, with eyes still closed, he began.

It was like a dance, the swords gracefully swung back and forth as he moved to an unknown rhythm. The tempo picked up, the swords soon swirling so fast they blurred Ari's vision. He kicked out, extending one sword parallel before he lithely flipped, the swords spiraling overhead. She held her breath, afraid to say anything to disrupt him. No one wanted to lose any fingers today.

He landed in a crouch, his feet not touching the red sand. His swords froze, crossed above his head. Toward her. Cabyll opened his eyes, his green gaze sparking.

A sly smirk spread over his face as he recognized her. "We meet again."

She jumped back, startled. Her hands clenched, holding back from smoothing her dress again. She had chosen an asymmetrical summer style outfit. Not too fancy, but just enough to be cute and adorable. And cute and adorable she could be. She smiled and waved back.

Straightening her shoulders, she walked out into the training yard, the sun beating down, thick and heavy, her breaths becoming shallow. Warmth poured into her, almost burning. But soon, it became pleasant. She hated hot weather because it melted her makeup and it made her hair sticky. But today? She was surprised she actually liked the heat. When did that start? Whatever the case, she lifted her head, eyes closed, soaking in the warming rays. Mentally she shook herself.

Come on, time to lure an Assassin.

When she finally reached him, he was bent down, cleaning his swords. Giving him a big smile, she clasped her hands behind her back, hoping she looked cute. She trilled out, "You're a super CEO."

He chuckled, his voice deep. "I do not understand the term." Not looking at her, he kept wiping his blades meticulously. They gleamed in the morning light.

She tugged her hair before tucking a strand behind her ear. "Sorry. I just meant you're an expert." She gestured to the scimitars. "With those."

Without a word, he sheathed them with an audible hiss before slowly getting up. He began some stretches, loosening his hands with a few shakes. "I have to be." He bent forward, winking. "If I don't, then I won't be deemed the 'Assassin of the Veil', would I?"

Her cheeks heated. "Um...How does one affect the other?"

Cabyll pursed his lips, his hands reaching over his head, lazily stretching his muscles. "Do you know how someone inherits the title?"

She shook her head. Maybe it's a vote or...

"In the Guild, the title of 'Assassin of the Veil' is only handed down through combat." He paused, indolent. "The current holder's death is required to gain the title."

Her mouth opened slightly. *Oh....*

"Who was it?"

He tilted his head. "Who was what?"

"The last Assassin of the Veil." *The one you killed*, she refused to say out loud.

He pursed his lips, his eyes slightly narrowed, before responding slowly. "That...is a story for another time."

Ari blinked. How could she respond to that?

He put up his hands, his tone suddenly soothing and smooth. "I didn't mean to startle you. You humans startle easily you know that?"

She swallowed, keeping her smile in place. "Sorry, it's not typical conversation."

He grabbed a towel, draping it around his shoulders as he picked up a cup, taking a long sip. "The Veil is a dangerous place."

"So people keep telling me."

"Why don't you heed their advice?"

"Because it is too much fun here." She twirled around, letting her dress billow in the warm breeze. "Even though there is danger, the magic and beauty beat it."

Cabyll's eyebrow quirked, a knowing grin tilting upward. "Not because of Prince Dain?"

She smiled shyly, looking at him through her lashes. "No, Dain sometimes forgets me." She purposely pushed her lower lip out in an enticing pout. "I get lonely sometimes."

She refused to admit how her chest tightened saying it out loud.

"I'm sure that's not the case," he bowed. "Whatever is pulling him away must be quite important indeed to stray from your side. Even now, you are glowing with that beautiful dress."

She smiled brightly, her heart skipping. He noticed! "You like it?" She twirled again for good measure.

He laughed, his voice smooth and dark. "How could someone not like it when it is meant to catch the eye?"

Ari fluttered her eyelashes. "I'm glad you think so. Sometimes I feel like Dain's gaze is not even close to where I am."

His gaze grew shrewder, his voice lazily seductive. "Maybe he's simply looking for something?"

"Maybe..." she coyly replied, trying to keep her heart calm.

He stepped forward, rubbing the towel against his neck. He was so close she could reach out and touch him.

She held her breath, her heart beating fast.

He tilted his head. "I could help you know." He lifted the cup again, taking a slow drink. "Whatever he's looking for. More help will relieve the burden so he won't be distracted and can put his attention to where it belongs."

Her breath froze. Did he know something?

He winked, giving a soft chuckle. "Those trade agreements are tricky." He extended his arm toward her.

Her breath escaped in a relieved sigh. Of course, their cover story was for trade. She had almost forgotten as her initial fear of discovery dissolved.

Ari lightly rested her hand on his forearm, finding herself being led around the training yard. It reminded her of the romantic novels she'd bury herself in. When was the last time Dain took her for a stroll? She couldn't remember. She blinked, his patient gaze resting on her, waiting for something. *Oh darn!* She was so focused on him, she forgot he asked a question.

A flush crept up her cheeks. "Sorry! What were you saying?"

"Are you okay? Your face is red."

She lifted her hands up, sputtering. "No, no! I'm fine really. Just the heat."

They stopped for a moment near the edge of perimeter. She found the source of the water she heard earlier. Straight down in a sheer drop, was a spring. The teal green water lapped softly against smooth stones. And right in the center, there was a swimming hole. A very *deep* swimming hole. Ari couldn't figure out how deep it went but the beautiful teal water became dark blue, almost black.

She gulped softly, moving away from the edge slowly.

Cabyll gave a contemplative look, steering the conversation. "I suspect this is a hotter environment than what a human body is used to. Do you need a drink? Has Prince Dain done anything to secure your comfort? Or...anyone from the Council?"

She hunched her shoulders instinctively before forcing a smile. "I'm fine really. Dain has been very great throughout all this. Even when I mess up sometimes."

He grinned. "I cannot imagine you 'messing' anything up. You act as if you are the sun."

She blinked, taken aback, her palms sweaty. Unbidden, she asked. "More so than Lily?"

Cabyll stopped, frozen. "I would not say she is the sun." His playful look shuttered down, turning his gaze away. "I prefer not to talk about her."

She pursed her lips, patting his arm. "I get it. She can be really difficult. You probably had such a hard time with her. I always tried to help her, you know. But, she can't make friends. It's cause she's too serious, she drives everyone away." Her big blue eyes widened in mock pity. "I did everything I could for her, honest. But she always refused to listen because she was jealous of me. I couldn't take how pathetic she was, it was really kinda sad."

His arm tensed under her hand. "Jealous huh?" His gaze was unreadable, boring into her. "And coming here freed you from her?"

She smiled wide, her heart swelling. "You understand."

"More than you know," he murmured, soft but deadly.

Ari's eyes widened. His eyes were swallowing her up. Was he learning forward?! Was he trying to kiss her? Dain faded from her mind as her gaze was centered on the fae before her.

She closed her eyes, waiting.

Abruptly, he turned away, steering her around the training yard, the red swirling sand at the border of their feet. He stopped, a red circle surrounding them and removed his arm. He sighed, pinching his nose. "I can't do this."

Ari frowned, confused. "Um, Cabyll?"

"Don't!" He snapped, running his hand through his hair. He grumbled to himself. "I used to be good at this, what did she do to me?"

"What's going on?" She twisted her hands, a pit settling in her stomach.

He sighed, arms crossed, his playful demeanor gone. "Look, you do not seem to want anyone hurt. So...tell me, is there anything you know about Dain's plan?"

She frowned. "You're not talking about trade, are you?" His silence was her answer. Her nostrils flared. "You want to know about the vessel and the fire, don't you?"

He nodded, resolute, his eyes calculating. "You catch on quick. So... What do you know?"

Why would he be asking her these things? He was so focused on her earlier. What changed? Unless...

She clenched her fists. "Lily forced you into a deal, didn't she?"

Cabyll shook his head. "That's not actually-"

She chewed her thumb, her mind racing. "She tricked you. You would be helping me if it wasn't for *her*!"

He ran his hand through his hair. "Listen, you really..."

Anger boiled inside her, drowning him out. Lily was *still* butting into her life! Here she thought she got away, but no. Now Lily was interfering in other lives, tricking Cabyll into her schemes. How selfish could Lily be?!

Breathing hard, she stepped back trying to calm herself.

He raised his arm out. "Behind you, the sand."

Too late, she stepped into the red pattern. The supposedly *boiling* sand. Cold reality settled in her bones.

Uh – oh...

With a yelp, she tried to jump but her heels catching on the soft granular particles. Her stomach flipped, her arms pinwheeling as the inevitable weightlessness pushed her backward. She gasped, her breath catching as her back met flush against unforgiving ground.

"Don't touch it!" Cabyll's voice muffled over her ringing ears.

Groaning, her hands automatically reached out to regain her balance. She blinked, red sand coating her palms.

"Get up!"

She ignored him, staring at the red grains sifting through her fingers. Any minute she should be burning. But, she wasn't. It was warm, like being wrapped in a heated blanket. And it wasn't unpleasant. Quite the opposite, she could just snuggle into it forever. She wanted to bask in the heat. As it filled her up, so too did her anger.

Cabyll should not be tied down by Lily. He was too good for her! Even now, the fae assassin was making sure she was okay. Could she really say that about Dain? He almost let her be eaten. Twice! He left her alone for days. Cold and lonely. Now, she was warm, powerful, and had the attention she craved.

That she deserved.

A red, orange haze obscured her vision, clouding everything. She was meant to glow, to burn. Strong hands grabbed her shoulders, pulling her up.

"Wake up." A few mumbled words were muffled...something like, "...I promised. She would never forgive me..."

She blinked, the red haze fading. Confused she gazed around her, finding she was back into the shady alcove at the edge of the training grounds. Cabyll was in front of her, holding her shoulders.

"What happened?" She rubbed her head, trying to grasp the faint strand of something that tingled the back of her mind. But it disappeared as another headache formed.

"You touched the red sand. You could have been burned," Cabyll shook his head, frowning. "You should have been burned."

She looked down at her smooth, unblemished hands. No blisters, no burns, nothing marred her skin save for a slight red tint.

"Why did you not burn?" he muttered, echoing her inner thoughts.

"It's none of your business," she snapped, pulling back trying to hide her panic. She had to see Dain, he would know.

She pulled away, ready to leave.

"Wait," he called out.

She turned, the blood pounding heavy in her chest.

He continued, his tone warning. "Lily is worried about you. Be careful when mingling with the high fae."

Her shoulders slumped. *Always Lily. Stupid Lily.*

She shook her head. "Lily isn't worried about me. What she needs to do is stop interfering." She smiled at him, sincere. "But I'm glad you're looking out for me."

He frowned. "That's not-"

A familiar, smooth voice interrupted.

"And what happened here?"

Dain stepped into the arena. She jumped, hurrying over to him. His arms opened as she ran into them. "What happened Ari?"

She laughed awkwardly into his chest. "Nothing. I was clumsy and I fell on the red sand and-"

"The red sand?" His eyebrow raised, his tone sharper. He grabbed her hands, inspecting them. Silently he shared a look with Cabyll. "Why are you not burned?"

She shrugged. "I don't know, guess I was lucky."

"Lucky indeed," he murmured silky. He wrapped his arms around her shoulders, turning her to head back inside. He called over his shoulder. "Well, old friend, I must take Ari back. She should be attended to."

Cabyll nodded, gritting his teeth. "Of course...your highness." He bowed to Ari slightly. "Stay safe."

"Thank you Cabyll," she replied, grateful. She wanted to tell him more, but didn't dare to as Dain's keen eyes were watching.

He nodded silently, then disappeared.

Dain grabbed her hands, whisking her through the various corridors until they arrived back to her room. He ushered her in, slamming the door behind them. He whirled around, his expression intense.

"What happened Ari?" he demanded. "Tell me everything."

She wrung her hands, confused. "I *did* tell you. I fell..."

He waved her off, "Not that. Did you manage to charm Cabyll?"

Disappointment sank into her chest. *Oh...that...*

"He was opening up to me," she began, hesitantly.

"And what did you find out?" he interrupted, impatient.

She kept her eyes down. "Nothing, he stopped talking. I think Lily has him locked in a deal."

She risked a peek at his face.

His face was unreadable. He tapped his chin lazily. "Hmmm... Anything else?"

"No. He was focused on asking what I knew about the fire. I suspect Lily asked him to find out." She pouted, biting her lip at the thought of Lily.

"Wait...he asked that?" He grabbed her roughly, shaking her. "Are you sure?"

She nodded, afraid to say anything else.

"He must know what I'm doing," he mumbled, beginning to pace back and forth. He kept talking to himself. "If that's the case, then my brother must know. Which means they discovered I have the vessel, which means..."

He snapped his fingers, calling out.

"Aput!"

Aput materialized, bowing low. "Yes, your highness."

"It seems my brother and that interfering human are looking for the fire. They need to be stopped at all costs."

Aput nodded. "Yes, your highness."

"They cannot reach the Council," Dain's eyes sharpened, "is that understood?"

Aput's gaze remained on the floor, their antlers tilted forward. "Understood."

Ari grasped Dain's shirt lightly. "Dain!"

She dropped her hand when he turned around, his eyes cold. "Sorry.

But...I found out my brother is with them. At least, I think so." She clasped her hands, pleading. "Can you stop them, just so they don't bother us? Maybe send them back home?"

He blinked, his gaze melting. He smiled softly, patting her head lightly. "Of course, my dear. I personally won't see them come to harm."

She smiled, her shoulders sagging with relief.

Dain ran his hands over her shaking shoulders, giving them a reassuring squeeze. "You must be exhausted. Why don't you get some rest?" He gently turned her around, steering her toward the bed.

She nodded absently, shivering. After the training ground, she was suddenly ice cold. She missed the heat. Her gaze strayed to the cord around Dain's neck holding the vessel. Her brain thumped, the beginnings of a headache. That would make her warm, she just knew it.

She leaned forward. If she could just touch it...

Dain scooped her up in her arms, laying her gently on the bed, dispelling her thoughts as he whispered, "Rest my dear." He gave her a quick peck on her forehead. "I'll take care of everything."

Her eyes drifted shut, the blankets engulfing her. Yes, rest would help. She snuggled into the warmth, burrowing deep. Her mind drifted off, so focused on staying warm that she didn't hear Dain whisper to Aput.

Dain glanced over to find Ari asleep, eyes closed. He peered at her, as if he could uncover her secrets. Why did the red sand not burn her human skin? His eyes narrowed. He would find out, and soon. He ignored the small prick in his chest at her limp form, so still on the bed. Her face, porcelain and pale, practically glowed.

His lips turned downward. She was so fragile. Crossing his arms, he pulled his gaze away, staring out the window in silence. Over his shoulder, he softly commanded. "Aput, get Hunapo and the Maero. I *cannot* have anyone stop me this time."

The Ijiraq protested calmly. "Your highness, are you sure? You know the Maero are unpredictable."

Dain paused, his shoulders trembling as if an invisible force shook him. Aput merely stood still, understanding for what it was. Another vision. Soon the tremors subsided. Dain sighed softly, running his hand through his hair.

"I'm sure," his voice was rough and tired. "Hunapo will not be able to resist fighting a Sentinel."

Aput paused, their voice wary. "A Sentinel?"

Dain kept staring outside. "That human girl had help from the ancient Thunderbird. My current vision says there is a new Sentinel among their ranks. One that I must be wary of. I'm positive they are one and the same."

Aput hummed in thought. "Then you are correct. The Maero won't say no to hunting a Sentinel," their voice deepening in warning. "They live for the hunt."

Dain nodded, his hands clenching behind his back. "Tell Hunapo what you must, but make sure they never make it here."

Aput's soft voice questioned. "Unharmed, correct? You promised Miss Ari."

"I said *I* would personally not see them harmed," Dain paused briefly, his voice calm. "Don't make me 'see' anything."

"Are you sure? Your highness....Dain. Speaking as your old friend, if Miss Ari finds out-" Aput warned.

His flippant tone dissipated, his voice taking a soft growl. "Don't Aput..."

A whispery sigh echoed, the Ijiraq bowed. "As you wish...your highness."

A tinkling sound rang within the room as frost began blanketing the walls. Dain turned back to Aput, his eyes glowing almost white. "It's time to hunt."

Chapter Eighteen

"ARE...WE...ALMOST...THERE?"

Brandon stopped, his hands on his knees, gasping for air.

"Almost, young human. Come on, you are supposed to have energy." Waru jumped a few more rocks, barely breaking a sweat.

Brandon groaned, wiping his nose. "Dude...seriously, I have energy in spades. But now it's washed away after hiking up a mountain for the last few hours. A freaking mountain dude!"

Waru huffed, clearly disappointed. "We will work on your endurance when we return."

Lily held her chuckle as Brandon groaned louder. The big fae had taken Brandon under his wing, determined to turn the young man into a warrior. Last night Brandon thought it was an awesome idea, until his first 'official' training began. Now all he did was complain how bad of an idea it was.

Spyke appeared beside her. "How are you doing Lily?"

She wiped her forehead, the sweat trickling down her back. She hoped her wobbly legs weren't noticeable. "I'm doing okay, but I can empathize with Brandon."

When they left the Menehune village, dragging a woozy Ang, the sun was peaking up over the horizon. Now, it was high overhead, light filtering down through the thick palms of the coconut trees. They were hiking upward for a while, but Lily couldn't gauge how far they walked, or how close they were.

Spyke frowned, his keen gaze taking in her trembling form. He was warring with himself, probably on whether to stop.

She completely understood. Even now time was slipping away faster than sand through fingers. The last thing she wanted was to be a burden. The fae were not winded, if you didn't count Ang's blurry eyes. By comparison, the humans sported pink, sweaty cheeks and soaked shirts. The differences were stark.

"It's okay Spyke." She held up her hands. "Scout's honor." She crossed her fingers, hoping to reassure him.

He frowned, scratching his head. "What does a scout have to do with this?"

Ang pushed past him, rolling her eyes. "Forget it, you wouldn't understand. If Lily says she's fine, she's fine. If she wasn't, she'd tell us." She gave a side-glance. "Right sissy?"

Lily smiled, ignoring the small prick of guilt. "Yes, I would."

Ang nodded. "Then it's squared. Let's keep going." She lightly punched Brandon's shoulder as she continued on. "Get moving slow poke!"

"Am not!" Brandon yelled back, pouting. But that lit a fire as he brushed himself off to run after her.

Waru put his hands on his hips. "Do not fret humans. We should reach our destination soon."

He paused, before giving a loud cough. "Oh…" another bigger, exaggerated cough, "it seems like I need to take a breath as well. Maybe we should rest a moment?"

Spyke palmed his face. Lily covered her lips, hiding her smile. She nudged his shoulder. "Gotta give him points for trying right?"

He groaned before reluctantly agreeing. "True."

She cupped her mouth. "We're good Waru, but we appreciate the gesture."

Waru straightened up, his ailment miraculously cured. "Then let's be off!"

Lily laughed, running to catch up with Brandon. His reddened cheeks were glossy with sweat. She fished out her canteen and handed it over. "Here, you need to drink."

"Thanks Lil." He gulped the cold water down greedily. He sighed, wiping his mouth. "I hope we get there soon."

She nodded, refusing to bring up that they still had to get back to the Council after this.

One problem at a time girl. Just focus on what you can do right now.

Waru's voice echoed ahead sharply, past a canopy of ferns that lay ahead on the path. "Watch your step."

She pushed through the ferns, the path opening. Her eyes widened as she jumped back. "What the-"

The view revealed a sharp cliff dropping down into a canyon, the jungle canopy below. In front, Waru stood at the edge of a rope bridge which arched above the canopy, connecting to the other side of the jungle ravine. The soft trilling of birds echoed through the treetops as the wind rocked the makeshift bridge slightly.

Lily gulped, unable to move.

Waru, already halfway across the bridge, called out. "The bridge is fine. Keep moving."

She stared down, unable to see the bottom. Only dense foliage filled her vision. She bit her lip, her chest tightening. Her feet refused to move.

Yeah...nope. Why heights? I HATE heights! If I was a bird, heights would be great, but I wasn't born a bird, was I? Nope I wasn't!

Brandon's brow furrowed, worried. "Hey Lil, you okay?"

She swallowed, distracted by the view. Was the sky getting fuzzy? "Um, yeah...sure..."

Merda! Move feet...move!

A warm presence appeared at Lily's frozen side.

Spyke leaned down with a whisper, his voice encouraging. "It'll be alright Lily. Look forward, and don't look down." He nodded to Ang, who stayed back with Brandon. "Can you take the rear?"

Ang nodded back, keeping her arms crossed. Spyke moved past Lily and stepped onto the bridge. He moved a few feet inward before turning back.

"I'll be right here," his voice was low and soothing. "You can do this."

Lily took a breath, trying to remain calm. *Easier said than done...*

"Just focus on me," he insisted.

She grasped the rope tightly, taking another deep breath through her

212

nose. Her feet were still leaden, but she slowly began to step onto the bridge.

One step...two steps.

Her brain went to autopilot as she slowly made her way forward. Every time she got close to Spyke, he'd move further away, forcing her to keep moving. He grinned, speaking randomly about the birds, the weather, many other things that meant nothing. Normally, she would be smiling at the big hulking warrior talking about little birds. That is, if she wasn't so petrified that beneath her feet was nothing but air.

With clenched knuckles, she managed to shuffle herself halfway onto the bridge. Waru was already on the other side, scouting ahead. Lily envied that. How did he get there so fast? Did he skip across?

Behind her, there was scuffling. She hadn't felt bridge move. What was going on? Maybe Ang was giving her time, which she appreciated. Just when she started to breathe a sigh of relief, that's when Brandon spoke.

"Oh..." his voice dropped. "This is L..."

Lily frowned. If Brandon was saying that, something was wrong. Spyke's eyes widened as he slowly pulled his club from behind his back. He reached out his hand, motioning to her.

"Lily, I hate to rush you, but-"

Her heart stuttered, afraid to turn around. "What's happening?"

A loud roar came from behind.

Merda...

Ang cried out, "Run Brandon! Get over the bridge!"

Lily's body shook as the bridge moved. She clutched the ropes tighter to keep steady, the frayed edges digging into her palms. Brandon footsteps got louder as he got closer. She risked a glance over her shoulder.

Brandon was coming in...fast, his eyes wide with panic.

Her breath shortened. "What happened?"

Brandon gulped. "I heard like...a cry in the bushes. I thought someone was hurt."

He reached her as another roar thundered behind them. He flinched, clenching his eyes.

"Brandon!" Lily shouted, jostling him.

"I thought someone was hurt Lil. Honest!"

His pleading eyes were desperate as he repeated. "I didn't play a prank. I went to help and then this thing came out-"

Another roar combined with a pained grunt had Lily trying to look over Brandon's shoulder.

"No Lil!" Brandon tugged her back to focus on him. "We have to keep going!"

His panic fueled her. She pushed around him and her mouth gaped open.

Ang was guarding the bridge, her feet splayed in a defensive stance. She swayed back and forth, unsteady, holding her side. Her gritted face was caked with blood, rivulets running down her neck and side. Her steely gaze centered on the creature that towered over her.

Lily froze. The noise around her muffled until all she could hear was a high-pitched ringing.

It stood about eight feet tall. Standing on two feet, the creature was humanoid, but covered in massive blue-black fur. Its large hands and bare feet sported wicked claws. A tattered loincloth draped around its waist.

Wicked yellow, sharp teeth gleamed in the light, dripping steaming saliva. Prominent ears and a mane of blue-black hair ran down its back. Red eyes glowed menacingly at them. To Lily, it looked like a weird werewolf. Did they have werewolves here? She shook her head. At this point she couldn't rule anything out.

The creature's lip curled as another growl reverberated in its chest.

Ang hissed back, but her unsteady legs made her intimidation tactic a fail. Lily moved forward, but stopped when the changeling barked.

"Lil...if you don't move, I swear I'll not bathe for a week and sleep in your bed!"

She blinked, struck by the absurdity. *Okay...noted...*

Spyke yelled at them from the other side of the bridge. "Lily! Brandon! Hurry! She cannot hold the Kaupe for long."

The what?

"No need to tell me twice," grumbled Brandon, as he ran across the bridge at a breakneck pace.

Lily didn't take a step, still in a state of shock.

Spyke pulled Brandon up onto the ridge and Lily was still on the bridge.

"Lil?!" Ang yelled over her shoulder. The creature tried to get onto the bridge, its eyes laser focused on the humans. It kept pushing Ang to the side, but she held on desperately. "Normally I'd be touched by your sentimentality," she gritted out. "But, now is *not* the time! Get...your butt...in gear or so help me!"

Lily turned back, but the movement was too quick. The height loomed over her, her head spinning. Bile rose up in her throat, her heart stuttering, vertigo rising. She had to walk, but fear took root. When the acid rose up into her throat, the Kaupe frantically sniffed before giving a bone chilling howl.

She shivered, dots pebbling her skin. It was the kind of howl that predators gave when finding a tasty prey. Her fear rose, and with it the howling increased.

"What's happening?" Brandon asked.

"Kaupe thrive on fear." Spyke projected his voice, commanding. "Focus on other emotions! Do not let fear rule you."

Her eye twitched. *Seriously?!*

"Totally get it. Not afraid here," quipped Brandon.

She ignored them, focusing on the task in front of her. She clenched her hands as the bridge swayed. The Kaupe howled again against Ang's grunting. She flinched, halting as cold realization set in.

Oh...it must be me. Can't have one fear to myself can I?

Her feet were lead, heavy and bulky. She grunted, stepping forward, her thighs trembling. At the rate she was going, she'd never make it. A voice echoed in her brain, but it wasn't her own inner voice.

What are you, deaf? It's one foot in front of the other. Get going!

Cabyll's deep voice reverberated in her brain. Why was she thinking of him now?!

"Jerk," she grumbled, gritting her teeth.

Regardless, his snarky tone got her angry. Even if it was by sheer defiance to prove to the imaginary Cabyll she could do it, the progress she made across the bridge was significantly faster than a few seconds ago. She crossed over the halfway mark, desperately trying to ignore the animalistic grunts and howls behind her. Brandon's voice reached out to her.

"You're almost there Lil. Just a little more!"

She let out a long breath. Looking up, Spyke's encouraging gaze filled her with hope. She was going to make it! Then, his eyes widened slightly.

Oh no...that can't be good.

A pained howl raised goosebumps along her arms. That wasn't the Kaupe. Brandon's panicked cry struck Lily's heart. She whipped around.

Ang fell to the ground, bleeding heavily. The Kaupe stood over her, its chest heaving. She blinked, her brain not catching up.

Ang?

She must have made a noise, as the creature's gaze snapped up to meet hers. Its frothy maul trembled, its long fangs glistening, and its red eyes gleamed with an evil mirth.

Everyone screamed behind her.

For a brief moment, the shock blossomed into a cold fire. She contemplated pulling out her bow and shooting right between its eyes. Her fingers itched, leaving the rope.

Cabyll's voice pierced into her rage.

Not now human! Are you dumb? Run!

Dropping her hand, she turned and ran. Her arms pumped, her sluggish blood slowly moving through the anger and fear. She zeroed on Spyke's outstretched hand.

Almost there...

With a snarl, the Kaupe leapt onto the bridge. Lily collapsed, the bridge swaying dangerously. Splinters cut into her knees and palms as she hit the floorboards hard, gasping as her stomach dropped. Spyke's grunt cut through the hazy panic.

"Hold on!"

She blinked. The bridge heaved upward, her feet scraping to keep purchase as the canyon yawned below. Her arms trembled, fingers biting into the wood as the ravine filled her vision. Everything went sideways.

She held on desperately, her knuckles white. At this rate, she'd die by falling off the bridge. Her fear mounted, staring at the dark canopy of trees underneath her. The bridge swayed back to the center, the force of weightlessness punching her in the stomach.

The Kaupe's footsteps approached, its claws scraping the wood while the growling transformed into an evil snicker.

The Cabyll voice yelled in her head again.

Did you have memory loss? They like fear. Stop being afraid!

"Easier said than done," she mumbled to herself. She must be dying. That was the only way she could rationalize she was talking to herself and an imaginary Cabyll. She would kick him when she saw him.

If she saw him...

"What are you guys doing? Can't you go get her?" screamed Brandon.

"The bridge is close to collapsing young one. If we go out there, we'll all fall to our deaths," Waru replied. He yelled out, "Young Sentinel! Just move a few more feet forward and jump. We will catch you!"

Brandon protested. "Are you crazy dude?! Can't you see she's terrified and you're telling her to jump?! Against a monster that gets power boosts from fear?"

Waru barked back, "What else can we do? She can't stay put."

Spyke's calm voice cut through. "Lily...focus on me." Her eyes jerked up to meet his. He nodded, sincere yet earnest. "I won't let you fall."

Nodding back, she grasped onto the rope. With a grunt, she lifted herself up, shaking madly. The bridge kept swinging, but it was lessening. Her heart thudded, her chest heaving. She tensed, ready to jump.

A sinister chuckle breathed hot against her neck.

Oh no...please no...

Gulping, she looked up...and up.

The Kaupe stood above her, snickering. Saliva dripped off its fangs as it leaned toward her throat.

Lily gulped, the vein in her neck pulsing against her throat. Her brain told her to kick it between the legs, but her body wouldn't move.

She clenched her eyes shut, waiting for the chomp. But...the Kaupe's long fangs didn't sink into her neck. Instead, a pained whine filled the air.

Hesitant, she cracked one eye open. The Kaupe flinched, wiping its eyebrow, as a cut began to form. A rock rolled off the bridge. She heard Brandon whooping, yelling at Waru to throw another one. Her brain kept yelling at her to get going, but the red eyes held her in place. It was weirdly reminiscent of Oktena, which was not a fond memory.

The Kaupe's nostrils flared, its growl promising retribution to the others across the bridge. It was that arrogance that flipped something in Lily.

She growled back.

It recoiled, surprised. And it was that precious moment Lily needed as a high-pitched warrior whoop tickled her ears.

"*Hakaka!!*"

Suddenly, two little figures fell onto the Kaupe's head, pushing its ears over its piercing eyes. She shook her head, not really believing it. Pika and Peni clung to the Kaupe's furry ears, pounding on anything their fists could reach. The Kaupe grunted, stunned. Lily wasted no time.

She kicked between its legs.

It howled in pain, stumbling forward.

"Poke its eyes Pika!"

"Did you just shove a stick in its nose Peni?"

"Focus Pika!"

"*Akau!* You got it!"

Peni caught Lily's eyes. "Go Sentinel! We'll hold him off." The little Menehune saluted, holding tight like he was riding a bucking bronco.

She nodded, beginning to run, but a familiar weightlessness caught her.

"Uh-oh," said Pika.

"That crazy Kaupe is suicidal! He's cutting the bridge," shouted Peni. "Jump!"

She tensed, the bridge falling beneath her. She had no choice. Holding her breath, she jumped.

She reached out for Spyke's hand. Her stomach flew up to her throat as gravity took hold. Her eyes squeezed shut as she began to fall, images of smashing into trees passing before her eyes.

A large hand engulfed her wrist, a deep grunt thundering above her. Her breath caught before she slammed into rough dirt, any remaining air whooshing out of her lungs. Spyke grunted again.

"I got you, Lily."

Her stomach scraped against the side of the cliff as Spyke lifted her to safety. She gasped as thin arms encircled her. Brandon sniffed into her hair, his arms shaky.

"Lil?" He whispered brokenly. "You okay? Please...tell me you're okay."

She patted his back, willing her heart to slow. "I'm okay, promise." She jerked back, finding Spyke and Waru. "But Ang? And the Menehune. What about them?"

Waru pointed across the broken bridge. Lily squinted as the hazy figure of the Menehune came into view. They were flying. Her eyes narrowed.

Flying?

As they came in closer, they weren't flying per se. They held their hats, the updraft lifting and carrying them over the canyon. They gripped Ang between them, drifting across the chasm.

Lily breathed a sigh of relief as the Menehune landed safely, Ang lying prone on the ground.

"Waru, see to the changeling," ordered Spyke.

Waru nodded, pulling out something from his clothes and leaning over Ang.

Pika and Peni dusted themselves off, giving each other high fives.

Pika snickered, making air jabs. "Did you see how I punched that Kaupe in the eye?"

Peni snorted. "That's nothing. I poked his eardrums. The amount of gunk in those ears would have made even the stoutest warrior cry."

"Guys...you were awesome!" Brandon held up his hand for another round of high fives, laughing. The Menehune lifted their noses proudly.

"You won't be seeing that dog anytime soon," remarked Peni.

Pika nodded. "Yeah. He tucked his tail between his legs as he fell off the side."

A faint, angry howl rose behind them. Everyone froze, slowly turning.

A large, clawed hand appeared on the cliff's edge.

Lily's mouth dropped.

Is this some horror movie where the bad guy doesn't die?!

Peni and Pika paused, taking in the claws. They gulped, walking back.

"Um...I...I think this calls for a retreat," stammered Peni.

"Yup, time to run," agreed Pika.

Spyke's muscles bunched, his body zeroed in on the cliff. "Waru, how far?"

Waru easily picked up Ang, slinging her over his shoulders in a fireman carry. "Not far."

Spyke called over his shoulder. "We need to go."

"We could take it," Waru growled in protest.

"Remember the mission," he snapped. "Protect the humans."

Waru paused, then rolled his eyes. "You are right." He cast a backward glance at the cliff, a look similar to regret. "But it would have been fun." Without another word, he took off with Ang into the foliage.

Lily shook her head, frustration pooling in her belly. Fun? There was nothing *fun* about this.

Peni and Pika clapped their hands together, needing no encouragement. The two took off in a blink after Waru.

The angry grunt grew louder, dirt crumbling away from the edge. Another clawed hand burst upward, grasping the ground, large furrows digging into the earth. Lily and Brandon remained behind Spyke, who still stood guard.

Lily reached back to grab her bow. "Brandon, go!'

Spyke spoke behind his shoulder, cautioning. "This is not the time Lily. Get ready when I give the word."

"What's the word?" asked Brandon, clutching his hands.

The jungle was silent, not even the birds sung. Everything held their breath.

Spyke's chest heaved, his muscles straining.

"Now!"

He did a backflip, the soft earth breaking under the pressure. Lily's mouth opened as the fae soared about their heads, landing effortlessly behind them. She coughed as his large arms wrapped around both of them, lifting them on each of his shoulders. Before she could respond, Spyke turned, sprinting.

Instantaneously, the Kaupe soared in the air, landing on the ground where Spyke had been. Its eyes shooting daggers at Lily. She gripped Spyke's shoulder tighter.

The creature roared in anger, bending over on all fours, chasing after them.

Fronds hit Lily's face, the emerald trees a blur. She gasped, her stomach slamming against Spyke's shoulder. Her bow was still out, bouncing against his back.

Gritting her teeth, she pulled the bow as high as she could, trying to keep steady. Brandon was panicking at her side, yelling things she couldn't make out. Spyke must have felt what she was doing, his voice ringing out.

"Let it fly Lily!"

She bit her lip, trying to focus but failing. The Kaupe took up her entire vision, the bouncing movement making her eyes tear up. *Just please hit something!* She pulled the arrow back and, not focusing, just let it go.

Luck must have been on her side. The Kaupe skittered to the side, hitting a tree, a pained howl piercing her ears. Savage pride filled her.

Take that you piece of –

Brandon tapped her, pointing. "Ah...Lil. I think you just made it angry. It's coming faster."

He was right. She may have slowed it down, but it was catching up, and fast. Its red eyes practically glowed in rage...at her. Its howl grew so loud it pierced her eardrums. She flinched as she desperately held onto her bow, unable to cover her ears.

Brandon clapped his hands on his head, his voice warbled. "Spyke dude? Are we close to wherever we need to be? Or like can you smash it?"

Spyke grunted, his legs pumping. "Almost there..."

Lily felt, rather than saw, when they reached wherever "it" was. It was like being pushed through Jell-O as a gelatinous pressure skated over her skin. She held her breath, just in case.

When she finally took a breath, Spyke skidded to a stop with a jerk. Her lips paled.

Because the Kaupe didn't stop.

She pushed Spyke's shoulder, her panic flaring. "Ah...Spyke? It's not stopping."

A flash of fang and red engulfed her vision as the Kaupe launched itself at them.

But instead of colliding, the Kaupe slammed against something. It yelped in pain, its face smushed, before sliding down. Lily frowned. What is that? A force field?

Cautiously, she reached out, one finger extended. It hit something, the air shimmering. Her lips pursed. Wait...it was an invisible wall.

The Kaupe howled in rage, shaking its head. It paced back and forth, looking up and down, trying to find a way in.

A calm voice spoke out behind them.

"Do not worry. It cannot enter."

Lily turned around and gasped.

Chapter Nineteen

SUNLIGHT BROKE THROUGH THE TREES IN SCATTERED BEAMS. Large, gnarled branches reached up through the canopy, framing a beautiful tropical pool of stunning turquoise water. Several small waterfalls rushed down in various levels, one stacked atop the other, to cascade into the pool. The water rushed to the side to indicate another waterfall below, out of Lily's sight. She backed up, the view was stunning.

"Don't get too close," the voice warned.

Lily jumped, the Kaupe standing behind her. It slammed against the barrier again, frustrated.

The voice continued, amused. "I understand you have business with me."

She blinked, turning around. Her gaze focused away from the striking scenery to the even more impressive fae before her. She rubbed her eyes to make sure she wasn't imagining things. Unicorns? The impossible existed in the Veil, but *unicorns*?

Upon closer inspection, the fae before her was sadly not a unicorn. It was hard not to compare since the fae sported a large horn that reminded Lily of the fantasy creatures she loved as a little girl.

The fae was female, her soft features surrounded by waves of golden blonde hair with gradient caramel tresses. Her upper body was humanoid while her lower body was a cream-colored horse. Her beautiful face was dusted with a blend of cream, caramel, and blonde fur. That same fur dusted all over skin that wasn't covered by a dark brown tunic. Lily would have thought she was a centaur, but centaurs didn't have horns in the middle of their foreheads. A beautiful ivory horn was centered above doe-like golden eyes.

Those eyes fixated on Lily, smiling at her in mirth.

"You have never met one of my kind, have you human?"

Lily shook her head, afraid to speak. She didn't want to offend anyone. Especially someone that had a sharp horn, heavy hooves, and weapons strapped to their back, the curve of a bow and wickedly pointed arrows peeking out over her shoulder.

The fae tilted her head, tufted ears flickering. "My apologies, I should have addressed you appropriately, young Sentinel."

Flustered, Lily put her hands up. "Oh, that's okay..."

"You may call me Isa," supplied the fae, her smile returning.

Lily smiled back, ignoring the shocked faces around her.

Waru coughed, interrupting them. "Forgive us Anggitay. If you know who the Sentinel is, then you must know why we've come."

Isa pawed the ground, her dark brown hooves digging into the dirt. A breeze blew, shaking the leaves. Her ears twitched outward.

"The Emerara has been whispering," she replied, her lip turning downward. "Do you not think that your tromping and traipsing in the Emerara was subtle? Did you not think it would not speak to me?"

Waru bowed his head. "You are correct Anggitay. Can you help us?"

Isa snorted, crossing her arms. "I do not help, you know this. Not even with his highness. I bargain." Her gaze returned to Lily, a soft smile forming. "Though for the young Sentinel, I could be persuaded."

It didn't escape Lily's notice the difference in how Isa spoke between her and Waru. While Isa seemed kind, an eager glint shone in those doe eyes. Maybe it was her imagination, but they seemed a little too eager. Perhaps a little...hungry. It was unnerving. She clocked the wariness in Waru's stance, his eyes following Isa's every step. His eyes caught hers over Isa's shoulder. His head gave the barest hint of a shake, warning her.

Tim's voice whispered faintly in her thoughts.

Be careful...

Her eyebrow went up. *So NOW you talk to me?*

Tim responded reluctantly. *The encounter you had with Namaka made me weak. I couldn't reach you until now.*

She winced, embarrassed. *Oh...I'm sorry. I didn't know.*

The Thunderbird's thoughts warmed her. *You are still learning. Remember, I am tied to your soul. It takes practice and control. Now...I need to continue to rest. Remember what I said. Be careful with this Anggitay.*

As the warmth left her, Lily chose her words carefully.

"It is an honor Isa. Truly, it is. Though I am merely a human, I will adhere to the rules of the-" she paused, glancing at Waru, "Emerara?"

He nodded imperceptibly. She let out a small sigh of relief.

Isa cocked her head, assessing the group. Her doe eyes were unreadable, black and limitless. "You are a very polite human. I approve."

With a quick turn, she called out to the waterfall. "Hari...come out!"

A growl vibrated the trees before a large rustling parted the ferns above the waterfall. Out from the jungle, emerged a panther.

"Duuuude..." Brandon breathed out.

With an uncanny stillness, it stood motionless at the top of the waterfall. Watching them. The animal was a cross between a few creatures, the most prominent she could identify was a panther. Its dark, brown body was broad, almost bearlike. It sported a sleek lion type mane.

Lily shuddered. The most unnerving thing was not the creature's massive size, but the milky white eyes that stared back at her.

Isa called again, "Come here Hari, we have guests." She turned back with a small smile. "We must properly greet them."

The creature growled low, its massive muscles bunching. Hari dropped down lightly, the water splashing around his gigantic paws.

"A Glawackus," breathed Spyke, his eyebrows furrowed. "So that is how the memories are taken."

He quickly closed his eyes, gesturing to Lily and Brandon to do the same. "Close your eyes."

"A what?" asked Brandon.

"I said, close your eyes!" he snapped.

Isa's laugh rang out. "Oh, there is no need for that. Hari can control his power."

Hesitant, Spyke opened his eyes. He remained in front of Lily and Brandon, putting himself between them and the Glawackus.

"Oh, how cute," replied Isa. "Do not worry warrior, I'm here for business."

Spyke crossed his arms, his voice resolute. "I'm fine where I am."

Isa shrugged. "To answer your question little human," she continued, motioning to Brandon. "A Glawackus is a unique creature that has the power to steal memories."

Hari came up to her, rubbing against her side, purring. "Glawackus have been given a terrible reputation and were driven out of all the territories."

She glanced at Lily while she scratched Hari's chin gently, cooing. "Poor thing, he came to me as a cub. Lonely, without a home or a family. So...we became family."

"And you taking in a Glawackus had nothing to do with your love of shiny things and he can remove any memory of taking what you want?" Spyke asked drily.

Waru coughed, hitting his chest.

Isa kept stroking Hari's fur. "Be careful with your insults, warrior," her voice took a dangerous edge. "I may love beautiful and shiny things, but I strive to keep a code unlike my birth family. And you do not have the time to barter words with me."

Waru took a deep breath. "Can you help us Anggitay?"

Hari purred again, butting against her hand. Isa cooed again, scratching his ears, unperturbed. The group waited, holding their breath, before a pair of high-pitched voices rang out.

"Oh man did you see that Kaupe fall on his face?"

"He is fuming." snickered the other.

Peni and Pika entered the lagoon, laughing merrily together. They paused, taking in the group.

Peni waved. "Hey Isa!"

"You're looking furiously fiiiine." Pika snapped his fingers, giving her a wink. "Get it? Fur?"

Lily gaped. What was Pika thinking?!

Isa remained quiet, but her doe eyes twitched. She gritted out softly, "You two..."

"Yup. Us two!" Pika replied proudly. He smoothed his hat, clearing his throat. "What a coincidence we're here. You, me-"

"You're helping this group?" Isa interrupted; her eyebrow raised.

"Uh...Pika," Peni warned. He tugged at his brother's arm.

"Yup!" replied Pika, ignoring him. "And how lucky we're here. Its fate don't you think? I just knew you couldn't forget about us, together, by the shore."

Isa simply stared, pawing the ground.

Lily wanted to palm her face, silently begging. *Read the room Pika.*

Pika continued, his eyes dreamy. "Why don't we spend some time together by the coconut grove?"

Peni put his hands up, placating. "Forgive him Isa. He really didn't mean to play that prank on Hari, honest."

Pika frowned, confused. "But he looked awesome in blue."

Hari growled, bending down as he slowly stalked the oblivious Menehune.

"Pika!" Peni warned, elbowing him in the gut. He bowed hastily. "We're really sorry to interrupt."

Isa held up her hand, stopping Hari from pouncing.

Peni continued. "We'll keep an eye out for the Kaupe while you talk with these folks. They are really nice, honest."

With a tug on Pika's arm, they disappeared as Pika yelled out, "Don't forget. Meet me later my sweet, beautiful doe!"

Isa patted Hari's head a moment, halting him from going after the brothers. She sighed. "That fool. If he weren't so innocent, I'd have Hari snack on him."

Waru coughed politely. "Apologies Anggitay. But back to the issue at hand."

Isa shook her head. "I can do what you ask," she paused, "for a price of course."

Waru nodded, fishing something from his satchel. "His highness prepared a gift to bargain."

"*Not* from him." She waved her hand. Her gaze centered on Lily. "But we could make a bargain little Sentinel. What do you say?"

Lily blinked, pointing to herself. "Me?" What did she have? She had nothing. Absolutely nothing.

A greedy glint twinkled in Isa's eyes. "I've never bargained with a Sentinel before."

Lily rubbed her temples, counting to ten. Anger and shame gurgled up her throat.

What is up with this whole Sentinel thing?

So far, she needed help from drowning, from being eaten by monsters, and almost falling off a bridge. There was this expectation with the title of 'Sentinel' that she was something huge. But she wasn't. She wasn't bitten by some radioactive animal, dumped in a tank full of chemicals, or even hit with cosmic rays. She was just her. Plain, ordinary, Lily. And, quite frankly, she was getting exhausted by all the pressure.

"Is it a big deal to bargain with me?" she asked warily.

Isa clapped her hands. "Not with you by yourself no. But," she flipped her hair braid over her shoulder, "it is your role as a Sentinel."

She lazily tapped her fingers on Hari's head. "You see, I'm a collector of sorts. I want to obtain the most beautiful, the rarest, things I can find. A high fae prince's memories is a pretty rare item."

Her eyes burned, greed overshadowing. "So, I must have an equivalent in order to return it."

Lily frowned, already not liking where this was headed. "And how could I do that?"

"I've never made a bargain with a Sentinel. They stay on their side of the Veil, guarding your world. And even in my rare encounters with them, they would never even entertain a bargain."

Lily bit her lip. *Probably cause they're too smart.*

But she found herself asking anyways. "Why?"

Isa smiled, her teeth too white. "Because they knew better."

Lily smacked her lips. Yup, she knew it.

Isa leaned forward. The scent of cloves, sandalwood, and spices wafted across Lily's nose causing it to wiggle.

Isa giggled.

Lily pinched her nose, her eyes closed. "And why do you think I would then?"

"Because you're desperate," she replied, very matter of fact.

Lily could kick herself, because Isa was right. What other choice did she have? They needed Prince Kye's memories and they were running out of time.

"One lesson to remember when you're in the Emerara little one." Isa's eyes were bottomless, a black abyss that sent shivers down Lily's spine. "Sacrifices must be made. Whether it is your body or mind, you lose a piece of yourself to gain something when you're within Emerara's heart."

Lily's teeth ground together. This was a bad idea. A really bad idea.

But what other choice did she have?

Sighing, she replied, "What do you want?"

Lily ignored the triumphant gleam in Isa's expression. It was hard, really hard. But she buried the anger and frustration, focusing on the task at hand.

Isa clapped her hands excitedly. "You are just the sweetest." She trotted a moment, her tail flickering as she pondered. "Now...what do I want," she mumbled.

The pregnant pause filled the glade. No one spoke, no one moved, not even a purr from Hari.

Lily shuffled side to side, the suspense killing her. What would Isa choose? She hoped it didn't involve her organs, first born child, or something else creepy. She fingered the ribbon in her hair, a gift from Ari, absently. It had grown into a nervous habit since her stepsister left.

Isa gaze followed her hand. Her eyes gleamed, greedy and eager. "That!"

Lily looked up, confused. "What?"

She pointed hungrily at the ribbon in Lily's curls. "I want that."

Lily paused, her fingers grazing over the silk. She knew mentally that was easy. It *should* be easy. It was just a ribbon. Not her life or a body part. Easy peasy.

But...it wasn't.

It was the only thing Ari had given her in genuine kindness. It helped ground her, center her. It reminded her how kind Ari could be. That they were sisters. As silly as it sounded, that scrap of cheap silk meant so much more.

Isa seemed to notice her hesitation. Her eyes eagerly ran over Lily, almost with a manic glint. "Are you unsure? Do you not want to bargain?"

229

Everyone stared at Lily. The pressure was thick, pressing down on her. She clenched her fists, her face flushed. Why was it always up to her?

A warm hand grabbed hers, another fell on her shoulder.

Startled she looked up. Brandon held her hand, giving her an encouraging look. "You're not alone Lil."

Spyke's large hand warmed her shoulder, his smile supportive. "Yes, you do not have to do this if you do not want to." His gaze hardened on Isa. "We can always retrieve the memories another way."

Ang coughed behind them, clutching her side. "Yeah, what he said."

Lily's heart warmed, settling in a steady rhythm. With just those words of support, her hesitation melted. She stepped forward, undoing the ribbon, her curls falling around her face. Clutching the scrap of fabric, she marveled that it was lighter than she thought it would be.

"Here you go," she said, holding out the ribbon toward Isa.

Isa reached out, eager, but Lily pulled back slightly.

"I'd like to ask for one more thing." She gestured over to Ang, who was breaking out in a clammy sweat. "Can you heal her?"

Isa's ears went back in confusion. "You want the changeling healed?"

She nodded.

Isa shook her head. "The ribbon is not enough for both. I would need something else." A sly glint stole over her. "A memory perhaps?"

Hari purred louder, his tail flickering.

Lily balked, holding her first instinct to run.

Isa clucked her tongue, pinching her fingers together. "Just a small one."

Ang coughed again, protesting. "Lil! Don't be stupid. She could take any memory she wants. I don't deserve it."

Lily bit her lip, her brain swirling. Ang was pale and sweaty, struggling to stay upright. She clearly needed help. Resolved, she straightened her shoulders. "If we agree to a memory, it's one that I am willing to give. I will be aware what I give you."

"Lil!" snarled Ang. "What are you doing?"

"Yes, this isn't necessary," protested Spyke. He gestured to Waru. "Can't you heal her?"

Waru, unmoving, shrugged his shoulders. "The Sentinel is speaking

230

warrior." His face remained emotionless, assessing her. "What will you decide young human?"

Brandon squeezed her hand, keeping quiet. It was all the encouragement she needed.

"A memory of my choosing Isa," she repeated.

Isa tapped her chin, sharing a look with Hari who purred deeply. She nodded. "This is acceptable with us. What are you willing to part with? It must be a worthy memory."

Lily took a moment, thinking. Isa wouldn't accept a mundane memory like a trip to the grocery store. She also didn't want to give a memory involving a person because what if Isa wiped out all her memories of that person. She wracked her brain. What could she part with? Her memories made her who she was.

An idea formed, small but growing. Her eyes cleared. *Maybe that one...*

Silently, she walked up to Isa, gesturing her to lean down. Curious, Isa leaned forward. She cupped her hands, whispering into the Anggitay's ears.

Isa's eyes widened, her lips parting. She reared back, her ears twitching. "Are you sure young Sentinel?"

She nodded. "Can you please heal Ang first."

Isa shared a look with Hari again. With a wave, she gestured Ang forward to the pool.

Stumbling, the changeling hit the water, falling to her knees with a loud splash. Her eyes were shuttered, her body swaying.

Isa circled her, chanting softly. The water glistened and swirled around them. Water droplets rose, dancing across Ang's skin.

Lily gasped. The water beads were stitching and cleaning off the wounds. The wounds were still visible, but they had healed significantly until only a thin red line remained.

Isa inhaled deeply, her shoulders relaxing. "The pool helps somewhat, but I'm afraid any poison or infection from the Kaupe's claws is another matter. This is the best I could do," she admitted sadly. "She still needs attention, but she's better than she was. She will be fine as long as she gets to a healer."

The changeling stood, giving an audible sigh of relief. Soon, a scowl graced her face as she came back to Lily as she barked out. "You're too nice!" She flicked her finger at Lily's forehead.

Ignoring her, Lily and Brandon threw themselves at the changeling, wrapping their arms around her. Startled, Ang stood a moment, before hesitantly patting their backs.

"You're both hopeless," she mumbled, burying her head in their necks.

Lily grinned, replying with a whisper. "We're in this together sis."

Ang, silent, clutched her tighter.

Lily knew without a doubt, at that moment, it was worth it. She whispered again. "You smell terrible."

Ang chuckled softly. "You're such a germ fanatic."

A voice cut in. "Eh em..."

Isa motioned Lily toward the pool. "Now for your end of the bargain."

Ang held Lily tighter, a soft snarl forming.

Lily patted her arm. "It's okay," she whispered. Ang shook her head, but reluctantly let go.

Lily walked to the pool, the water caressing her ankles. It was warm, pleasant.

Isa stood tall, her tail whipping back and forth. Her hand reached out. "The ribbon?"

Her curls cut into her eyes, the wind dancing them around her face, but she ignored it. With a calm she didn't know she possessed, she dropped the ribbon into Isa's grasp.

Isa clutched the silk, taking a large sniff. Pleased she tucked it into her satchel. Wordlessly she motioned for Hari to move forward.

With an almost gentle tone, she said, "Just stare into Hari's eyes. Do not fight him. It hurts less when you do not fight."

"Will it hurt?" Lily asked.

Isa's sympathetic gaze confirmed Lily's fears. "It will not be easy. You will not remember what you lost, but you will remember you chose this. You will remember that you chose which memory to give. And remember why you chose to do this." Her head tilted slightly. "I do not give this grace easily Sentinel, but I have grown fond of you in this short time."

"I appreciate it Isa," she responded genuinely.

232

Breathing deep, she closed her eyes to prepare. Knowing she couldn't delay it further, she shook herself. "Okay, I'm ready.

When she opened her eyes, Hari's milky white eyes caught hers, unblinking. They began to glow as a cloudy gray mist emerged, blanketing over her. The mist fractured, strands spiraling around Lily. The strands circled around, until they reached into her ears and eyes. It tickled, like a feather brushing against the shell of her ear.

Lily breathed in audible relief. Maybe this wouldn't be as bad as she thought.

That was before she felt the tug.

It was a soft tug, a pull no stronger than a baby lightly pulling your finger. Then it grew. And grew and grew. The strands wormed their way in her head, slithering and sliding. The tugging increased, the memory unwilling.

Lily winced, trying to remind herself why she was doing this.

It's okay. This is for Ang. I can part with this memory…it's okay.

A soft, loving voice whispered, *Starlina, I love you…*

Wait, whose voice is that?

The tugging pulled harder. She held her head, the pain throbbing and pounding.

The soft voice began to sing, *Abua – your mother will gently kiss you. Don't be afraid of bad creatures in the forest. Your mother is forever guarding…*

She shook her head, trying to place the voice but unable to. Where had she heard Starlina before? Wait…what was she thinking about again?

The tugging paused a moment.

She panted, sweat beading down her forehead, her curls sticking to her neck. Her head bobbed, a brief sigh of relief escaping her lips. It was finally –

Then came one last yank with such a force, Lily's eyes rolled back into her head. She vaguely heard someone screaming before realizing it was her as darkness claimed her.

233

W*here am I?*

Lily's head was fuzzy. She peeled her eyes open, her body swaying. She wasn't in the pool anymore. Where was Spyke? Brandon? Ang? There was no one.

And nothing.

She stood in blue darkness, water puddling at her feet. She could feel the water, but not see it save for ripples that escaped beneath her when her foot pressed down upon the water. Horrors of being trapped in her mind a few months ago with the Owl Sisters wrapped around her.

Rubbing her arms she turned around; afraid something would jump out of the dark. But this darkness was different. It was calming, not oppressing. It reminded her of a meditation room, the ones that had water fall from the walls. Even now the trickling tinkling of droplets fell around her. Not enough for rain, but just enough for calm to seep into her bones.

Am I still in my mind?

Yes, child of Kanaka, a soft, ethereal voice whispered in the darkness.

Lily rubbed her temples, a small ache forming. She opened her mouth, but no sound came out. The unfamiliar voice chuckled.

You are in your mind child. Voices work differently here.

She held back from rolling her eyes. *Okay then, who are you?*

I have many names, but I believe the one you are familiar with is Namaka.

Lily paused, taking that in. *The sea goddess?*

Yes, little one. Over here.

The ripples from the puddles beneath her swirled. They extended, growing larger until they rose into a column. A graceful hand pierced through, parting the wet sheen as a woman emerged from the depths.

She had olive skin, with arresting hazel eyes that were surrounded by a cloud of brown curly hair that fell down her back. Lily frowned. Something was off, but she couldn't quite place it. Then it hit her.

The woman was perfectly ordinary.

Not ethereally beautiful, not even stunningly beautiful. By no means was the woman not pretty. Even now the delicate crinkles around the eye and full lips gave the woman an adorably cute and happy appearance. She had gotten used to the fae (the women especially) being over-the-top supermodel gorgeous. The woman in front of her seemed humanly normal.

It gave her a strange comfort.

Namaka's eyes crinkled, warm and amused. *You were not expecting me to look like this were you?*

The words stuck in her throat, still in shock of the situation. Hesitant, she shook her head.

This is not my normal appearance child. I chose this from your memories to give you comfort in my presence. She chuckled, the sound like waves crashing against the shores. *I'm told I tend to have an 'intense' personality.*

Lily frowned. What memories? She didn't recognize the woman in front of her.

Hmmm, continued Namaka. She pursed her lips. *I see now. You chose well for your memory to give to the ho'omana'o stealer. The memory chosen was deep in your subconscious that you would not normally pull up. You are a very clever human. A worthy Sentinel for the great Thunderbird.*

Lily's eyes widened. How could she forget about Tim? She grasped the pendant, hoping against hope for that familiar warmth. But it was strangely cool, as if sleeping.

Namaka confirmed her fears.

I have placed us in a time sphere for this...private conversation. He cannot enter. Though...I anticipate he will be angry. But, I needed to speak with you and we have little time. I promise you are safe with me, little one.

How can I be sure? she asked, finally getting her 'voice' back.

The sea fae nodded, approval evident. *Good, keep questioning. That will keep you alive in our world.*

How are you in my mind?

Namaka smiled, pointing to the bracelet. It glowed brightly, a soft pulse thumping against her wrist.

This keeps us linked. Since you are unconscious, it is easier that I may speak with you. Her smile faded, her gaze growing serious and more intense. *I said before, we do not have much time and there is much to tell you.*

She waved Lily to come closer. Reluctantly Lily padded through the water, reaching the fae's side.

Namaka nodded. *I know what the traitor fae prince is attempting.*

Yes, Lily replied, *Waking up a creation maker right?*

Depends on how you look at it. Creation, destruction. They are two sides of the same coin. She looked solemn, and her eyes eerily ancient.

Lily took a soft gulp, goosebumps pebbling over her skin. *You're one of them too, aren't you?*

That is why I came to you in this form. Even now I feel your anxiety rising.

She put her hand over her heart, eyes sincere. *Remember child, I promised you were safe with me. I will never say I have been perfect in my extremely long existence but now, my only goal is to keep the world whole. Safe. However, this prince...he has no comprehension on who, or what, he is going to unleash.* Her eyes bore into Lily's. *If he succeeds, both the Veil and your world will burn.*

Burn?

Namaka held out her hand, water droplets dancing upon her palm. *Let me tell you a story. Something that has been lost to history.*

The water turned into two figures. Lily squinted. They looked like children, two young girls to be precise.

Namaka began.

Long ago, there were two sisters. They were different in every way but balanced each other. They were the mirror of the other, their powers polar opposites. Regardless, they lived their lives together, along with their other siblings. They danced and dreamed of the world they were creating.

The two figures moved, the water swirling. They morphed into larger, adult versions.

As the sisters grew older, their differences became stark. They began to move in different directions, creating the world based on their respective roles. The oldest did her best to be responsible and cover for her younger sister's mishaps.

However, the youngest proved impulsive and her temper was fierce. It got to the point where the eldest needed distance and space. But, the sisters always kept their bond and love for one another. Their bond was tighter than most, sometimes their love raging to fights, but they always calmed.

The figures disappeared. Another figure appeared, male. He approached one of the sisters with a bow.

Soon, the older sister found love. He was a human. A mighty warrior and sorcerer. He made strides to impress the elder sister, who was bound by rules and responsibilities. With his courtship he won the love of the elder sister, and they married. She taught him the magic from the Veil, which was different than what he knew. He was the first human sorcerer to learn creation magic. The eldest was happy...she was loved. She was finding a life of her own.

The couple were embracing, until the other sister emerged, tapping the male on the shoulder.

However, the youngest did not like this. She approached her sister's husband. She was beautiful, fiery, and fun. She never bore the weight of responsibility as her eldest sister; the one who always helped her. Always looked out for her. Being human, the sorcerer was swayed by the younger sister's beauty. The sorcerer betrayed his wife, leaving her to marry the younger, taking the magic and all the knowledge taught to him. Then, he became irresponsible with the magic taught to him.

A pause. Namaka's voice hitched before she continued.

The eldest was heartbroken. Then came the anger. And with it, came storms and floods. Instead of creation, destruction arose. Betrayed, the eldest chased after her sibling, their powers raging against one another.

Soon, the eldest was winning, as she forced her sibling and ex-husband to hide in a volcano.

Namaka paused, breathing deep.

The eldest, in a moment of clarity, realized the results of her actions. Humans were being affected by floods and fire.

The main figures merged in the water, splitting into hundreds of tiny people in various states of panic.

Namaka closed her eyes, a tear falling down her cheek.

They were homeless, dying, crying out in despair. The anger fell from the eldest, shame and regret taking root. This was not what she wanted. Her power held responsibility. So...she left. The floods ceased. Her sister and ex-love were left in peace.

Or so she thought...

Time passed, and the world spun again, and the sorcerer abandoned the youngest sibling. He claimed he was placed under a love spell. When the spell lifted, he felt remorse for leaving his first and only love. But, when he tried to leave, the youngest sibling raged.

She raged against humans, calling them fickle, weak, and untrustworthy. Fire reigned from the sky. Rivers of lava covered the forests and farms.

Soon, the smoke blocked out the sky. The youngest sibling joined other evil creatures with the sole purpose of dominating both the Veil and the Human world. Darkness fell over the land while horrors emerged from the deep dark.

It was then, the ancients along with powerful humans created the Accord. The eldest sibling knew the alliance wouldn't be strong enough to defeat a creation maker. It was her duty to bring balance back to her sister's destruction. Her sibling was her other half. Creation, destruction. So, she aligned with the fae and humans and sealed her sibling away.

There was a pause, Namaka staring into the distance, her eyes vacant.

Lily cleared her throat softly. *What happened to the eldest? Did she find her love again?*

Namaka shook her head, her hair falling down. *He died trying to help seal away the evil creatures. More precise, it was the youngest sibling's fire that seared his soul.*

Did he tell her how he felt? Lily paused a moment. *The eldest sibling I mean.*

Namaka's eyes shimmered. *He did, with his dying breath. But he died before she could give her forgiveness.*

Lily wiped away tears. *Did the sisters find peace?*

Namaka smiled sadly. *Unfortunately, the youngest's rage flamed too great. Even the eldest couldn't calm her, when in the past she could have done so. To save the worlds, the youngest was sealed without any reconciliation. To this day, the two sisters always feel the absence of each other.*

Lily's heart ached. It was one of those sad tales where no one wins; everyone lost something. Before she could think, she had rested her hand over Namaka's.

The fae goddess's eyes widened.

Lily squeezed gently. *You must feel pain every day.*

Namaka's eyes glistened. *You are very kind. Take this advice, young human. Never lose your kindness. No matter what you will encounter in the future. I foresee your path will not be easy.*

She shrugged. *What life is?*

Namaka chuckled. *The Thunderbird has mentioned your humor.*

So...what does this mean for Dain?

Namaka's lips tightened, her eyes growing cold. *If the prince releases the youngest sibling, all realms will be destroyed. She will not rest. Her fire and rage have been burning ever brighter since her imprisonment.*

Her eyes caught Lily's. They swirled, as if the waves themselves were alive within their depths. *Creation makers cannot be controlled. And this prince is a fool to think she will listen to a mere fae prince. She wants revenge on every living thing. Complete and utter destruction.*

Lily's chest tightened. How was Namaka so sure? And even then, what could they do against a goddess? Maybe it was a silly question, but she had to ask. *How do you know?*

Namaka's eyes grew vacant again, her voice drifting. *I feel her. Every day.* She turned back. *My sister is an unstoppable fire.*

Well...crud...

Oops! Did she say that out loud? She wasn't sure anymore what were thoughts and what was her voice in this weird space. But that didn't matter. Namaka confirmed what she suspected. The imprisoned creation maker and Namaka were sisters. This was so much worse than a horned serpent.

She straightened her shoulders. *Is it bad of me to assume you will help?*

Namaka sighed, regret lacing her words. *After the others were sealed away, I voluntarily sealed myself as well.*

Lily's lips pinched as she strained to keep her face neutral. Of course there would be no help, how silly of her to ask.

A sad smile graced her face. *Yes, I chose to do this. The worlds were ever growing and changing. And when the High Beings erected the barriers between the worlds...well...as creation makers, we fulfilled our purpose. I did not want to follow my sister into despair.*

Her head tilted, gesturing toward Lily's wrist. *But, while I may not be fully awake, I did pour a bit of myself into the bracelet you wear. I did this as an emergency if someone was foolish enough to try to awaken my sister.*

So, what do I do now?

Listen inside your heart child. If my sister awakens, you will need my help. Just listen for me.

Lily nodded, not trusting herself to speak. While the fae goddess made sense, the answer was far too vague and cliché for her liking. She couldn't rely on simply listening for a goddess. The best thing she could do was stop Dain before he could free Namaka's sister.

Namaka eyes grew distant. *The Thunderbird is impatient and will not wait any longer.* She grabbed Lily's hands and gave a comforting squeeze. *This is where we part keiki...for now. I will be with you when you need me.*

The bracelet glowed brighter as the darkness began to fade. Namaka's parting words echoed in Lily's ears.

Remember little keiki. Keep your love for your sister. Remember, keep yourself afloat and do not drown in anger.

And Lily woke up.

Chapter Twenty

ARI WAS IN A WONDERFUL DREAM. SHE WAS DANCING WITH Dain, and they were laughing. Halfway through, Dain morphed into Cabyll. Her smile grew while Cabyll's deep green eyes sparkled down at her, mischievous and alluring. He leaned over and then-

Tap, tap, tap.

She groaned, the dream dissolving into a haze. She rubbed her eyes, her hair sticking to her forehead.

Tap, tap, tap.

Frowning, she sat up. The warm wind blew in from her open window. Then, a pebble appeared, rolling on the floor.

Tap.

Another one came from the window, falling onto the floor again.

Tap.

Ari's eyes widened. Was it Cabyll? Was it like one of those movies where the suitor couldn't be away and tried to come in through the window? Excited, she threw off the covers and ran, peering over the side.

"*Nipote...*"

Her lips downturned. *Busted...*

Below was Aunt Raven. She was hanging on the wall.

Wait...

Ari rubbed her eyes. The wall?! Sure enough, her aunt was climbing

241

up the wall, pebbles in hand. How in the world did she get up there? Looking down further, she noticed Raven was supported by something.

She squinted, trying to make it out in the dark. An animalistic pant broke the same moment Ari made out the outline of the dire wolf. She couldn't believe her aunt was not only scaling the wall, but on the back of a huge wolf.

Ari shook her head. Her mom told her Aunt Raven was a bit of a daredevil, but she brushed it off. She had only seen Aunt Raven two, maybe three times. She figured her mom was exaggerating. True, her stepdad's sister travelled the world. But not once did she imagine her aunt was this fearless.

Or insane.

"*Nipote*," Raven chirped, interrupting her thoughts. "A little help would be lovely sweetie."

She glanced down, her head bobbing. "Uh..."

Raven raised a single eyebrow, her tone deadpan. "Your hand *nipote*."

Ari flushed, her cheeks red. Duh, of course. "Sorry!"

On autopilot she reached out and grabbed her aunt's hand. With a small tug, her aunt lithely jumped onto the ledge into the room. With a soft grunt, the wolf came following behind.

"Whew!" Raven wiped her brow dramatically, though Ari couldn't detect a speck of sweat. "That was a workout. Do you have some water sweetie, I'm a little thirsty."

She raced and grabbed a small cup, pouring some water from the pitcher. As she placed it into Raven's hands, she frowned. *What am I doing? She's the one who barged into my room!* She opened her mouth to say so, but Raven walked past.

Raven circled, her eyes roaming the room. "So...this is where you're staying? It's pretty nice sweetie." She took a small, leisurely sip. "You seem to have everything you need."

Suddenly, Raven's eyes narrowed. "What am I supposed to tell your mom, hmm?"

Ari's mouth was still open. Wow...she went right for the jugular. She swallowed, coughing lightly. "Well, you see...the thing is..."

"I'm waiting dear," she replied, her voice syrupy sweet. She took another long sip. The wolf padded to her side, rubbing against her ribs as she casually scratched its ear.

Ari swallowed, gathering courage. Whether courage in front of the massive wolf that her aunt dismissed like a puppy or her aunt herself, Ari wasn't sure. She clenched her hands. "I found love Aunt Raven."

"Uh – huh." Raven kept petting the wolf.

"And...I decided to be with him." She clenched hands tightened.

Raven merely blinked; her expression remained neutral. "So, let me get this straight. You found love?"

"Yes."

"With a fae prince?"

"Yes."

"And you just decided to live with him?"

"Yes!"

"How long have you known him before you did this?"

She paused. "In the beginning? Total? I guess a few hours."

Raven's eyebrow shot up; her hand froze above the wolf, causing him to whimper, nudging her hand. But, she refused to move, sucking in her teeth. "A few...hours?"

Ari protested, "Yes, but...that doesn't mean anything. It was love at first sight. We knew we were meant to be. I love him and he loves me."

Raven stared blankly, not moving. Then she clucked her tongue, her mouth opening, closing, making huge motions. The wolf whined, slinking back. Ari didn't blame him. Her aunt was experiencing a breakdown.

The wolf moved next to the window, sitting on its haunches, keeping alert.

Ari frowned. Was something wrong with Raven? She looked like she was choking, or a really bad game of charades. Finally, Raven took an audible deep breath, fanning her face.

"*Dio mi aiuti con gli adolescenti,*" she mumbled into her hand.

With a forcible shake of her shoulders, Raven cracked her neck before fixing Ari with a pointed stare. "Okay, I get it. You love the hot prince. But, did you even think about how your mom is feeling right now?"

Ari gulped, her throat tightening to the point she almost choked. She didn't want to think about her mom. She should just ignore Raven;

pretend she didn't care. But, in the quiet dim light, a question that kept tickling the back of her mind she had ignored for months came rushing out. "Is...is she upset?"

Raven rubbed her forehead. "Dear, your mom loves you. You know she'd want you home."

Ari ignored her sinking heart with the lack of answer. Maybe her mom really was upset with her. "Dain needs me though." Her gaze returned, her eyes bright. "I'm important you know! Besides, you're in love too, right? With Okena?"

Raven ran her hand through her hair, twirling a long strand through her fingers. "Yeah, lots of love going on in this place. Cupid is just firing arrows left and right."

Ari frowned, her brows furrowed. "Do you love him?"

Raven's face softened. "There are many kinds of love dear. And we are in different stages of our lives, sweetie. You are just starting to live yours. It is important you understand," she put her hands lightly on Ari's shoulders, "you need to love yourself first before finding someone to love. I think that's something you're still working on."

Ari tensed. She shook her head, pushing her aunt's hands away. "I'm fine. So you can save the lecture." Her body shook, her fingers digging into her palms. "And just for your information, I *know* I am amazing."

The words tasted ashy in her mouth even as she repeated. "He loves me because I'm special!"

Raven nodded, putting up her hands in surrender. "I get it. Just remember, you're important to us too, sweetie."

She crossed her arms, turning away. "I think you should go."

Raven started forward, her expression worried. "*Nipote*, I know we haven't gotten to talk much. I will help you any way I can. You just tell me."

She backed up, putting distance between them. She glared. "What do I need help for? I told you I'm fine."

Raven sighed, biting her lip. "Okay. But we're here."

"I don't need anything from *you*," she barked, her annoyance growing. Who was Aunt Raven to tell her what to do.

Raven's eyes widened before narrowing. "Watch your tone, Arianna Ambrosino. I'm still your aunt."

"It's Greene!" Ari yelled back.

Raven threw up her hands with a growl of her own, startling the wolf. "Ugh! *Per amore di tutto cio che e santo*!! And to think everything your siblings are doing for you and you are acting this way!"

Ari stopped, suspicious. "What?" Maybe it was her paranoia, but she had to ask. "What are you talking about?"

Raven's mouth dropped open. She closed it with a snap and groaned, rubbing her forehead. "Well, that's outta the bag." Her eyes pierced Ari before she sighed deeply. "They're here sweetie."

"Here?" she asked again, stupidly. She already knew that, but how did her Aunt know? Her fears bubbled up. Her aunt couldn't mean...

Raven waved her hands impatiently. "Yes, here. As in...in the Veil."

"You know?!"

Raven smacked her palm over her face. "They love you sweetie. We only want you home, safe."

Ari frowned, wanting to confirm. "Tell me, don't lie. Is Brandon here?"

The look on her aunt's face said everything. Ari balked, her stomach dropping. What was Brandon doing here? Mom let him come? Wait...did she even know? She winced. Painful images of the day her father didn't come home pierced her memory. Her throat closed as she desperately tried to dispel her mom's distraught face that flashed through her mind.

She paused as another thought wormed its way in.

Did that mean Cabyll deceived her earlier? She chewed her lip. No, it couldn't be. The fae couldn't lie. She looked into his eyes, she could tell.

Couldn't she?

Her blood warmed. He was worried when she fell on the fire sand, more so than Dain. She shook her head, her face flushed as her heart thumped harder. Her fingers began to shake, heat pooling down her throat, choking her.

"I think you need to go now," she strangled out, turning away.

"Ari," Raven reached out, concerned.

Without turning back, she threw her hand out to grip the bed sheets. She clenched her eyes shut, gritting out. "I said, get out!"

She struggled to breathe, the heat welling up inside her. She was afraid she'd rip the sheets, her knuckles straining, going white. Would

245

Dain be angry if she tore the sheets? The vague thought burned away as the boiling anger rose.

She gnashed her teeth, her skin practically crawling. Raven's presence lingered at her back. Why was she taking so long to leave?! She opened her mouth to yell again when a breathy, sad, sigh whispered behind her. Then, the soft padding of a wolf's feet.

Then silence.

Wary, she turned around to be greeted by nothing. Her aunt must have jumped out the window again. The wind blew softly into the room, cooling her heated cheeks.

Ari blew out a frustrated breath. Why couldn't she be left alone? Why couldn't *they* leave her alone? Her traitorous inner voice whispered.

Because they love you.

She shook her head at the stupid thought. Lily was stupid. They were all stupid. Stupid, stupid, stupid! She didn't need them. She was beautiful, special, and loved in this magical world. Why would she want to leave? Dain was a prince, and he loved her. Maybe he never said the words, but he did. She just knew it. Besides, all magical romantic stories had hurdles. She only needed to get through hers and she would have her happy ending with Dain. Together. And she'd be a queen. It would be perfect. *He* was perfect.

Then, another voice, not hers, warmly whispered in her mind.

He may seem perfect, but he is still a male. They all betray.

Ari frowned, tugging her ear. Why would she think that? Dain wouldn't betray her. Unbidden, memories of Uktena and Yarramundi sprung forth. Where was Dain then? She had been terrified, and he wasn't there for her.

She scrubbed her arms, trying to remove the traitorous thoughts that sparked the edges of her conscious. They smoked and fumed, gathering oxygen and glowing brighter. Her palms began to sweat...again. She didn't deserve such fear. Who was *he* to do that to her? He needed *her*! Smoke flamed her mind, logic growing hazy.

Then, a pair of striking green eyes peaked through her fearful thoughts, dispelling the smoke and dousing the flames.

She took a deep, calming breath. Yes, Cabyll wouldn't betray her. Wait...she shook her head. No, not Cabyll. Dain needed her. He only needed to see she was loyal to him. He was like one of those princes in her books. The one that was cold and cruel, but eventually her love would thaw him. She would be the only special person to change the cold Prince of Prophecy.

Only her.

Her body swayed, the heat dispelling somewhat. She wiped her forehead. She needed a cool glass of water. Yes, that was it. She simply needed something to drink and eat.

I'll call for Aput. Then I can eat some delicious cookies and a drink. Then I'll talk to Dain tomorrow. Yes, that's what I need. If I see him, it'll be okay.

She stepped out of her room, pushing all the bad thoughts out, focusing instead on hopeful thoughts of happily ever after.

She failed to see the burnt finger trails on her comforter, the soft smoke trailing upwards, disappearing into the wind.

Chapter Twenty-One

LILY WOKE UP TO VOICES ARGUING ABOVE HER.

"Lil?! Can you hear me? Guys, is she okay? Spyke?!"

"Isa, if you have harmed her, I am honor bound to-"

"Step back warrior. I have done nothing. Hari knew not to kill her."

"Sissy you're such a fool!"

"Humans are so frail..."

Lily's head ached. It was like her brain had gone through a meat tenderizer and then put in a ten-speed blender at the highest setting. She winced, the voices rose, blending together. Everything was swirling, the setting sun her pierced her eyes.

A familiar warmth centered in her chest.

My Sentinel, are you okay?

The Thunderbird's comforting voice embraced her. She sighed, physical relief flowing through her limbs. *Yeah, I'm okay. Though my head hurts.*

You gave up a memory. A precious one at that. It is natural your head will ache.

She knew she wouldn't remember, but she asked anyways. *I know it was a subconscious memory, but, do you know what I gave away?*

No young Sentinel. I am not privy to your mind except what you show me.

Well, that was good to know. At least she had some privacy. It was the little things, right?

Tim continued, his voice concerned. *But, I could not reach you. You were blocked from me, which is worrisome. I noticed the energy blocking me felt familiar.* He paused. *Was it the sea goddess?*

Yes, she spoke to me saying Dain is trying to release her sister. She claimed she will help, but...I dunno...she was vague.

A whispery sigh tickled her chest.

Such is the way of creation makers. As old as I am, they are far older. And highly powerful beings who have the gift of creation also fall prey to destruction. Even I cannot understand their minds. So...let us focus on what she told you. You mentioned her sister?

Yes...

The Thunderbird's displeasure rumbled through her very soul. *I had my suspicions, but she confirmed it. Though I cannot express whether I am relieved I was correct, or more worried.*

What do you mean?

Tim cursed. *That fool of a prince is trying to awaken Pele.*

Is that her name?

Yes, Goddess of fire and volcanos.

She groaned. *Well...that's just fine and dandy now, isn't it? He couldn't have picked the goddess of roses or birds or something?*

The Thunderbird was silent, not laughing at her sarcasm for once. His nerves raced down her spine, causing her to shiver.

Young Sentinel, Tim's grave tone perked her ears. *I was alive when the battle between Namaka and Pele took place. I remember the devastation. When creation makers battle...it was the worst I ever witnessed in my long life. The destruction alone...*

Tim trailed off, unable to continue, the pain palpable. Lily's heart hurt witnessing the normally stoic being in such obvious pain. She cleared her throat, attempting a cautious joke.

Well...Dain sure knows how to pick 'em doesn't he?

Tim gave a reluctant chuckle, a faint blanket of warmth covering her. His somber tone pricked her skin.

Lily...it is imperative we stop him.

She knew they had reached another level of bad news. Probably because Tim called her by name. It reminded her of when her father called her by her entire name, confirmation name and all, when something was about to hit the fan. Yeah, this situation was already not good, but this just took it to an upper level.

He continued, pulling her from her thoughts.

We will continue this later. First you must get up. The others are worried about you.

"Pushy..." she mumbled.

The chorus of voices resumed as the Thunderbird's thoughts faded. She squinted, her arm moving slowly over her eyes, trying to block out the blinding sun. "I'm good guys. But, can I get a little help up?"

Before she finished her question, several hands pulled her upright. The voices peppered her with questions. She winced, unable to gather her thoughts or pull out who was asking what.

Rubbing her temples she pleaded, "Give me a second please? My head is throbbing."

Isa's voice took center.

"It is due to the memory extraction." Her eyes were bright, unshed tears filling them. "Hari showed me. For you to part with such one," she bowed low to Lily, "you are one of the most selfless humans I've seen in my entire life. Thank you for gifting such a precious memory."

Ang crossed her arms, shooting a glare at Isa. "She shouldn't have had to do that period," she groused out. Her gaze zipped to Lily, her voice harsh. "We thought you were dead. You just dropped and-"

Lily interrupted, "Namaka came to visit me."

Might as well rip off the band aid.

The whole group fell silent. Hari and Isa exchanged a cautious glance.

She continued, "We can't wait anymore. We have to stop Dain." She turned to Isa. "I hope I'm not being rude, but I need the prince's memory, please."

Isa nodded. Without prompting, Hari padded forward, his eyes glowing.

Lily flinched subconsciously.

Isa clucked soothingly, whether it was meant for Hari or Lily, she didn't know. A large opalescent tear beaded up at the corner of Hari's milky white eyes.

Isa motioned forward. "Take it, human."

Lily cautiously reached out beneath the devil cat's eerie eyes. The tear welled up, becoming larger and larger. With a forward bow, Hari closed his striking eyes, the tear falling.

She jerked back, expecting it to splash all over. Instead, it was solid, landing safely in the center of her palm. Lifting her finger, she gently poked it, wondering if it would break. It was hard, like a jewel. She held it up to the light, beautiful colored swirls moving within the tear.

"Be careful," Isa warned. "Memories are fragile and precious. If that breaks before being back in the prince's hands, his memory will be forever lost."

Brandon peered into the jewel. "Why is it so fragile?"

"Why wouldn't they be delicate?" Isa cocked her head. "Memories make up who we are, they are a blueprint of our lives. When you live the long life of a fae, your memories are all you have left. Therefore, every memory is a pearlescent treasure. As much as they are strong, they are easily breakable. Memories can be lost, forgotten, ignored. You could easily lose a part of yourself. They are precious and rare."

Her gaze caressed the pearl, an eerie smile spreading her face. "Which is why I love collecting them."

Lily nestled her other hand around the pearl, worried to leave it out in the open. What Isa said made sense, memories helped shape who we were. The pearl suddenly seemed more fragile than before. How in the world would they get this large jewel back safely?

As if he read her mind, Waru reached out with a small pouch in hand. "His highness anticipated this. Place the memory in here. It is magically sealed to protect it from breaking."

She placed the tear inside as carefully as she could.

"So, if it fell it wouldn't break?" asked Brandon.

"That is correct," replied Waru.

Brandon's eyes gleamed a moment, a mischievous grin spreading. "Are we sure? Should we test it?"

Ang elbowed him, hard. "Do not even *think* about it."

He flushed, ducking his head down, mumbling an apology.

Spyke interjected. "Since we have what we came for, we need to leave." His keen gaze caught Ang. "Are you well enough to move?"

Ang snorted. "What no overnight stay?"

She gave an exasperated groan at the blank stare she received. "I deserve a month's supply of honey for this."

Brandon clapped her on the back, oblivious to her wheeze. "Not a prob Ang! We got your back."

Isa looked up, the sky darkening to a violet cranberry hue. "It is getting dark. You are welcome to spend the night if you must."

Lily chewed her lip. On the one hand, they needed rest. She hoped Ang was alright, but nagging uncertainty crawled over her skin. The changeling was pale, her face too drawn out for her liking. But on the other hand, Namaka's worried gaze speared into Lily's memories. Was it really worth taking a breath?

But, as fate turns out, she didn't have to make the decision.

Pika and Peni came running in, clutching their hats over their heads. Their big eyes were wide and anxious. They skidded to a halt, a dust cloud hovering over them.

Pika coughed, waving his hands. "Um, Isa...darling? Wonderful, beautiful creature ever to set foot...or hoof...in my life."

Isa sighed, her hooves pawing impatiently before she growled out. "What did you two do this time?"

Peni put his hands up. "Nothing this time Isa, we swear."

"I'll have you know I'm always innocent thank you very much." Pika put his nose up in the air with a humph.

"Pika...focus!" Peni smacked the back of his brother's head. "Look we were minding our own business, only making fun of the Kaupe-."

"Just *little* jokes." Pika pinched his fingers.

"But," interrupted Peni, "we noticed something."

Isa rolled her eyes. "And that is?"

The brothers twisted their hats in nervous tension, not answering.

Peni sighed, finally replying. "Maero warriors appeared. They joined with the Kaupe."

Silence infected the grove.

Lily and Brandon shared a glance, confused. He shrugged at her, giving her the, *your guess is as good as mine,* look. But it didn't escape her notice the slight paling of Spyke's face. Even Waru's carefree vibe vanished.

"Maero? Here?" Isa stepped back, agitated. Hari tossed his head, growling.

Her tail flickered, her tone growing urgent. "It is no longer safe. You need to leave, now!"

Waru stepped forward, cracking his knuckles. "Menehune," he ordered. "Describe the Maero for me."

Pika scratched his head, but Peni replied. "They looked normal for Maero...but the largest one seemed different."

Waru's voice lowered, deadly and dangerous. "Tell me. Did any of the Maero sport *Ta moko*? Any tattoos?"

Peni nodded. "The large one had some on his forehead and around his eyes."

A low growl reverberated in Waru's chest, the veins in his throat pulsing. He stared off, his mind somewhere else. Only one word slipped through his bared teeth. "Hunapo."

Spyke frowned, crossing his arms. "Someone you know?"

Waru didn't answer, his burning eyes unfocused.

Spyke barked. "Waru! Will you be focused on *this* fight? Or are you unable to meet this challenge?"

That snapped the Māori warrior out of it. Shaking himself, his eyes calmed, his breathing evening out. He rubbed his forehead, weary. "Apologies, my mind drifted a moment."

He caught Spyke's gaze and held it, something unspoken traveling between them. "I will be focused, do not worry."

Ang cracked her knuckles, her upper lip curled. "We gonna fight?"

Spyke and Waru both shook their heads.

Waru responded, somewhat disappointed. "This is not the place for a battle."

Brandon scratched his head. "I thought you lived for the fight dude."

Waru chuckled, tousling Brandon's blonde hair in a very fatherlike gesture. "That is correct young warrior. Normally I would be thrilled for this fight. This indeed would be a challenge." Then he sighed, his shoulders slumping as if a huge weight fell on them. "But this Maero... Hunapo, he is not honorable. Our mission is to get you safely back." He cracked his neck. "Though I will not mind if they try to catch us."

"Obviously," Ang grunted before she clapped her hands. "Well, if that's that, let's go guys."

Lily jumped into action. She grabbed her pack, tucking the satchel

253

holding the memory close to her chest. The group gathered their supplies quickly before a distant howl permeated the glade. Her heart thudded against her chest. That howl was familiar. Way too familiar for her liking. It grew louder, a war-like whoop accompanying as it cackled into the night air.

Isa notched her bow, her lips pinched in a firm line. Hari hunched low, growling at her side. She gestured behind her. "You must hurry. They are breaking through."

"But where can we go?" asked Brandon, looking around. "Last time I checked, the bridge was where the bad guys are. Oh wait...the bridge that is not there anymore."

Isa nodded over her shoulder. "At the edge of the pool, the water trails down. Follow that. The Menehune should know it."

Pika pursed his lips, before his eyes lit up. "Oh yeah! You mean down the waterfall?"

Lily's heart dropped.

Pena slapped a hand over Pika's mouth, muffling him.

A waterfall? Seriously?! She had enough water to last her a lifetime. But from Spyke and Waru's neutral expressions, she gathered it was that or fighting. Groaning, she steeled herself. She really didn't want to fight the Kaupe again.

Isa's apologetic gaze pleaded with Lily. "It is the fastest route. It is the *only* way, young Sentinel."

She turned back, raising her bow as the howling grew louder.

Spyke tugged Lily's arm toward the pool. She frowned. Why wasn't Isa coming with them? She pulled away, calling out. "Wait! Aren't you coming?"

A smash followed by a louder war whoop answered her.

"They broke through," Isa muttered. She shook her head, not turning to Lily. "Hari and I will distract them while you escape."

"But, what about you?" asked Lily.

Isa's relaxed tone belied her tense shoulders. "I have Hari, remember? We should be okay."

Lily didn't want to point out that Isa didn't say it was a definite guarantee. The fae couldn't lie. Before Lily could protest again, Isa barked over her shoulder.

"Thunderboy! Take your charge and leave."

Spyke scooped Lily in his arms, dangling her over his shoulder. She wanted to pound against his back, but instead she clutched the memory tight against her chest as Spyke's heavy footfalls pounded in the water.

She could only yell in the haze as water splashed against her eyelids. She squinted, making out faint figures approaching the parameter of the grove.

"Be safe Isa! You too Hari!"

Isa called over her shoulder, her face obscured. "And you as well young Sentinel. I hope to see you again. Protect that memory."

Lily rubbed her eyes, trying to dispel the ache. Hari's eerie yowl answering the Kaupe's growl was the last thing she heard before fronds slapped her face, obscuring everything. Tree branches whipped against her cheek as Spyke ran fast along the water's edge.

She coughed, her chest smacking against his back as Spyke suddenly stopped. The world righted itself as she found herself back on her feet.

Shaking her head to clear the dizziness, she spotted the rest of the group. There, by the cascading water, stood the Menehune brothers. Next to them were a few little boats made from smooth Koa wood. Pika and Peni motioned with their heads to sit down.

She took a big breath, trying to quell her racing thoughts. She could have her breakdown later. For now, she had to protect the memory and time was not on their side.

Pika jumped up and down, flailing his arms. "Sit, sit! Faster everyone!"

Lily stood, uncertain where to go.

A gentle hand steered her. "Over here Lily," said Spyke calmly but firmly. "You sit in front of me."

She just got settled onto the bench in the boat when another howl tore through the night air.

Goosebumps pricked over her skin. *Seriously? Is this thing a zombie or something?*

Her legs started shaking. Thankfully she was sitting in a boat because she would have fallen on jelly legs. Could they outrun them? What would happen if they were caught? She couldn't identify anything other than fear. Just the image of the Kaupe made all rational thought flee.

Some Sentinel I am, she lamented. *If Cabyll was here, he'd tell me to get my act together. Come on. Get your act together, Lil!*

"Lily." Spyke reached out in front of her, grasping hold of an oar. "Excuse my reach, but I'll take it from here." He stared straight, his head above her. "Whatever you do, protect that memory."

That snapped her back to reality. Her cold hands wrapped around the satchel, holding it tight. She nodded. This is what she could do. Brandon gave her a thumbs up, sitting with Waru in the boat in front of her. Ang's angry glare speared the Menehune she was stuck with.

Pika and Peni yelled out at everyone.

"Ready?!"

Brandon raised his hand. "Uh...dudes. Do you know what you're doing?"

"Of course. We do this all the time," replied Peni.

Pika nodded. "Yup. When we played pranks on Hari just the other week-"

"AND we're off." Peni pushed his oar forward. "Whatever you do everyone, just keep your heads down."

"Why?" asked Ang suspiciously.

"Just the trees, and the rocks, and the drop." Pika pushed his oar faster.

The boats jostled in the water, their speed picking up. Lily's heart evened out. This wasn't so bad. It reminded her of very calm white-water rafting.

Waru glanced behind him. "Will this go any faster?"

Pika waved him off. "No worries it'll happen in just a few-"

A rustling in the fronds near Lily had the hair prickling up her arm. She turned to find two familiar frightening red eyes nestled in the green foliage.

She yelled out, fear coating her voice. "Spyke!"

The Kaupe growled, jumping out of the trees, preparing to launch itself from the bank.

Spyke, without missing a beat, twisted the oar to smack the Kaupe hard across its jaw. Stunned, the monster flew backwards into the fronds.

"Menehune!" Spyke's growl increased. "We need to go faster."

256

"Oh crap!" Ang's freaked out voice reached Lily's ears. "This drop is-"

And then nothing but Pika and Peni's howling whooping echoed in the air.

"Wait! What happened?" asked Brandon.

He tried to peer over when Waru took his big hand and smashed Brandon back into his seat.

"Hold on little human." Waru pushed his oar faster and soon their boat disappeared, Brandon's screaming fading.

Lily twisted, but the water didn't show where they were going. Or what happened to the others. Lily cursed how short she was.

Spyke gasped, his height enabling him to see what she couldn't. His arms wrapped around her.

"Don't forget to breath Lily," he whispered urgently into her ear.

What in the world?

The boat teetered, and all she could see was mist. She couldn't see the bottom the drop was so high. Brandon and Ang's screams were faint, echoing below.

Her feet automatically started backpedaling, as if she could stop the boat.

Nope! Nu-uh! Does this Sentinel stuff come with compensation?

The boat moved as if in slow motion. She leaned back against Spyke, clutching the satchel. Movement caught in the corner of her eye.

A man with a long ratty head of hair covering his face appeared from the fronds. Yellow, blunted teeth bared at her. He held a frightening stone club in his meaty hand. But it was his eyes that were the scariest. They were the eyes of a hunter.

A hunter that found his prey.

"Sentinel!" The wild man howled, lifting his club right as her boat fell over the edge. As she screamed the entire way down, clenching her eyes, the wild man's guttural voice chilled her trembling limbs.

"Run *tangata iti*! I will find you little girl!"

Intermission

"*Dai*! Come on!"

Raven threw a pillow out the window, her anger falling as fast as the descending lump of cloth. Aka butted her thigh, rubbing against her in silent assurance.

She winced, immediately contrite. Maybe that was not the best idea. That and charging in, confronting Ari. Kye told her to keep a low profile.

"What happened?"

Kye's deep voice growled in the shadows, causing her to jump. She placed a hand over her hammering heart. Squinting, she tried to make him out in the dim light.

He's a big guy, how in the world is he so quiet?

She sighed, knowing the jig was up. "I went to see Ari."

Kye groaned. "We talked about this-"

"I know, I know. 'Keep a low profile'," she mimicked in her worst deep voice.

No way was she able to copy how Kye sounded. His was too rumbling, too deep, too...growly. Why was that growl so shivery?

She flopped onto the bed, grabbing the remaining pillow and smashed it into her face. Her voice muffled as she bit out. "It was just so hard."

A faint creak, then a dip in the bed made her heart stop. A resounding whine and warm fur pressed against her side. She relaxed.

Oh, thank the saints, it's Aka.

His gruff voice bit out, sounding closer. "And our story?"

She kept the pillow over her face, she wasn't in the mood for his angry, judgmental glare. "Yes. Don't you worry your big handsome head. She only asked how much in *love* we are. Your prowess in sweeping me off my feet has remained intact."

Kye cleared his throat. She smiled under the pillowcase. While she was not able to see his face, she could tell he was clearly flustered.

He coughed again, grumbling. "Well, that's good. After making such an abysmal mistake visiting her, we can't afford another. Did you find anything useful?"

She took a few breaths. *Abysmal? I'll give you abysmal you two bit, stick up your butt –*

"Only that she is head over heels for Dain," she replied instead. "That guy can do nothing wrong in her mind. He really has her wrapped around his finger. You know, I think he's emotionally abusive."

He ignored her. "Did you tell her anything else?"

She bit the pillow to keep herself from snapping. "No...I did not." Her chest tightened by the lie, thinking of Ari knowing the other kids were in the Veil.

Kye's rough voice continued, interrogation mode on. "Because if you revealed even the slightest-'"

His voice stopped as he got hit with a satin clad pillow cover. Raven sat up, her face flushed, eyes narrowed. "Do you think I don't get it?! I am not a child!"

He frowned, flicking the pillow to the ground. "Then why would you do something so reckless?"

"Because she is family! She is a kid, K-"

"Okena," he hissed, his eyes motioning around the room.

She sucked her lip, her mistake striking her upside the head. They had to be careful at all times since Kye could not guarantee no one was watching them. Even when alone, in their own room, they had to be acting.

She briefly shut her eyes, taking a steadying breath. "Okena," she continued calmly. "She's a kid who is alone...probably scared. I wanted her to know she has someone who is thinking about her. Someone who cares. That her family will be there when and if she needs it."

The prince pursed his lips, his glamour still in place. "I do not understand." His eyes were genuinely confused. "You keep speaking of family. Why do you go to such lengths for them?"

She blinked. "Don't you have family?"

"Yes, a few siblings."

"Are you close?"

"We do not live close to one another."

"No...I mean. Did you grow up together?"

"For a few hundred years, but we had separate mothers."

She rubbed her temples, groaning. "Okay. Let's backtrack. When I said close, are you close with anyone?"

Kye raised his eyebrow. "That is a silly question. You are close to me currently."

"Not physically close. Emotionally close!"

He remained silent.

She tried again. "Are any of your siblings kind? Do you like any of them?"

Again silence, before Kye quietly responded. "I guess...you could say I have a brother I respect. He smiles a lot."

"Okay, let's go with that. What would you do if he was in trouble?"

"What I am doing now. Finding out the culprit and bringing them to justice."

He's hopeless... Raven palmed her face before letting out a sigh. "Well, that's as good as I'm gonna get. Just think of it that way. I'm just trying to make sure Ari is fine and find the culprit."

He grunted, lifting his nose. "Seems like you are expending unnecessary energy."

She counted to twenty, slowly. "Dude...the only thing you got going for you is you're hot."

"I am not hot. It is quite chilly this evening."

She threw up her hands, falling back on the bed. "Okay fine!"

Aka curled up to her side, his glamour wolf form still in place. She sighed deeply, her hands delving into the soft fur, hoping the softness would quell her mounting frustration.

Kye sat down next to her, their thighs touching. She tensed, burying her face in Aka's neck.

He clasped his hands in front of him, silent. His gaze focused downward, his fingers twisting. "I understand I can be...what is the word?"

"Emotionally awkward?" she mumbled.

Kye grimaced. "I was going to say rough."

He gave her a sidelong glance. "I am a warrior. Honor, code, strict rules to follow. That is all I've known. I do not do well with," his gaze locked onto hers, "emotions."

Silence passed between them.

He continued, his voice rumbling. "I have been rather...ignorant of your devotion to your family."

"You mean clueless."

His gaze cut hers, eyebrows drawn together before he continued. "I understand loyalty though." He tousled his hair, grunting before he mumbled out. "I do admire that about you."

She sat up quickly, nudging his shoulder. "Aww, is this you apologizing?"

His ears flushed as he cleared his throat. "I am just saying. I may not understand you sometimes, but I've come to admire you...Raven."

She smiled, her eyes crinkling.

He jerked as she wrapped her arm around his waist in a light hug. "You're such a softy aren't you," she chuckled.

Time stopped a moment, the quiet of the evening only being interrupted by Aka's panting.

"I forgive you," she whispered.

Another beat of comfortable silence ensued. Finally, Raven broke it as she voiced what she most feared.

"The third day is tomorrow."

Kye didn't answer.

She continued, her anxiety mounting. "What if they don't get here in time? What if something happened?"

His eyes held hers. "Trust them Raven. I admit, I may have doubted your...family earlier, but the girl has courage and resolve. She will not give up so easily." He chuckled. "I suspect stubbornness runs in your family. With that alone, I trust she will succeed."

Raven, while comforted by those words, still trembled as her unvoiced fear overshadowed her courage.

"But what about the bad apples here? Do you think we can stop Da- I mean-Mr. D?"

He snorted at her bad nickname. "I have my suspicions, but no proof yet. I almost have what I need."

"Care to share?" she asked.

He shook his head. "Not yet."

She tensed. Progress was great to hear, but with no evidence it was only speculation. The scientist in her knew they needed evidence.

Frustration pooled out of her eyes. Suddenly weary, her head landed on Kye's shoulder, her warm tears melting into his side.

She squeezed her trembling arms. "I need my family safe."

Kye's heavy, warm arm rested lightly on her shaking shoulders, pulling her closer to his chest. His head leaned atop hers, his voice ruffling her hair in an oddly caring gesture.

"We will keep them safe."

She sniffed before she whispered. "But what if we can't stop him?"

His lips brushed the top of her head. "We...I *will* stop him." Kye's voice deepened, rumbling into the night. "Or die trying."

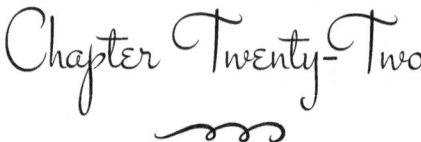

Chapter Twenty-Two

I'M GONNA DIE.

Lily's mind blanked. Her heart dropped down past her stomach, all the way down to her toes. The little boat kept falling faster and faster down the mountain, with no end in sight. Her voice was raw from screaming. Only her aching jaw remained opened in horrified silence.

Her vision was a blur of water droplets, dark branches, and the endless night sky overhead. She didn't know what was more terrifying. The drop itself or that she couldn't see the bottom of the waterfall...yet.

Spyke's large arms held her tight. If he hadn't, she was sure she would have been thrown from the boat by now. Her frozen arms still death-clutched the satchel holding Prince Kye's memories.

Focus on what you can do Lil. Her thoughts admonished her shaking brain.

And, of course, where was Tim? Lily could only guess he was still sleeping, since he was silent throughout the entire amusement park ride of doom. Lily's logical side understood he used a lot of energy with the exchange with Namaka and this was a natural event, not a magical one. But her emotional side didn't care. It kept saying, *What good is having a tremendously powerful spirit when he sleeps all the time?!*

"We're almost to the bottom," Spyke yelled into her ear. "Brace yourself!"

She clenched her eyes shut as she covered the satchel, holding her breath.

Her body jerked forward, the boat lurching before eventually righting itself. Cold water splashed her face, her galloping heartbeat drowning out the rush of the waterfall. Trembling, she slowly opened her eyes, squinting as they gradually adjusted to the darkness.

The water...the water was glowing.

Literally glowing with blue and green speckles. Every movement caused a cascade of glowing light, which dissipated, to re-emerge again when the surface was disturbed. It was beautiful. Unbidden, Lily wished she had a camera to capture the brilliance. She bet Cabyll never saw something like this.

She shook herself, mentally smacking herself. *Focus, Lil. We have a werewolf monster and some kind of crazy jungle man after you. Focus!*

"Do you see the others?" she asked.

"Yes," Spyke pointed. "Just ahead." The boat rocked as he moved back slightly to resume rowing, heading toward the bank. "Let's hurry."

With a slight tinge of regret, she turned her back on the incredible water as they reached land. Carefully, she cradled the satchel as she hobbled out of the boat. She tripped, catching herself on wobbly legs before she fell face first on the gritty sand.

Blinking, she found herself at the edge of the jungle, facing the open sea. The waterfall had thrown them down the mountain, through the jungle, until it eventually dumped out into the sea.

She shivered, an uneasy feeling of being exposed taking root.

"Dude. That was awesome!" Brandon whooped, jumping up and down, running toward them. "That beats an amusement park any day."

"Humans have parks for amusement?" asked Waru.

Brandon clapped Waru's back, then winced shaking his hand. "Waru, my man, we need to get you on a rollercoaster one day."

"Roller...coaster..." Waru pondered a moment, before giving a wink. "Someday we shall."

Ang growled, impatient. Her hand flew down in a chopping motion. "Not to interrupt, but we should get moving right?"

Waru nodded, giving a deep, resigned sigh. "You are right changeling." His gaze rose up to the sky, peering behind them. "Looks like we have double bad luck."

"You mean Isa? Are you missing her?" asked Pika, wide eyed. "I'll have you know warrior that I'm pursuing her. Should you even *think* about-"

"No silly." hissed Peni. "He means we're being chased by the Maero."

"And the time," Waru pointed skyward.

"Don't tell me." Dread pooled in Lily's belly. "Is it the third day?"

"When dawn rises." Waru frowned slightly. "I do not understand why you told me not to speak of it, then asked the question. Are humans always this contradictory?"

Ang palmed her face.

Brandon shook his head. "Wait...dawn? How long is that?"

Spyke strode forward, his club on his shoulder. "A few hours." His eyes narrowed before settling on Waru. "Think his highness has any allies that can help us?"

Waru stood a moment, thinking. He cupped his mouth, giving a war call that echoed in the distance, crashing against the waves. He didn't move, not one inch, his ear raised slightly before he whispered. "They should come soon."

"As well as those crazy guys after us. Everyone heard that," groused Ang.

Waru shrugged. "It was necessary. With the Maero on our tail, we won't make it without assistance." A pregnant pause ensued before Waru continued in a confident tone. "They should be here before our enemy."

"Ah...you sure man?" asked Brandon, wary.

Spyke kept walking forward. "Regardless, we keep moving. Help will come, but now is not the time to be idle." His lips downturned, apologetic. "I'm afraid we must cannot stop to rest."

Lily shouldered her pack, her legs pinching back to life. "It is what it is." Her heart beat inside her ribcage, gently pushing against the satchel. A constant reminder of the fragility of their package.

Brandon called over to Pika and Peni. "You guys coming?"

The Menehune scratched their heads.

"We didn't think that far ahead," answered Pika sheepishly.

Peni rolled his eyes. "*You* don't think."

"Only on days that end in day," Pika replied smugly.

Lily interrupted. "You don't have to if you don't want to. It's getting dangerous."

Pika scoffed. "You mean exciting!"

Peni shrugged. "Dangerous, exciting. Banana, banana right?"

She schooled her face. *No...not really. It's really not.*

"Suit yourself," Ang snapped, moving forward. "Come on! Let's go before more things wanna kill us."

"You're so chipper Ang." Brandon ran to catch up to her.

"You'd think a deadly waterfall would keep you quiet for five minutes," she grumbled back.

Ignoring her, Brandon shouted. "Onward!"

Lily shook her head. Normally she'd be smiling or chuckling at Brandon's antics. But he hadn't seen who...or what...was chasing them. Even now the image of the fearsome warrior burned her mind.

And those eyes...

Goosebumps peppered her arms. That look was only described in movies and stories. Never had she seen it in real life...until today.

The eyes of someone obsessed.

She knew, without a doubt, that warrior would never give up. So that meant she was going to keep moving as fast as she possibly could to get back to her aunt, Cabyll, and Peri.

And hoped and prayed they stayed ahead of the Maero.

The moon and stars sparkled overhead as the group continued to trudge along the sandy beach and the moon dipped faster and faster toward the horizon. No one slowed down, their movements quick and quiet, save for her and Brandon's soft panting.

"We're close." Waru pointed straight ahead.

There, far in the distance, a large structure loomed high above them. It rose above the cliffs, overlooking the ocean, a portion carved into the mountain.

Lily's shoulders sagged. It was so high. Why was it so high?

Ang snorted, frowning. "How are we going to get up there?"

Lily was glad Ang asked the question. Last time she checked, she hadn't gotten a pair of wings on this trip. Free climbing was not on her list of skill sets. Plus, she was carrying a memory that looked like it could break if you so much as breathed on it wrong. Somehow, she didn't think climbing cliffs was what Isa had in mind when she instructed them to keep it safe.

"When our help comes, we will be able to get up there no problem," replied Waru.

"Well, it isn't here yet, is it?" Ang snorted, crossing her arms. "There's *no* way the humans can get up there."

"I'll agree with Ang on this one," inserted Brandon. "My forte is catching air from a ramp, not a cliff."

"No need to worry young human," Waru reassured. "You may be very weak, your constitution soft-"

Brandon frowned. "Um, I wasn't going with that-"

Waru continued, "Your baby hands can barely hold onto dirt let alone stone..."

Lily jumped in. "Waru, will the help be here soon?"

Waru stared off in silence, as if listening for something. He finally nodded.

"Does that mean we wait at the cliff?" she asked. "Can we even afford to wait?"

Spyke hummed, rubbing his chin. "I do not believe we have a choice. The only alternative is to carry you and Brandon up the cliff." He glanced at the satchel, frowning.

There was a great risk if they did that.

A chilling howl reached Lily's ears. Her blood thickened, turning to molasses in her veins.

No...no, no, no!

How were they so fast? Her shoulders shook, afraid to turn around. Instinctively she hugged the satchel, protecting it. Her heart jumped sluggishly as a fiery hand clasped onto hers.

Spyke dragged her gaze to his, his warm hand engulfing hers.

"They're here," he growled.

She nodded. *Pretty much gathered by the horror movie howl.*

Ang's lip curled. "Think we can get up there?"

Waru eyes narrowed. "No chance now. They will be here in minutes."

Spyke peered into the darkness, his hand over his eyes. "I spot ten, eleven...no twelve Maero."

"Don't forget that Kaupe," added Ang, her voice lowering to a soft growl.

Brandon gulped. "Uh...guys? What do we do?"

His alarmed face tugged at Lily's heart. He shouldn't have been involved in this. He should be at home, safe. This was all her fault. What if something happened to him? She'd never forgive herself.

Spyke patted her shoulder. "We will protect you both." Almost as if reading her mind, his voice lowered. "He will be safe, on my honor."

Lily's shoulders loosened slightly - not by much, but a little. But she couldn't depend solely on them. She needed to help, too.

Cabyll's voice echoed in her mind.

Are you just going to stand there? Or are you going to do something?

She gritted her teeth, his voice snapping her senses back into place. Straightening her shoulders, she carefully rested the satchel on the sand. She took out her bow, getting it ready. The faint dots in the distance were growing, the howling getting louder.

"Brandon?" Lifting the satchel back up, she handed it out. "Take the memory."

He frowned. "What Lil? You're not seriously gonna fight them, are you?"

"I have to do *something*."

"But Lil-" he protested.

The dots grew even larger. So large Lily could now make out the angry, terrifying faces of the Maero warriors, one in particular. Her heart thumped loudly.

She yelled, hoping her fear didn't make her voice tremble.

"Take it Brandon! There's no time!"

Reluctantly, he grasped the satchel, moving behind Ang. Lily turned her back to him, drawing her bow taunt. Her cold fingertips burned against the string, the stinging pain keeping her fear at bay.

"So, what's the plan everyone?" asked Ang.

"Waru and I will take out the Maero and the Kaupe. You keep the humans safe," said Spyke, slinging his club over his shoulder.

"Oh...that's all?" Ang's sarcasm was fierce. "Why don't you take out a hoard of Pookas while you're at it!"

Waru cracked his knuckles, then his neck with a loud snap before he

269

whirled his club in a lazy circle. His lip quirked up in a grin, anticipation evident on his face.

"This will be a good fight," he said. "My muscles need some exercise."

Lily's temple throbbed. *Why do they look so happy? What is happy about fighting?*

"Idiots," Ang grumbled.

"But," Waru continued, his voice turning serious. "You leave Hunapo for me."

The warrior's playful eyes dimmed, narrowing into flints. "He is *my* fight."

Spyke nodded silently, his own club ready.

Brandon pipped up. "So...you guys are saying you can handle like a dozen of these big guys? On your own?"

Both Spyke and Waru raised their eyebrows before Spyke answered. "We would not be considered warriors if we couldn't."

Waru shook his head dismissively. "You say the silliest things."

Brandon's eyes glazed. "That's so Gucci!"

Ang hissed, her nails lengthening into claws. "Focus morons! They're here."

Sure enough, the Maero had indeed arrived. They stood in a row, silent, the waves crashing to their side. The Kaupe frothed at the mouth, its angry eyes on Lily and Ang. No one said anything, each group assessing the other in a chilled silence.

Finally, the largest Maero, the one Lily saw earlier, stepped forward. Hunapo.

He chuckled darkly, his voice gravel and stone. "Looks like we meet again Māori dog."

Waru's nose twitched. "Hunapo...I didn't think you'd ever show your face again."

He gave a dismissive wave. "The hunt is all. You should know this."

"There are honorable hunts, and then there is viciousness and cruelty." Waru shook his head. "You never learned the difference Hunapo."

Hunapo's face hardened, his hairy eyebrows dipping down to cover his eyes. "And everything came so easy for *you*. *You* got the blessings from the gods simply by being you. While *we*," he thumped his chest, sneering as the others behind him whooped in unison. "*WE* work and train hard so that we were allowed to even step in your shadows. We are just as much warriors as you."

"Do not blame your failings on others," barked Waru. "Take responsibility for your actions. You and you alone caused your downfall."

"And why was that?" Hunapo balled his fists. "What can one do when fate forgets you?"

"You rise above and make your own."

Hunapo sneered. "Typical Waru. So lofty and self-righteous. You are ignorant because you and your people were always favored. Your blindness is laughable." His eyes narrowed. "You know why you anger me so? Because you think we are so different."

"I am nothing like you," Waru growled.

"Because you are weak!" Hunapo pounded his chest. "We will not be shackled by rules and chains you call honor anymore. The hunt makes *everyone* equal. The hunt is ALL!"

Waru barred his teeth. "The *hunt* does not involve women and children."

Hunapo's dark chuckle gave Lily's goosebumps goosebumps. With supreme effort, she forced her eyes to stay focused on the Kaupe, even as they began to water.

The Maero leader smirked. "You're still angry about that?"

His cruel laugh grew. "After all these years, you still haven't found another wife? We live for hundreds of years Waru. You'd think you'd have another family."

Lily's heart stopped. The jovial warrior she saw the past few days had disappeared. A haunted, burning anger flared inside him so bright he practically vibrated with it.

Ward's soft, menacing tone chilled Lily's bones as a cold, desolate smile slowly upturned his lips. "I cannot wait to slice your smirking face."

Hunapo scoffed. "I only want the humans. The Sentinel specifically. Hand them over."

"No." Spyke's firm answer brooked no argument.

"It was an order, not a request." Hunapo shrugged his shoulders. "But still, if you don't want to do this the easy way...we *love* the hard way."

Lily blinked. Faster than she could imagine, Waru launched himself at the Maero leader, giving him a resounding punch to the jaw. A crack echoed, the Maero leader's jaw slightly tilted. Without saying a word, Hunapo took one hand and snapped his jaw back into place. He rubbed his cheek dismissively, as Waru growled in his face.

"Stop talking," ordered Waru.

And the talking stopped.

Chapter Twenty-Three

"MISS ARI, IT IS TIME TO AWAKEN."

Aput's voice permeated her dreams of fire and smoke. She woke up, her hair sticky with sweat, her mouth dry. Confused, she took in her surroundings. It was still dark. Why was it still dark? And what were those dreams she had? Goosebumps peppered her forearms. More and more she felt less like herself.

"Aput?" she called out.

The Ijiraq appeared. They bowed, their voice whispering. "It is almost daybreak on sacred Imbolc. The Council is gathering for a special meal before the sunrise ceremony."

"Ceremony?"

Aput nodded. "Honoring the sun. It brings the light and fire back into the territory. His highness has requested that you be dressed appropriately."

A dark voice crept in her thoughts, piercing her brain.

You mean dressed like a naïve doll for his amusement...

She frowned, rubbing her temple to dispel the sharp pang. The angry thoughts were getting louder. She shook her head, dismissing them. Dain wanted to make a good impression, that's all. Cold sweat beaded on her brow.

She wiped her forehead with a trembling hand.

Aput curious eyes met hers. "Miss Ari? Are you alright?"

She forced a weak smile. "I'm good Aput. It's just hot in here."

Aput tilted their head, their voice confused. "It is actually quite cool. Miss Ari...are you sure you're well? Do you need to rest more?"

She waved her hand, holding back the acid in her throat. She gritted her teeth, pulling her lips in, what she hoped, a placating smile. "I said I'm fine. I'll get dressed."

Aput nodded. "Very well," They gestured to the bed, a beautiful dress appearing on the sheets. "His highness must not be kept waiting."

Mechanically, she got up, reaching for the dress. Wild thoughts danced in her unconscious, burning brighter and louder.

Soon, he will wait for me. When the fire begins...

If you could ask Ari what she remembered on that night, reflecting years from now, it was the vision of candles burning bright in the twilight.

Thousands upon thousands of candles glowed within the calm darkness. A cool wind blew into the dining area, the starry sky frozen overhead. Dreamy wisps of basil, blackberry, and bay incense danced in the breeze. A large table was laden with greenery, more candles, and an abundance of blackberries, jams, cheeses, and savory breads.

Through the incense and candlelight, faint figures danced in merriment. Firelight played upon their faces, ping ponging between ethereal and cautionary. Beauty and danger.

Nafanua dragged Peri onto the floor, the larger warrior picking up the little fairy and twirling her around. Their laughter bubbled as little Mo'o servants hid smiles at their antics. Okena and Raven were off on the side, speaking intently with Tane.

Kamohoali'i interrupted, pulling Raven onto the floor. The shark god ignored Okena's dangerous frown, dipping the human into a series of impressively smooth moves that surprised Ari considering how large the fae was.

Tane's little owl perched upon the Thunderboy's large wolf. Ari was oddly reminded of Aesop's fable of the lion and the mouse.

It was strangely heartwarming.

She smoothed her ruby gown, darkened to a cherry hue in the dim light. The corset hugged her curves and flared out in a shimmery skirt.

Squinting, she spotted Dain amongst the throng. Impeccably dressed, he wore a crisp icy white dress shirt and matching pants that shone brilliantly even in the candlelight. His golden hair was tousled, burning embers that sparked something in her heart. Now was the moment where Dain's brilliant eyes would find hers and give her a loving smile.

But...they did not.

He was standing with Kamehameha and Hi'iaka, the latter shining gloriously in a form fitting dress made of crimson and orange leaves which accentuated her glowing caramel skin. Dain leaned down to whisper in her ear, causing Hi'iaka to giggle, her smile sensual. Ari rubbed her chest, a burning ache sparking.

He toys with you...

A voice cut through the fiery thoughts. "Ari?"

Cabyll was at her side, his bright eyes assessing. The fire in her thoughts swirled, shifting. Was he worried? He must be! Out of the corner of her eye, she peered back at Dain, who was still speaking with the other members.

Her face flushed.

Now is the time to toy with him...

Turning her attention back to Cabyll, her lips peeled back in a sugary smile which belied the dry tongue that stuck to the top of her mouth.

"Cabyll, are you wanting a dance?"

He shook his head, his lips opening to respond, but...Ari couldn't make out what it was. Her heartbeat thumped too loudly in her ears. Instead, she focused what he wore, which was incredibly handsome.

He wore a verdant linen tunic and pants. The tunic, outlined with silver, was opened at the neck. His emerald eyes glowed in the twilight, his dark hair swallowing up any remaining light. She blinked, realizing they were standing in silence as he looked at her questioningly.

She gave an apologetic smile, tilting her head coyly. "Sorry, I was thinking of something else. Are you sure you don't want to dance? The music is dreamy."

And it was. Even now, Ari was swaying to the beat, her hips moving on their own. A vague thought teased, reminding her this was not her. Usually, she didn't dance by choice. But somehow, right now, the music called her. Telling her that she was beautiful.

Powerful.

"Wouldn't you want to ask Prince Dain for the first dance?" He gestured over to the prince, whose gaze was finally upon them.

Dain's shrewd eyes caught hers. Ari could sense the prince was analyzing the scene. Those crimson eyes bore into hers, but instead of feeling bashful – as she normally would – her skin crawled. It was annoying.

She scoffed, ripping her gaze from Dain's surprised one. She fluttered her lashes. "I asked *you*, not him. I can ask who I want to dance with."

Cabyll frowned. "Are you alright? You seem a little...different."

She giggled, moving closer, ignoring his shocked expression. He took a small step backward, but that didn't deter her. "I'm more myself than I've ever been."

Warmth rushed through her limbs, moving her ever closer to the fae assassin.

"And that is?" He asked warily, taking another step backward.

She kept moving forward, unperturbed. "Don't worry Cabyll. I know you're only stepping away because of the deal you made."

"What are you-"

In her haze, her shoe caught the hem of the dress. Her vision tilted, as she shut her eyes expecting to hit the floor. But it never happened.

Strong arms lifted her up, Cabyll's green eyes meeting hers.

"Are you okay?" His eyebrows furrowed.

She leaned in, whispering against his neck. "I promise I'll free you from her."

His gaze narrowed as he abruptly pulled his hands away, stepping back. A tiny voice in the back of Ari's mind peeped out that it looked like he was angry, but the languid, warming haze enveloping her spoke louder, knowing it had to be out of concern for her safety.

A deep voice cut through Ari's thoughts. "Ari?"

She turned to find Dain at her side, arms crossed. "I was told by Aput you were not feeling well."

She flipped her hair over her shoulder, giving a small smile. "As you can see, I'm fine."

His usual smirk dipped downward briefly before his neutral mask returned, his eyes shrewd. "Are you?"

She gestured toward Hi'iaka. "Better than you."

Dain's eyes traveled, his lips tilting upward in a suave half smile. "Ah...my *petite oiseau*, if you wanted me to yourself you only needed to tell me."

He reached out, taking her hand and placing it upon his forearm. His eyes focused on her, but he addressed Cabyll. "Excuse us Cabyll, I must attend to my human."

Cabyll gave a small, stiff bow before heading off toward Okena.

Ari pouted, looking through her eyelashes. "I didn't want him to go yet."

Dain squeezed her hand slightly. "I believe you played the part of wooing him quite enough. We are at the end of the play remember?"

She held herself back from rolling her eyes. "And did you get all your players?"

He blinked at her sharp tone. He paused a moment, gathering his thoughts. "I got as much as I could. But it shall be enough I believe." He leaned forward. "Are you sure you're alright?"

Burn...

She lifted her chin, her voice deepening. "I'm better than I've ever been."

Something sweet and smokey filled her nose, like a flower that stayed out in the sun for too long. She inhaled, deeply, her eyes widening.

Dangling from his neck, sparkling like a blood ruby teardrop, was the jasper jar. From Dain's height, the jar was almost at her eye-level. Winking. Waiting.

A familiar tug pulled her stomach, her fingers itching to cradle the warmth again.

Dain's eyes followed her gaze, resting on the jar. In a rare moment, his tense shoulders relaxed. A soft sigh escaped his lips, an unconscious little smile forming.

"It is very beautiful, isn't it?"

She nodded, unable to say anything else. It was taking everything within her not to rip the necklace off his throat. The angry voices thumped in her ears.

He is not worthy of it!

A surprised gasp escaped her as her vision filled with Dain's arms circling her. Carefully, the prince lowered the necklace over her head. The smooth jar rested on her collarbone, warming up almost immediately. Why would he part with the vessel now?

He looked down at her, still smiling softly. "We will have the fire. In the meantime, I think you should wear this for the evening." He winked. "Red looks exceptionally radiant on you."

Her fingers rested on the vessel, the warmth seeping in almost immediately. A slow pulsing, almost a rhythmic thumping, caressed her. It filled her up, warming her, embracing her. The smoky, languid feeling from earlier cascaded down, enveloping her in a dreamy, heated haze. This is what she needed. This was what she deserved.

And soon, they will all know it.

She smiled, wrapping her arms around the prince's neck. She reveled in his surprised expression. Not that she could blame him. She never was this bold. Not until now.

She leaned up, her mouth near Dain's neck, whispering coyly. "Shouldn't you get this party started?"

He paused; his eyes indiscernible. Then, he tilted back his head, laughing. "Intriguing...whatever has become of you my dear?" He raised a hand, stopping her. "It doesn't matter. It is Imbolc, you should have a bit of fun. And I must say, I am immensely entertained."

He winked, his eyes sly. "Yes, let us begin."

Dain waved his hand, the music coming to a halt. Attention turned to them as the prince bowed low. In a loud voice he proclaimed.

"Dear council members, as a show of our appreciation for your hospitality, I have prepared some entertainment on this sacred twilight before the dawn of Imbolc."

With a theatrical clap of his hands, a group of fae dancers poured into the room. Dressed in brightly colored leaves and flowers, their hair wild and free, they moved with an almost waterlike grace into position. The rhythmic deep notes of several drums beat softly. The dancers moved, as one, into a hula.

Ari scanned the room. Her aunt sat, mesmerized by the performance. The dancers quickened their pace, their hips moving like lightening as the tempo increased. If she was honest with herself, she was fixated too. An almost hypnotic call to join.

Dain's warm hand on her arm was the only thing stopping her.

His breath tickled her ear. "Watch this."

He gave a sharp clap. More dancers appeared carrying long sticks. Bemused, Ari's eyes widened as flames licked the wood, catching fire. The dancers began twirling and leaping, the fire dancing around in various patterns. Dimly, she noticed a Mo'o servant handing out glasses of sparkling liquid. As a Mo'o reached her, Dain stopped her.

"Please get the human wine." He gestured to the glass. "It was requested that the humans present would have normal beverages to keep their wits. Do you mind my dear?"

She shook her head, pleased by his thoughtfulness. Soon, a glass of wine appeared before her. Before she could take a sip, a biting voice cut in.

"Arianna Greene. How old are you again?"

Raven marched up to them, snatching the glass out of her hand. For someone who was engrossed in the music, her aunt had the eyes of a hawk.

Remember, she's not your aunt, she sharply reminded herself.

Dain raised his eyebrow, laughing. "You intend to treat her as a child forever?"

Raven pursed her lips. "I only want her to keep her wits. Regular wine or not."

Dain put up his hands in surrender. "I will not interfere, I assure you. I do not intend harm to my *petite oiseau*." He gestured to the wine. "You can try it yourself if you doubt me."

Suspicion poured out of Raven. With a beat of hesitation, she sniffed the glass before taking a small sip. Mulling it over, she must have deemed it fine, as she reluctantly nodded.

Ari reached out again, but Raven wagged her finger. "It may be fine missy, but I can't in good conscience let you have it."

Ari held back her annoyance, the fire warming her insides. She was ready to argue when Dain's palm engulfed her shoulder, stopping her. His lips turned upward into a satisfied smirk.

"Miss Ravenna, I must say. You...truly...are a human that looks out for your family." He squeezed Ari's shoulder lightly. "It is comforting to see my little human has so many looking out for her."

Raven blinked, keeping her expression neutral. "Ari is family."

Dain nodded, his lips upturned in a smirk. "Of course."

He bowed slightly, putting his hand over his heart. "Apologies, if you excuse me, we should watch the show before it ends. The ending will be quite spectacular."

The dancers picked up the tempo, the fire dancing madly. Ari stood, transfixed. One wrong step, one wrong move, and the flames would be out of control. Her head tilted, following the blazing pattern, her gaze engulfed. How strange. Something so small and seemingly harmless could grow into an inferno and completely destroy everything. How easy would it be to let it go. Let everything soar, burn it all away.

Her cheeks warmed, blooming.

Let it burn...

Far too soon, the music ended. The dancers paused, the fire still glowing in the night. The candles flickered and danced. They seemed to grow, change, and bend in the shadowy moonlight. A quiet pause ensued before fiery clapping engulfed the room.

A piercing, encouraging whistle jostled Ari's attention. Peri removed fingers from her mouth, giving a war whoop, pumping her arms. Vaguely, she heard the little fairy shout.

"That was amazing! You are all beautiful. Well, not as gorgeous as my girl Nafanua here."

Merry laughter and smiles filled the space, but to Ari it seemed far away. Was it warm in here or was it her? Dain's cold presence usually calmed her, but tonight it was bothersome. She flinched when his icy fingers patted hers and held a sigh of relief when he removed himself to move to middle of the dance floor.

He extended his arm, giving a jaunty bow. He gave a roguish grin, captivating everyone. "Are you all having a good time?"

Incoherent yells of affirmation greeted him. The prince's smile widened as he continued. "As we know, on this sacred eve...we welcome the changing of the seasons. Winter is falling back to sleep," his arms moved fluidly, ice crystals dancing in the air above him, "and we welcome the emergence of the light." The ice melted, warm rain puddling around him. "As the sun rises, we too will rise with the fire."

Suddenly, a strong wind blew, a majority of the candles flickering out in one breath. The orange flames sputtered, but then grew higher, taking on a sinister glow. The darkening flames spread over Dain's face; his grin too wide, his teeth too bright.

"This is the time to remember the ancient ones. The ones that encompassed the primal elements themselves. It is time to reclaim what is due us and resurrect those from the beginning."

The wind shifted. Smiles withered, the laughter dying. Nafanua was the first one to step forward.

She frowned, her large hands crossing against her chest. "That is dangerous talk your highness."

He smirked. "It is only dangerous to those who aren't fully enlightened."

"Or to those who do not understand and respect dangerous forces," she countered.

He dismissed her, his hand waving languidly. "I knew you were too idealistic Nafanua. That is why I did not even bother to speak with you." His eyes narrowed, a sneer gracing his lips. "But it is time for you to give me what I came here for. Tell me...where is your piece of the fire."

Nafanua's eyes widened. "You sly little *gata*! You did not learn from your mistakes with Uktena, now you wish to unleash destruction herself?"

Dain inspected his nails, his tone flippant. "So, you refuse?"

She growled, bending into a fighting stance. "Of course!"

Dain groaned, rolling his eyes. "Why am I not surprised. But it does not matter, I have more than I need."

He snapped his fingers.

Nafanua gasped as a figure appeared by Dain's side. A familiar voice gave a breathy sigh.

"You really are quite loud, even when in denial Nafanua."

Nafanua hands unclenched as her lips opened in shock. "*Uo*?!"

Tane towered over Dain. An unreadable expression glided over his face. Ruru chirped sadly, ducking within his braids.

Nafanua stood in silence, her mouth agape. Peri put a comforting hand on her shoulder. The little peri fairy bared her teeth. "I would think the so called 'Forest God' of the South would want life, not destruction."

Tane's lips curled, his nose upturned. "Insolent peri fairy. Things are not always so simple. I do wish for life to thrive."

Only then did Ari notice the council member appeared weary, like a weight was pressing down as his shoulders fell.

He gave a drawn-out sigh. "Sometimes," his eyes opened, bitter. "you must burn it down to give life a chance."

"You can't mean that Tane," protested Nafanua.

"While you sit here and drink yourself stupid, the humans are eradicating life as we speak," he barked, his voice rising. "How long do you think it will take before that poison spreads to us? We need to scorch the land to eliminate the disease to allow for our world to endure."

Peri rolled up her sleeves. "Just say the word Nafanua and I'll take care of this bozo."

She yelped.

Large vines wrapped around the little fairy until she was covered in bright red hibiscus. Peri struggled, ripping a vine or two until a huge flower slithered upward, wrapping around her shoulders, the petals facing her. With a burst, the flower poured a pink powder over Peri's eyes. She squinted, coughing. In only a few seconds, her eyes glazed over, unblinking, until they closed. An unladylike snore was the only indication the little fairy was alive.

A high-pitched giggle rattled Ari's ears. Hi'iaka tapped her chin delicately. "Now, now, snoring isn't very ladylike."

Nafanua bowed her head, disappointed. "Not you too Hi'iaka."

The beautiful fae scoffed, flipping her hair. She moved toward Tane, her hips sashaying. "Tane may have noble purposes, but mine is just simple."

"And that is?" growled Okena, taking every detail in.

Cabyll slowly flipped a knife in the air, silent. His wordless gaze met Okena, who shook his head.

"Power." Hi'iaka tugged a flower from her hair, cradling it in the palm of her hand.

"I am a magic hula fae for goodness sakes. And for that, the man I wished to be with rejected me. Why?" She clutched the flower, the frayed petals falling to the floor. "Because I was not a warrior. I wasn't deemed strong enough."

Nafanua palmed her face. "You're telling me, you turned traitor on his highness because you still pine for him?"

Hi'iaka's face flushed. "I have *never* been turned down."

"He did turn you down, flat," Nafanua deadpanned.

"Yes, he did. You were upset for years," answered Tane, rolling his eyes.

Hi'iaka hissed, her teeth clenched. "Shut up both of you!"

"This is a stupid reason to unleash the goddess and you know it," barked Nafanua.

Hi'iaka walked up to Nafanua, her eyes cold and angry. With a feral hiss, she slapped the warrior fae on the cheek. "I do not care! Soon, Prince Kye will regard me as the strongest fae. He will regret rejecting me."

"Highly doubt it," Okena mumbled.

Nafanua stood stock still, the light imprint fading from her face. Her eyes blanked, a neutral mask obscuring her typical jovial face.

She leaned forward to coldly whisper in Hi'iaka's ear. "Just remember, I *let* you do that. You will not have another chance."

Okena stepped forward, his gravelly voice cutting. "I think that is quite enough."

Dain smirked. "Yes, I do believe it is *Okena*." He snapped his fingers. "Come on. Chop, chop! I haven't got all day. It's time to end the charade...brother."

Okena glared, reluctantly removing a ring from his finger. With a glimmer, Okena vanished and another man emerged. The large wolf had also disappeared, transformed into a furiously large cat. A collective gasp filled the room.

Ari frowned. The man before her was intimidating, towering over everyone, save for the shark god. Corded muscles everywhere, bunched up and tense. Deep, violet eyes glowed in the candlelight, narrowing on Dain. His arms were crossed, promising power and danger.

Raven stood, unmoving, the entire time they transformed. Judging by how her aunt didn't react when the glamour dissolved, she must have known. Ari bit her lip. Raven kept it from her. She chewed her lip harder, holding back the anger.

The council gasped, all of them bowing, even the traitors. Hi'iaka's eyes widened, her face paling. She reached out instinctively. "Prince Kye, you're...back?"

Ari held in her gasp. This was Dain's brother?

Kye cracked his neck, ignoring her. "Well then, *little* brother. Guess you figured it out sooner than I anticipated. We have a lot to talk about." He cracked his knuckles, his eyes beginning to glow. "But first...I think I need to impose some manners on you."

Dain held up his finger, tsking. "You were always so impatient. Ever since we were children, you always wanted to fight someone, smash something, take someone's head off." He sighed. "You know, it has become quite predictable. This time," he clapped his hands, "I suspect you'll be begging for my help."

Kye frowned. "You are delusional if you and those traitors think for one moment-"

Cough, cough...

The coughing behind them stopped the prince mid-sentence. Slowly, he turned around, the light dying from his eyes.

Ari gasped, panic settling in her stomach.

Raven hunched over, grasping her stomach fiercely. Blood trickled down her lips, splattering onto the floor. The cat ran to her side, trying to steady her, whining anxiously. Her eyes were unfocused, her trembling hands grasping at the cat's fur as her legs gave out.

Kye made a dashing leap, catching Raven in his arms before she hit the floor. His eyes were wide, his gaze catching Dain's smirk.

Kye yelled out, his voice thundering. "What did you *do*?!"

Dain shrugged, inspecting his nails. "Do? A simple poison really."

Kye's eyes glowed, the air growing cold and damp. Ari shivered, that icky feeling coming back, twisting her insides.

The prince raised his hand, water forming and narrowing to sharp needlelike spears. With a grunt, he threw his arm out, the water spears slicing through the air toward Dain.

"Nu uh," tsked Dain, lifting his finger. The spears stopped, frozen in midair, almost touching his nose. He gently tapped the spears, the frozen water shattering. "You try anything else, and she dies."

Kye's lip curled, his breathing ragged. He clutched Raven's still form as water pulsed around him, gathering like a storm.

Dain shrugged his shoulders. "Do what you want. It's her funeral."

Kye frowned, his eyes indecisive as they briefly flickered back to Raven's crumpled form.

Dain put up his hands in a flourish.

"Let me distill this down for you, dear brother. You try to heal the human, she dies. You fight me, she dies. But by all means, I know you love to wield your fist first so do give it a go."

Cabyll and Nafanua stepped forward, but Dain slashed his hand down, irritation dripping. "I *hate* repeating myself. If *anyone* tries *anything*, the human dies."

Nafanua growled. "You coward. You resorted to poison? How despicable." She spat on the ground, disgusted.

Dain just shrugged. "I will do anything to achieve my goal. I'm not bound by the lines of, what you deem, morality. Now," his eyes narrowed, "enough of this game brother. What do you choose?"

"What do you want Dain?" interrupted Cabyll, calmly palming his dagger.

Dain's lip curled upward. "It's simple really." His gaze fell on Kye. "Bind your powers big brother, and I give your human the antidote."

Kye knelt down, his massive arms cradling Raven gently, his eyes fixed solely on her. Ari scarcely made it out, but she thought Raven gave a weak thumbs up.

Another sputtering cough emitted from Raven, more blood escaping down her chin. Kye shook his head, his eyes sad. Much to the surprise of everyone in the room, he stood up, Raven still cradled in his arms.

Cabyll shook his head. "I don't think this is wise Prince Kye."

Kye hard eyes bore into Cabyll's. "What would you do? If you were me."

Cabyll kept silent, his dagger momentarily stopping.

Kye nodded. "As I suspected."

Nafanua blinked, surprised. "Your highness, there are millions of lives at stake. You taught us sometimes the hard choice is still the only choice to make."

Kye sighed, taking in Raven's pale form again. He looked up, his eyes like violet ice.

"You *swear* Dain," he gritted out. "Swear an oath that if I bind my powers temporarily, you will give the antidote at the same time."

"Temporarily?" scoffed Dain.

"You know if I bind them too long, it will affect us all," an unspoken warning passed between them, "even you. And not for the better."

Dain grumbled, reluctant. "Fine, fine. So...until noon then?"

Kye nodded, opening his mouth -

"NO!"

Hi'iaka paled, her hands shaking, her lips trembling.

"No." She repeated, her lips turned downward into a malicious sneer. "For a human? I, who am the most beautiful, you reject. But you'll bind your powers to save a weak human?!"

Kye shook his head. "You, Hi'iaka, were never beautiful in my eyes."

"But to sacrifice your power?" she protested. "You're one of the most powerful fae that our world has known. And you're shackling yourself...for a *human*?"

He roared, his voice firm and commanding. "No one...*nothing*...will change my mind."

Ignoring Hi'iaka's stunned expression, Kye slowly, and carefully, laid Raven on the floor. He returned upright, taking a deep breath. He closed his eyes, the tendons tense in his throat.

"Anytime now," Dain called out impatiently.

Kye eyes snapped open, a glowing violet illuminated in a haze around him.

The candles dimmed and flickered while the air became colder, damper. Shimmering water droplets formed, swirling around him. Faster and faster they sped, until the water began to glow a vivid purple. Then, the haze surrounding him grew dimmer, the water absorbing the glow. The violet aura around him faded as the droplets disappeared with a soft popping sound.

"It's done," answered Kye.

His eyes narrowed on Dain, cold and angry. "The antidote...*now!*"

Dain scoffed, waving his hand. "Yes, yes. Your theatrics are amazing. But before that," he motioned over toward the remaining council members. "I have been waiting long enough for your answers."

Silence held with bated breath. Kamehameha was standing on the side, his arms crossed. With his helmet on, Ari couldn't make out the Nightmarcher's expression. He strode over to prince, stopping momentarily when he passed Kye. Maybe it was her imagination, but the Night-marcher seemed focused on Raven's pale face. Slowly, he reached up, plucking something small from his helmet.

Nafanua yelled out. "Kamehameha, no!"

The Nightmarcher sighed deeply before turning to Dain, placing the item in the prince's palm. His voice whispered around the hall, without him turning around. "Death comes to everyone. So does life. My purpose is to make sure the cycle does not break."

"But millions will suffer," protested Nafanua.

"Millions suffer now as well. To live can be suffering. To receive death can be merciful. Who am I, who are *we*, to make those ultimate choices? No choice is ever easy. To live with a choice is a heavy burden." His head tilted slightly, motioning toward Raven. "And if I must make such a choice, it shall be one I can endure living with for this long immortal life."

Nafanua shook her head, her beseeched gaze landing on Kamohoali'i. The shark god lumbered up, his eyes bright. "As I told you before Prince Dain, this is dangerous. I refuse."

Dain shrugged. "Well, I guess I could always give the word to my... associates...who are watching your son..."

Kamohoali'i growled, growing bigger in size. Ari flinched, backing away.

Gone was the laughing councilman. His face morphed, his lips peeling back as rows of needle-sharp teeth emerged. Midnight black hair fell to the floor in chunks, his balding forehead pulled back. His black eyes grew empty.

He spoke, an animalistic growl booming. "You go too far!"

Everyone stopped. Even Tane and Hi'iaka froze, their eyes wide and wary.

Dain crossed his arms, scoffing. "Honestly? I would think *you* of all the fae here, would want to see this day."

The anger within the shark god burst like a balloon. His great shoulders sagged as Kamohoali'i shook his head, saddened. "I was young. Foolish."

He looked to Kye, his indecision growing.

Dain examined his nails, his voice lilting. "I hear your son is learning how to spear fish right now."

Kamohoali'i closed his eyes, his face pinched. Gritting his long teeth, the shark god bowed low before Kye. "Forgive me your highness."

Kye nodded, his attention still focused on Raven. "I understand, old friend."

Kamohoali'i straightened, breathing out resigned sigh. With his meaty hands he reached up, and with no hesitation, ripped a large tooth from his mouth. Reluctantly, he handed over the torn tooth.

Ari covered her mouth, turning away from the gruesome sight.

Soon, everyone focused on Nafanua. Her gaze shifted from Peri to Raven. She pinched her nose, sighing.

Her angry gaze bore into Dain's before she removed a ring to throw it, hard, at his chest. She hissed, her voice dripping venom. "I hope when you wake her, she burns your vapid face."

Dain effortlessly caught the object. His smug smile grew wider. "I thought my face was handsome."

"Weak," she gritted out, her anger turning to pierce Hi'iaka. "Physical beauty alone has nothing of value in this grand universe."

Dain shrugged. "Regardless of your ridiculous thoughts, thank you so much for your cooperation. I will not forget it."

"Brother," Kye interrupted. His lips peeled back in a snarl, bending down to clutch Raven closer who, Ari noticed, was becoming a sickly gray. "The antidote!"

Dain sighed, his fingers tapping his forehead. "Yes, of course." Turning his back to the group, his hand delved into his shirt. He pulled out a small glass vial. With a flick of his wrist, he threw the vial over his head. Eyes wide, the group followed the precious container that was on a collision course to meeting the stone floor.

Dain smirked over his shoulder, "I said I'd give it to you, I didn't say how."

An animalistic growl tore through the group. The large black cat leapt into the air, startling everyone, particularly Hi'iaka who yelped daintily and fell on her backside. With a lethal grace, the cat caught the vial in its mouth, before landing softly on its paws.

The cat turned toward Kye, dropping it in the prince's palm. With a last plaintive whine, the cat butted Raven's pale face, before curling up on her side.

Ari's heart broke a little. Even the intimidating prince looked lost, his bleak eyes meeting the cat's mournful gaze. "I know Aka," he whispered. "I know."

Kye poured the antidote into her aunt's slack mouth, but the liquid started to spill down her chin. His gaze widened, before bending over, sealing his lips over hers. He pulled back, his thumb trailing over her cheek.

Maybe it was wishful thinking on Ari's part, but she swore she heard the prince whisper as he bent over Raven's slack body, "Yell at me, admonish me, berate me, insult me. I will take it all, as long as I hear your voice. I will even kneel before you, so your focus is only on me. As long as I can see your bright gaze which rivals the sun."

Nothing happened.

Kye gritted his teeth, his eyes clenched shut. He pulled Raven closer, his head buried in her hair before looking up.

His furious gaze caught Ari's, startling her. "Are you happy? She gave up everything because she loves you...because they love you. What more will it take for you to open your eyes?"

Ari gaped, unable to speak. Why was he mad at her? What did she do?

Dain's arm draped over her shoulders. "Do not blame my little human brother. She had no idea."

"What do you mean?" asked Kye suspiciously.

Dain whistled a little tune, the toe of his boot flicking a discarded wine glass. Ari frowned, not understanding.

Dain tapped her shoulder softly to the music. "I figured protectiveness ran in the family." The glass flew with a decisive kick of his boot. "And turns out, I was right."

Kye glared. "You poisoned the wine?"

Dain shrugged. "I poisoned all the human wine."

Ari's mouth gaped open, her chest caving in as her heart bottomed out. Only one thought kept repeating in the haze.

He poisoned **my** *wine?!*

Kye spoke what she couldn't. "What about your human? She could have died Dain."

Dain's neutral tone pierced Ari. "I made a calculated move."

His raised eyebrow clinically took in Raven's limp form. "I deduced she would protect her family. It was quite touching...really...to see her

289

running up to drink the wine instead of Ari." His scientific gaze assessed Raven, cataloguing her as if he could piece a puzzle together. "Your human sacrificed herself for her family. You should be proud brother, she has a strong will...for a human."

Kye growled, his violet eyes icy chips. They sparked, unable to glow to their full potential because of his binding. "Brother... when I am whole again, you will regret making me your enemy."

Dain dismissed him with a wave of his hand. "She's just a human Kye."

"And yours?" Kye gritted out, "How do you think she feels that you used her?"

Ari's throat stuck, her eyes glued to Raven's gaunt pallor. That could have been *her*! Did Dain care? Didn't she matter?

Dain squeezed her numb shoulders, his voice sounding far away against her ringing ears. "My *petit oiseau* understands the ultimate plan. And she is just fine as you see."

"What if I wasn't," she whispered brokenly.

He peered down, as if finally noticing her for the first time. His tone was nonchalant, almost flippant, as he said simply, "I had the antidote."

Her mind kept skipping. *That* was his excuse? That was how he rationalized it? She blinked, her vision filled with only her aunt's lifeless form. She looked like Sleeping Beauty.

Mentally Ari shook her head, telling herself it wasn't real. Her hands, and heart, were frozen, unable to grasp anything. Everything kept replaying back. Yes, it was part of Dain's plan, but she never thought he wanted her hurt. But, this time? *This* time, he planned it! There was no 'mistakes' on this. And his apathetic attitude that she could have died was just the final straw.

Enough!

The fire roared, melting the frozen, broken parts of her heart. Red and hot, the numbness pricked her, blazing. An inferno crested inside her chest, threatening to burst. The unfamiliar voice, and her voice, snarled as one.

He does not care! After all you have done, what an ungrateful, weak prince.

Cabyll's voice cut through the fire, briefly. "Then let the human go Dain. You have what you want."

Her charred heart thumped faintly. The roaring flames dulled slightly by Cabyll's calming voice. The inside voice whispered mysteriously.

That fae's soul is of noble fire. He deserves to be at our table.

Dain's hand squeezed harder, his voice steely. Ice crystals crackled in the air. "She...is *mine*."

She tensed. *Why does he say that now? He doesn't get to say that after almost poisoning me!*

She chewed her thumbnail, wanting to throw off his arm, but she stopped. The voice whispered, its cunning logic spreading in her ear.

We still need this prince, weak as he is. Let him finish his work. Then, his weak ice will melt under our blaze.

She frowned. This didn't seem right. But...

Give in, the voice whispered. *Fall into the warmth of my embrace little human. I will keep you safe and warm. You will be powerful and beautiful...as you were meant to be. We will punish those that wronged you. All you need to do, is fall into me. Let my fire consume you.*

Inside, the fire slithered and wove around her. A misty haze filled her mind, clouding her logic. Yes, she deserved this. She would be in control this time. She would be the one Dain listened to for once.

Yes, that sounds good, she agreed.

A small electric jolt hit her heart where the pendant lay. Slowly, a languid warmth flowed into her veins. It filled her up, like a cup. She became lighter, but stronger. Warm, but solid. The oddest sensations where she felt everything, yet nothing. The voice spoke, louder and happy.

Well done mea liilii, it praised. *Let us begin the show...together.*

Ari lifted her hand. Somehow it was brighter, smoother. She laid it on Dain's cheek, startling him.

When she spoke, her voice was more melodic and soothing than before. "Do not frown so Dain. I am here, and I will be."

Her gaze turned back to caress Cabyll, who brows furrowed as she continued to smile. The poor man didn't know it yet, but he would be hers soon.

Dain's eyes widened, as if seeing her anew. And she was. She was new, beautiful. So beautiful she glowed in the dying candlelight. She had rose from the ashes and burned so bright she had a hard time containing herself.

Not yet, warned the voice. *We mustn't burn too brightly too soon. Patience little one.*

Dain blinked a moment, confused. "Ari, did you dye your hair by chance?"

Her innocent eyes widened. "Oh? Did I?"

"Yes, your blonde hair looks...almost pink."

She laughed softly, tugging his arm. "It must be a trick of the light. Come now, we mustn't dawdle. Let us take everyone to the site, my prince. The sun is almost up."

He stared at her, unmoving, before shaking his head. "Yes, yes you're right. Guards!"

The Adlet guards suddenly appeared from the shadows, ready for the next command.

Cabyll crouched, his hands grasping his scimitars. Kye speared him with a look, shaking his head.

Cabyll's eyes narrowed. "I can take them," he gritted out.

"Remember why you are here," Kye ordered. "Think of the others. Think of Lily."

Hearing her name, Cabyll's eyes clenched shut. He began to lower his scimitars.

Dain's eyes glowed. "Oh yes...let's talk about the sister..."

Cabyll growled, his arms tensing as his hands clenched the handles.

Ari gripped Dain's arm, smiling languidly between them. "Now, now. Let's not have a fight."

Dain eyes dimmed, a roguish smirk turning upward, belying his icy tone. "Never let it be said I never listened to a lady's plea."

Cabyll gritted his teeth. With reluctance he sheathed his swords. "You are correct Prince Kye. I need to think of Lily."

Ari's nails dug a little into Dain's arm. Why would he say Lily's name? It must be the deal they made. She wanted to break it and have Cabyll to herself.

Not yet, the voice reminded her. *The time isn't right yet.*

Relaxing her grip, she smiled sweetly up at Dain. "Can we go?"

Nodding, he snapped his fingers. "Take them up to the site."

As he escorted Ari up the hallways, he whispered. "I hope you are not mad. I had no other way to gain their cooperation. I would not have let you die."

She kept smiling, tucking her head into his neck. "I am not mad."

Lie.

She continued, "We will make a new world remember?"

He sighed, seemingly relieved. He rubbed his chin against the top of her head. "Yes, a new world."

She burned inside, hot and molten. Her hair fell over her arm, an ombre pinkish red staining the bottom of the strands. A hot smile peeled her lips as the voice, her voice, burned.

A new world, yes. I will burn this world...and you...and make it anew. Into my world.

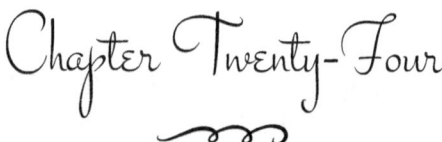

Chapter Twenty-Four

L ILY GRIMACED, ANOTHER ARROW FLYING ONLY TO BE swatted away by a Maero warrior. She wiped her brow, frustrated.

Waru and Spyke were amazing. They fought as though they were comrades for decades, not days. They coordinated their moves in sync, so accurately they cut through the Maero with little effort. As soon as Spyke sent one warrior sailing through the air, Waru was right behind him to block a blow. From what she could tell, they had already taken out about four warriors.

She stared at her bow. But why couldn't she? Not saying she wasn't trying, but even when she managed to get an arrow in a few arms and a foot, that didn't slow down them down. At this rate she'd lose the bet with Cabyll.

Don't think about him, she reminded herself ruefully. *Four down, still eight to go.*

And that didn't include Hunapo or the Kaupe, who eerily waited behind the others, their attention focused on Waru and Spyke. She refused to acknowledge her tight chest when the empty, soulless gaze of the Kaupe flitted her way.

"Guys...hurry up!" Ang yelled as she clawed one warrior near her and Brandon. She spun, giving a forceful kick at another warrior that tried to sneak from behind.

WHAM!

Another Maero warrior flew over their heads, landing into the far sea.

Waru gave a loud war whoop, his eyes wider and brighter. He laughed over his shoulder to Ang. "Good fighting technique *taitamariki*."

Ang kicked the fallen Maero warrior she clawed, knocking him unconscious. "I'm not young knucklehead!"

Spyke, who was lifting another warrior high over his head with ease, called out in warning, "Waru...get ready."

Waru's eyes gleamed as he knocked another warrior out of his way, his club ready. "Throw the *paru* my way Thunderboy."

"Dude." interjected Brandon. "Is he going to..."

Spyke threw the unconscious warrior as Waru pulled back his club and let it fly, sending the massive warrior so far he became only a speck in the distance.

Brandon pumped his fist. "Home run! Man, that's so cool."

Lily groaned inside, her gaze still focused. She breathed deep, notching another arrow.

Five more to go...

Spyke slammed down his club, knocking another warrior into the earth as sand erupted in a gritty cloud. He wiped his chin, a small cut gracing his jaw.

"How are you holding up Lily?" he asked over his shoulder.

"Oh...just fine," she replied shakily as she launched another arrow over his shoulder to push back a warrior who tried to sneak from the side.

Spyke nodded in approval, taking a moment to throw a massive punch at the offending warrior, knocking him unconscious. "Your skills are improving."

"Less talking, more hitting!" Ang yelled, pushing Brandon further behind her.

Three more...

A familiar voice tickled her mind.

Shall we give them a taste of thunder my Sentinel?

Lily smiled, the familiar warmth rushing through her pendant.

Sounds good to me.

Forgive my lateness, his voice was contrite.

Lily's guilt surfaced. If she had trained more he wouldn't have been late. She shook herself.

Nothing to forgive.

She raised her bow again, calling out to Waru and Spyke.

"Guys? Think you can get them closer?"

Ang threw up her hands. "Closer?! Are you crazy?"

Spyke looked up, pausing a moment, before nodding.

Waru immediately picked up her thought, his whooping laughter was answer enough. Soon the remaining three warriors grouped up, heading toward them.

Lily notched her arrow.

Ready when you are Tim!

Energy rushed through the pendant, racing down her arm, through the bow. The arrow lit up, electric blue energy radiating from the arrowhead. She vaguely recalled Hunapo's eyes widening, his lips opening to give a command that was drowned out as she let the arrow fly.

A thundering boom lit up the sand, dust exploding everywhere.

As the sand settled, a crater of glass emerged from the dust cloud. Spikes of glass gave a cold warning of the immense power of the Thunderbird.

The Maero warriors stood silent, their figures frozen in glass.

Ang blew out a soft whistle. "Woah...good job sissy."

Brandon whooped. "Heck ya!"

Lily lowered her bow, adrenaline coursing through her veins. She tried to stamp down the euphoric feeling that she contributed...finally. The Thunderbird's voice brought her back to reality.

Stand ready little one. I believe this battle is not over quite yet.

Hunapo roared, beating his chest. He slammed his fist against his heart until it bloomed red. He stomped his foot, lowering his shoulders in a terrifying stance. The Kaupe mirrored him, emanating an eerie howl that trailed over the waves.

Echoing, fading...into silence.

The groups stared each other down, the tension palpable.

Ang subtly moved Brandon further backward toward the cliff. "Ugh! Okay can we *please* get moving?" She motioned her head for Lily to follow.

"Not yet vermin." Hunapo pulled a conch shell from his side.

Waru blinked, his eyes widening in recognition. "Don't be a fool Huanpo."

With a sneer, the Maero warrior rose the conch to his lips, blowing an unnerving call across the seas.

Lily waited, goosebumps prickling her skin.

Then the waves moved.

It wasn't the fact they moved. Waves normally move. Back, forth, back, forth. This...this was different.

The waves bubbled and frothed. The sea appeared to be on fire from underneath, steam rising from the depths. Then, before she had a chance to process, the waves parted, revealing a horde of creatures.

Walking on two legs, the creatures were slightly hunched over. They sported greenish white skin that glowed inward with an unnatural phosphorescent light as ocean water slicked off their backs. Their feet were webbed and their hands, that sported spears and tridents, ended in sharp claws. They were bald, with bulbous eyes that blinked with a third eyelid, similar to reptiles. Their mouths were wide and lipless, almost like a frog.

Waru cursed. "*Wairangi*. He summoned the Ponaturi."

Brandon hummed a moment. "Um...who?"

Ang spit on the ground, disgusted. "Water goblins."

Brandon's eyes widened. "Awesome. That's super cool."

He flinched as Ang shot him daggers with her eyes. He cradled the satchel closer. "I mean...it'd be cool...if they didn't wanna fight us."

Ang pinched the bridge of her nose, mumbling under her breath. Lily suspected she was counting to ten.

Spyke growled, his voice deep and thunderous. "We're trapped."

Lily's heart dropped as she realized what he meant. In the confusion, she failed to notice *where* the water goblins had appeared.

Behind them, blocking their way to the cliff.

The horde of goblins chittered among themselves. She shivered, their voices were scratchy, grating against her arms.

Hunapo snickered. "Nowhere to run now, little *rapeti*." His voice rose. "For the hunt!"

Ang rolled her eyes. "This guy is just dumb isn't he."

"More like obsessive." Lily gingerly pulled out another arrow, twisting around to focus on the goblins, who were slowly, sneakily... advancing.

Now's a good time to come back Tim, she thought.

The Thunderbird breathed heavily in her mind.

I'm...I'm being blocked little one. The sea goddess's bracelet...her power clashes with mine.

Suddenly, a blinding pain tore through Lily. She gasped, clutching her chest, her arrow falling into the sand. A cold torrent washed over her. Images splintered in her mind of smoke, destruction, terrified screams, and a column of fire.

Namaka's urgent voice broke through the painful void.

Something is wrong mea liilii. My sister...she...

Another wave of wracking pain enveloped Lily, forcing her gaze up the cliffs. Namaka's response echoed hers.

I think...my sister. She's awakening. Hurry Sentinel hurry!

Spyke's worried gaze caught hers. "Lily?"

The Thunderbird's voice came back, weak.

I cannot use my full power as you are still tethered to Namaka with that bracelet. I am sorry my Sentinel.

She groaned, wiping her brow. What bad timing. Now she didn't have Tim to help grill some fish goblins. Another painful tug pulled her gaze back toward the cliffs. Her heart sped up. What was going on up there?

She tried desperately to keep her voice from trembling. "Um... Spyke? My 'Sentinel' mojo is out of juice. What do we do?"

For the first time, the Thunderboy was speechless. Whether it was due to what she said, or the situation, she didn't know.

The Kaupe growled low, bringing them back to the present. Its claws were outstretched, a trail of salvia dripping onto the glassy sand. Without warning, the large monster leapt over the group, landing in front of Ang and Brandon. With precise movements, it raised its claws, ready to slash Brandon, who stood petrified.

"Brandon!"

Ang threw herself in front of him, taking the full brunt of the Kaupe's attack. Brandon held her as her legs buckled, falling with her onto the sand. The Kaupe towered above them, snorting deeply in a chilling animalistic laugh.

Hunapo chuckled darkly his eyes victorious. He raised his battle club high.

"There is nowhere to run. Even the 'great' Waru and a Thunderboy are no match against all of us. Just accept your fate."

Lily glanced around. Brandon huddled behind Ang, clutching the satchel tightly in one hand, grasping a rock in the other. His tearful, angry gaze stayed on the Kaupe.

Spyke did a back flip, soaring above them to land in front of Ang and Brandon, facing the Kaupe. Waru kept his position blocking Hunapo.

But there were still the water goblins. They advanced, their spears and tridents ready. The ocean crashed, the waves thundering in Lily's ears.

Her hands shook, almost losing her grip on the bow. She thought of Kye, her aunt, Ari. Were they safe? Namaka's vision showed they needed to get up that cliff. The destruction if they failed was just...well it wasn't an option. Her worried thoughts strayed to one central fear, her teeth pinching her bottom lip, hard.

Where was Cab?

She mentally smacked herself. *Focus Lil. Focus!*

Waru yelled, "I accept nothing but a warrior's fight!" He pounded his chest. "We fight. Fight til we cannot anymore!"

He stomped his feet, screaming loud, letting his tongue fall out. He gave a glance to Spyke who moved beside him. Taking his cue, Spyke followed Waru's movements; they slapped their thighs, their chests, their war whoops and screams increasing in challenge.

Hunapo stood silent, his teeth bared.

When the war cries died down, Waru glanced over his shoulder, giving her a wink. "I am proud to stand beside you little humans. You are tougher than I gave you credit for."

Taking a breath, she picked up her fallen arrow. Notching it, she held her breath against the string, pulling it taunt. Her eyes narrowed.

I'm not going down today.

Before she could let the arrow fly, a screeching howl of the water goblins trailed over the dunes. Terrified, chittering screams filled the air.

Lily frowned. What was causing that noise?

Brandon pointed beneath her, his voice shaking. "Ah...Lil? Look down..."

She grimaced. *No...I really don't want to...*

But she did, reluctantly.

Darkness. A never-ending, deep, dark pit was beneath her. But...it was solid. She gingerly pressed her foot and, sure enough, it was hard.

She gasped.

The pitch black, starless hole began to spread, growing wider and wider until it encompassed the entire group.

WHAM!

A ponaturi got sucked into the pit. The dense ground underneath it suddenly collapsing, pulling the water goblin down as it screeched in terror. Suddenly, long black tendrils struck out from the pit, wrapping themselves around more goblins, pulling them into the inky blackness.

She steadied herself. "Ah...Waru? This isn't the help you called for, is it?"

He shook his head. "I do not know this magic. Be vigilant for we still have a fight to win." And with no further ado, he threw a punch at Hunapo.

Chaos ensued.

***

Spyke started fighting the Kaupe, dodging its massive jaws. Ang pulled herself up, raking her claws against the water goblins that came from behind. Even Brandon rallied himself, throwing stone after stone, hitting goblins in the eyes as much as he could. And the dark, foggy tendrils whipped up around them, dragging goblins to the dark unknown.

Lily tensed, a presence appearing at her back. She whipped around, ready to use the bow as a club when-

"Woah there darlin'! Give me that bacon without the sizzle please."

Her eyes widened, her mouth dropping open, not believing her eyes. "Randee?"

Randee chuckled, giving a wink, sans makeup this time, brilliant smile wide. Before Randee could say another word, she dropped her bow, rushing in for a hug.

Randee let out an 'oomph' before banding arms around her, rubbing her trembling limbs. "Hush now Lily pie, it's alright. And it's Randy with a 'y' right now darlin'. Left my heels behind today and put on my big boy pants."

He chuckled, taking a finger to wipe a tear she didn't realize trailed down her cheek.

She smiled, squeezing him tighter. "I'm so glad to see you."

"Likewise girl," he brushed back her curls in a fatherly gesture. His smile faded. "Sorry I couldn't get here sooner. Some things came up."

She shook her head. "You're here now."

Randy gave a small sigh. "Still, you look like you could eat your sorrow by the spoonful. I don't like you lookin' like that Lily girl." He looked around, taking in the chaos. "I gather you're in a bit of a bind huh?"

Oh yeah...almost forgot about that.

She stepped back, picking up her bow. With a renewed confidence, she pulled back and let an arrow fly. It soared true, knocking back a goblin that tried to sneak up behind Randy.

He whistled low, nodding in approval. "Look at you, charging to hell with a bucket of ice water. Dang darlin' call me impressed. Even Cab can't deny you're improvin'. Speakin' of that handsome devil, where is he?"

She pointed upward, toward the cliff. Randy clucked his tongue, taking a breath.

"Well, can't say I'm surprised." He crossed his arms, wagging his finger. "But he should've stayed with you."

"There wasn't time," she protested. "What's important now is we have to get the memory to Prince Kye so we can help the others. I think the goddess is waking up."

She raised her wrist where the bracelet glowed brighter. She ignored Randy's shocked stare. "Long story Randy, but Namaka can talk to me, and she's saying her sister is gonna wake up. We need to get up there before the sun rises."

He groaned, palming his face. "Well girl, sounds like this problem is as big as a yellow-jacket in an outhouse. But," his eyes lit up with a gleeful grin, "you don't ever disappoint."

He cupped his hands over his mouth, calling out into the chaotic black darkness. "Didn't I tell you they wouldn't be boring?"

A deep, smokey chuckle tickled Lily's ears. "You were right *Arenyen*."

The black tendrils swirled and danced, wrapping themselves together for a moment. They pulsed a few times before pulling away, revealing a tall, slender man. The fighting stopped as overwhelming dread and death pressed down on the group.

Lily clutched her chest, the constricting nausea almost too much, before it subsided. She could see the figure clearly now, and she held back the prickling fear that skated down her spine.

He was extremely tall and willowy, but his movements assured taunt muscles. He wore black trousers, a crisp white cotton shirt that was unbuttoned around his neck. A black frock coat trailed down, little wisps of grey smoke edging around the shoulders. Dark ebony skin stood out against the white shirt, a series of necklaces dangling from a strong neck. Long black dreadlocks framed a face that held strong, prominent features that was topped with a crisp black top hat.

He was strikingly handsome with full lips, a chiseled jawline, and large yellow eyes. Even the white face paint that resembled a skull didn't deter his striking countenance. In one hand he sported a smooth, obsidian cane topped with feathers and a skull. His other hand clutched a smoking cigar, which he languidly put to his full lips, blowing smoke rings into the air. Those same lips pulled back, revealing a glowing, pearly white smile.

The Baron had come to play.

Randy winked, breaking the silence. "Looks like you folks could use a little help."

Spyke eyes widened. "*Masauwu...*"

The Baron chuckled low, blowing another smoke ring. His voice was syrupy, like dark molasses. "Did I interrupt the party? Do not stop on my account *moun k ap viv yo*. You living ones just keep on playing and I only wish to join your lovely dance."

Hunapo growled, locked with Waru. "Why are you here death dealer? And why is it I cannot move?!"

The Baron raised his eyebrow, or what would have been an eyebrow under the face paint. "You all cannot move because I will it so."

His gaze traveled Hunapo up and down as he scoffed, "You are rude, but I will graciously answer your other question. I go where death calls. Death..." his yellow eyes glowed eerily, "is everywhere."

He walked slowly, his cane echoing each time it rapped against the glass sand. "But in particular little ones...death is most interested in this place." His gaze traveled up to the cliff. "And I go where I'm called."

"What called you?" asked Lily.

The Baron tilted his head, assessing her. "Who called me, to be more precise." Her gave her a flirty wink. "One of my colleagues. There is more than one who dances with death *cheri*. He warned me of a threat of overwhelming death that could be unleashed."

Lily frowned. "But wouldn't that be good for you?"

The Baron took another long drag of his cigar. "Too much of a good thing is not good *bel*."

He strode up to Lily, taking her hand. She flinched, for the Baron's hand was surprisingly warm. He leaned over her palm, bowing low. His glowing gaze quirked up at hers, giving a roguish twinkle. "May I be of assistance little Sentinel?"

She gulped. Everyone around her was still frozen, their fearful eyes taking in the exchange. Randy, the only other person able to move, gave her two thumbs up.

Lily held her twitch.

You gotta be kidding me...

But what other choice did she have. Remembering all her lessons in polite courtesy from her Nonna, she tried to give a small smile. She really hoped it looked like a smile. Inside, it was more like chewing nails.

"Yes, please Baron. We would all appreciate your help. We really need to get up to the Council."

Straightening, the Baron towered over her. He did another short bow, leaning over his cane, his other hand tipping his hat in a courtly gesture. "*Jan ou komande.* As you command little *bel* Sentinel. I will help a little."

She paused, "Oh?" was all she could say. "I'm sure you could finish this quickly."

The Baron straightened up, laughing. "You are delightful little one." His cane rapped softly. "I could...but..." He gave her a chilling wink. "Where is the fun in that? I can't do all the work for you."

She blinked, somehow reminded of staring at a cat...and they were the mice.

He took another drag of his cigar. A great smokey gust of cloves billowed over the group, unfreezing them.

In the confusion, the Baron twirled his cane, tapping it on the floor loudly.

His laughing voice gave an eerie chill down her spine. "Time for some fun, *timoun yo.*"

Tendrils sprang forth in a flourish, spearing and wrapping around as many water goblins as possible, pulling them into the dark hole, their screams fading away.

Lily shook herself, trying to dispel the sinking feeling of her decision. Did she make the right one? Did she make a mistake? She would never know, but the deal was done.

Feeling ten pounds heavier, she pulled back her bow, launching another arrow.

Randy patted her shoulder, as if he read her mind. "Don't worry darlin', no one ever said right thing was always something to be happy about."

He cracked his knuckles, winking. "Now...I should do my part."

With a jump, he twirled in the air, throwing his arms out. Webbing shot from his fingertips, encasing several goblins that tried to surround Ang and Brandon.

Brandon gave an excited shout. "That is so awesome. You're like Spider-"

"Don't say it," Randy interrupted, landing near them. He pulled the webbing taut, giving another twirl, trapping the goblins before launching them at the Baron who sucked them down into the abyss.

He dusted his shoulder, giving Brandon a pointed stare. "Don't you dare snap my garters with that comparison. I'd sooner hug a rose bush than be compared to anyone, anything, but me."

"But why?" asked Brandon, throwing a rock at one goblin.

"Because," Randy caught the rock in webbing, throwing it to further knock into several goblins. "I am amazingly awesome and fine as boomtown silk."

As the battle continued, the tide slowly turned. Now that the Baron and Randy had arrived, they stood a chance. But, this couldn't last forever. Even now, the faint stirrings of dawn were beginning to blend with the twilight. They needed to get up to the cliff, and fast. A voice called up above.

"Did someone call for a ride?"

Flying above the group, Peni and Pika sat on two large...Lily squinted.

Snakes?

Two enormous snakes flew through the air, the little Menehune on their backs whooping with glee. They were unlike any snakes she ever saw before. Other than the obvious size, their scales gleamed in the twilight. Various shades of reds, oranges, yellows, blues, and purples twinkled.

Lily rubbed her eyes. It was a rainbow – a rainbow snake.

Should I be surprised by this point?

"Holy moly," Brandon gasped. He yelled over at Waru, "Dude, if this is what you call help, this is fire!"

The rainbow serpents landed with a resounding thud onto the sand, dust flying everywhere. Lily scrubbed her hair, sand falling out. She would need a long soak. Whenever that would be.

Peni yelled, his hand outstretched. "Come on everyone, get on!"

A goblin tried to jump her, but another tendril shot out, ripping the goblin away. The Baron tipped his hat, an eerie smile on his face. "I shall buy you a little time, *son bon?*"

She gave him a grateful nod.

Ang threw Brandon onto the snake's back with a graceless thump. She took a stance in front, guarding both the snake and Brandon.

Lily turned around, ready with another arrow. However, a large hand wrapped around her waist. Startled, she pulled her arm back to throw an elbow when Spyke's rumbling voice broke through the adrenaline.

"Lily!" he shouted. "There is no time. You must leave."

With great care, he lifted her onto the rainbow serpent's back behind Brandon before he jumped behind her. Randy joined them as well.

Spyke yelled over the snake's massive head.

"Waru, we *must* leave!"

But Waru was too busy fighting Hunapo. The two massive warriors clashed, their clubs smashing against each other so hard sparks flew. Their faces were feral, animalistic growls rumbling in their chests.

Waru glanced behind him as Spyke called out, then staggered back, taking a hard punch to the jaw.

Hunapo took advantage of Waru's distraction, using his momentum to shove the Māori warrior. Waru stumbled, falling backward onto the glass sand. Before Waru could right himself, Hunapo took a dagger and stabbed it into the warrior's thigh. Waru gritted his teeth, stuck on the ground.

Lily gasped, reaching for her bow. Spyke pushed her hand down, shaking his head.

"He needs to finish this fight, Lily. Do not dishonor him."

Hunapo snickered, his club resting on his shoulders. "I will take great pleasure in finishing you off."

Waru clutched his leg. "You are a dishonorable cur."

Hunapo dug into his ear to clean something out. "Once you are gone, I will get my prize."

His gaze settled on Lily. He raised his club aiming it at her in a promise. "I will bring honor by having a Sentinel head as one of my conquests."

Waru growled. "No!" With grim determination, he pulled his leg up, the dagger embedded inside. Faster than Lily could imagine, he ripped the knife from his leg and slammed it into Hunapo's stomach.

The Maero warrior howled as Waru jumped, landing in an unsteady crouch. Waru swept his injured leg across Hunapo's feet. The massive warrior collapsed with a thunderous boom, unmoving. Waru got up, slightly limping, and brought his club down on Hunapo's chest.

Waru roared, raising and slamming the club down again, and again. "This is for my wife!" Another thud. "For my child!"

Lily gripped the bow tighter, whispering shakily. "He's going to kill him."

Spyke shook his head. "Such is the warrior way. Waru wants to avenge his family so they may be at peace."

She shook her head. "This isn't right," her shaky voice grew more hysterical.

Spyke remained quiet, the sounds of fighting surrounding them. The Baron was doing splendidly at holding back the goblins, but it couldn't last forever. They had to leave.

Lily's pleading eyes tore into him.

Spyke sighed, calling out. "Warrior! Remember your orders."

Waru stopped, the club raised overhead ready to deliver another blow. His lips were peeled back, his teeth bared, chest heaving. As if in a trance, his eyes began to clear, rational thought returning.

He shook his head, turning back. "Forgive me," he whispered to the breeze.

His gaze moved down at the crumpled Maero warrior, taking one last glance before spitting at his feet. "My family is avenged...you dishonorable *poaka*." He turned his back, ready to mount the riderless serpent.

Brandon yelled out. "Waru!"

With inhumane reflexes, Waru dodged the oncoming attack from behind. But, he wasn't the target.

Hunapo, clutching his stomach, had taken his wicked dagger and raked it against the serpent's rainbow scales. A heart wrenching howl tore from the poor serpent. It flailed, its tail smacking the ground erratically.

Waru stared, horrified. "What have you done?!"

Hunapo gritted his teeth, his eyes mad. "We...are not...finished!" He raised his arm to slash the serpent again.

Waru jumped, grabbing Hunapo's arm. "Blasphemer! You have harmed the Rainbow Serpent. How far into the pits of Rarohenga will you go? How far will you stain your soul?!"

Hunapo struggled to break out of Waru's grasp. "You will *not* leave. This is *my* hunt!" He grunted, then whistled loudly.

The Kaupe jumped onto the wounded serpent's back, slashing madly with its claws. It gave a ferocious howl that gave a bone chilling harmony against the serpent's plaintive wail.

Hunapo's wild eyes caught Lily's. The Maero warrior growled, a terrifyingly manic smile in place.

"You...are *my* prey!"

Her heart went cold as grim realization set in. He would never give up. He would sell his soul to prove he was the best, like catching the prized deer. There was no redemption for this man. With only slight

307

regret, she lifted her bow and sent an arrow flying. It struck true, hitting Hunapo's palm causing the dagger to fall to the ground. His surprised eyes met hers.

Lily lifted her chin, pulling her shoulders back. "I am *no one's* prey!"

Waru shook his head at both Hunapo and the Kaupe. "You will both be cursed for this. If the beloved serpent dies..."

Sure enough, the serpent thrashed, knocking Pika off. It cried and wailed, and laid down onto the sand, growing still. Its brilliant opalescent eyes closed. They did not reopen.

Everything...and everyone...froze.

Pika slowly approached the fallen serpent, resting his hand on the dimmed scales. Tears streamed down his face as he wiped his nose. The other serpent gave a mournful wail at the loss of its mate.

Lily clutched her chest. How could such a beautiful song be so heartbreaking? She patted the serpent's side, even though it was but a superficial comfort.

Peni rubbed his eyes, clearing his throat. "Pika...get on!"

With a respectful bow, Pika jumped onto the other serpent's back.

Lily wiped her cheeks, her lip trembling. Shaking herself, she yelled out. "Waru, we have to go."

Waru pressed his lips together. With resolute determination, he whipped around giving a resounding kick that sent Hunapo sailing backward. His shoulders were shaking as he climbed on the remaining serpent, a weary sigh escaping as unshed tears burned in his eyes.

"Wait...where is Ang?" Lily's frantic gaze scanned the field, finally spotting the changeling on the other side of the fallen serpent.

The Kaupe, still on top, looked down and found her. Its gaze returned to Lily, uncertain.

Ang cupped her hands, yelling out. "Hey ugly, I'm still standing! And I'm right over here. You're not so tough, are you?"

Lily wanted to scream, but her voice choked. What was she doing? *Stop it Ang!*

The Kaupe whipped its head down, its nostrils flaring with steam as its red eyes narrowed. An angry rumble reverberated in its chest as its lips peeled back. It tensed, ready to spring.

She notched her bow, desperately trying to keep from shaking. "Ang, come on. Peni, get the serpent to her please!"

Peni nodded, nudging the reigns. The serpent tried to rise, but it was having difficulty. He turned back, his worried gaze sinking Lily's heart. "We're getting too heavy."

"Do I need to jump off?" asked Waru.

Peni shook his head. "No, we should be fine. We should be," he muttered to himself.

Ang noticed the serpent's struggle. She looked to the sky, seeing the rising colors peeking through and sighed, her gaze catching theirs.

She gave a small smile. "Guys, I got this! You get going."

Brandon shook his head, not understanding. "What are you talking about Ang? You're coming."

The Kaupe howled, jumping at Ang, but was blocked by a wall of tendrils.

The Baron clucked. "She is right, little ones." He pointed to the sky. "You do not have time to do both. I cannot hold it for long."

"Help her!" pleaded Lily.

Her heart bled when the Baron slowly shook his head.

"Aww, don't do this Baron," Randy sighed sadly.

"Someone's life thread is not meant to go up that cliff." He crossed his arms over his chest, his tone soft but chilling. "I may bend the rules *Arenyen* but I do not break them. And as you are now, your serpent cannot carry all of you." His deep gaze met Lily's, curious. "What choice will you make?"

She shook her head vehemently, her eyebrows pinched. She couldn't leave Ang. She just couldn't!

Ang broke through Lily's panic, a sad, almost resigned, smile filling her vision. She clutched her side. The wound had opened up again.

"You don't have to make a choice. Go save your sister Lily," she said, her smile pained.

"But," Lily protested.

"Don't make me repeat myself," Ang barked, furiously wiping her eyes. "Just leave already."

Brandon hiccuped. "Don't say that Ang." His desperate eyes found Lily's. "She's coming right Lil?"

He didn't wait for her answer, turning back to Ang. "You're coming with us, and you'll hit me on the head again for crying like this. And I'm gonna prank you so hard for making me this upset."

Ang snorted, her voice breaking as a few tears escaped her eye. "Don't make me hit you later."

She shrugged her shoulder, giving a half grin to Lily. "Take care of him, will you? He's too trusting and this place will eat him alive."

Lily nodded woodenly, afraid if she spoke, she'd fall apart. But that didn't stop her shaking, holding onto herself by a thread.

Ang nodded back, an understanding between them. She took a shaky breath. "Look, I never had a home," she began, giving a cynical laugh. "How ironic you insane kids are the closest thing to a family I got." She snorted, wiping her chin. "For what it's worth...I'm glad I was part of yours while it lasted..."

She gave a heartbreaking smile, her eyes glossed with unshed tears. "Bye Sissy."

Peni made a clucking sound, ordering the serpent to rise. It lifted from the ground, but Brandon protested, ready to jump off. Lily lurched forward, holding him tight. Tears streamed down her face as Ang sadly waved goodbye.

"NO!" Hunapo screamed, staggering to his feet. "I will find you! I will NEVER stop and when I do catch you I'll-"

Abruptly, his tirade stopped. Tendrils wrapped around his mouth, his throat, and his waist. The Baron rose up in the darkness, tapping his cane softly. His eyes danced over the still serpent before briefly closing in repose. He bowed low in reverence to the beautiful creature before turning to the group. He folded his hands on the top of his cane, leaning forward slightly.

His voice carried over the sand.

"Ladies and gentlemen, it has been a pleasure." He gave Randy a wink. "You were right *Arenyen*. This group was indeed entertaining, but I am afraid the fun has run out." He gestured sadly to the fallen serpent.

His gaze chilled as it caught Hunapo. The yellow orbs narrowed in a calculating glint. His voice frosted over, shivers of smoke and ice skated over the group, the full force of that icy anger centered on the fallen warrior.

"You are indeed cursed now *nanm*." A chilling, sadistic grin spread on the Baron's pallid face. "And it is time for me to collect, *son bon*?"

Hunapo's eyes widened, fear entering them for the first time. He struggled against the bindings but could not move. The Baron snapped his fingers, just once, and with a chilling scream the Maero warrior disappeared.

Lily flinched, closing her eyes as if they could block out the terrifying sounds.

Waru's long sigh tickled her ears.

"It is finally over." He gave a slight bow toward the Baron.

The Baron tilted his hat to the group with a gentlemanlike smile. "Good luck *ti fi espesyal*."

The Baron paused, blowing a kiss in Lily's direction. "You call Baron Samedi again little Sentinel when you need a warm final hand. *Byen!*"

Then, he too, disappeared in a cloud of smoke and darkness along with the tendrils that melted into the earth.

Lily held back her unease at the parting image of taking death's hand.

The Kaupe howled in anger, the rest of its prey was escaping. As the tendril wall disappeared, it tensed, ready to jump after the serpent. Ang clutched her wounded side, her claws lengthening, and gave an answering roar, attacking the Kaupe midjump. They both fell, missing the serpent as it flew upward.

The serpent soared high up the cliffs, leaving the ground far below. Lily squinted, trying to keep her eyes on Ang but she could barely them out as they became specks. She wasn't sure who was winning. Ang was wounded, incredibly so. Her breath shortened. The Kaupe was just too strong.

She jerked hearing Brandon's soft sobs puncturing through the rushing wind. She leaned over, wrapping her arms around his hunched frame, his body trembling. She tucked her chin into his shoulder.

"It'll be okay," she whispered. "She'll be okay."

Brandon hiccupped, refusing to look at her. "No...no it won't. Why, Lil?!"

She paused, unable to answer. She clenched her trembling jaw, her tears spilling down his neck. "I...I don't know."

Brandon reached out, grasping her hand tight. His voice shook, wavering with desperate hope. He pulled up the satchel. "Is it worth it?"

She squeezed his hand, trying to give him some comfort even when she didn't know the answer. "We just have to make it count. We need to find Ari, Aunt Raven," she looked at the towering cliff, the blush of dawn creeping ever closer, "and stop whatever is coming."

The two held each other close, mourning. Her tears had to be fleeting, because when they reached the top...all bets were off.

Chapter Twenty-Five

ALMOST THERE KEIKI...

Ari's inner voice had morphed, changing into something she could not discern from her own. It was deeper, sultry, and confident. Her body thrummed, the growing warmth becoming more tolerable...ironically the hotter it became.

Dain and his guard had 'escorted' the remaining council members, Prince Kye (who was still holding an unconscious Raven), and Cabyll to the training grounds. Peri was left behind, still frozen below.

Dain's Adlet wolf guard silently surrounded the prisoners, who were bound and gagged. Normally, Ari would have been concerned for the little fairy and her aunt. But weirdly, at that moment, she shrugged it off. Things like people seemed unimportant right now.

The wind whispered against the hot sand, the red stones smoking slightly in the predawn air. Rushing water scraped her ears, a sound she once considered soothing, had become nails on a chalkboard. She ran her hands down her pebbled arms, moving as close to the red stones as she could. She needed to be closer to the heat.

Ah...that is better. She closed her eyes, basking in the warmth for a moment.

More...I need more.

"Ari?"

She peeked one eyelid open, slightly irritated. Who was bothering her now?

Dain stared down at her, his eyebrow furrowed. "Ari? Are you listening?"

She gave a languid smile. "Of course, I'm just closing my eyes a moment." She waved her hand, dismissing him. "You may keep doing what you're doing."

His eyebrows turned further down. "I *may*?"

She patted his chest. "You better hurry, the dawn is coming."

He speared her a sideways glance before holding his hand out. "The pendant my dear."

With a drawn-out sigh, she plucked the necklace off, handing the jar over. He abruptly turned his back and moved to the middle of the training ground.

She gave a small smirk behind his back. *What a clueless fae he is...* Little did he know the pendant was useless now.

Aput appeared by her side. They tilted their head. "Are you okay Miss Ari? You do not seem yourself."

She hummed, giving a slow sensual grin. "I'm more myself than I've ever been. I do appreciate the concern." She waved her hand with a shooing motion. "Go on, help him."

Aput gave her a perplexing look, if the Ijiraq could show emotions. Nevertheless, they slinked away by Dain's side, keeping watch.

Ari's gaze moved over the prisoners, her eyes lingering on Cabyll. He remained stoic, his eyes not meeting hers. Instead, they glinted, clinically assessing his surroundings. He didn't pull at his restraints, nor did he growl like the others. He was serene in his confidence, as if he could break free at any moment.

What a good little assassin, her new inner voice purred.

She padded around the edge of the sand, ducking behind Tane and Hi'iaka. No one would notice a little human.

She rolled her eyes as, sure enough, no one paid her any attention. Her eyes clocked Prince Kye who did notice her, but he dismissed her, his attention focused on her unconscious aunt. With a silent ease, she slid next to Cabyll.

His gaze briefly darted at her, but his focus remained on Dain. He

314

frowned slightly, whispering from the side of his mouth. "What are you doing over here?"

She covered her mouth, hiding her smile. "Why wouldn't I be?"

"As much as I enjoy a good word play, this is not the time. Will you free me?"

She tapped her chin, her hair swirling around her. Was it her imagination or did it seem her hair was longer? She gave a singsong chuckle. "I would love to, but it isn't the right time...."

His eyes narrowed. "What do you mean?"

Ari giggled softly, pressing her finger lightly to her lips. "Shsshh. No spoilers." She winked. "Just watch."

Dain circled the red sands, arranging and placing the pieces in the center of the training grounds. He looked up toward the rising sun, his eager tone breaking the tense silence. "Any moment now."

He gave a slow victorious smile, his eyes gleaming as the sun began to peek over the horizon.

Nafanua tugged against her bonds, baring her teeth. "It is not too late! Do not do this." Her desperate gaze hit Tane, who refused to look at her.

A feminine groan from behind had Ari whipping around.

Raven scrunched her eyes, groaning louder. Her eyes cracked open, groggily taking in her surroundings. The antidote was working.

Ari ignored the flush of joy that briefly traveled down her chest.

Raven shook her head, confused finding herself in Kye's arms. Her foggy gaze cleared, moving around. "What happened?" Her voice was dry and papery. "Um...let me guess. We're in a pickle, aren't we?"

Kye pulled her close, his arms refusing to let her go.

Ari scoffed. This was only a formality, a pretense. The prince was too strong, even if only by brute strength. It was obvious he could break free at any time he wished. Why he kept himself detained was beyond her understanding.

He keeps his promise to save that human, whispered the new voice in her head. *He's honorable. One of the few...*

"Much has occurred while you were asleep," the prince softly replied.

Raven pushed at him weakly. "Well mister tall, handsome, and brooding. Let me down."

"No," he said, matter-of-fact.

Raven gritted her teeth. "I said...let me down."

He refused to look at her. "Your legs are weak."

"But-" she protested.

"Raven," Kye growled, clutching her tighter against him. "You almost died."

Her mouth dropped open. "...okay..."

Dain groaned loudly, then barked out. "Will you both be quiet?"

The sun rose above the skyline, kissing the ocean landscape beyond. Bright hues of pinks, yellows, and golds illuminated the training ground. The steam rose higher into the air as Dain murmured ancient words into the wind. The sunlight reflected off the pieces, creating a beam that bounced from one to the other, in an intricate pattern. The light bounced faster and faster, finally landing on a particular vein of red sand.

Dain stepped forward, placing the pendant upon it. Steam and fire rose up, filling the jar until it pulsed with an amber glow. Dain's eyes gleamed in excitement.

"Come forth Pele, Goddess of Fire, creation maker, life giver and end bringer!"

Everyone waited...

But nothing happened.

Dain frowned, glaring over the pieces again.

Tane coughed lightly into his hand.

"Did you speak in the correct enunciation?"

Dain glared. "What am I, a child? Of course I did."

Tane shrugged. "I understand. But you must have done something incorrectly. I went through the ritual with you step by step."

"Maybe you made a mistake," Dain snarked.

Tane lifted his nose in the air, his voice pompous. "I *never* make mistakes of the academic variety."

Nafanua snickered, then grunted when she earned a kick from an Adalet guard.

Hi'iaka sighed, examining her nails. "Not the time Tane."

She turned to Dain, gesturing to the captives. "What do we do now your highness?"

Dain ran his hand through his hair. "I'm trying to think...give me a moment."

The voice whispered in Ari's mind. *Let's help the poor little prince along, shall we?*

She smiled, leaning over to whisper in Cabyll's ear. "I think it's time now."

With a flick of her finger, Cabyll's binds were magically undone, burned into ash. He looked at his wrists, then back at her, shocked. She chuckled. He was being so cute in his confusion. Honestly, she didn't understand how she did it and frankly she didn't care. Instead, she reached out to cup his cheek.

He sidestepped, avoiding her touch just as Dain shouted out. "What are you doing?!"

Ari smiled, asking her voice. *Now?*

The voice laughed. *Yes, mea liilii...*

...Now...

A powerful surge of warmth ran through her, from the bottom of her feet up to the top of her head. She breathed deep, elated. Everything was clearer, brighter, sharper. Colors she never even knew existed danced along her eyelids. She could hear the thick thumping of molten magma snaking underneath the crust of the earth, winding and swirling in a magnificent rhythm. It was glorious.

She was glorious.

With another flick of her fingers, the necklace snapped out of Dain's grasp, rushing into her hand. With smooth, precise movements, she put the pendant back on, the jar pulsing softly like a heartbeat. Her lips peeled back into a divine smile as she slowly took off her shoes, walking through the red sand to make her way to the center.

"What am I doing?" she repeated his earlier question.

Humming to herself, she tapped her chin. She paused a moment. Her fingers were slender, her nails a brilliant red hue as if freshly painted. She stared dreamily at them. How beautiful they were.

She giggled. "I'm doing what I want."

Dain shook his head, confusion evident. "My dear, what are you talking about?"

Aput nudged Dain, their voice slightly shaking. "Your highness...her hair."

For a split second, a look of dismay crossed over Dain's handsome features. Then she blinked and it was gone. Must have been a trick in the light. Why would he be upset? This was what he wanted after all.

Everyone's stares bore into her. She held in her chuckle at their widened, shocked eyes. Gasps rang around. What were they worried about?

Curious, her fingers grasped a few strands of her long hair. It had turned a beautiful strawberry pink, transitioning to an ombré of the deepest scarlet she ever saw. She moved her head slowly, rubbing the locks back and forth.

How pretty...

Dain reached out, a stilted smile on his face, his eyes appearing sad. "Oh...What do you wish for my dear? Or should I say, my *Akua*?"

She chuckled, the sound becoming deeper, like her new inner voice. "What I wish?"

He nodded, extending his arm out in a gentlemanlike fashion.

She sauntered up to him, her hips swaying languidly. The group's eyes were on her, but they remained frozen. Unmoving. As she got closer to Dain, her normal inner voice tried to convince herself she that she cared. That she loved him. But the voice was getting weaker, so she simply ignored it.

Instead, she ran her hand up his neck, cupping his jawline. His eyes closed briefly as she leaned forward, her other hand lightly resting on his chest.

"What I wish," she whispered, "is to be completely free."

Both hands warmed, smoke emanating from her fingertips. Dain's eyes widened, realization dawning almost too late. He pulled back, jumping out of her arms. Frozen fractals blasted out of his body, uncontrolled, to douse the flames that tried to spread across his chest. His normally stoic, cunning face deteriorated. His eyes widened in horror as he clasped his still smoking cheek.

"Pele," He whispered, awe and horror mixed. "How? How did you possess her?"

Ari giggled, the flames pulsing brightly around her. That was when another voice spoke through her.

Deeper and ancient.

"Because she wanted to be *seen* young Prince. To shine so brightly that all of you would bow beneath her light. Besides, did you really think that *you* were worthy of awaking me?"

Ari/Pele twirled around, a stream of flame burning her dress until only the warm red/black color remained. Scarlet Lehua blossoms bloomed from the ash, dotting around the skirt up to the bodice. She raised her eyebrow at the insignificant fae before her.

She pointed to the ground. "Kneel."

Tane immediately kneeled. No one else moved.

She exhaled, counting to ten. Sometimes servants needed to know their place. She flicked her wrist. Spirals of flame and magma danced around her, like vines. They shot outward, wrapping themselves around the prisoners.

Kye put out his hand, gritting his teeth. The flames stalled, hovering in midair.

Ari/Pele frowned. That was surprising. How could he do what most could not, even when bound? Well...it didn't matter. She raised her hand again, the flame burning hotter.

Kye's nose twitched, his eyes rebellious. Her lip quirked upward, daring him. With a resigned sigh, he slowly put Raven down but refused to let go of her hand. With a moment's hesitation, he gently went down on one knee. He tugged on Raven's hand, pulling her down reluctantly with him. Soon, the others followed suit.

She smiled, her hair flowing around her. She clucked her tongue as her eyes took in the kneeling group. They centered on Cabyll, taking note of his clenched hands.

"Oh, that won't do for you," she tsked.

With another flick, gentler this time, a fire tendril slithered out. It wrapped itself around Cabyll's waist, tugging him forward.

Sparks flew from his eyes as he went to grasp his scimitar. It did nothing against the fire as the vine secured itself around him, pulling him toward her. He struggled, but the tendril tightened around him.

She cocked her head, shushing him. "So fiery. You are worthy indeed. You use both action as well as speech." She raised a brow at Dain, smirking. "I like that in a consort."

Cabyll's eyes flashed again, belying the suave response. "How could I ever presume to be a worthy consort of one such as you?"

She giggled. "Such a flatterer." She leaned forward to purr in his ear. "I do like a chase."

"I will not attempt a chase such as this." He pulled against his bonds, gritting his teeth.

"You can resist...for now," she gently moved a lock of hair behind his ear. "But all men I choose eventually become mine."

She didn't wait for his response. Her eyes jumped upward as something crested over the horizon. Whatever it was, it was flying toward the training ground. She squinted her eyes, making out the shadowy figures riding a monstrous serpent. She gave a delicate snort. They would all kneel before her in the end.

A low rumbling of the earth greeted her.

She smiled. Daybreak had come.

Chapter Twenty-Six

LILY SQUINTED, THE BRIGHT RAYS OF THE SUN WARRING against the whipping wind. Her eyes stung. She wasn't sure if the tears were from the wind or not, another parting vision of Ang stabbing her chest. Her stomach flipped and flopped. The serpent's ride upward was not smooth, but what did she expect. It wasn't like she was taking a taxi.

She grimaced, pressing on her stomach to hold in the rising bile. How much longer would it take? All she could make out was stone and sand as they kept climbing higher and higher. She pinched her lips together, not wanting to wait anymore. If her mind strayed, it would go back to Ang's face.

She couldn't handle that.

Brandon was hunched over, his shoulders shaking. She suspected it wasn't from the cold or the whipping air. His head ducked as he reached up to covertly wipe his eyes. Lily's heart cracked and bled, but she had to tuck it away. She didn't have the luxury to crumble and weep.

Amidst Brandon's soft sniffling, a calming voice yelled in her ear over the rushing wind.

"Almost there." Spyke tapped her shoulder, pointing upward. A faint edge appeared on the wide expanse of the cliff. "We don't know what we'll encounter when we arrive, so be prepared."

She nodded, breathing deep. She reached out, shaking Brandon gently. "Brandon, I need the satchel."

With a jerk, he numbly handed her the memory. She winced at the sting that jabbed her chest witnessing Brandon's desolate face. Her hands clutched the satchel tighter.

I never should have let him come with me.

"Everyone." Waru's bellowing voice interrupted her desolate thoughts. The warrior started to stand on top of the serpent, crouched low with his club ready. "Brace yourselves!"

With a cry, the serpent soared, the cliffs disappearing. Brilliant light blinded Lily as daybreak broke through the clouds.

When the haze cleared, she peered down. Her heart leapt with a faint, desperate hope. Did they make it?

A huge arena lay before her. Intricate swirls of red and gold were inlaid in the ground, making a beautiful indescribable pattern. On one edge of the cliff was the ocean and beach. The other side was a large mountain with a winding river that ended in a deep well. The arena had several figures dotted around the swirls.

She squinted, trying to make them out but she was still too high. One figure stood from the rest. There, in the middle of the arena, was –

Ari?

Lily frowned. It looked like Ari, but somehow not. Did she change her hair? Ari's hair was golden, never an ombre of golds, pinks, and reds. And call Lily crazy, but she knew that hair didn't defy gravity. But Ari's was floating around her body.

And that's when she noticed next to Ari...stood Cabyll.

Her eyebrows furrowed. Why was he so close to her? Wait... She rubbed her eyes. Was something wrapped around him? She couldn't tell from the height, but the faint blue sparking light around his body spoke volumes.

Someone's ticked off...

Peni and Pika both gasped.

"Oh, that's not good," said Peni.

"About as good as a rotten banana," quipped Pika.

Waru growled, pointing downward. "Looks like we're almost out of time."

Lily followed his finger. Prince Kye, her aunt, and several others she couldn't recognize were also bound. They looked relatively unharmed, with wolf-like figures surrounding them.

Oh geez, this definitely isn't good.

Then she noticed something else. Or rather, didn't notice someone.

Her heart began to thud.

"Um, Spyke? Where's Peri?" she whispered.

He shook his head. "I don't know, but it'll take more than those beasts to take her out."

His confident tone soothed her anxiety-riddled heart. She couldn't take losing another friend.

"Don't worry Lily." He reached around, covering her hand reassuringly. "She'll be here. I'm more worried about the person who detained her."

He mumbled that last part to himself, but she could hear it. She covered her mouth, hiding the uncharacteristic giggle that tried to spring up.

Waru growled, his nose twitching. "What I am concerned with is why his highness is allowing to be detained."

Sure enough, as they got closer Lily noticed the shackles.

Waru continued, "He could easily take out those weak Adalet guards."

Her stomach flipped, the serpent suddenly dipping drastically to the side.

"Evasive maneuvers engaged," shouted Peni.

Pika screamed, shaking his head violently. "No time, no time!"

"Boys! This isn't some outer space show ya know," yelled Randy.

"Hold on everyone!" Pika pulled on the serpent's head feathers.

Lily's throat closed as the serpent took a sudden dive downward. An uncomfortable warmth rushed over her head. She turned, trying to figure out what happened. The ending trail of smoke behind them was proof enough.

She blinked.

Oh...that can't be good.

It was a fireball. A legit fireball! And it would have hit them if Peni hadn't acted so. quickly.

You've gotta be kidding me!

Randy smacked his lips loudly, grimacing. "Um, guys and gals?

Hate to be the party pooper here, but, if my eyes are correct, and they usually are cause they're amazingly sharp like that. I'm sorry to say Lily darlin'...but I think the source of that fireball was that little sister of yours."

Well...crap...

Reluctantly, Lily held her stomach, risking another look down. Sure enough, Randy was right. Flames danced and licked across Ari's skin, intricately weaving themselves around her like ribbons. Yeah...that was new. Definitely not a good sign. She grasped her bracelet, hoping to hear something other than her own freaked out inner voice.

Namaka...what's happening?

The bracelet pulsed softly, the sea goddess's voice faint. *It seems my sister has possessed yours. Her awakening is happening more quickly than I anticipated.*

Lily held her breath, that little info nugget rolling around in her brain. There were so many questions swarming. She filed away most of them, especially the one of *how* the creation goddess possessed Ari. Instead, she tried to focus on one major question. *Is my sister still in there?*

There was a pause. *She is. I can feel a human soul is still in the body, but she's fading. You need to hurry keiki.*

"Uh...everyone?" Peni's shaking hands held the reigns. "She's ready to fire again." He looked back, apologetic. "We can't lose another serpent."

Waru and Spyke nodded. They shared a look before Spyke pulled Lily into his arms. She gasped, her brain slowly grasping the situation as Spyke gave her an apologetic look. Waru grabbed the still silent Brandon, who gave no protest.

Randy rolled his eyes, running his hand over his head with a dramatic sigh. "What? Doesn't anyone think I need saving?"

He held up his hands at the resulting glares. "I know, not the time. Sheesh, young folks today are so serious."

Standing up, he gave a quick salute before he jumped off the serpent, heading to the arena below.

"Hold tight," Spyke murmured, his arms tensing.

Lily turned, wrapping her arms around his neck. She gave a quick glance to Peni and Pika. Would they be okay?

The Menehune saluted her jauntily, their faces split with big, reassuring smiles.

"Don't worry Lily, we'll see you soon," assured Peni.

Pika gave her a quirky grin. "Yup, this is too awesome to miss!"

She briefly counted to ten. These fae had really odd ideas of entertainment.

"Let's go!" yelled Waru. He bunched his muscles, and jumped.

Lily held her breath as Spyke launched them into the air. *So, this is what skydiving must feel like.*

Her stomach jolted as her entire body squished in a free fall. She wanted to scream, but the rushing air cut off her voice. Her nose twitched. There was a lot of falling the last three days, and she was over it.

The ground rushed to meet them, faster and faster. Actually, it was coming too fast. Why weren't they slowing down?!

Lily squeezed her eyes shut, bracing herself. With incredible skill, the warriors landed on their feet, the ground splintering beneath them. It reminded Lily of one of those superhero moves you only could see with special effects. Randy followed closely behind as he lithely landed, giving a short bow.

Showoff...

Spyke set her down gently, slowly removing his arms. She wobbled, her feet finally finding purchase, albeit on shaky legs. That's when another set of warm arms surrounded her.

"*Nipote!*"

Lily almost broke down right then and there. She held the small hiccup, closing her eyes to block out the tears. The familiar warm, comforting coconut smell enveloped her. She leaned into her aunt's arms, stifling a sniffle. She discreetly rubbed her eyes.

Her aunt pulled her face within her hands, examining her.

"Are you okay? You're not hurt, are you?"

She smiled, her voice trembling. "I'm okay Zia Raven."

Her aunt squeezed her cheeks before going to Brandon. She took in his vacant eyes. Her worried gaze whipped to everyone, her voice turning icy. "What happened?"

Waru sighed, shaking his head. "It's a long story."

"Where's Ang?" Raven interrupted, looking around.

No one spoke, all eyes downcast unable to meet Raven.

Raven's mouth opened, grasping the gist of the silence. Without another word, she gathered Brandon into her arms. Without any resistance, she led him backward toward the others – Lily assumed – council members. Raven rubbed his arms soothingly. "We'll talk later." She motioned toward Ari and Dain. "We have other problems at the moment."

Ari raised her arms, a charming smile in place. "Ah. You missed my welcome gift. Did you like it?"

Lily stared, trying to process the Ari in front of her.

That...was a welcome gift?

She continued, "Well...it does not matter. More subjects to kneel before me. I am waiting to be worshipped."

Lily frowned. Ari's voice was all wrong. It was too deep, too mature. Her mannerisms, *everything*, was different. "Ari? Are you okay?"

Ari tapped her chin, her eyes glazed for a moment. Her voice returned to the normal, higher tone Lily was used to hearing. "Lily?" Her confused gaze began to narrow. "So...you did make it here after all. Why don't you just go home?"

Oh, they were not starting out on a good note. Lily held up her hands, trying to keep the peace. "Ari, I think you're being possessed by a fire goddess right now. I know it sounds crazy, okay? We're here to help you."

Ari...or Pele...laughed, her voice getting deeper again. "Help? Me?" She spread her arms out. "I am better than ever! Not only am I beautiful, but now I am someone to be respected." Her eyes narrowed. "And I do not need to be watched over and babied by you...or anyone else."

Cabyll pulled against his bonds, his eyes boring into Lily. "Hey...not to interrupt but if you have a plan, do it fast will you?!"

Lily tensed, squeezing her hands as she blew out a breath. She understood he was in a bind, but seriously? She should speak logically, rationally.

"And a hello to you too." There was no way she could explain away the sarcasm in that sentence. She could have kicked herself.

You haven't seen him in three days girl. But nope...had to be snarky didn't we?

326

His eyes widened, sarcasm dripping from every pore. "Oh! Because *this* situation requires pleasantries?!"

Ari frowned, wagging a finger at her. "You will not speak to my consort like that."

Lily blinked, taken aback. "Excuse me what? Consort?"

Cabyll ducked his head, groaning. "Let me explain..." he began.

"When I am fully awakened," Ari interrupted, a mean girl smirk gracing her face. "I will free him from his bond with you and he will be mine."

Lily's brain skipped a moment...once, then twice. Bond? What was she talking about?

Ari continued. "Did I mention he cannot wait to be my consort," she lifted her nose, scrunching it in disgust, taking in Lily's disheveled appearance. "Taking one look at my beauty compared to you, how could he not?"

Lily's eyes widened in disbelief. *How...HOW did Ari manage to find someone that was more self-centered than her?*

She rubbed her forehead, forcing herself to breathe out...slowly. "Cabyll, what did you do?"

Cabyll rolled his eyes, scoffing. "Why are you asking me? I can't help my looks and my charm are irresistible. I've told you thousands of beings have fallen in love with me. Well...most..." His cheeks flushed under Lily's narrowed gaze. "I only gave her a few little superficial compliments, nothing meaningful."

Dain barked. "Did you flirt with my human?"

"Enough!" Ari...or was it Pele...interjected. "I recall you asked for me to flirt as well."

Dain, stunned, remained silent as the sun rose higher. Another rumbling shook the ground, the sound growing louder.

Waru took advantage of the distraction. He looked over his shoulder, still in a crouch, his question addressed to Kye. "Your highness?"

Kamohoali'l echoed Waru. "Yes, what is your command, your highness?"

Kye shook his head. "I'm bound Waru. I still have to wait until the time limit expires. Did you retrieve what I asked?"

Waru called over his shoulder. "Lily, now is the time."

She mentally smacked herself. *Right...focus Lily.*

She gave Cabyll a quick look. The 'oh we are going to have a talk when this over' look.

His eyes widened, his cheeks still flushed.

But before she could even reach for the satchel, a tug pulled her forward. A fire vine wrapped itself around her calf.

"Oh...we weren't done talking," Ari purred as she yanked her arm back.

Lily fell backward, the air whooshing from her lungs. She quickly turned around onto her stomach, discreetly cradling the satchel.

Spyke reached out to grab her hand. She stretched, her fingers grasping, but the vine was too strong as it pulled backwards.

"Lily!" yelled Cabyll.

Her hands pulled futilely at the ground, her fingernails digging furrows in the sand. She turned onto her back, grabbing the vine in an attempt to pull it off her, but to no avail. Soon, the fire vine dragged her at Ari's feet.

Her eyes widened, staring up at her stepsister. Her voice cracked, dismay bleeding into her tone as she finally could take in her stepsister's appearance. "Oh Ari, your eyes!"

Ari's eyes, once a beautiful blue, were becoming a ruby red, the crimson hue bleeding into the blue. She just laughed, tossing her hair back, unconcerned.

Cabyll pulled, the vines struggling to hold him. He gritted out, "Let her go."

Ari shook her finger, tsking. "Now, now. Don't strain yourself darling. You will soon be free of her."

Her hand reached out, longer than a normal human hand...ending in pointed, blood-red nail. Lily flinched as those long nails grazed her cheek.

Ari whispered, "Just do me one, simple thing my consort."

Cabyll simply watched, waiting.

Ari smiled smoothly, tapping Lily's nose playfully. "Tell her you don't care about her."

Jerking back, he frowned, genuinely surprised. "What?"

"Tell her you do not care about her. That you never did," she repeated patiently. Her finger rested on Lily's curls, twisting it around and giving it a forceful tug. "Tell her that you noticed *me*. You were a gentleman to *me*. That you are *my* consort."

Cabyll's face evened to an unreadable mask. "How could I dare to assume that I could ever be your consort."

Ari giggled, tossing her hair over her shoulder. "You are *very* good with your words Assassin. I'm feeling generous, so I'll answer your question." She spun around, humming. "You are strong, but smart enough to be a worthy fae who understands power. This weak Prince," she sneered at Dain, "does not appreciate that, nor does he appreciate me."

"Now my dear," Dain cooed, holding up his hands, trying to step forward.

"Don't," she hissed. The flames flickered menacingly. "The only reason I haven't incinerated you into dust is because you are somewhat still useful. I must fully awaken before I reduce this world and make it into my will."

Lily remained silent, filing the information away. So, the goddess wasn't fully awakened. That meant Ari still had a chance. They could still free her. But...how?

"Does that mean you will be part of the cause, Goddess of Flame?" Dain made a short bow, keeping a watchful eye.

Ari...or Pele...chuckled, another rumbling shook beneath the earth.

Lily swallowed, almost choking. *That can't be good...*

Ari/Pele scoffed. "The cause?"

A wicked smirk pulled the corner of her red lips. "Young prince, I have lived eons. That 'cause' you speak of from so long ago," she paused, her eyes narrowing, "I only agreed to lend my power then for what was promised to me by..." she trailed off, shaking herself. "It does not matter. This time, I will follow my own path now. I will not be part of any plan but my own."

Dain's eyes widened, a flicker of genuine fear crossing his face.

Lily would have laughed seeing the prince get his dues. He really didn't seem to have thought of a scenario where the goddess wouldn't help him. She couldn't say she was sorry for the prince after all the stunts he pulled, but she could be a teeny bit empathetic.

A teeny tiny bit.

Ari/Pele continued, waving her hand to dismiss him. "Now stay quiet and guard me like a good little boy."

Nafanua mumbled under her breath, "Should have burned his face..."

"Now," Ari/Pele ignored the others. She turned back to Cabyll, motioning toward Lily, "tell her."

Cabyll looked at Lily, silent.

She waited, chewing the inside of her cheek. Just a few words and it was over. But Cabyll merely stared at her, his green eyes never leaving hers.

She bit her lip.

Why isn't he saying something?

She decided she should say something, anything, to break this awkward silence. "He doesn't care about me like that Ari. We're friends, so let him go."

Ari/Pele gave a pretty pout, glaring at her. "No...I want *him* to say it. I want you to be devastated to know that he cares about me more than you."

Lily's eye twitched. *All around the mulberry bush, the monkey chased the weasel...*

She gritted her teeth. "Why is that important?"

Ari/Pele smiled, deadly. "He danced with me, you know. It was a beautiful dance. He's so good on his feet, and his hands were strong as they held me, comforted me..."

Lily's blood pressure rose. She rubbed her face, tugging her hair in frustration.

POP goes the weasel...

So much for self-preservation in front of a goddess.

Her angry gaze caught Ari's, her voice challenging. "Seriously? Of all the shallow things I can think of, and you're worried if another guy likes you over me? Get off your high horse Ari! There are more pressing matters. Like an apocalyptic fire goddess inside you."

Silence.

"Ah...Lil darlin'," warned Randy.

"*Quella e mia nipote*," Raven smiled proudly.

"*Not* the time Raven," Kye hissed as he stepped in front, blocking Raven from the goddess.

Ari/Pele's breathing turned shallow. She clenched her hands. Her rose gold hair swirled above her. Her voice dropped, whispered low and lethal. "*What* did you say to me?"

Lily bit her lip, realizing her mistake. *Well...shucks...I shouldn't have done that.*

Cabyll, eyes wide, ordered, "Lily...roll!"

She didn't need to be told twice. She tucked and rolled, holding the top of her head as fire whipped above, singeing a few curls. The acidic smell of burned hair soured the air.

She smacked her head a few times, making sure no fire remained.

Che cavolo! I better not be bald or I swear I'm ripping those red locks out of Fire Goldilocks.

"You are a very rude girl." Ari/Pele sighed, her hand falling. She smoothed her hair, shaking herself. "Look at what you made me do."

Examining her nails absently, the goddess gave a small pout. "I think I chipped a nail...oh!" She looked at her hair, her eyes widening.

Lily followed the goddess's gaze, but couldn't figure out what she was focused on.

Ari/Pele continued, annoyed. "This just won't do."

Shaking her head, she snapped her fingers, her eyes darting to the Adlet guards. She pointed, her blood-red nail jabbing the air. "You!" She crooked her finger. "Come here."

The wolfen guard stood still, confused. They looked back at each other, then over to Dain, awaiting orders. Dain reluctantly gave a small nod.

Slowly, the guards moved forward.

"Kneel," Ari commanded.

The guards, hesitantly, kneeled down.

Lily, still on the ground, craned her neck. What was Ari doing?

Without another word, Ari/Pele threw out both her arms toward the guards.

Lily's eyes widened, horrified. If she could sink herself further into the ground and hide, she would have.

Ari's eyes had become opaque, glowing golden tinged with crimson. Her hair whipped around her, the scarlet tresses creeping upward, over-taking the rose gold hue until red strands reached her mid-back. From her eyes and hands, more fire vines appeared. But, these were different. A shimmering red gold that was more ethereal, fierier.

The guards frowned, their unease growing. One, the tallest, tried to rise. However, like a snake, the tendrils struck out, wrapping around the guard. He struggled, but to no avail as white smoke emanated from his chest. His breathing grew heavier, strained, his eyes beginning to glow the same color as Ari's.

The smoke emanating from the wrapped guard grew. Several strands stuck from all over his body as the white smoke trailed upwards, trying to escape to the sky.

But that's when things got weird.

Well...weirder in a sense because Lily already placed this as one of the top two weirdest things she had seen so far.

The smoke from the guard was being dragged back down, straight into Ari/Pele's mouth.

She was eating it.

Lily gagged, tasting dirt. The guard began shrinking, as if he was deflating like a balloon. The last of the smoke left his body, and with a choking gasp, the guard stopped moving. The tendrils released him, leaving behind a humanoid-shaped husk that fell onto the floor with a sickening thud.

If this was a movie, someone had just clicked the start button after a long pause.

The other guards scrambled up, ready to run. But it was no use. Ari tilted her head and tendrils lashed out to wrap around the rest of the guards. Yells, curses, and howls scraped Lily's ears while the guards struggled to get away. More white smoke was sucked into Ari/Pele at a faster rate.

A fae with antlers near Dain cried out, motioning to the guards.

"Your highness. Shouldn't we do something?"

Dain gritted his teeth, turning away from the screams. "Let it be Aput."

The screaming suddenly stopped as more hollow thuds hit the floor.

Lily, shaking, took in the scene. She was thankful she was still on the ground because she would have been struck down in sheer horror.

Ari...no...Pele stood amongst the guards' lifeless bodies that were strewn about the yard...and began to glow. Her hair grew longer, shinier. Her face glowed, an ethereal light shining from within. She was even more gorgeous than before, if Lily could even fathom it. Ari was

332

taller, her limbs more muscled and smoother. And her hair...the red was climbing even higher. The opaque glow in her eyes dimmed, returning to their blended red/blue color.

She smacked her red lips with a satisfied hum. She practically purred, a vision of contentment. "That hit the spot." She turned to Dain. "I appreciate the use of your guards."

"That hit the spot?" Lily whispered, dumbfounded.

Namaka's voice whispered back in Lily's mind.

My sister is not fully awake. She needs more energy.

Lily shook her head, not understanding. *She needs energy? Was that the energy?*

Hurry little one! Namaka shouted. *We need to stop the energy transference.*

Lily tried to keep her face neutral. *What happens to Ari if we don't?*

There was a pause.

Mortal bodies are not meant for us. Pele will burn your sister's body away to make way for the new one growing inside her.

Lily gasped, her fingers dug into the sand. *Are we talking like butterfly cocoon stuff?! Like shed an Ari skin?!*

Well...to put it mildly...yes.

Her stomach dropped, heavy lead sinking her further down.

Well...things just got a lot more complicated.

Chapter Twenty-Seven

"As much as I'm glad to be of assistance your majesty," Dain interrupted smoothly. He moved forward cautiously, stepping over the bodies, to give a small bow to Ari...well...Pele. "But, the guards were necessary for the prisoners. What would you like me to do with them?"

Ari touched her lips, not sorry at all. "Oh, silly me. I can fix that, since you were generous with your men."

She winked, then blew a kiss. Black smoke rushed out of her lips, enveloping the fallen Adlet guards. As if pulled by strings, the guards rose up. Their heads jolted, cracking unnaturally as their eyes shone bright red. Black smoke trailed from their bodies in faint wisps.

Lily slowly pulled herself up, but still kept to a low crouch. She shuddered, wrapping her arms around herself. Those were not the eyes of the living. Those were the eyes of the dead. At least in all the zombie movies she watched.

I'm never going to look at a zombie movie the same again...

Ari tapped her chin, pursing her lips as the zombie guards stood silent.

As if in afterthought, she motioned to a dark figure near the bound members. "Don't be upset Kamehameha. They're my creatures, purely my own creation. I did not steal their souls or any others from the dead I promise."

The dark figure shook his head in sadness. "These are not the dead. These are cursed creatures of your making."

"They're mine," Ari hissed, her eyes narrowing. "And something from me is not cursed unless I say it's so."

"Wait..." interrupted Lily.

She smacked herself inwardly when the goddess's burning eyes caught hers. She should have stayed quiet, but she already opened her big mouth. "Did you really just make zombies? Ari, are you out of your mind?"

"What I am is none of your business." Her voice turned sharper. "Speaking of, we never spoke as to *why* you are here Lil. And don't you *dare* say it's just because of me."

Lily closed her eyes a moment, breathing out slowly. *Be polite...be polite.*

"Anytime Lil," she barked.

Lily raised her eyebrow, unable to hold back the snark in her tone as she gestured to her fallen form. "Can I at least get up?"

Her inner voice barked.

Girl...did you forget that Ari is possessed by a goddess who can smite you on sight? And now she can make you a zombie. Mind your manners!

Ari sighed dramatically, wagging her finger up slightly. The vine tugged and pulled Lily up.

Lily shook herself, wiping dust and sand from her pants.

"I'm waiting." Ari crossed her arms, her nail tapping against her forearm.

Lily put up her hands. "Fine. I'll tell you. We're here because," she motioned to Dain, "of what he was planning. To stop him." She couldn't help but mutter, "But it seems like you're doing the work for him."

Ari leaned forward, tilting her head slightly. "But why *you* Lil? You're just a human." Her eyes glowed softly, a seductive smile that was definitely not Ari's creeping upward. "Or..." the goddess's deeper voice took hold, her eyes falling onto Lily's pendant. Her head swayed slightly, her voice singing. "Maybe...you're more than that."

Lily bit her lip, refusing to take the bait.

Ari's fingertips grazed Lily's cheek, her voice taking on a creepy, laughing lilt. "Look at little Lily hiding something." She chuckled dryly. "You did well little one," the fire goddess's eyes burned, "but I'm not easily fooled...little Sentinel."

Dain's eyes widened as did some others in the room. Lily refused to look at anyone, she kept her head straight. But she couldn't help cringing when Ari/Pele leaned forward, their noses almost touching.

"What else are you hiding?" the goddess whispered, her warm lips brushing against Lily's cheek, burning a trail down Lily's skin.

Lily winced, pulling back.

Ari/Pele grabbed her arm, nails digging in painfully. And...oh man it hurt. It really hurt, but the more she pulled, the more those talons dug in.

She grimaced, trying everything to not look down at the satchel, her bracelet...basically not look at anything. But, she must have given something away as Ari/Pele's eyes widened, a triumphant smile splitting her red lips. She reached into Lily's backpack and plucked something out.

Lily froze, holding her breath.

"Do you really think this will help you?" Ari/Pele chuckled darkly, raising their fingers.

Lily blinked, schooling her face. It was a parcel of herbs from Papa Remy's store.

Ari/Pele continued, dropping the herbs one by one onto the floor. "Vervane, dill, nightshade, mugwort..."

She sighed...almost in disappointment...before crunching the herbs with her foot, a faint burning waif of smoke curling upward. "Did you honestly think these plants could stop a creation goddess?"

Lily remained silent, giving silent thanks to Papa Remy. It may not be what he intended, but those bits of dried leaves just saved her.

Ari frowned at the silence. With a huff, she turned her attention back to Cabyll, her demeanor softening.

"Now my consort. Let us both be free of all our constraints. Break free of her by breaking her heart."

Cabyll glared, shaking his head.

Ari's long fingers wrapped around Lily's throat. Lily gasped, a slow pressure forming as those fingers began squeezing.

Lily tried to breathe slowly, but her heart wouldn't take the lesson as it beat frantically against her chest. She reached up to grasp Ari/Pele's fingers, attempting to pry them off, but the grip was too strong.

She choked, tucking her chin downward to get a breath. What would she give to just be somewhere, *anywhere*, other than here. She tried to also ignore the pang in her chest seeing Ari's cold face. The same face Ang wore...who was nothing but kind to her for months.

Stop thinking of Ang. Focus Lil.

"Wait!" He grunted, struggling with the vines tied around his wrists.

Ari/Pele paused; her fingers still wrapped around Lily's throat. Lily winced, the pressure steady against her windpipe.

Ari/Pele rolled her shoulders delicately, her tone patient. "Yes, my consort?"

Cabyll lifted his wrists, motioning toward the vines. Her gave her a suave smirk. "Can you take this off?"

Ari/Pele nodded, the vines disappearing. Rubbing his wrists, Cabyll stretched, his muscles taunt. Ignoring Lily, he moved to stand in front of the goddess.

Lily did a double take. Was it her imagination or was Ari now the same height as Cabyll? Could it be the transformation was not only changing her inside, but physically outside as well?

He bowed gallantly, his voice smooth as satin. "Your generosity is overwhelming."

"Flattery will get you many places dear consort." Ari/Pele preened, tapping her lips. "Would you like a sample?"

He gave a roguish smirk. "I prefer to wait for my rewards."

"Then what do you ask for?"

"I only ask you to let her go." He gestured to Lily, giving a dismissive shrug. "She is still your family, correct?"

Ari/Pele tapped her lips again, in thought. "Hmmm. I suppose you make a logical point."

He put his hand over his heart, bending his head. "Then, your Majesty-"

"Call me *ahi nani*," she purred, spearing a side glance at Lily, a triumphant gleam in her eye. "It means gorgeous fire."

Lily held back her eye rolling at the snarky tone. She was not in any position to snap back. She also tried to ignore the intrusive thought that

Cabyll and Ari looked good together. Too good. It was like looking at two models.

She pinched her lips, an unfamiliar ache in her chest. Giving herself a good shake, she reprimanded herself silently. *This is the dumbest thing I've ever...*

Cabyll's lip quirked up in a half smile. "Okay, *ahi nani*." He gave Ari/Pele a flirty wink that made Lily grimace, holding in her disgust.

He held out his forearm in a gallant gesture while he motioned flippantly at Lily. "Would you like me to tell her to get lost?"

Ari/Pele trilled, a pleased smile gracing her face. She let go of Lily's throat to grasp his arm.

With a thump, Lily hit the ground, her knees scrapping against the sand. She gasped, rubbing her neck.

Ari/Pele raised her eyebrow. "That won't be enough. I don't want her to harbor any ridiculous notions. She needs her to learn her place. I now want you to say you hate her and you never want to see her again. Then," she reached out, patting his broad chest lightly, "I'll let her go."

He stood still, his muscles tight. "I'll tell her," he responded cautiously, "and she gets to leave?"

Ari/Pele fluttered her eyes. "I promise."

Stiffly, Cabyll turned to Lily. His gaze took her breath away, it was burning into her. She held in her trembling, berating herself. She expected this. It made sense for him to say it so they could leave safely. But that didn't stop the anxiety creeping up her spine.

She took another shuddering breath. Ari was so wrong about them. They were friends. Simply friends. He didn't feel that way about her, she was sure of it. But it didn't make it hurt less as her heart braced to hear the words. Would he be cruel? Would he be cold?

She held her head up, ready, refusing to let her eyes cloud with tears.

Cabyll bent over her, his strong fingers catching her chin. She winced as he tipped her head back, her throat raw. His eyes were hard, almost tormented, as he ground out. "I will *never* feel the same way about you as you do about me."

She mutely nodded, her heart thudding. It was an odd choice of words. Maybe he was being dramatic.

"Say you hate her," pressed Ari/Pele.

Cabyll's eyes flashed. He pressed his lips firmly together. "I...ha...I-" he stopped a moment, grimacing.

His angry gaze tore into Lily as he growled out. "I despise this!" He ducked his head, his free hand gesturing between the two of them.

Lily's heart cracked a little. *Remember*, she reminded herself. He was her friend. Surely, he didn't despise their friendship. But...he couldn't lie. So, something was true. He despised her somehow. She tried desperately to keep reminding herself they were friends. It still didn't dispel the sharp ache that pierced her chest. It hurt.

A lot.

Ari/Pele saw Lily's pained expression. She clapped her hands and giggled, twirling around. She rushed forward, lying on Cabyll's back.

He stiffened, removing his hand slowly from Lily's chin, his fingertips brushing softly against her jaw. He straightened up smoothly, but slightly to the side forcing Ari/Pele to jump back.

A rakish smile plastered on his face once again, he took Ari/Pele's hand, bowing over it. "How was that, *ahi nani*?"

"You did splendidly my consort. I can see her heartbreak from here." He flinched, but Ari/Pele didn't notice. "Now!" She clapped her hands, spinning away. "Prince Dain, I need more energy."

"Excuse me, *ahi nani*," interrupted Cabyll. Ari/Pele whipped back, surprised. He continued. "Shouldn't we let the mortals go first as you said?"

Ari/Pele paused, a slow smile forming. "You are so right my consort. Best get them out of the way."

Suddenly another fire vine whipped out, wrapping around Lily's throat. She coughed, surprised, the tendril tightening around her. Her eyes briefly met Cabyll. His own were widening in panic and confusion.

Voices rose up, protesting. Vaguely Lily could hear her aunt screaming, Randy calling out.

Another voice cut through the noise.

"Ari...STOP!"

Through blurry eyes, she could make out Brandon moving forward. Somehow, he snapped out of his shock, taking a few hesitant steps forward.

Ari/Pele paused, the tendril holding Lily's breath.

"Brandon?" Ari frowned, her voice returning to normal. "Is that you?"

Brandon wrung his hands. "Ari, what's happened to you?"

She shook her head, her voice wavering. "You...you shouldn't be here."

"Ari, please. You gotta stop this fire lady from taking you over exorcist style." He took another step forward.

Ari reared back, shaking her head. "No. You need to leave. I'm finally happy."

"You're happy?" He threw out his hands. "Ari you made zombies!"

Ari frowned, hissing. "I'm powerful...beautiful! I'm special. And I will get everything I deserve."

He put up his hands. "Look, I get it. I know it's not been the same since dad died."

"Stop it," she gritted, backing away.

He took another step forward. "But you can't let that change you this way. We need to go home to mom."

Ari put her hands over her ears. "I said stop it!"

"I miss him too!" he yelled, startling everyone. His voice quieted. "Every...day. But Ari...we have people who love us, family and friends. We can't lose any more. Please...Ari, stop this." His eyes were begging. "*Please*, don't hurt Lil."

Lily gasped, trying to swallow and winced, her throat burning. She hastily gulped a precious breath of air.

Please listen to him, she silently begged.

Ari clutched her head, her hands trembling. Her hair cascaded over her, covering her face. A deeper voice of the goddess whispered.

"You don't have to lose your family little one."

Ari's voice whispered back, teary. "What do you mean?"

Randy whistled low. "Whoee, she's dancin' in the hog trough."

Lily hated to admit he was right. Ari talking to herself was a scary sight to see.

Pele continued, *"You saw what I did with the guards. We can bring your father back little one."*

"Wait...we can bring my dad back?"

"Yes...just listen and follow me. Let us be free like we planned, and we can return your father from the land of the dead."

340

Lily's heart went cold. They were entering into dangerous territory. She wanted to scream out, but her speech was garbled.

Don't do it Ari. Don't listen to her!

"You cannot do that Pele," Kamehameha echoed Lily's thoughts, crossing his arms. "The dead must remain dead."

"He is right," Kye agreed, his voice firm. "Even you cannot change the ancient laws."

Ari's eyes glazed. "We can bring him back, we can bring him back," she whispered frantically, her voice growing louder. "Yes...yes!"

She straightened, her eyes bright red, narrowing on Lily. The tendril tightened further, her voice deepening, becoming Pele again. "I am the creator. I am the destroyer. Laws do not apply to me."

"No!" yelled Brandon.

"I will bring our family back Brandon, you just watch," Ari gave a crazed smile, ruby tears spilling down her cheeks. The red in her hair creeped higher as she transformed again into the hybrid of the goddess and Ari.

Cabyll cautiously placed a hand on Ari/Pele's shoulder. "You said you'd let her go," he whispered. "You gave your promise."

Maybe it was the trick of Lily's hazy eyes, but Cabyll seemed tense. Almost pleading.

Ari/Pele closed her eyes, leaning into him. "I did promise."

The tendrils lightly lifted Lily a smidge. It was faint, but enough for only Lily to notice. Without anyone catching what was happening, ever so slowly it moved, edging her over the cliff.

Lily's stomach dropped as her feet scrapped the cliffside. Her eyes welled with tears. As much as her heart refused to believe it, her logical side always won. In that cold, weightless moment, she knew she only had seconds. Quickly, she fished the memory pearl from the satchel, gripping it tight.

Please let them catch it, she begged silently.

"I'll let her go," said Ari coyly, keeping Cabyll and the others distracted.

Then, the tendril lifted Lily high in the air, moving lightning fast until she couldn't see ground anymore. Her legs dangled, kicking fruitlessly to find ground again. The vine, still around her throat, loosened a smidge to allow her to peek over her shoulder. Fear coated her insides as she found herself swinging over the edge, the deep, endless water churning below her.

I swear, in the afterlife I'm going to write a complaint about how many times I was dropped in the last few days.

A choked chaotic laugh escaped her lips. Her inner voice really was amping up its defense mechanisms this time.

Her sad eyes turned back to the group. Her blurry tear-filled gaze could vaguely make out their expressions. Dread, anguish, fear. She knew they wouldn't make it in time. Her lip quivered.

Tim, if you're there. I'm gonna need a miracle.

But the Thunderbird was silent, too exhausted to reach her.

Lily gritted her teeth. She made a quick show of pulling at the vine at her throat, getting the pearl ready.

Ari/Pele cackled, but suddenly shook her head. Ari's blue eyes came back, frowning. "I don't want to do this..." Her eyes caught Lily's, indecision warring, her limbs shaking. "Lil, but...my dad..."

Ari winced, clutching her head.

"We shouldn't do this," Ari protested. The familiar red glow came back into her eyes, the goddess speaking to her.

"*You want to be free? Your father? Being special? You know this is the only way.*"

Ari groaned, her voice strained. Regret laced her words as she gritted out, "I'm sorry Lil..."

She straightened, her eyes back to a blend of red/blue. The deep voice of the goddess rang out, the lilting apathetic tone returning.

"Goodbye young Sentinel. Nothing personal, I just don't like competition."

Lily was only able to mouth an, *I love you,* tears streaking down her cheeks before the tendril withdrew.

Cabyll's eyes widened in horror, realizing too late what was happening. He ran forward. "Lily!!"

Lily flailed her arms, but instead of reaching out to Cabyll's outstretched hand, she threw the pearl toward Kye.

"Catch!" she screamed, her voice breaking.

Her fingertips grazed Cabyll's, but then nothing but air greeted her.

Shouts answered her.

"Lily darlin."

"*Nipote*!!"

"Little Sentinel."

"*Nooo! Naui Haneul!!*"

Weightless greeted her as she found herself falling down the cliff, heading toward the abyss. More screams and howls followed her down the fall. Most of all, she could hear a heart wrenching roar accompanied by blue lightning streaks that flew high over the cliff.

She closed her eyes, tears falling upward, bracing herself for the fall.

Her body hit the water with a force that knocked the breath from her lungs, swallowing her into the watery blackness. By reflex, she opened her eyes, squinting at the salty sting. She kicked, desperate to move upward, but the abyss dragged her down. A heavy weight, like a too heavy blanket, settled over her.

Then darkness...

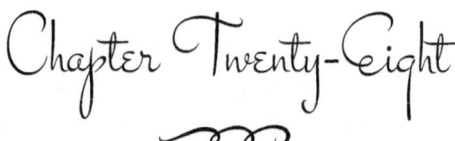

Chapter Twenty-Eight

IT WASN'T COLD.

Lily assumed dark water would be cold. Didn't dark water mean no light? No light meant no heat. It should be freezing as she sunk further and further down, the abyss pulling her into its arms.

But it was warm.

Like a cozy blanket wrapping around her, Lily had an odd sense of comfort. And the quiet. Oh! How quiet it was. If Lily could breathe a sigh of relief, she would have. No more yelling, no more anger. The unbearable pressure of expectations and duties floated away. It was so easy to let go.

For a moment, Lily sat quietly in the warmth of the abyss. Her eyes closed, savoring the blissful quiet.

Snap out of it Lil. Move your feet! This is no time to give up.

She frowned. There went her bootcamp inner voice. Why couldn't it just stay quiet and let her be?

A deep voice replaced her inner one.

Are you really going to let some water beat you? I thought you were stronger than that bul gat-eun kkoch. Besides, we still have a bet human.

She mentally sighed. Both her inner self and imaginary Cabyll was right. It wasn't time to give up. She tried to control her heart to keep it calm. If she panicked, it was over.

She opened her eyes to the darkness. Taking a quick glance around, the saltwater stinging briefly, she found nothing.

Her legs kicked, barely making a dent in the water. Bubbles escaped her mouth, the peace giving way to a slow burning in her chest as her lungs constricted, growing tighter. She only had a minute, maybe less, before lack of oxygen shut her body down.

She kicked again, using her arms to propel herself upward. The weighted blanket of water, which had recently been comforting, was now constricting. It tugged at her, impeding her efforts and drawing her downward. She squinted, a water current rushing over her and blinding her momentarily.

As she stared into the indigo abyss, her lip quivered. Her heart fluttered, the pain increasing. Panic crackled at the edges of her consciousness. What could she do? Her dismay was overwhelming as she tilted her head upward, no sunlight visible.

Her bitter tears were invisible, melting into the saltwater around her. Some great Sentinel she was. What good was she? She couldn't even swim properly. Her aunt could have taken care of this. Even Peri could have done something. Her chest constricted again, pain flaring. She was not worthy of being a Sentinel.

A faint pearlescent light appeared below. Her gaze drifted downward, resting on her bracelet. It glowed, the soft pulse growing.

Ah...keiki. Do not despair.

Namaka's voice surrounded her, warm and maternal. Lily's heart pulled, the tears flowing faster. Layers of compassion and empathy flowed, calming her rapidly beating heart, even though her lungs burned.

The image of Namaka appeared, floating in the dark ocean. Her dark hair glided in the current; her kind eyes distraught as she took in Lily's appearance. Lily knew she must have looked a mess covered in bruises, struggling for air. The goddess cupped her hands and blew. A bubble took shape, growing and expanding. It grew so large it encompassed Lily.

Lily fell as the suspension of the water disappeared. Salt stung her cuts and eyes. She coughed, the cold stale air sweeter than anything she could imagine.

When her lungs quieted, her teary gaze met Namaka's. Her lips quivered.

I failed, Namaka. I couldn't stop her.

Namaka shook her head, her eyes pained. *Oh, little Sentinel. Do not fret. My sister is almost awake, but she is not fully free. There is time still. But...* She trailed off.

But?

Namaka's chest rose and fell, the reflection of a deep sigh. *With your sister almost fully possessed, you cannot stop her as you are now.*

Lily's shoulders slumped. She tried to stop this, but she was too late. It was only a matter of time she'd lose Ari. After that, destruction in a fiery blaze. Her head fell to her chest.

What can we do?

Namaka pursed her lips, warring with indecision.

A soft butt to her head raised Lily's gaze. Tim's small bird form flapped in the bubble.

"Tim?" Lily's whisper seemed loud in the dark, silent water.

The Thunderbird tilted his head, his eyes solemn. *You need to let Namaka take possession of you.*

"Wait what?!" Her confused gaze whipped back and forth between them. "But...can't you help?"

Tim's regretful eyes speared her. *I'm afraid my powers as they are, are no match for a creation maker.*

The goddess refused to look at her, rubbing her arm nervously.

"But," Lily protested, "won't I become like Ari? Couldn't I lose myself too?"

Namaka shook her head. *I promise, I will leave if I notice you are in danger. Unlike my sister who wants to gain control, I only wish to help.* Her worried gaze pierced Lily. *But, it is dangerous. I will not deny it.*

Tim landed on her shoulder. Lily chewed her lip, wincing as the salt water mixed with her torn skin. The Thunderbird squeezed her shoulder in his small claws, not hard enough to hurt, but enough to startle her.

My Sentinel, I understand how you feel.

Lily whipped her head away, refusing to look at him. *How can you possibly understand? You're immortal.*

A soft wing caressed her cheek.

You and I are bonded, young one.

Lily shut her eyes, pain spearing her chest. *You must be so disappointed you got me. I'm not a real Sentinel. I should have stayed home. This stuff isn't for me. I'm not a hero. I'm just a girl who wants to go to college.*

She rubbed her eyes, the tears flowing freely down her cheeks.

Do not cry. Tim's sympathetic tone somehow made her cry harder. *You are more a Sentinel than the ones that hide in their tower. I did not choose you for what you could do. I chose you for what you had already shown me.*

She scoffed, unable to hold back a miserable pout. *What? That I'm not perfect?*

Exactly. Tim's wings gently beat above her head. *Someone who is perfect cannot bend in adversity. They break when something too hard hits them. Those who are truly extraordinary are those that bend in the wind, that flow with the storm. One cannot be strong without being tempered. And you, my dear little Sentinel, showed more courage and heart in that storm than thousands I have seen in my life. Perfect is but a dream. Temperance and kindness forged through fire is once in a lifetime.*

His head butted hers, a small spark tingling down her head.

And you have such a soul. I do not expect perfect. Those who do are fools. We learn from our mistakes as they are natural as breathing. Grow from your mistakes little one and you will be the strongest Sentinel than you can ever imagine, should you choose that path. You are worthy, and do not let yourself think differently.

Lily sniffed, wiping her eyes, a smile forming. *Guess I should stop the pity party huh?*

A wing smacked her head slightly. *Everyone should have time to reflect. But, yes, you should stop this 'party' as you call it.*

Lily reached out, cupping Tim's cheek. *What will happen to you if she possesses me?*

The Thunderbird's eyes warmed. *That is the spirit. As long as you have the pendant, I will be safe. And as long as your soul remains, we will remain bonded.*

Will we be bonded? Lily directed her question at Namaka.

She shook her head. *Not in the way you are with the great Thunderbird,* she answered. *Ours is temporary.*

347

Tim gave a solemn squawk. *Creation makers cannot bond to humans. Their powers are too great. They can only stay temporarily, or they burn the soul away.*

She chewed her lip. This was too much too fast.

Tim rubbed against her head. *This decision, this path, only you can choose it.*

Lily stood quietly, the two ancients awaiting her decision. Could she help Ari before her soul burned? A shiver raked down her spine. Possessed Ari was truly scary. Would she be like that too? Uncontrollable? Violent? And she couldn't forget the main fear of dying by her soul being destroyed. She swallowed; her salty throat dry. Could she really do this?

Her boot camp inner voice yelled out.

Wake up Lil! You're surrounded by water. You're so far down in the depths there's no way you can get out on your own. There's really no other choice is there? Remember, your friends have your back. Your family needs you! So...get your butt in gear!

With a renewed determination her eyes met Namaka. She still had serious doubts of being a Sentinel. She really didn't know if this life was meant for her, but that didn't matter at the moment. What mattered was she was here now, and the choice was clear.

The goddess nodded, not needing another word. Her approving smile lit the dark waters. Was it Lily's imagination or did the cold begin to heat up significantly?

Namaka cupped her mouth, trilling a beautiful call that echoed into the waters. After a moment, a distant song rose from the depths of the abyss.

Lily's eyes widened.

A pod of whales drifted up beneath her feet to circle around them. Their song rose in a heart wrenchingly beautiful melody. A little calf swam to the goddess, rubbing against her playfully before swimming back to its mother.

One by one, other sea creatures appeared. Dolphins, sea turtles, glowing jellyfish. Even a shark. Lily shuddered. Well, it looked like a shark but was much too large – almost prehistoric. Hundreds of creatures surrounded them, each one swimming in front of Lily, pausing a moment before taking a position around the bubble. Their eyes focused on her, assessing her.

After the last one, the large shark, gave her an approving nod (after eyeing her too closely for Lily's liking), and the group of animals hovered in their circle, the song reaching a peak. Their gazes centered on Lily and Namaka and slowly, they bowed.

Namaka put her hand over her heart, unshed tears in her eyes. *Thunderbird, you have indeed chosen wisely. I can see what drew you to her.*

The goddess swayed with the current, her maternal smile and crinkled eyes glowing. With pure grace, the goddess bent forward, her eyes closed, and arms outstretched in a deep bow.

Lily was taken aback. She reached out, ready to protest for Namaka to get up, but Tim flew up in front of her, stopping her. His wings beat fast as he bent forward into his own bow.

Lily shook her head, her voice raspy. "Really, please. You don't need to do that."

Namaka's voice rang, ancient and bold, as the whale song rose to a crescendo. *Yes, we do. You are putting your soul on the line for others. For all of us. We respect and acknowledge your actions keiki.*

The goddess rose, pride radiating. *No...not child anymore. You are worthy to be my kai'i. Protector of not just the worlds between Veils, but of sea and life itself.*

The current swirled around Lily. The blue-green bioluminescence glowed brighter and brighter. The melody increased in volume as the rest of the animals called out, blending with the whale's song.

Namaka reached forward, the palm of her hand gently pressing against the bubble.

Will you make a pact with me kanaka uuku?

Lily waited for the familiar anxiety and uncertainty that plagued her for weeks. Somehow, it was as if all those feelings were washed away. She spared a brief glance at Tim, who gave a reassuring nod, removing any remaining doubt.

With no hesitation, Lily placed her palm on the bubble's surface, her fingertips mirroring the goddess. The water swirled, bubbles covering them. The light grew until all the creatures disappeared, the abyss glowing. The bubble burst, the water rushing over Lily. But instead of fear, she felt a cleansing wave wash over her. It filled her up, a cool warmth promising hope.

She was refreshed, clean, and new.

Namaka's voice rang out, no longer in her mind, but clear in the water.

"Let us go save your family...my Guardian."

Chapter Twenty-Nine

REWIND A FEW MINUTES...

Roaring filled Ari's ears. Her inner voice screamed the moment the tendril let go of Lily. She could even feel it remove itself from Lily's body. It was like watching a dream, unable to change anything.

Or more like a nightmare.

A vision of her dad, happy and laughing, pierced her. Then the vision morphed to him frowning, disappointment evident. At her! Then it turned to Lily's frightened eyes as she fell. Shame punctured her chest. Why didn't she stop it?

Because you are a coward, her inner voice berated her.

Voices yelled around her, overshadowing the white buzzing noise.

"No! Lily darlin!"

"*Nipote!!*"

"Little Sentinel."

"*Nooo!! Naui Haneul!!*"

Pain pierced her shoulder. Since the goddess was using her body, all Ari could do was sit and watch everything unfold while Pele was in control.

Pele twisted, clutching her shoulder. "Who dares?!"

Cabyll filled her vision. His eyes narrowed, burning a bright green.

Blue-white lightning sparked around him in a fury, his hands still holding one glowing dagger.

"My consort?" Pele shook her head in disbelief. "What is the meaning of this?"

Cabyll's eyes were vacant, cold and unyielding. "Bring her back."

She frowned. This didn't make sense. The bargain should have been broken. He shouldn't be acting this way. She pursed her lips, thinking. He must be confused. Yes, that's right. He's simply being honorable...as honorable as an assassin can be of course.

She gave a saccharine smile, pressing her hand against her wound as a healing fire spread from her fingertips. The fire licked her skin, mending her shoulder. "My dear Cabyll...do not worry. Things will be clear in time. Now, you won't be influenced by that wicked girl ever again."

Cabyll's shoulders bunched, his teeth bared. "I said...bring...her... back!"

Another lightning dagger was flung, but to no avail. Pele gently moved her hand, knocking the offending weapon aside.

"Cab, quit hollering down the rain. You need to think of Lily's family," Randy called out.

Cabyll shook his head, his eyes manic as he growled. "I need to save Lily."

Pele sighed, her arms crossed lightly. "She is gone my consort. Nothing, and no one, can escape the abyss."

She sauntered toward him, her beautiful lips clucking softly. "Do not fret. You will forget about her soon. Immortality makes memories fade." She reached out to caress his cheek. "You'll even thank me soon enough."

He reared back and bared his teeth. "Do not touch me!"

Pele paused, a small frown marring her perfect face. She tried to touch him again.

His eyes flared, electricity sparking. "Mark my words fire witch. As Master Assassin of the Veil I swear-"

Randy interjected. "Ah...Cab. Don't rile up the wagon master. Remember, it is still Lily's sister in there."

"If she's really gone, it won't matter what I say," he gritted out.

"Oh darling," Pele cooed, her voice scraping. Inside, Ari wondered vaguely if she really sounded so grating. "Your mind must be in shock from the breaking of the bond. Don't worry," she ran her hand lightly down his cheek. "I'll just confine you for a few decades and you'll be good as new again."

Cabyll's hands clenched, "Why you-"

She snapped her fingers. Fire tendrils erupted from the ground, holding him in place around his legs.

Cabyll unsheathed his scimitar, ready to hack at the tendril.

A whisper shouted in the air. "What have you done?"

Everyone turned.

Brandon had fallen to the floor, Raven clutching him. His heartbroken eyes slashed into Ari's soul with more power than Cabyll's lightning. Her brother's tears fell down his cheeks, his lip red and bloody from biting it.

"What have you done Ari?" he repeated, his voice cracking.

Ari's inner self struggled. She was doing this for them. She was going to bring their dad back. Then everything would be okay. He'd see. Everyone would see.

Her real voice broke through, thready and strained. "Brandon, I didn't mean...you have to understand..."

"Understand? You threw Lily off a cliff!" Brandon's accusing gaze tore at her.

She jerked back. Why was he so angry? She didn't deserve his anger. Everyone should be loving her. After all, she did all this for...

For you, her inner voice – weak though it was – lashed out. *You didn't do this for him. You did this for your own selfish desires so you could be the heroine in this story.*

Another vision of Lily's frightened face slashed Ari's chest. Her heart clenched, her body bowing over.

Pele's voice slithered in. *Don't listen to yourself. Just trust me little one. I'll make you shine.*

She clutched her head, eyes clenched. None of this made sense. The roaring buzz filled her ears again, her head spinning. Another rumble echoed amidst the white noise.

Dimly, a voice broke through the commotion.

"Cab, keep your saddle oiled and your gun greased. I'm gonna hog tie her up so we can work some magic to get Lily's sister back."

Ari moaned, the fire burning hotter. What was happening to her?

Hush little one. Just let go. I'll take care of everything. Let me deal with these pests.

Ari felt herself get pushed down inside her body again, unable to move.

Pele lifted her head, her eyes fiery, as webbing shot toward her. Pele lifted her hand, burning the web to ashes.

Randy whistled low. "Well shucks. I just got my ox in a ditch." He called out. "Anyone else got a plan? I'm plum out."

"Pests," Pele hissed. After all the grace she gave them. After all the kindness she showed. Well, if they didn't want her help, they may as well help her.

"Sister, do not do this." Kamohoali'i shook his head.

"You call me sister? *Now?*" mocked Pele. "You abandoned me."

Kamohoali'i's sad eyes only fueled her fire. "You were going mad. We could not let you help those who would destroy the world. You chose destruction back then, and you're following the same path now."

Pele raised her eyebrow. "I am choosing to burn down the world, only to rebirth it from the ashes. Cleanse it anew. You will see, my foolish brother. But first, I must take care of your companions."

Ari dimly protested. *Please...not Brandon.*

My dear, Pele sighed. *For one to be reborn, we must burn all shackles that bind you. We will rise from these emotional ashes, free of fettered mortal morality. Let us start fresh with no emotional ties.*

The goddess raised her hand, fire tendrils erupting from all around her. Her hair lifted, the warm breeze blowing. Another rumbling from a distance sparked a burning anticipation.

Soon...

"Well, my little *naonaos*...I won't crush you like the little ants you are. You will serve a greater purpose." She tilted her head. "It is a shame. I was being merciful you know, but now you will be used for something else."

She snapped her fingers.

Ari screamed inside from her mental prison as the tendrils whipped

354

out toward Raven, Brandon, and the rest. They snaked out, ready to catch, to wrap, to destroy.

BOOM!!

A resounding explosion lit up the arena as a wall of flame enveloped them.

Chapter Thirty

PAIN RADIATED FROM ARI'S ARMS AS SHE SNAPPED BACK INTO consciousness, the tendrils falling in ashen clumps against the sand.

A cloud of dust obscured her vision. But, too soon, the goddess regained control. Who would dare go against her? She was fire itself.

The dust settled, grey smoke dissipating. Pele's eyes widened. Prince Kye stood in front of the group, his hand outstretched. Fire licked his fingertips, dust falling around him.

"How?" asked Dain, his eyes round. His voice rose. "You should still be bound!"

Kye's chest heaved, his eyes glowing. He held out his other hand, the small memory pearl glowing, the light being sucked into his skin until it disappeared with a faint pop. His shoulders shook, his eyes pained.

"I am," he gritted out.

"But how?" Pele looked at her hands, her own flames flickering, uncertain.

Tane's eyes widened, the wheels in his head turning. "Oh…this situation has taken a different turn."

"Tane, explain," ordered Dain.

"Look at him your highness. Prince Kye is still bound."

Tane motioned to Kye's shaking shoulders, his split lip, and the sweat beading off his brow.

Aput drifted in, their antlers tilted. "I sense another power coming from him."

"Another power?" Dain's brow furrowed. "That is impossible."

"This is ancient," Aput continued, their voice hesitant. "Almost..."

Tane blinked, awed. "Almost like destruction itself."

"Destruction?" Dain's eyes widened, recognition forming. "That means..."

Fire sparked from Kye's fingers, jumping to the shackles that bound the others. They stood in awe as the restraints burned away, freeing them.

Kye grinned, his split lip bleeding down his chin. "Creation and destruction brother."

Kamohoali'i sucked in a breath, whispering, "It was true after all."

Pele fumed. "This is impossible!"

"It is not!" roared Kamohoali'i. "You know it's true, sister. You recognize your own power."

Pele jerked back, her face paling. "No," she wrapped her arms around herself. "This should not be."

Her panicked eyes centered on Kye. "He should not be..." She clutched her head, gasping in pain.

Ari's inner voice yelled out. *What is going on Pele? Who is he?*

The goddess's emotions swarmed through her. They were jumbled, warring between shock, dismay, and hesitant hope. *What are they talking about Pele?*

Kye cracked his neck, his fists clenching. Smoke tendrils emanated from him, black and red. His eyes glowed, sad and bitter. "Oh, but it is... mother."

Pele rubbed her temples, a grimace warring her red lips. "Do *not* call me that. There is no possibility that you are my son."

"You know enough to doubt," quipped Kye, his eyes hard.

The flames grew brighter, flickering along her arms. Pele gritted her teeth. Who was this boy to judge her? She yelled at the zombified Adlet guards. "Restrain them!"

Nafanua cracked her knuckles, pulling forth her hook. "About time."

Waru smiled. "I was getting bored anyways."

The warriors slammed into the guards.

357

Ari, ready to throw another tendril, grimaced as her inner mind split in pain as images filled her, hundreds of years of Pele's memories flooding in. A faint memory came into focus, like an old movie reel. Images of Pele, in her true form, holding a swaddling cloth and handing the bundle to an extremely large, red haired, bearded man. In a flash, the memory was gone. Ari felt the anger rise in the goddess as Pele ground her teeth.

Her hair rose, more flames and tendrils erupting. They clashed with another wall of flames. Kye's hands were raised, his violet eyes burning.

Equal parts fury and panic warred inside her. The goddess's deep voice boomed. "Step aside." Another shuddering rumble echoed her panicking heart. All she needed was a little more energy.

Just a little...more...

Kye stood firm, though his shoulders trembled under the weight of the fire. "You will have to kill me." His bitter eyes bore into hers. "Can you do it mother? Kill the being you created?"

Ari felt her heart--or was it the goddess's heart?--crack. Her feet lifted off into the air, the fire swirling around her. The figures below her scattered, leaving the prince alone, standing tall.

Like little ants...

The goddess's voice rumbled. "Remember this child. I find no pleasure in this form of destruction."

Ari trembled. *You can't kill him!*

Little kanaka, you must burn away your naïve thinking. We do what we must for the sake of freedom.

Ari panicked, fear rising. *Think of the cost. My family!*

Even now, the betrayal in her brother's eyes tore at her. Aunt Raven ran forward, gathering him in her arms. What would this do to her brother? She only wanted her father back. It wasn't just for her, but for him! And here he was staring at her as if she was a stranger.

There was a pause, a weary sigh echoing within, her body suddenly weary.

...Child, you have just begun to live. I feel it within your body, I feel it within your soul. Know this young one, to choose to live means at times, sacrifices must be made. Your mind can only comprehend a few decades. I have not lived an eternity without sacrifice. And I choose to live and live the life I choose.

But...he's your son.

The weary voice hardened. Ari's chest burned hotter, hardening into ashy fragments. *I do not know this child, so therefore he is not my family.*

But –

Enough kanaka!

With a heavy heart, she raised both arms. Flames flickered and licked within the space between her hands until a fireball appeared, growing and expanding. Once this fireball hit, anything in its path would be reduced to ash and dust.

Ari's heart splintered between the terrified gazes of her brother and Aunt Raven and the rising, all-consuming burn of the goddess's fire.

"Farewell," she whispered.

The fire left her hands, the ball of flame barreling down toward the group. Wetness trickled down her cheek, tears she didn't know if they were hers or the goddess.

Another cold, wet, drop tracked down her face. Then another. And another.

She frowned. Another drop disappearing on her lips. It was salty.

She smacked her lips, the taste lingering on her tongue. Too salty.

The drops fell faster, the sunlight dimming. The sky darkened. A cascade of coolness poured over her. Her gaze traveled upward. A huge torrent of water suspended above them, a big ocean wave hovering...waiting. Before she could blink, the wave crested over her head, barreling downward.

The ocean wall slammed down, cutting off the others from the goddess. It also caught the fireball in its path, the water sizzling and steaming until the fire dissolved and the zombified guards disintegrated into dust.

Waru shouted out. "Your highness, did you do this?"

Prince Kye shook his head. "My water is still bound. I did not do this."

"Then who..."

The air grew heavy, the pressure dropping at an alarming rate. The scent of crisp sea salt and sweet tiare flower filled the air. A pillar of water rose, higher and higher, behind Ari. As if the abyss itself awakened, the water swirled in an intricate pattern that branched off in a kaleidoscope of fragmented droplets. Through the shimmering pool, a figure rose, hidden within the depths.

The goddess's voice was soft, but the beginnings of an angry, inhuman growl filled Ari's throat.

"This scent. I know this magic..."

The figure emerged from the pillar, feminine and graceful. Dark curly hair cascaded down sun kissed shoulders that gleamed with a pearlescent glow, as if pearls were crushed and rubbed onto the skin. Deep eyes, fathomless and dark, opened.

Cabyll's eyes widened, his mouth opening slightly. He started forward, only to be held back by Randy who grasped his arm. Randy shook his head in warning.

Cabyll yelled out, but his voice was muffled by the roaring water. Though one word was clear.

Lily...

Ari turned away, unable to watch the pained look in Cabyll's eyes that tightened her chest. She focused on the figure instead. Her eyes widened in shock, taking in the sight. Inside she was relieved, wanting to cry.

It was Lily.

Lily was alive! But, she didn't seem like herself. Her dark eyes centered on Ari, a sapphire blue glowing behind the brown.

The goddess inside Ari grew again, pushing her true self further down. Bitterness, envy, happiness, and fear ravaged her mind. Ari gasped at the sheer force of the conflicting emotions. The fear was new. She should never be afraid, especially not of Lily.

Why was the goddess afraid?

"Sister..." Pele rasped.

Lily's voice rang out, ancient and endless. "Yes...sister." She tilted her head, her eyes swallowed by the brightest blue of the oceanic depths. "We meet again."

Silence.

"Merda." Raven took the words out of everyone's mouth

Chapter Thirty-One

LILY WAS FLYING, IN A COLUMN OF WATER. HUNDREDS OF feet in the air.

This is so weird.

Actually, everything was weird. After her pact, it was as if she was playing a video game in the first person. And her, the character, was moving on their own like in a video sequence. Namaka's voice echoed inside.

Yes, it is...weird is the word you used? But, it looks like my sister and yours are not in agreement. Unlike them, we will work together.

She was right. Ari's lips were pinched, a sheen of sweat over her skin. It was as if Ari had eaten something rotten, and her insides were tearing from within.

Namaka's concerned voice echoed inside her. *Your sister is fading faster than I anticipated. My sister is currently in control, do you mind...*

The unspoken question lingered.

This was it. The goddess had a point and Lily was determined they would work together. *Yes, Namaka. Let's get our sisters back.*

Pele yelled out. "Why are you here?"

Namaka's mouth pinched in disapproval. "How could I not? I could hear your tantrum from the farthest reaches of the Veil."

Pele stomped her foot. Another rumbling echoed in the jungle. "Always with the judgement. Why are you here Namaka?"

The goddess sighed, the sound like wind blowing against the sea. "You're in pain."

"I'm angry!"

"You're always angry. If you're not flirting, you're screaming."

"I'm passionate!"

Namaka held up her hands. "Of course you are."

"Don't placate me sister," Pele groused out sarcastically. "You're here to stop me and my fun. You're always such a spoilsport."

"Someone has to be responsible."

"You're a prude." A sly, snarky grin peeled back from Pele's lips. "That is why Aukelenuiaiku chose me. You are boring, an old maid."

A thunderclap broke the sky. Namaka's eyes narrowed. "Do *not* speak his name."

Pele gave a saccharine smile. "Do you want to know what he whispered to me in the dead of night? Of how you were like a cold fish, while I was his burning star?"

Lily could feel the storm rising within the goddess. *Remember,* she called out. *She's just trying to upset you. You remember what you told me right?*

The goddess breathed out slowly, the thunder quieting.

"I remember," she whispered. Then louder. "Pele, do not forget. Aukelenuiaiku was under a spell." Her eyes lowered in pity. "He never loved you."

Pele reared back, her beautiful countenance terrifying as she hissed. "It's a lie. Humans lie. *Men* lie! They will do anything to be forgiven."

"When have I lied to you?"

Namaka's question startled Pele. She stood there a moment, unmoving and flustered.

Namaka reached out, pleading. "It is time to heal ourselves. Please, come with me. We can go back to where we belong."

Pele stood quiet, chewing her lip softly. She rubbed her arms, indecision evident.

Namaka continued in earnest. "The best time to have planted our healing should have been thousands of years ago. The second-best time is now. Let us put away the destruction sister. Let us be at peace."

Pele's nose twitched. She looked up, her expression hardening, eyes blazing. "At peace? At peace?! After what they did to me?"

She clenched her hands, her mouth pinched. "They imprisoned me, Namaka. *You* helped them."

Namaka grimaced, her eyes sad. "You were in a rage, you weren't in your right mind sister. It was the only way-"

Pele's eyes smoldered with contempt. "I was trapped, confined. My life-fire was muted. It was torture."

Namaka eyed her warily. "*Kaikamahine...*"

Pele slashed her hand down, cutting her off. Her eyes glowed, fire licking her fingertips. "I will not go quietly. I will make them suffer as I did before there is any peace."

We're losing her, warned Lily.

"Sister..." Namaka pleaded. "Do not do this. I do not wish to fight."

Pele's eyes narrowed. "I don't care what you wish." Her clenched hands opened, fire tendrils shooting downward, into the earth. "I will be free and make the betrayers pay."

The rumbling grew louder. The arena shook, tremors in the earth growing. Lily winced as a blast of heat spread out. The group fell down, save for Kye and Kamohoali'i who stood on braced legs. Raven clutched Brandon tightly to her, their eyes worried. In front of them were Randy and Cabyll.

Sweat beaded Cabyll's brow as he struggled to remain on one knee, his scimitar held steady in a protective stance in front of the humans.

His mouth was turned down in a grimace, teeth gritted as he held on despite the tremors. But his eyes were focused on Lily. They were manic, almost desperate. Much different from his cool and roguish twinkle.

Lily's chest caved. She wanted to reach out and ask why he looked so upset. What happened that made him look like he wanted to rip someone apart? She wanted to tell her aunt she was okay. Give Brandon a reassuring hug. Maybe if she just spoke for a moment, it could help...

Namaka whispered inside Lily. *You can reassure them at a later time. There are more pressing matters such as-*

Lily/Namaka turned, following the trail of tendrils.

Is that? Lily's heart stuttered.

The jungle.

It was dwindling. The verdant green was turning a sickly yellow. Fronds and canopy cover blackened and fell, the leaves dissolving into ash and disappearing into the wind. Trees fell down, withered and broken. The cries of animals tore into Lily's heart as birds desperately tried to fly but dropped like stones.

"The forest..." whispered Tane, who had emerged from hiding amidst the fighting.

"Coward," hissed Nafanua. "Are you happy?"

Tane refused to look at her. Ruru gave a plaintive hoot, burrowing into Tane's hair.

"No Pele...stop this madness," yelled Kamohoali'i, his pleading eyes turning to Namaka. "Sister! You must stop her."

Lily's stomach dropped. *Namaka, what is she doing?*

Lily's whispered question returned a freezing fractal response.

She is trying to awaken Him.

If Lily had the control to move her body, she knew her nose would flare. *Umm...not to be a pesky little human with tons of questions that apparently, I cannot comprehend according to all you guys, but...that's not helpful.*

There is no time kai'i.

Namaka raised her arms. The water swirled, solidifying into a spear.

Lily hesitated. Namaka whispered. *I promised you. Your sister will live. We just need to stop her concentration.*

With a grunt, the spear flew.

It shot through the air, ripping through several tendrils with a satisfying hiss. Water exploded in a large circle where the spear landed, dosing the flames.

Pele's eyes blazed as she bared her teeth. "Come fight me then Namaka!"

Namaka sighed, a sad weariness pushed her shoulders forward. She shook her head, covertly wiping her eyes before raising them.

With a forged resolve, the sea goddess thrust her hand into the water column. With a glow, the water stretched and shaped. As if an invisible weapon-smith was forging the water, soon a long double-bladed halberd manifested from the oceanic waves.

Pele answered in kind. With as sinister smile, fire grew from her palms forming two large, wicked looking weapons. They were similar to a ping-pong paddle but covered in blazing teeth.

Pele rolled her shoulders, tilting her head with an eerie crack. She twirled the daggers.

"It has been so long since my leiomano has tasted flesh and blood." Her eyes glowed red. "You ready...*sister*?"

Namaka shook her head. "I will never be ready to fight you." She slashed the halberd, the waves behind her separating. The waves narrowed into spear-like points. "But as you will, dear sister."

The water spears zipped down in a blink. Thankfully the water dissolved within the water barrier, leaving Lily's friends and family safe.

Pele, however, gritted her teeth, putting her weapons in front of her in a protective stance. Fire surrounded her, but that didn't stop water from breaking through, slicing her.

Pele rubbed her cheek, a cut blooming on her perfect face. "My turn," she hissed. She crouched, before launching herself into the sky in a fury of fire. With a warrior cry, she spun with an almost beautiful dancelike grace. She paused in midair, before falling down with her weapons pointing downward.

Right toward Namaka.

Namaka's halberd flew upward, crashing into the leiomano; the energy powerful enough that it rang out for miles. The goddesses gritted their teeth at each other, neither one refusing to back down. With a flurry, Namaka twisted, the halberd spinning around her body to force Pele to jump back.

"You always were like this sister," Pele hissed, venom pouring into every word as she threw her leg out. Fire flamed from her feet as she flipped backward, catching Namaka in the face. "So calculated, so boring. You have nothing but ice water in those veins."

Namaka grunted, wiping her cut lip. "And you let your emotions cloud reason. So much so, you delude yourself within a fantasy world of your own making."

"At least it is *my* fantasy and not the whim of someone else!"

Down below, someone cried out. Was it Raven? "What can we do?"

"I hear ya cluckin, but can't find your nest girl. That's nuts and suicide."

"She's right Randy, we need to do something."

"Cabyll, I'm afraid we cannot intervene."

"Kye, don't you dare stop me or I'll shove my scimitar somewhere you won't like! Where's that peri fairy?"

"Per won't let a spell stop her. She'll be here. But what about you, councilman? Aren't you their brother? Will they listen to you?"

"I never got between my sisters in the past, I will not do that now, Thunderboy."

"Are you happy now Tane? You got what you wanted. Do you see the devastation out there, you numbskull."

"I am not happy, Nafanua. This is not what I imagined, but what can we do against creation makers?"

"Your highness, you must take cover. Dain? Are you listening?"

"She is beautiful, Aput."

"Miss Ari is disappearing, your highness."

"...I know, but one shines the brightest right before the dark."

Namaka spun around, a roundhouse kick effectively knocking Pele off. She raised her arms, the halberd over her head. The ocean column rose, whipping around to encase Pele in a bubble.

With a soft blow of her lips, Namaka whispered something that even Lily couldn't understand. The water cracked and solidified into ice. With a thunderous whistle, the ice bubble fell with a thud onto the ground.

"Time to cool off," Namaka whispered to her frozen sister.

At first, nothing happened. Then, a red glow emanated within the ice bubble. It grew and grew, small cracks appearing. Suddenly, the ice broke, frozen fractals splintering in all directions.

Pele emerged, shaking off icy dust. The red in her hair receded slowly, black splotches of frostbite dotting her arms. She staggered forward, dragging one blackened leg.

Lily protested. *You gave her frostbite?*

It will be fine Guardian. Your sister holds my sister's healing ability. She will be well.

Pele's chest heaved, her teeth chattering. Steam rose from her body, the black spots disappearing. She gritted her teeth as she snarled. "I... HATE...when you do that."

"Then stand down. Leave the humans and this place," ordered Namaka.

"Make me!" Pele shouted, then coughed. She fell down to one knee, her body shaking.

Namaka raised her arm again.

Don't kill her please, Lily pleaded.

"Stop!"

Dain's voice rang out as he came through the water barrier, his eyes intense. He walked up to Pele, still leaving some distance between them. If Lily could tilt her head in confusion, she would have. What was he doing? His hair was messy, his eyes bright. Very unlike the cold composure she was used to seeing from the icy prince.

He raised his hands, beseeching Namaka. "Would you really kill your sibling, oh great creation goddess?"

Namaka shook her head. "How impudent of you, young prince. Do you need a reminder of all of *your* recent deeds?"

"I did them to save my family." He spread his arms wide. "To save all of us from the poison of the human world."

Namaka raised her eyebrow. Lily would have too. His family? Really? But...the fae couldn't lie. How could he say that so easily?

Dain continued, "Humans have nearly destroyed their world. They consume and eliminate everything in their path. Instead of tolerance, they spew hate and anger. They blame everything and everyone but themselves. Even when they understand their destructiveness, their apathy or resigned attitude to their fate is prevalent. I cannot have our world be destroyed as a byproduct of their greed."

The ocean goddess crossed her arms, skeptical. "You say the human world will be destroyed, but aren't you the one wishing to destroy it?"

"I am merely doing my duty. I have been given prophecies for a reason. It is for our people to return." He gestured to Ari/Pele. "Your sister is necessary to sever our ties to that diseased world before it spreads and infects ours. Do not hurt her."

Pele snickered before a cough racked her chest. "Are you really afraid for me silly prince...or this human?"

Dain didn't answer, she continued. "I doubt it's for this human. You never appeared afraid when she almost was eaten by Uktena, or Yarramundi." She laughed cruelly. "Actually, you were the one that initiated those encounters, correct? What makes you think for one second that she believes your halfhearted attempt of being a hero now?"

Dain stood there, frozen, like someone punched him in the gut.

Pele smiled sweetly, wiping her bloody chin. "Aww. Cat got your sly tongue? Do you feel conflicted now? Don't worry...I can take that away easily. If you really want to be helpful, then you would give everything to sustain this body, wouldn't you?"

In a split second, that moment of hesitation, changed everything.

With a flash, Pele whipped her hand out, shooting a fire tendril at the prince.

"Your highness!"

THWAK!

Chapter Thirty-Two

No, ARI'S INNER VOICE GREW. *No, no, no...*

She winced, pulling herself back into her body.

Pele yelled, pounding at the back of her mind at the sudden switch. Ari squinted, her eyes adjusting to the light, her limbs not used to being in control. And that's when she saw the scene in front of her.

Aput.

Aput had jumped in front of Dain, taking the fire into their chest. The Ijiraq staggered a moment, the tendril pulsing and pulling energy. Ari could only watch in horror as the energy coursed through her body. Aput stared at her, their grey eyes clenched in pain.

With a panicked yelp, Ari pulled her hand back, desperate for the tendril to release. With a sickening slurp, it pulled away, disappearing with a whisper.

Her mouth opened in horror as Aput's knees buckled, falling forward. Dain caught the Ijiraq in his arms.

She scrambled forward, falling down on her knees next to them. "Aput?!"

Aput tilted their head, their antlers swaying. "Miss Ari? Are you... back?"

Hot tears streamed down her face. "Yes, I am Aput. I'm here. You're gonna be okay." Her desperate gaze met Dain. "Aput's gonna be okay right?"

Dain's closed his eyes, shaking his head.

Ari's trembling hands grasped Aput's long, clawed tips. "Then... then...Pele can help. She can bring back dad, she'll bring back Aput right?"

She whipped around when only silence greeted her. "RIGHT?!"

Kamehameha appeared to her side, gently resting his hand on her shoulder. "The goddess of fire can only bring bodies back, not their souls, child."

Ari shook him off, bending over Aput. "No...no! She said she could bring him back! She wouldn't lie right?" Her stricken gaze met the Nightmarcher. "Please," she whispered.

Kamehameha's shoulders fell. "Where there is life, death is inevitable. I am sorry."

Ari bit her lip. No! This couldn't be right. It just couldn't. Maybe if she allowed Pele to take control again they could –

A light squeeze of her hand brought her back to the present. Aput pulled her hand, shaking their head. "Miss Ari. Please," they gave a shuddering breath, "do not call her."

Aput turned to Dain, raising their other clawed hand. Dain took it, his jaw clenched.

"Your highness," Aput began, giving a small cough. "All my life, I lived a cursed life. My purpose was to abandon the innocent. For centuries I lived that life, bringing lost children hope only to abandon them in the snow and ice." They coughed again, wheezing as the blackened tendril spread further up their neck. "Imagine...thinking there was only one way to do any one thing." They chuckled dryly. "How difficult life was."

Dain shook his head, covertly wiping his eyes. "Do not speak Aput. We need to heal you."

Aput sighed, ignoring him. "Then...when I saved that child and abandoned by my tribe...and you found me...that was the moment I started living." Aput took a deep, stuttering breath. "I swore that day, I would never abandon anyone again."

"You fool," groused Dain. "Don't speak like that."

Aput chuckled. "Better to be thought a fool than have pride cloud my eyes." A pause, their breath whistling, the sickness spreading further. "Please your highness. Before I leave this world, do not let your pride cloud your eyes."

Their eyes caught Dain's. "There is more than one way to do any one thing."

Ari panicked as Aput's eyes dimmed. "No! No Aput! Please, I'm sorry. I'm so sorry!!"

Aput smiled softly, their voice softening. "Do not blame yourself Miss Ari. I have lived a long time, some good, some bad. But...meeting you, it was part of the good. Do not doubt yourself. Just remember, do not judge others so quickly and do not abandon those who love and trust you like I did in the past."

Tears coursed down Ari's cheeks, burning a salty path to land on Aput's large, furry nose.

The Ijiraq blinked, surprised. "You shed tears for this cursed being. Truly, you are a marvel, Miss Ari."

"You are my friend Aput," she whispered brokenly. "I don't want to lose you."

"And you are mine Miss Ari."

She hiccuped, her throat tight. "I messed up Aput. Everyone is probably so mad at me, and they should be." Her voice choked. "This anger, what I became. I'm afraid..."

Aput closed their clawed hand over hers. "If you are afraid, change your way. As for me? Death is another journey. Do not shed too many tears for I do not deserve it."

"Yes, you do." Dain gritted his teeth. "You are always so prim and proper. You deserve a warrior's send off, not this pathetic death."

Aput chuckled, then coughed as the sickness racked their body. "Look out for him Miss Ari. As you can see, he is selfish, short-sighted and does not take care of himself. I even have to remind him to wash his hands-"

"She gets it," grumbled Dain.

"But regardless," Aput continued, "Like all of us villains and monsters...we all still crave love and friendship. Please remind him to stay on a steady path."

Ari was silent. How could Aput ask her to do this? Even when Dain treated her the way he did. Watching the prince, her heart tugged as the tears fell down his cheeks. Could she really do it? Aput stared at her, unblinking...waiting.

She nodded.

The Ijiraq's shoulders relaxed as if a large weight left them. They smiled at Ari, relieved and grateful. Aput turned to Dain. "Your highness, please forgive me for leaving you first. I swore I wouldn't abandon you."

"You haven't. You haven't," Dain repeated over and over, his jaw trembling.

"I had no purpose in my long, wretched life...until you. Thank you both for bringing meaning to my life."

And with one last, shuddering sigh, the Ijiraq finally rested.

"He's gone," whispered Dain.

Ari shook her head. Still on her knees, she clutched her head and bent over.

No...no, no, no! Pele! Why did you lie to me?!

Pele's voice slithered in, resigned. *I told you the truth child. Only not the entirety.*

So, you can't bring him back?

I can, but not the way you wish. Ouch! What is this?

What is what?

This feeling? It's like a pain, but it's so sharp. We haven't been injured. Why does this body hurt so much?

It's called grief. Ari winced, her chest caving in. *Aput was good.*

And your prince, he feels this too?

Even now, through Ari's eyes, they watched as the prince – who was holding Aput's body – throw back his head and wail. Ice crystalized down his wet cheeks and snow billowed around him.

Yes, Ari admitted solemnly, *this is grief Pele. This is what we are doing to all these people.*

How do we stop this feeling? I do not like this.

We need to stop Pele. Ari sighed. *This is wrong.*

The fire inside her diminished, flickering uncertainly.

They are not as selfish as I thought, the goddess reluctantly admitted.

We are selfish. Ari's lip trembled. *People can be selfish, and cruel. I just realized that in many ways, we are all not that different from each other. I've been selfish. I've been cruel. But, we are not just one thing. We can be kind and funny. And some* – her gaze flickered up to Lily – *are loyal and caring, even to people who aren't nice.*

You are growing a conscience child. A heavy sigh echoed inside her. *Maybe I should not be so emotional as my sister said.*

The hope that flared within Ari sputtered as quickly as it came.

But my freedom is more important.

Ari shook her head. *No! Stop!*

I'm sorry child, I am taking over now.

Chapter Thirty-Three

LILY STARED DOWN AT ARI, HER HEART CLENCHING.

Do you think Ari is okay?

I do not know. Namaka's uncertainty did not sit well with her.

Ari was bent over the large humanoid caribou. Her shoulders shook in grief, then immediately stiffened. With a few jerks of her arms, bones cracking, she stood up.

Ari/Pele's hair rose, whipping around her, the red tinge growing higher, almost to her ears. Her eyes went opaque, her arms outstretched, nails lengthening.

Chills skated down Lily's arms. Time was running out.

An idea popped up. *Can you give me a moment Namaka?*

A pause. *Are you sure kai'i?*

Yes, but can you lend me something?

With a jolt, Lily was back in control of her body. Thankfully, the goddess had agreed for Lily to use the cool creation maker powers since she was still suspended in the water spiral. She closed her eyes, willing herself to come down to the ground. Her feet landed gently on the surface.

She approached Ari, holding her palms out, keeping her tone soft. "Ari? Are you there?"

Ari struggled, jerking slightly but still unmoving.

She tried again. "Ari? Please answer me."

A pained grimace stole over Ari's lips. "Lily..." Ari choked out, "run away."

She shook her head. "I won't leave you."

Ari's lip trembled. "I can't hold her back. She won't stop Lil. I'm sorry...so..."

"It's okay," she reassured. "We'll separate you two. Just hold on a little longer."

"It hurts." Ari's pained voice tore at Lily. "The fire...it hurts Lil." Even now, the rising flames flickered around Lily, the heat burning her nostrils.

Ari choked, "I miss my mom..." Her eyes welled up. "I want my mom..."

Tears filled Lily's eyes. With a few quick strides, she ran up, wrapping her arms around Ari.

"Lily!" Cabyll's panicked voice dimly penetrated her senses.

But it didn't matter. Ari was in pain, and she would not leave her. The fire welled around them, but Namaka's power protected her. At least for the moment.

She squeezed Ari tighter. "You'll see her, I promise."

Molten tears burned down Ari's cheeks, falling onto Lily's hair with a sizzle as she begged.

"Leave, please Lil."

"Family does not abandon each other," she whispered, hugging her tighter.

Sobs tore through Ari, her body jerking. "I can't...she's..."

Then, the goddess burst forth.

With a scream that reminded Lily of a volcano, Ari's mouth ripped open, a beam shooting upward. Fire exploded; tendrils burst forth into the earth.

Lily clenched her eyes, a water barrier encasing her as the flames engulfed them, pushing her away from Ari.

The energy from the emaciated forest pulsed from the fire tendrils, a vibrant orange red glow within them. The earth exploded as power rolled, tearing through the dead jungle. It was heading toward the mountain until the earth cracked up the side of the steaming volcano.

Lily shook ash off her shoulders, assessing the situation. The force of the blow must have been too much for Ari as she was on the ground, unconscious. Thankfully, the rest were protected by Namaka's still active water barrier.

With a quick wave of her hand, Lily let it fall, allowing the group to move.

Randy whistled low, wiping his brow. "Uh...folks? While I'm sure we can all agree poor Lily's sister is missin' a few buttons off her shirt, I think it's safe to say this situation is lookin' as friendly as a bramble bush."

Raven gestured to the fallen Ari. "What happened to her?"

"Is my sister okay?" asked Brandon, wringing his hands.

"Is she still your sister is the question, sweetheart," Raven reminded softly, her eyes uncertain.

Kamohoali'i sighed. "Too much energy was spent and her human body was too weak."

"She's not..." Raven trailed off, biting her lip.

Kamohoali'i shook his head. "No, she is unconscious. The human still lives as well as my sister."

A bright flash of violet light erupted from Kye. He cracked his neck, rolling his shoulders. "Looks like my binding has ended."

His voice rose, barking orders. "Subdue the traitors now."

In a few seconds, Waru, Spyke, and the other council members overtook Tane and Hi'iaka.

Kye stepped to Dain, who was still kneeling over the body of Aput. He shook his head, solemn. "Brother, it is over." Dain wouldn't look at him, his eyes were glazed, unfocused.

Lily breathed out slowly, her eyes still on Ari. Was it really over?

BOOM!

The crack on the side of the volcano increased, splitting further apart.

Randy clucked. "Well...she just done tip over the outhouse didn't she?"

"Not the time spider," groused Cabyll. "We need to fix this mess she made."

He called out to Lily, his voice rocky. "Are you okay?"

Lily couldn't do anything but nod even though she really didn't know the answer to that. Was Ari okay?

She jolted as a pair of arms encased her, the scent of sea and salt surrounding her. Cabyll buried his chin on top of her curls, rubbing the top of her head slightly.

His gruff voice was soft, his tone accusatory. "You seem determined to worry me to death."

Lily awkwardly patted his back. "I didn't mean to worry you. To be honest, I wasn't sure how things were going to go there for a minute."

Cabyll pulled her in closer to his chest as he growled low in her ear. "I thought I lost you, Lily."

She tensed, afraid to bury her face in his chest. Her heart thumped against her ribcage as she whispered. "But you didn't."

His growling grew more intense. "I was ready to burn it down...for you."

Her eyes widened. She cleared her throat, putting her hands on his chest. "Geez, you certainly go to bat for your friends."

His gaze lingered on her, but she refused to look at him. She didn't want to see his face, she was still too afraid after what he said earlier. His hands tightened around her waist as if he wouldn't let her go.

He pulled back, ignoring her, but he still held her lightly. He tilted his head, his hair falling over his intense green eyes. His long fingers reached up to grab one of her wayward curls, rubbing it between his thumb and forefinger. His eyebrow lifted. "Care to explain the dye job?"

She followed his fingers. Her curls were tinged blue at the ends.

"I made a deal, but don't worry." She put up her hands when Cabyll's shoulders tensed, his eyes glowing. "Namaka and I are in a temporary contract."

"Lily darlin', I'm sure you already know the issues of wagering your soul on this," warned Randy.

"Her soul?" Raven yelled. Lily could swear steam was coming out of her ears.

"I'm fine," she reassured everyone, stepping away from Cabyll's arms. "I know it's not ideal, but it was the only option."

"We must trust her." Kye stepped forward, staring her down. "She has proven capable thus far."

Namaka's voice peeled out of Lily, the blue eyes of the goddess glowing. "My nephew is quite wise."

"Is that..." Brandon trailed off, his eyes widening. "That's kinda cool, in a weird exorcist way."

Randy scratched his neck. "Not gonna lie darlin', that's kinda creepy."

"Sister," Kamohoali'i bent down, peering into Lily's eyes, as if he could find Namaka. "It is good to see you, bad circumstances as they are."

"Aww. Baby brother! How I missed you," Namaka reached up and rubbed the top of his smooth, shark head. A rumbling chuckle came from the shark god. "We must talk when this over."

"What do we do with the fire goddess?" Waru nodded to the unconscious Ari.

"My sister still possesses the human. I must pull her out, and we will leave together." Namaka clutched her chest, her legs a little shaky.

"Sister?" Kamohoali'i's concerned gaze scanned her.

Namaka shook her head, waving off his arm. "I am fine."

She breathed out, her breath shaky. Her intense blue eyes caught theirs. "But I need to leave Lily soon. I do not wish to hurt her."

Cabyll crossed his arms, his eyes narrowing on Kamohoali'i's hand that was resting on Lily's back. "Then do it, and fast."

Before Namaka could move closer, a loud crack echoed around them. It was coming from the volcano.

Fissures rumbled and expanded, magma pouring out in waves. Bubbles of lava and exploding rock flew through the air, slamming into earth. The dry, dead jungle began catching fire, the oppressive heat bearing upon them.

Namaka's eyes widened, her mouth agape. "*'A'ole*...this cannot be..."

"This isn't good," Waru affirmed.

Raven's cry stuck in the air. "*Dio mio*! What is that?"

A huge, clawed hand clenched the top of the volcano. And by huge, the taloned hand was about the size of a football field. Magma poured out as the top split open. Emerging from the molten depths, a gigantic figure slowly pulled out from the lava.

Skin of blackened hard magma adorned with wicked spikes scattered down its back. Pupil-less orange eyes filled with lava glowed eerily against the ash covered darkened sky. Soon the figure lifted itself and pushed through the volcano, breaking the front of the mountain. Lava seemed to be in its veins as openings in its rib cage glowed with the molten magma. A sharp jaw sporting wicked rock fangs opened to bright orange lava. The titanic monster roared, more lava spewing down its jowls, burning a path of destruction down the mountain.

"She succeeded. Pele summoned him," whispered Namaka, fear evident in her eyes.

"Who?" asked Brandon.

"Deimos," answered Kamohoali'i reluctantly.

Nafanua gasped, clutching her hands. "May the gods have mercy on us. She unleashed chaos incarnate."

"Still clueless folks here," quipped Brandon.

"Deimos is a Cherufe demon," explained Kye. "A monster that fuels volcanos, they are the definition of chaos and destruction."

"I always told Pele he was a bad choice for a pet," sighed Kamohoali'i.

"PET?!" Raven blinked. She wagged her finger. "We need to have a serious discussion when this is over about what is considered an appropriate pet."

"Our father thought taking care of a creature would help Pele learn compassion for others." Namaka closed her eyes, rubbing her forehead. "But Deimos had a greedy appetite. She never fed him enough. It got so bad he needed to be put into a slumber to preserve the natural balance of the world. Now that he's awake."

She took a shaky breath. "I'm afraid his appetite will be insatiable."

"What do we do sister?" asked Kamohoali'i, his eyes worried.

Waru cracked his shoulder. "Your highness, I am willing to fight."

"That is suicide Waru. Even I cannot fight him as I am." Kye shook his head.

"What if I helped you?"

The group turned to Dain, whose eyes – bloodshot – focused on the demon.

"What are you saying brother?" asked Kye, eyebrow raised.

Raven glared. "Yeah, what are you saying? Didn't you want this to happen?" She motioned to the unconscious Ari. "You were willing to sacrifice Ari...again! Kinda hard to believe you."

Her accusatory tone caused Dain to flinch.

Kye shook his head at his brother. "Even if we combined our strength, it wouldn't be enough against a Cherufe demon."

Nafanua argued. "But we cannot sit here and do nothing."

Spyke and Waru cracked their knuckles simultaneously. Both their eyes sported a warrior determination.

"I can try to put him back to sleep." Namaka frowned. "But...Lily's body...I used up too much energy."

"What does that mean?" asked Brandon. "You're a goddess right? Just nail that titan wannabe to the wall."

Namaka chuckled. "You are a spirited one." Then she grew solemn. "I could, in theory. But...in this body, that would mean..." she trailed off.

"Lily would die, wouldn't she?" Raven bit her lip.

Namaka refused to look at her but nodded. "I promised her I'd keep her safe."

Lily whispered inside. *But if we don't do this, what would happen?*

The goddess took a few seconds to respond. *Deimos will consume this world...and move past the Veil into yours.*

We can't let that happen!

Lily, I promised you and the Thunderbird...

Namaka! Lily's sharp inner voice cut through. *I cannot let my family die.* A flicker of Ang's face flashed in her memories. *I don't want anyone else to get hurt.*

You know what you're saying kai'i?

Lily and Namaka both watched as the massive fire demon roared again, his taloned hand grasping at several hundred trees. He ripped them from the ground with a sickening lurch and devoured the helpless plants and animals in his flaming mouth.

Lily firmly responded. *Yes...we need to stop him.*

A large hand fell on Lily's shoulder. "What is going on sister? You're quiet."

Namaka shook herself, reaching up to hold Kamohoali'i's hand. "I was speaking with Lily. She is willing."

Raven protested. "But that means she'll die."

Cabyll shook his head, baring his teeth. "She's not martyring herself again! I swear Lily I'm gonna-"

The ground shook under them. This wasn't the typical rumble they were feeling throughout this encounter. It was different. More localized.

And louder.

Spyke smacked his lips, blowing out a long, drawn-out sigh. "I don't think you need to worry about that anymore." He hoisted his club on his shoulder, very relaxed.

"What are you talking about Thunderboy?" asked Waru.

The thunder grew louder, until a loud boom echoed underneath them. The group, save for Spyke, looked around but found nothing. Suddenly, the earth exploded on the side of the arena, chunks of debris falling into the abyss. The wind picked up, whipping around them in a fury.

The scent of cool peppermint permeated the air, shocking Lily back to herself.

Her eyes cleared, focusing on a cloud trail that zoomed overhead. She peered into the trail, trying to focus on the dim light. "Is that...is that Peri?!"

Spyke smiled, a deep chuckle rumbling. "I told you not to worry about her."

Randy's eyes widened, giving a low whistle. "Well, I'll be darned."

Even now, the cloud trail was zipping faster and faster, straight toward Deimos.

Cabyll shook his head. "Look, I know she's strong – she's a peri fairy after all – but still. This is an elemental, primordial being. Does she really think she can-"

BOOM!

With a flourish, Peri had slammed straight into Deimos, bursting a hole through his thick, hard shell. Lava bubbled out, running down Deimos's side.

The demon roared, bending over in pain.

"Take out that thing..." trailed off Cabyll, his mouth frozen.

"That's Per for you," shrugged Spyke.

"Are you sure she is not part demon?" asked Dain, brows furrowed.

"Holy moly! That's some superhero mutant stuff going on there." Brandon pumped his fist, giving a whoop.

Waru raised his eyebrow, giving a small nod of approval that Kye shared.

"That is no ordinary peri fairy," said Kamohoali'i, eyes wide.

Nafanua chuckled with pride, folding her arms. "She certainly is not."

Another thunderous boom, resulting in another gaping hole, rang out. This time the chaos demon clutched his face, his jaw removed.

Lily flinched. "Can he be killed?"

She jumped as Tane's large presence appeared at her back.

"Primordial beings such as the chaos demon cannot be simply "killed"." He rolled his eyes, acting like he was speaking to a toddler. "They can only be secured by a sealing or sleeping."

He is really pompous isn't he.

Namaka chuckled inside. *Want me to freeze him?*

Lily refrained, but it was definitely tempting.

"Then what she's doing is for nothing?" asked Brandon, frowning.

Kamohoali'i gestured with his large hand. "Not for nothing. Look human child."

At first glance it did seem like Deimos was hurt, but the holes seemed smaller. Soon the holes closed up, lava pouring over the hole and hardening into a magma skin. It was healing itself. Tane was right, this creature couldn't die. But then what was Peri doing to it?

"Look," repeated Kamohoali'i.

Peri continued to fly back and forth. Large gaping holes opened and closed simultaneously. With each healing, Deimos walked slower, became less agitated. The bright light of the magma dimmed, flickering softly.

Lily gasped, understanding what Peri was doing.

"Is it getting sleepy?" asked Raven, frowning.

"Impressive, for a peri fairy," rumbled Kye.

Nafanua pumped her fist. "Brillant Peri!"

"Of course the peri fairy is *playing* with a chaos demon," snarked Cabyll.

"That's Per for you, always wants to have fun," quipped Spyke, a faint smile quirking upward.

"Would you look at that," breathed Waru, smiling.

Deimos moved back toward the volcano. His mouth opened wide, but no roar came out. It was almost like a yawn as he fell backwards into the mountain again. He crumbled and melted down into the magma, the cracks hardening as he disappeared back into the heart of the earth until only wisps of ashy smoke trailed over a blackened, cold lava.

Lily's lips split in a smile. "She did it."

Spyke returned the grin with a confident wink. "Yup, she did it."

A voice yelled from above.

"Whew! Time for some cool down stretching."

Peri flew down with a dainty thud, flinging her long hair back. She stretched one arm above her head. She took a quick look around, her eyes widening. "Oh...my...Lily pie?! Spykie poo! Did you see what I did?!"

Spyke chuckled. "We did Per."

Peri giggled. "Now is the time to praise me."

Nafanua clapped her hands. "You were amazing." She winked at Peri. "Name your reward and I'll grant it."

Peri blushed, grinning wide. "Can we go have one of those little warm drinks that Lily calls lattes."

A voice interrupted. "How?"

The group turned at the plaintive question.

Hi'iaka, who had come out of hiding, her beautiful hair messed up, flower adornments askew. She brushed her shoulders, dust flying.

"How did you get out of that? No one can escape my magic."

Nafanua scoffed. "Have you no shame? You really are full of it Hi'iaka."

Peri's blinding smile vanished. Her eyes narrowed as a cruel smirk ticked upward. She wagged her finger. "Oh, there you are, you naughty little princess."

"This...this was not supposed to happen!" Hi'iaka shook her head, biting her lip. Her wild eyes caught Kye. "Your highness, I did this all for you...for us. I *deserve* to be at your side. I'm sure if you think about it, you can see I'm the best one to be with you."

Kye stepped forward, motioning her closer.

Hi'iaka's eyes widened as she smoothed her hair. She shuffled toward him.

He stopped her when she got within touching distance, leaning down. "I have thought about it."

Her hopeful eyes broke when he continued, his voice growing colder. "Hi'iaka, you are hereby banished from serving on the Council.

Vacate this realm immediately." His eyes sparked, resolute. "Never darken my sight again."

Hi'iaka's mouth opened. "But, your highness..."

Kye spun around, flicking his hand toward Peri. "Envoy to my brother, dispense with your justice as you see fit."

Peri smiled, jumping up and down clapping her hands. She cracked her neck then her knuckles, bouncing lightly on her feet.

Hi'iaka protested, still reaching out to Kye's back. "No! You can't! I am the most beautiful being in this realm and deserve-"

CRACK!

Peri's fist flew so fast Lily couldn't see it. Hi'iaka suddenly took to the air, the force of the blow so intense she flew for miles backward until she was out of sight, her screams echoing in the distance.

Peri wiped her hands, giving out a satisfied sigh. "No one tries to trap me and gets away with it."

She clapped her hands one more time for emphasis. "So...what did I miss?"

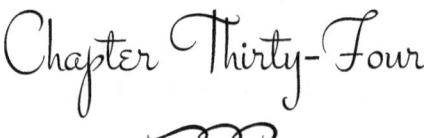

Chapter Thirty-Four

THE GROUP WAS SILENT A MOMENT BEFORE ANOTHER VOICE broke the silence.

"I never thought I'd see Deimos fall asleep from playing."

Ari had woken, but looking at the red eyes told Lily it was Pele.

The goddess rubbed her head, her shoulders tense. She eyed Lily warily.

Lily took a breath. *Namaka, can you end this?*

Yes kai'i. One last time.

Lily felt her consciousness being sucked back into the sidelines as Namaka took the reins. Namaka shook her shoulders, tossing her head. With a deep, steading breath, she moved forward until she was arm's reach from Pele.

Pele raised her arms, bracing herself for another fight. She looked weary and wary. "I warn you Namaka, just because Deimos is gone doesn't mean..."

She stopped mid-sentence as Namaka wrapped her arms around her.

Pele's lip quivered, her arms frozen. "What are you doing?"

"Something I should have done centuries ago," whispered Namaka.

"Don't think this will change anything." Pele's trembling hands hovered over Namaka's back, belying the venom in her words.

385

Namaka hugged tighter. "As a smart human said, family doesn't abandon one another."

Pele gave a choked laugh, her eyes welling up.

"I'm so angry," she whispered.

Namaka's voice lulled like a soft wave. "I know, I know."

"He really loved you," Pele's voice cracked. "I thought...It was wrong of me." Her eye pleaded. "I'm sorry, I'm so sorry sister."

Namaka leaned back, cradling her sister's face in her hands. "We're here now."

"You are right," Pele sighed. "Maybe I should let go of the anger."

Namaka let out a relieved breath. "It is time to rest. Let us go where we belong."

Pele closed her eyes, her arms wrapping around Namaka finally. "Yes, I'm ready to rest."

The sisters turned to Kamohoali'i. They both reached out their arms. With only a half second hesitation, the large shark lumbered forward, towering over the two women.

Without a word, he engulfed them in a bear hug. After a long moment and a loud sniffle, Kamohoali'i backed away, wiping his eyes.

Dain's angry voice cut through. "You cannot leave."

Everyone turned back at him. He stood stiff, hands clenched. His curls burned bright as his eyes began to glow. Frost coated him like a light blanket, spreading out from his feet as he took purposeful steps.

Pele looked at her sister for a moment. The two shared a nod before Pele peeled away. She clasped her hands, staring down the prince.

"I cannot give you what you want, young prince."

Dain gritted his teeth. "I lost..." He shook his head, his eyes pained. "People sacrificed for this. You need to do what was promised. What I have *seen*!"

Pele shook her head, backing away. "Centuries ago, many of us were foolish. I...I was foolish. Thinking the only way to obtain my desire was to obliterate my obstacle." Her remorseful gaze scanned the group. "Do not be fools like this old goddess."

"Where will you go?" asked Kye.

Pele's mouth parted, so many words to say, before softly replying. "To where we began."

Kye cleared his throat. "For how long?"

Namaka replied kindly, "Long enough nephew. But we will be watching over you."

Pele twisted her fingers, suddenly at a loss. "May I...I know I have no right but..."

Her tearful eyes caught Kye. "May I hug my son, one time?"

With a hesitant nod, Kye opened his arms. Pele flew to them, giving a hug that made even Lily's heart clench within her subconscious. What would it have felt like to remember her mother's hug. Was it warm?

Covertly wiping her eyes, Pele backed away. Namaka placed a hand on Pele's shoulder. "Ready sister?"

She clasped hands with Namaka, giving her a nod. The two goddesses began to glow, their auras growing brighter in the ash covered sky.

Pele took one glance back at Dain and the others as she imparted one last word.

"A word of caution, young ones. This fight of yours is not over. The evil behind this is still working in the shadows."

Her eyes were intense, the bright red burning into them as she scanned the entire group. "Do not always trust what your eyes tell you. What you see may not be what is real."

The glow became unbearably white, enveloping Namaka and Pele until the last sight of them were the sisters' heads touching, eyes closed as Namaka's whisper drifted into the air.

Thank you, my Guardian. Be well.

"Lily? Lily! Wake up!"

Lily peeled her eyes open. She groaned, every muscle in her body aching. This was the worse pain she ever felt. She lifted her heavy arm slowly, the bracelet catching the light.

It no longer glowed. The stones looked normal, the iridescent shine dulled against the bright sun.

Wait...the sun?

Her eyes opened wider. The dark, ashy clouds that covered the sun had disappeared. The bright, oceanic blue sky filled her senses, and the cry of birds tickled her ears.

"Lily?"

She shifted toward the voice. Her aunt and Brandon stood over her. Smiles spread across their tear-streaked faces. Raven pulled her up, holding her gently.

"You're okay! You're okay," Raven held her tightly.

"Ari?" Lily croaked out.

"I'm here Lil." Ari appeared beside Brandon, her gaze unsure.

She lifted her hand, gesturing Ari over. The entire family fell together in a huge hug, their laughter, tears, words of love overlapped each other. Lily swallowed, her throat tight. Finally, they were back together. Everyone was okay.

Save for Ang, her traitorous mind whispered.

Raven coughed, wiping her eyes. "Come on you two, up you go." She pulled Ari and Lily to their feet. "It's time to leave this place and go home."

"Are you gonna tell mom?" asked Brandon warily.

Raven blew out a strand of hair from her messy head. "Brandon...do you really think they'd believe it? Plus," her pointed look made the kids stare down at their shoes. "I think you all have enough guilt and weight to carry around. No need to add more at the moment. I'm just glad everyone is okay."

Lily lifted her head. The other council members surrounded Dain and Tane.

She caught Waru's attention. "What's going to happen to them?"

When Waru got a nod from Kye, the warrior immediately restrained Tane.

"Tane," Kye's voice boomed. "For the crime of betraying your oath to safeguard this realm, punishment would be stripped of your rank and banished."

Ruru squeaked, burrowing himself in Tane's long braids. Tane sighed low, reaching up to scratch the little owl gently. "I understand. I have committed an offense. Truly, I was blinded by my ideal of the past that I failed to see the possibility of the future." His black eyes closed, bending his head slightly. "But, I would like to give recompense...if I may your highness."

Kye wordlessly nodded, allowing Waru to let Tane go a moment. With a turn, the tall fae moved to the edge of the cliff, overlooking the burnt and ruined jungle. The little owl flipped his wings, floating above Tane.

Tane poised a question to his companion.

"Ready Ruru?"

"Quork-quork!"

Tane opened his arms, his swirled tattoos glowing. His eyes, once black, changed. The yellow pupils grew until his eyes glowed a bright yellow. His feet began to grow, like roots until they drilled into the earth, holding him in place. Ruru flew fast and far, his wings beginning to glow the same light. A yellow mist descended from where Ruru flew, to be met with a rumbling from the earth.

Lily gasped in awe.

The blackened jungle broke away, falling into pieces. New, green shoots began to emerge from the soil and soon a beautiful bed of green started growing.

Tane put his hands down as Ruru flew back, tucking himself into Tane's braids. He bowed low to Kye. "It will take time, but at least the jungle has a head start now to heal." He looked up, remorse evident. "For what it's worth, I am sorry."

Nafanua crossed her arms, refusing to look at him.

Kye watched a moment, silent. Then he put his hands on his hips. "In light of this development, you will still be stripped of your rank Tane, God of the Forest. But, instead of banishment," Tane's head snapped up, surprised. Kye continued, "your penance will be fixing what you have destroyed. Fix this jungle and make amends to the creatures you hurt."

Tane bowed low. "Thank you, your highness."

"Sorry to break up the warm and fuzzies, but what about him?" Randy jerked his thumb over to Dain, who had a blank look on his face.

Kye waved his hand. A pair of cuffs forged from fire emerged. He threw them at Waru, who effectively handcuffed the still unmoving Dain.

"He will answer to the royals," Kye answered. "He will be secluded and have time to...reflect...on his actions."

Raven nodded, gesturing to the kids. "Well, I guess our work is done here. Time to go kids, *andiamo*."

"Are you really going to leave?" Kye asked, suddenly appearing behind Raven, his gigantic frame towering over her.

She looked up, giving a hesitant smile. "I have to get these kids home. That was the whole reason why we came."

"And now?" He asked quietly.

Aka moved forward, purring loudly as the panther rubbed against Raven's legs. With a shove, the panther pushed Raven forward. She yelped, losing her balance, only for Kye to catch her. He held her gently, his large arms surrounding her.

They stared at each other a moment, silent.

Lily's eyes bugged out. *Oh...my...* What in the world happened these last few days?

Randy whistled, nudging Cabyll while whispering loudly. "Ohh!!! That panther is smart as a whip Cab. Take some notes, you're gonna need them."

"Shut up," Cabyll hissed.

Raven's face flushed beet red. She coughed, putting her arms out to straighten herself, and put distance between them. "You're pretty smooth, Muscles."

"I'll be anything you want Raven," he answered seriously.

Randy fanned himself. "Oh man, is it getting hot in here?"

Cabyll gritted his teeth. "...will you be *quiet* Spider?"

Raven blushed, shaking her head. "I need to get home. But," she paused, her lips quirking, "that doesn't mean I won't see you again right?"

Kye's lip tipped upward, giving a satisfied grin. "Soon," he rumbled.

He reached out, tucking a strand of hair behind her ear.

Randy whistled again, loud and bright. "Well, hate to break up the love here."

He gave two thumbs up to Raven with an exaggerated wink. "Don't you worry darlin' I promise we'll paint the town and the front porch soon, but," he pointed upward, "our ticket home is on its way."

Sure enough, a brightly colored rainbow serpent flew above them, the sunlight gleaming off its scales in a brilliant hue. Lily smiled to hear the familiar laughter of the Menehune.

The Menehune waved, laughing brightly. "Hello! Need a ride back home?"

Randy clapped his hands. "Alright, everyone aboard the flying snake."

Brandon and Ari got on the serpent, Ari giving one last backward glance at Dain. The two locked eyes, but neither said a word. Ari turned her back, grabbing Peni's hand and climbed onto the serpent.

Lily turned to Spyke and Peri. "Are you two coming?"

Spyke shook his head. "We will finish our mission and help Prince Kye clean up the aftermath. Then we will report back to Prince Jacy."

Lily ran and hugged him. "Thank you both...for everything."

Spyke hesitated a moment, before his large hand softly patted her head.

His voice was gruff, awkward. "No need to thank us, Lily."

"Yeah, don't thank him," Cabyll snarked. "You seem to be a little more handsy since last I saw you Thunderbrat..."

Peri stuck her tongue out. "Take your jealously and fly off the cliff Cabyll." She turned to Lily beaming. "No need to thank us cause we're just awesome. And we'd punch a demon for you girl. Wait...I just did."

She giggled and pushed Spyke out of the way to envelope Lily in her arms.

Lily chuckled, holding her tight. "Yup, you showed him Peri."

"I did, didn't I?" Her proud smile beamed.

"Okay break it up." Cabyll grumbled as reached over and caught Lily's wrist, pulling her away.

Peri pouted. "Stupid Cabyll. Such a party pooper."

He rolled his eyes. "Go flirt with the warrior woman already."

As Peri huffed, stomping her foot, Spyke put his arm on her shoulder, giving Lily a reassuring smile before turning Peri away. "We'll see you soon Lily."

Cabyll remained tense until Spyke and Peri walked away, leaving them alone.

Lily stood, shuffling her feet, as he kept silent, staring at her.

Geez why is he so quiet?

She cleared her throat, trying to fill in the silence. She fingered her curls nervously. "So, is my hair still blue?"

He tilted his head, frowning. "No, why are you asking that?"

"Cause you're brooding and staring. Is something wrong?"

He shook his head. "I just wanted to look at you a moment. Making sure you're really okay." His mouth pinched in disapproval. "You tried to pull another foolish stunt."

She sucked in her bottom lip, contrite. "I know, I know! But if there really any other way to-"

He grabbed her shoulders, shaking her. "You are so reckless!"

Her gaze snapped upward, startled.

He growled, low and dark. "You always put yourself at risk. You're a headache, stressful and foolish." His hands squeezed lightly, keeping her still.

He sighed, exasperated. "You are a mystery, yet the most certain thing I've ever known."

Then, he gave her a blinding smile that made her heart stop. His eyes were bright, glowing with an intensity she couldn't describe. Suddenly he pulled her close, burying his head between her neck and shoulder. His breath was hot, inciting goosebumps prickling down her arms.

He continued, his lips rough against her throat. "I can't tell you how relieved I am that you're alright."

Before she could respond, he pulled back, his fingers coming up to her cheek. They trailed down to rest on her neck, wrapping around a stray curl.

"I'm sorry I worried everyone," she managed to croak out, her pulse beating fast in her throat.

"Don't *ever* do it again," he warned. His fingers tugged her curl, hard enough for her to move her head. "You have no idea what I was going to do when I thought something had happened to you."

She frowned. "What like ask for a duel or something?"

His lip quirked upward. "We're not so civilized Lily." His hand tore through his hair. "I would sooner electrocute and burn this world to ash than have seen you hurt."

Her eyes widened. *Woah...that's kinda extreme.*

"Burn the world?" She forced a laugh, lightly patting his shoulder in jest. "Just so I wouldn't get hurt? Isn't that ironic? I would get hurt by simply being burned."

He leaned toward her, his forehead gently meeting hers. He whispered low, "I would never let a flame touch you."

Her face warmed. She could only imagine her beet red face and bugged out eyes. *What is up with him right now? This is more flirting than he's ever done.*

She pulled back, disengaging from his arms, trying to calm her heart. *Remember Lily, he's a flirt. He just thinks of you as a friend. He must just be trying to get a reaction out of you.*

She put her hands on her hips, raising her eyebrow. "You're laying it on pretty thick. You know you don't have to put the fake charm on with me. I've never been the type to swoon over your pretty lies, you know that."

He tilted his head, leisurely folding his arms, looking the epitome of a swoon worthy rouge. "Who said I'm fake or lying Lily. I stretch the truth, bend it, manipulate it to my advantage. But...I never lie. And I won't lie to you...ever."

Her mouth fell open in disbelief. What in the world happened in the last few days? "Did you hit your head or something? You said you despised me!"

She could have kicked herself when her voice cracked.

He rubbed the back of his neck, grimacing. "I didn't mean it that way...I meant-"

He bit his lip, halting himself. His throat bobbed before his eyes narrowed as they centered on her face. "When you fell into the abyss, I was swallowed up with you. Your...sister." His nostrils flared. "I swear I would have-"

"She wasn't in her right mind," interrupted Lily. "It's not her fault."

"Don't." he warned. "Do *not* defend her after all she's done. You may be forgiving and kind, but I will not. She is nothing but dirt." He spit on the ground.

His voice deepened into a growl. "I refuse to let anything happen to you like that again."

They stared at each other. Lily jumped as a voice broke the tense atmosphere.

"Alright y'all, time to put the chairs in the wagon and head outta here."

Randy came over to Lily, reaching out his arm. In shock, she blindly took it to head toward the serpent. Randy paused, seeing Cabyll's glare and hearing his low growl.

He wagged his finger, tsking. "Don't snap my garters, Cab. You need a moment to cool down and Lily has been through enough today for you to goin' in like a house is afire."

"Randy..." Cabyll's warning died as Randy shooed him flippantly.

"I mean it Cab, you're acting like you just fell off a turnip truck. If you got enough horse sense, you'd tone it down a notch got it?"

Randy waited a moment before emphasizing. "Wash off your war paint *Assassin*."

Cabyll rubbed the bridge of his nose, sighing. "Yes, you may be right. Wait..." he paused, his eyes lighting up as something came to mind. "We still have a bargain, don't we?"

Her mouth dropped. *Oh geez...why now?*

She bit her cheek. "Um..."

"Think you can hit a bullseye?"

She blinked. "What? You mean now?"

His lip tilted up, his dimple out. "I can't think of a better time."

Her eye twitched. She was tired, achy, had gotten possessed, fell down a cliff, and that was just the start of the long, long list of issues she dealt with in the last few days. And he expected her to shoot on command? She glanced briefly down at the bracelet, suddenly wishing for Namaka's freezing spells.

She groaned inwardly.

Oh...forget this.

She fished in her backpack, her muscles aching in protest. She dug out the scarf and, stomping over to Cabyll, slapped the clothing in his hand. "There!" Her nose scrunched up. "I'm too tired, have it."

She lifted her head, turning back to Randy. But Cabyll's eyes still glowed, catching hers. She squinted, the sun blinding her.

"Oh," she mumbled. "Is the sun extremely bright or is it just me?"

"What do I care?" Cabyll raised the scarf to his lips. "Did I ever mention that I prefer the moon and stars?"

She looked at him, confused.

He gave her a long, slow wink. "I'll see you soon Lily. You won't get rid of me that easily."

Her cheeks burned. *Why that brazen...*

Randy tugged her forward, whispering in her ear. "Lily darlin', don't take too much to heart. Give him a little grace. Cab was a mess, we all were, thinkin' you bit the bullet."

He put up his hand chuckling when she opened her mouth to reply. "Don't apologize, I know that's what you were gonna do. But just know that man can ride the rough string when he's got his sights on something."

"Why are you saying that, Randy?" she asked.

He helped her up on the serpent. "Didn't know you, the one who tells the stories rules the world." His eyes glittered with mirth. "Your story has just begun girl. Keep being the one who tells them."

He is right my Sentinel, whispered Tim. *Let us continue to walk your path.*

A week later...

LILY'S DAD SLID A PLATE OF GRILLED *SARDE A BECCAFICO* toward her. He squeezed a fresh lemon over the rolled sardines.

"Here you go *fiore, mangiare.*"

He smiled kindly. "You haven't eaten much these last few days. I figured you were used to a lot of seafood being with your aunt, so I decided to make my great Aunt Ophelia's recipe. What do you think?"

Lily hesitantly removed the skewer from the rolled fish, taking a nibble. Normally, she would have loved the contrast of the savory bread-crumbs and salty parmesan with the slightly sweet raisins. But she could only vaguely taste it. Her eyes strayed to a plate of steaming maritozzi that was left uneaten. A familiar pang in her chest hit her again as it did several times since they came back from the Nalu Realm.

She forced a smile. "It's good dad. Thanks for making it."

Tony gave a relieved grin. "Good, for a minute I thought you all caught a stomach bug or something. First Brandon, then Ari, and now you wouldn't eat." He scratched his head. "I know Ravenna said it was jet lag, but you've been used to time changes, so I was worried."

She bit her lip, wanting to tell her dad everything, but it was not a good time. What would she tell him, anyway? Hey dad, fairies and monsters exist? She pushed down the guilt a little further, giving him a hug.

"Thanks, Dad. They'll get back to normal soon, I'm sure of it."

But the words felt dry in her mouth.

Brandon was outside, doing boot camp drills. He hadn't touched his skateboard since they came back. He had a singular focus: pushups, running, lifting, and practicing on the new punching bag he asked for.

The group had to come up with a good story when they returned. One change was, unlike Lily, Ari's hair had remained a stained ombre pink. A permanent reminder of her time in the Veil. It was almost like her DNA changed. Thankfully, Raven smoothed over Tabby's initial skepticism by saying she dyed it.

Speaking of Ari, she had changed in several ways. She stayed away from her phone, not wanting to interact with her friends. Instead, she clung to her mom and Lily, staying near as if they would disappear at any moment. Most times she could be found by herself sitting on the little bridge, basking in the sun. Her gaze constantly drifted to the woods, vacant and dreamy. Lily couldn't help but worry when Ari stared a little too long at the Veil.

Foolish.

Lily flinched as Cabyll's words came back to haunt her. She was indeed foolish. Foolish to think that Ari coming back would mean everything would return to normal. Nothing was back to 'normal'.

Raven had left, saying she needed to return to Italy to see Lily's grandmother. Lily thought back on the last interaction they had before Raven departed.

"Why are you going to Italy all of a sudden?"

Raven fingered her evil eye necklace, letting out a reluctant sigh. "I need to go see your nonna."

"Are you going to tell her what happened?"

Raven shook her head. "No, but..." She trailed off, her gaze spacing out a moment before shaking herself. "There are things I need to look into."

Lily raised her eyebrow. "Are you going to explain?" She pointed to the necklace. "You said we would talk about how you know about all this."

Her hands gestured to the kitchen where Brom and Alasdair were making afternoon tea.

"Yes, I promised you, didn't I?" Raven patted the seat next to hers. "Have a seat." She waited while Lily sat down before continuing. "What I'm about to tell you does not leave these walls."

Her aunt yelled over her shoulder, "That includes you two!"

Brom and Alasdair spit out their tea, giving mock salutes.

Raven nodded. "The women in our family. Well...let's say, some of the women in our family have been involved in the otherworld for generations."

Lily crossed her arms. "I think I need a little more than that."

A cup of steaming jasmine tea appeared. She gave a grateful nod to Brom.

Raven stared at her own cup, tapping on the handle. "Well...um..."

Lily frowned, taking a sip. Her normally articulate aunt couldn't get out the words.

Raven banged the table, knocking a few cups over. "Fine. I'll just spill it out."

"You spilled more than that," Brom huffed, trying to clean up the mess.

Raven sighed, pinching her nose. "Your nonna is a strega."

Lily blinked. "A witch?"

Raven rubbed her temples. "Yes, she's a witch. And her nonna was before her and so on."

She paused, not really comprehending. "Are you a witch?"

Her aunt shook her head. "No, I just happened to know about it that's all. With all my travels it's hard not to see the otherworld after your mother gives you wards of protection and charms to see them. Let me tell you, that was a surprise I wasn't ready for."

"Does that mean Dad knows?"

"Goodness no." She waved her hand dismissively. "He just thinks mom's superstitious and immersed in Italian country folklore. He doesn't believe that actual monsters and goblins exist." She called out, "No offense."

Brom puffed his chest out. "We are not goblins madam; I am a brownie."

Lily shook her head. "So, what are you going to tell nonna?"

"I need to look through her books. I'm glad Ari is back, but what the goddesses said bothers me. I have a feeling this isn't over. Don't you agree?"

Lily nodded, she had the same feeling.

Raven patted her hand. "Have you decided on the Sentinel Academy?"

Lily was pondering it, but she knew once she made her choice, her life *would be completely changed. But...she was still her. Still boring, predictable Lily. Was she ready for such a big step?*

Raven took her silence and squeezed her hand. "Follow your gut nipote. If you could take anything from of this journey, know that your gut hasn't steered you wrong. You are an Ambrosino after all."

"Fiore?"

Her dad's questioning tone broke her out of her stupor. She shook her head, dusting the cobwebs. "Sorry dad, what did you say?"

He showed her an envelope. Taking it from him, she could see the printed return address of Cornell University. She clutched the letter, biting her lip.

"Go on," he encouraged, his smile wide, "open it."

Nervous, she peeled the top open. Pulling out the letter she read in silence, taking it in.

Her dad rocked back and forth. "So? What does it say?"

"I got accepted," she whispered.

Tony clapped his hands. "That's wonderful!" He touched his chin in thought. "Hmm...so that means Arachstone or Cornell. Which one do you want to go to?"

She didn't speak, holding the letter tightly. Cornell was what she wanted, what she dreamed.

The road divides up ahead...what path will you choose young Sentinel?

Lily jerked, startled to hear Tim after all this time. He had been quiet, gathering his strength. His deep voice jolted her. She wasn't ready, was she?

...What if I fail?

Tim's comforting voice whispered.

Then do what you do best my Sentinel. Be the human that I know you are.

His reassurance and support bolstered her. She shook herself, bracing her shoulders. She focused on her dad, a slow, genuine smile forming. "I think I want to go to Arachstone."

Her dad's returning smile was warm and excited. "Then Arachstone it is." He pulled her into a hug. "I'm soooo proud of you *fiore*."

Lily found herself outside, wandering toward the bridge. Ari sat on the edge, staring off into the forest again, a book beside her. It was some kind of a diary or journal, opened with some scribbles written on it.

With a sigh, she plopped down next to her. "You're thinking about Dain aren't you?"

Ari blinked, still staring at the green trees. "Kinda. Not all the time though." She sighed, her voice wistful. "Lily...I miss being there. The magic, the wonder of it all."

Lily could understand. The Veil changed people.

Ari continued, mumbling into her knees that were pressed against her chin. "I don't know if I could go back to counting calories and talking about the latest fashion trends."

"You want to go back?"

Ari frowned, conflicted. "I don't know. I want to be with mom and Brandon...and you." She stopped, her mind drifting. "But I miss being there. I feel like I was more myself. Like, I didn't know how much I pretended to be someone everyone wanted me to be...until I left."

Her voice quieted. "Do you think I could have both? Be over there and have my family?"

Lily pondered a moment. "I guess...anything is possible."

"I wrote to you, ya know." Ari suddenly said.

Lily blinked, surprised. "What are you talking about?"

Ari motioned to her diary. "I would write to you sometimes, when I was in the Veil. Even though I knew you weren't going to see it, I guess...I still was comforted thinking I was talking to you." She tucked her hair behind her ear sheepishly. "Was that weird?"

Lily smiled, putting her arm around Ari's shoulders. "Not at all. Remember, you'll always have your family no matter what."

"But we're not real sisters," she protested. "How can you still be nice to me, after all I've done?"

Lily shrugged. "Blood is blood. But family, that is a choice." She squeezed Ari's shoulders lightly. "And I choose to be your sister, if you'll have me. Maybe...when you're ready, you can share those letters?"

Ari sniffed, giving a watery smile. "Yeah, I'd like that." She burrowed her face in her knees as Lily quietly held her.

"I'm sorry," Ari finally whispered. "About before. About Cabyll and the possession. I'm...lost, where I can't seem to find myself."

Lily didn't know what to do. Everything was different now. Ari was not thriving. Sure it was great she was back, but Lily knew her step-sister needed something that they couldn't give her. She needed someone to help her handle all the magical insanity she had gone through. That wasn't exactly an easy therapy session to find. But what could they do?

"I'll always be right here...to remind you of how good you are," Lily insisted.

Ari gave a watery chuckle. She wiped her eyes. "He only thought about you."

"Who?" she asked.

Ari gave a half smile. "Cabyll." She clasped Lily's hands. "I just wanted you to know. He only ever thought of you."

Lily blinked, trying to process that. She opened her mouth, but a voice cut in.

"Aww, well isn't this cute. Forgive me if I threw up a little bit in my mouth."

Lily's throat choked at the painfully familiar voice. She clenched her eyes shut.

It can't be...

Afraid to turn around, but finding she couldn't stop herself, Lily finally caved in. The light was blinding behind the silhouette, causing Lily to squint. But maybe it was the tears that began welling up that made the image blur slightly.

The figure put a hand on their hip, cocking it to the side.

"And what about me sissy? Am I chopped liver or something?"

Lily was speechless, the words sticking to her throat. Another voice pipped up.

"Hey guys, did you see the kettlebell? I can't find it."

Brandon walked up, his head down. He was re-taping his knuckles, his fingers bruised and blistered. The figure barked at him.

"What are you doing kid? You're not trying to throw a kettlebell at someone are you?"

He froze, his eyes slowly traveling up. His jaw dropped as the figure kept harping.

"I leave you for only a week and you're already causing trouble. I swear you're a magnet for it."

"Ang?" He choked out, the tape falling from his fingertips.

Sure enough, Ang stood there, a cocky grin on her face.

"Who else would it be?"

With a cry, Brandon launched himself at her, almost knocking her over. Lily cautiously got up, her lips trembling, before she ran over, too.

Brandon's stuttered voice was muffled. "We thought you were dead."

Ang sighed. "It'd take more than that to get rid of me." She returned the hug awkwardly before pulling away. "Sheesh, you guys are so emotional. Get off already."

"How?" asked Lily, unable to form more words.

Ang scratched her armpit. "How what?"

She shook her head. "All of it, but I guess start with how you got back?"

Ang pulled an item out of her pocket. She held it up, letting the sunlight touch it.

Lily gaped. It was Brom's sending stone. The one he gave her when she went to Arachstone.

Ang continued, flipping the stone deftly between her fingers. "I picked this off you when we were with the goblins." She gave Lily a sly wink. "Figured I'd need some insurance."

Lily smiled, giving Ang a nudge. "We're glad you're back."

Ang scoffed, hiding her face. "Well...not sure if I'm back." She gestured to Ari, who was watching quietly the entire time.

Ang raised her eyebrow at Ari. "So, you decided to stay?"

Ari tilted her head. "You...you look like me. Did you pretend to be me?"

Ang rocked back and forth.

Lily interrupted. "Only in the beginning Ari. But...Ang is her own person. Just like you are."

"This is weird," replied Ari, eying her doppelgänger cautiously.

Ang mirrored her with a cheeky grin. "Tell me about it. You know how hard it is to listen to Sam whine and complain about boys?" She crinkled her nose in disgust.

Ari laughed, her shoulders relaxing. "I get it." She stopped, an unreadable look in her eyes. "Do you like it here?"

Ang paused, thinking, before giving a slight nod. "Yes, I really do."

Ari pursed her lips, keeping quiet.

Lily held Ari's shoulder, asking gently. "You still want to go back?"

Ari nodded quickly. "Not permanently, but I feel like I need to go back. Nafanua sent a letter." She slid a scrap of paper out of her book, looking sheepish. "Sorry I didn't tell you sooner. She offered to help me handle my anger, to help me deal with this whole human/fae thing since she used to be human. I was thinking, maybe...if you guys are okay with it...I could figure that out."

She gave a hesitant glance at Ang. "Maybe Ang can stay here."

"I'm good with that," Ang quipped. She flicked her hair, transforming it to a pinkish ombre to match Ari.

"Slay," Ari whispered.

Brandon frowned. "Are you sure Ari? You just got home."

"It wouldn't be forever. I'd come visit. It's just...Brandon I need to do this." Ari's voice grew more firm.

Brandon looked at her before shrugging. "Well...as long as you aren't trying to destroy the world or anything I guess it's cool. Promise you'll visit alright?"

Ari nodded, standing up to give Brandon an awkward pat on the shoulder.

Lily gave a reassuring smile. "Stay safe. We're here for anything you'd need."

Ari beamed, throwing herself into Lily's arms.

Ang interrupted the moment to bellow out, "Hey guys? Think your dad made any maritozzi?"

❦

M*eanwhile...*

. . .

An eerie bird call echoed off the iron bars of the isolated prison. High in a desolate cavern, vast arches of black stone blocked out the hot desert sun. Carrion birds called out, eager and hungry.

They circled the blackened sun, keeping a watchful eye on the denizens within. The sharp vertical, almost smooth, sides of the cavern bolstered many small openings that were encased in black, wrought iron. Darkness pierced through the bars to cover a seated figure, stretched on the hard rocky floor.

His hair was messy with filth and dirt. Oil and sand dulled the once burnished copper strands. Iron gloves covered his hands, the soft hiss of burning skin was drowned out by the cawing of the vultures.

The once resolute, haughty crimson eyes were now a muddy terra-cotta, grief stricken and torn. Where there once stood a proud, confident prince only a husk, slowly decaying away, remained. He had forgotten how long he was there. Time was irrelevant. Nothing made him move or respond. Not the incorporeal guards that jeered at him. Not the smell of burning flesh. Not the blistering heat or the maddening darkness.

Until...

A puff of wind and the whisper of wings flapped against the prison bars. The prisoner ignored it. This wasn't new. Probably a vulture, crow, or harpy looking for food. He remained still, unmoving, until the bird finally called out. The prisoner blinked slowly. It wasn't the familiar caw or cackle, but an eerie blend of a hoot with a howl.

Dain raised his head.

There, before him, was something like a cross of a large barn owl and a raven. It was large, but skinnier than any regular owl found beyond the Veil. It flapped its large, grey-white wings, keeping a stoic stance in front of the bars.

Dain's tired eyes peered the darkness. The bird was not here for food. The bird transfixed its gaze on him as its rapacious beak opened, giving another eerie howl.

He blinked.

It was a Strix, a terrifying ill omen.

The prince shook his head, wanting to turn away. He was done with omens. He was done with destiny.

But the Strix wouldn't release its hold on him. It kept its eyes on Dain, almost giving a snicker.

And then Dain's eyes went white.

As the prince started convulsing, another vision taking hold, the Strix backed away. It had finished what it was set out to do and turned to fly high into the blackened sun.

❀

S omewhere far to the east in the Veil...

T he cherry blossoms were in bloom. But then they were always stuck in eternal bloom as the resident Aerico demons refused to allow for such beauty to wither and die. The fragrant trees surrounded a beautifully tall and statuesque wooden structure. Almost seven tiers topped the building, reaching toward the heavens. The bright red wood stood out against the setting sun as lanterns dotted the landscape and balconies with their warm glow.

The steady hum of fae and creatures chatting merrily accompanied by upbeat music thrummed within the walls. High up at the top of this structure, where the laughter dimmed and the music faded, a large office stood near an open balcony.

A woman sat at an ornate red desk carved with jade dragons, phoenixes, and other various creatures. Her youthful beauty glowed in the ember light of the lanterns. She sported long, beautiful, shiny black hair which was pinned up by a hairpin made of pearls and garnets. Her ruby lips sipped a cup of fragrant chrysanthemum tea as she peered over copious papers and notes.

An eerie howl mixed with a hoot greeted her from the balcony.

Slowly, the young woman got up, rearranging her kimono with impeccable grace and elegantly floated to the terrace. She took a moment to look down at the bustling fae town. The Strix was sitting on the railing, right next to her.

The woman clucked, her voice melodic with a singsong lilt. "What visions do you have for me today dear one?"

She held out her hand, palm up.

The Strix opened its beak. Something black and oozing dropped out with a sickening plop. It splashed onto the woman's hand, quickly absorbed until not a trace remained.

The woman smiled, giving a dainty chuckle. She took one, long blood-red nail and carefully scratched under the Strix's neck, causing the bird to close its eyes in happiness.

"What a good little one you are. We mustn't keep the prince idle for too long."

She turned abruptly, the Strix losing balance for a moment as it hastily flapped its wings to follow her back inside. The woman went to an adjoining table which held a chess-set. The pieces were placed in a game already in motion.

She sighed, flicking her finger at a Knight, causing it to slump over.

"It is quite unfortunate the Prince of Prophecy was caught."

She huffed in annoyance, her long nails trailing over the enemy pieces, hovering over a pawn. The Strix howled. "Yes, I think we all have underestimated the humans...especially that human Sentinel. She is proving to be more troublesome than initially anticipated."

The Strix flapped its wings, landing on a perch near the desk.

The woman tapped her chin, looking at the board. Her ruby red eyes glowed in the dim light. "Well, there is more than one way I suppose."

Her blood-red lips peeled back in a calculating smile. "I'm looking forward to their next move."

About the Author

Rachel Hawk is a full-time mom and wife while also working a full-time job. Whenever there is a sliver of time available she loves delving into fantastical tales of myth and folklore.

Rachel enjoys cooking up something new in the kitchen while blaring music on multiple levels of her house ranging from jazz to heavy metal. Dancing is an absolute must in the household - anything less is frowned upon.

Stories and tales of all varieties thrive in her home. Some days pirates, ninjas, or knights are running through the house - usually involving Rachel being turned magically into the final villain/boss of some variety, typically a dragon, and hereby defeated by her two little adventurers.

She lives in Maryland wine country with her husband, two questing children, and one large cat (third kid by proxy) Bucky.

Find her at:
https:authorrachelhawk.com/

www.ingramcontent.com/pod-product-compliance
Lightning Source LLC
Chambersburg PA
CBHW072337020726
47506CB00004B/913